For Tina,
Enjoy!

tar heel dead

Sarah R. Shaber

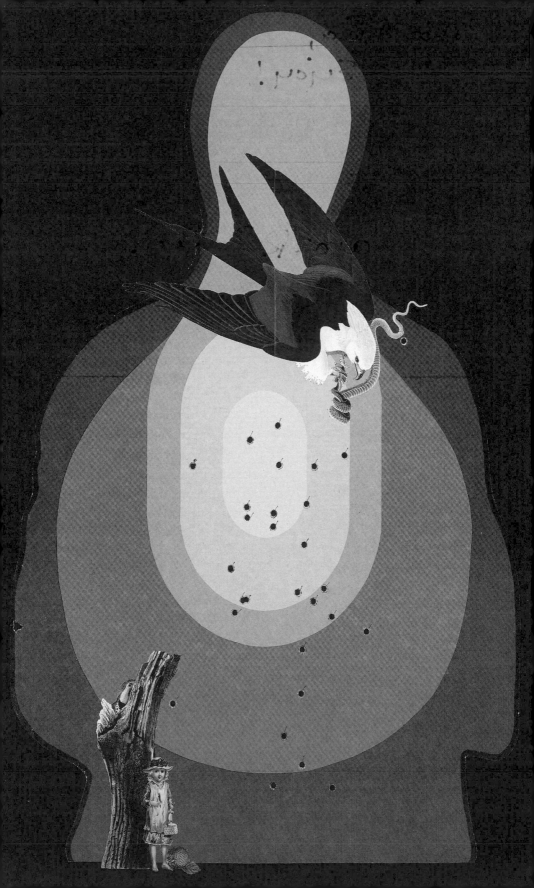

Tales *of* MYSTERY AND MAYHEM *from* NORTH CAROLINA

Edited by SARAH R. SHABER

Foreword by MARGARET MARON

The University of North Carolina Press

Chapel Hill and London

Manufactured in the United States of America

Designed by Richard Hendel

Set in Arnhem and Big Black types

by Tseng Information Systems, Inc.

The paper in this book meets the guidelines
for permanence and durability of the Committee
on Production Guidelines for Book Longevity of
the Council on Library Resources.

Frontispiece by Debora Greger

Library of Congress Cataloging-in-Publication Data

Tar Heel dead : tales of mystery and mayhem from
North Carolina / edited by Sarah R. Shaber ; foreword
by Margaret Maron.

    p. cm.

ISBN 0-8078-5604-5 (pbk. : alk. paper)

1. Detective and mystery stories, American—North
Carolina. 2. North Carolina—Fiction. I. Shaber,
Sarah R.

PS558.N8T36 2005

813'.087208'09756—dc22   2004027176

09 08 07 06 05 5 4 3 2 1

Dedicated to the

memory of "our beloved Liz,"

Elizabeth Daniels Squire

(1926–2001)

I'm a Tar Heel born

I'm a Tar Heel bred

And when I die

I'm a Tar Heel dead.

— "Carolina Fight Song"

CONTENTS

North Carolina stretches from blue-shrouded mountains to a crystal coast, and the landscape of its imagination has been equally stretched by Appalachian folktales and stories of ghost ships doomed to crash forever onto our treacherous shoals. Although multigenerational gatherings on the front porch on hot summer evenings are almost as rare as un-air-conditioned homes these days, stories that used to be told at such gatherings still persist as tales told at bedtime, during long car drives, or around fires built now for "ambiance" instead of as a primary way to keep warm.

Most of the tales are imbued with mystery, from the story of Tom Dooley (did he really murder Laura Foster?) to that of the Lost Colony (where did those first settlers really go?). Some are as ancient as the Brown Mountain lights, others as modern as East Carolina University's haunted guesthouse.

North Carolina is full of storytellers. We have Nobel Laureate candidates and those who publish in online E-zines read by maybe fifty people in a good month. Some North Carolinians joke that you can't throw a rock here without hitting a writer, which brings us to another mystery: Why is this state home to so many good ones? What is it that gives us such literary richness?

Webster defines a mystery as "something that has not been or cannot be explained . . . and therefore exciting curiosity or wonder." All we can do is lay out the evidence—such as this collection of short stories—and wait for a scholarly Sherlock Holmes to gather up the clues and give us a logical answer.

ACKNOWLEDGMENTS

I am grateful to Margaret Maron, who wrote the Foreword to this anthology and made many helpful suggestions.

Many thanks to Alice Ann Carpenter and John Leininger, whose mail and online catalog *Grave Matters* contained a number of the scarce books and magazines I needed. Without their help, I couldn't have located many of these stories. Jeff Hatfield of *Uncle Edgar*'s also found several rare stories for me.

Years ago, I worked for the University of North Carolina Press in both the editorial and marketing departments. These were my first jobs in the real world, and my bosses, Malcolm McDonald, then editor in chief, and Johanna Grimes, who recently retired as sales manager, were wonderful to me. I have many fond memories of my years there, and now I am honored to be one of the press's authors. This book would not exist if David Perry, current editor in chief, hadn't called me to suggest that I edit it.

INTRODUCTION   *Sarah R. Shaber*

here are two excellent reasons for compiling a book of mystery short stories by North Carolinians. The first is for the pure pleasure of reading the stories and taking delight in the literary success of fellow North Carolinians. The second is that it honors members of a vital part of our state's literary community by gathering a representative sampling of their work in one volume.

I have identified over sixty North Carolinians, both living and deceased, who could be called mystery writers. Obviously I couldn't include stories by all of them. Many only wrote novels. Some permissions obstacles couldn't be overcome. Others I just couldn't fit into this book.

Of course, this collection includes works by North Carolina's bestselling mystery authors. But you'll also find less well known writers represented here, stories that were essentially lost and required hours of research to uncover, and surprise selections by authors whom you might not know wrote mysteries at all. My intent was to include a variety of stories, some historic, some comic, some disturbing, some traditional, and some experimental. The oldest story was first published over a hundred years ago; the newest is my own contribution, written for this collection.

Locating copies of some of these stories resembled a scavenger hunt. I traced them through indexes, reference books, libraries, used bookstores, and the Internet. Over many weeks, I accumulated boxes of tattered old mystery magazines and a stack of dog-eared anthologies. I never did find a copy of the 1945 issue of *Ellery Queen's Mystery Magazine* that contained Manly Wade Wellman's seminal story. Instead, I located it by chance in an anthology published in 1970. O. Henry's "The Dissipated Jeweler" was apparently never reprinted after its first publication in 1896 in the *Houston Post*, except in his complete works, a battered copy of which arrived through interlibrary loan from a distant Wake County Library branch.

We all know that North Carolina has a surfeit of excellent writers, and we all wonder why the state is blessed with such literary bounty. Is it our storytelling tradition, the mystical congruence of several fine universities, or a secret ingredient in the barbecue? Whatever attracts writers here is equally attractive to mystery writers. No single mantelpiece in the state could hold all of the Agatha, Edgar, and Anthony awards won by our mystery authors. But these prolific and award-winning writers have received little attention outside the community of mystery writers and readers. The reason for this omission appears to be the trend to classify general fiction as "literary" and genre writing as just "entertainment." This is elitist nonsense. If "literary" means well written and meaningful, mysteries are literary too. As evidence, I offer *The Great Gatsby*, *Crime and Punishment*, and *To Kill a Mockingbird*, all crime novels!

In fact, understanding the mystery genre is important to understanding modern literature. Since Edgar Allan Poe wrote *The Murders in the Rue Morgue* in 1841, the mystery has become the most prevalent storytelling medium in the world. It's now the most viable written vehicle for exploring social issues, the subject of justice, and character.

North Carolina's well-known general-fiction writers have been featured in two previous University of North Carolina Press anthologies: *The Rough Road Home* and *This Is Where We Live*. Now *Tar Heel Dead* gives our mystery writers their due.

It's especially appropriate that an anthology of short stories should honor our mystery community. Until around 1950, the most popular form of mystery was the short story. Over 200 pulp magazines published crime stories by the thousands. The popularity of the novel slowly overwhelmed the short story, so that just a few magazines remain today, but we now see a resurgence in the form through anthologies like this one.

Several years ago, when I was visiting England, I gave a copy of my first mystery, *Simon Said*, to an airline agent in gratitude for an upgrade. She was delighted, saying, "My favorite—I love a murder!" Why are mysteries so popular? Crime novels outsell all other categories of fiction except best sellers, many of which are mysteries or their near cousins, thrillers. Michael Malone, one of our state's finest writers, has suggested that readers flock to mysteries in search of the stories they used to find in general fiction, which today tends toward introspection. Then there's the puzzle element of the mystery, the mental contest between sleuth and villain and between reader and writer, that is so intellectually stimulating. I have another theory. I think that human beings are so obsessed with death that they gain some release from this anxiety by reading fiction about murder. I compare this to a child who, though terrified of clowns, plays at dressing up as a clown.

Traces of the mystery can be found as far back as the classical Greeks. Dorothy Sayers, in her introduction to *The Omnibus of Crime*, reminds us of the mystery's hoary origins by quoting one of Aesop's Fables: "Why do you not come to pay your respects to me?" says Aesop's lion to the fox. "I beg Your Majesty's pardon," says the fox, "but I noticed the tracks of the animals that have already come to you; and while I see many hoof-marks going in, I see none coming out. Till the animals that have entered your cave come out again, I prefer to remain in the open air" (quoted in *The Writer's Handbook*, edited by A. S. Burack [New York: The Writer Inc., 1972], 223).

While readers consume mysteries like popcorn at the movies, writers love to write them. What is so appealing about the form to a writer? Some mysteries concentrate on crimes other than murder, but most are about an unnatural death. Since death is the deepest mystery of all, it follows that murder is the greatest injustice one human can inflict on another. Murder creates chaos in a community, which then unites to unmask the killer and restore moral order. The justice system, delving deep into motives and suspects' lives, uncovers secrets long buried within families and society. And the detective, whether a police officer or an unlikely amateur, often learns something important about himself or herself at the same time that he or she is fitting the puzzle pieces together. What luscious source material for a writer!

The classic tale of detection, which is still being written and written well, is about restoring order to a once well-ordered world that was disrupted by violent death. But now there are as many kinds of mysteries as there are authors' worldviews—from traditional whodunits to grimy police procedurals. Modern mystery writers emphasize internal character, motivation, and psychology more than the search for clues. You'll find several stories in this volume, including those by Margaret Maron and BarbaraNeely, that focus almost exclusively on the psychology of the main character. Lisa Cantrell's story is about the horror and finality of death itself.

The mystery form appeals to writers because, as Baroness P. D. James tells us, the mystery genre provides both reader and writer with a strong, comforting framework but "still says something about men and women and the society in which we live" (*The Mystery Writers of America Edgar Awards Program* [1999], 223). This anthology contains stories by writers as diverse as science fiction author Orson Scott Card and award-winning children's book author William E. Brittain.

A sense of place is essential to the mystery, even more than to other fiction. Setting creates atmosphere, illustrates character, holds clues, and contributes to the tension crucial to detective fiction. Evoking a sense of place exercises all of an author's descriptive muscles. What opportunities North Carolina offers a writer! From today's New South of the Triangle to the ancient Appalachians thick with laurel and pine to the coast saturated with the odor of salt spray, our state offers settings galore. North Carolinians' historical link to the frontier, the tragedy of the Civil War, and our obsession with family, race, and religion provide more than enough emotional material to last any writer a lifetime.

I won't review all of the stories and their authors in this collection since you'll be reading them yourself shortly. No two are alike. Enjoy!

Tar Heel Dead

DEAD IN THE WATER

Nancy Bartholomew

ne of the things I hate most about Sunday mornings is opening up the Bait and Tackle Shop for Freddy. On those Sundays when he's out fishing, hoping to finally get good enough to turn pro, I get stuck with the shop. Oh, don't get me wrong, I'd do most anything for Freddy. I saw him through his divorce, didn't I?

After I unlock the door, cut off the alarm, and turn on the lights, it's time to clean out the bait tank. I gotta grab the net and scoop out the floaters who didn't make it through the night.

There they are, bodies distended, eyes glazed over, swirling around the surface. I pick each slimy minnow up and toss it in the trash. The fish stink. Maybe it's fish fear. All those minnows, swimming in a tank, waiting to be used as bait, they gotta be scared. I know, you're saying they can't think like humans. Maybe not, but fish are mighty smart, else they wouldn't be so dang hard to catch. Just look at all the lures and plastic worms we sell. Even with the best equipment, you gotta have technique. Fishing's a skill. So tell me them fish ain't smart.

On this one particular Sunday morning, I set the coffeepot on to brew and headed for the back where we keep the live bait. I figured the hot coffee would be a reward for cleaning the fish tanks. By the time I finished, the coffee would be ready. There can never be too much coffee at six o'clock on Sunday morning.

I flung open the back room door, reached around for the switch, and started screaming. There, floating in a tank full of reddish water, was Freddy's ex-wife, Eaudelein. Her hair was fanned out around what had been the back of her head. It was now a bloody mess. I stared and screamed, turned and ran to the tiny bathroom, and heaved into the commode. I was shaking and crying, "Oh my God, oh my God." There wasn't a soul to hear me. I hadn't even switched on the "Open" sign yet.

I ran back out to the front, around behind the counter, and grabbed the phone. For a moment I couldn't remember how to dial 911.

"Oh Jesus, God," I screamed into the phone. "Get somebody over here quick. Eaudelein's dead."

There's only two cop cars in all of Barrow, and they both raced into the parking lot with lights flashing and sirens screaming. They don't get many chances to use their lights around here. I don't believe Wallace County had ever had a killing, at least not as long as I'd been there, and that was all of my forty-five years.

Randall Vaughn was the first one to get to me. He was the duty officer. Raydeen Miller came a close second. She wasn't on duty but keeps the police band on all night in her bedroom. She don't like to miss much. This was just the kind of situation she'd been waiting for all of her professional life.

"Patsy," called Randy, "you all right? What's this about Eaudelein bein' dead?" He was a comforting presence as he reached out to touch my shoulder. Randy'd been on the force for years; we all knew him, of course. He and I'd been in school together and even dated briefly in high school.

I finally got it all out, how I'd found Eaudelein in the bait tanks. As soon as I told him, he and Raydeen headed for the bait room.

"Oh my God," breathed Raydeen, turning white. Randy, also looking quite pale, said, "Don't anybody touch anything. I guess I gotta call the crime lab and get them to send out a mobile unit." Wallace County isn't big enough to have its own lab.

The next couple of hours became a blur of activity. The state boys arrived and started taking pictures, fingerprinting everything, including me. Then, after the medical examiner arrived, they hauled Eaudelein out of the water.

Randy and one of the investigators from the State Crime Unit, Detective Mertis, made me tell them the whole story in detail, over and over. They wanted to know who had keys to the store. I said I did and so did Freddy, of course, and Hank, Freddy's partner. There were a couple of part-timers who had keys, Willie Smith and Jim Roy Learner.

"Did Eaudelein have a key?" asked Randy.

"I really don't know," I said. "I doubt it, since she and Freddy are divorced. Maybe she still had a key, but I can't imagine her coming in here." She and Freddy hated each other.

"Where was Freddy last night?" asked Randy. Detective Mertis looked curious.

"You know, Randy, he was with me. We saw you at Blockbuster Video last night. We rented a video, went home, and watched it, then we went to bed around ten. Freddy got up around 3:00 A.M. so he could go fishing. The largemouth were supposed to be biting, and he's gettin' in as much time on the water as he can before the Bass Master Classic. He's tryin' to turn pro," I said in an aside to Mertis.

Randy and Detective Mertis exchanged a long look; then Mertis asked, "Where is Freddy now?" He spoke in a still, flat voice. It was my first indication that Freddy was a suspect. Later, looking back, I could follow his reasoning. But hearing the words come from him, in Freddy's shop, with Eaudelein lying on a piece of black plastic in the bait room, sent shivers down my spine. They didn't believe me. I'm about as trustworthy as they come. I don't look like a liar. Hell, sometimes I wish I did, but I look more like your mama. I'm plump and short, with a fresh-scrubbed complexion and pink cheeks. My hair went gray years ago. Give me a ribbon-racked apron, and I could be Betty Crocker. I drive their children to school in one of the four schoolbuses that Wallace County owns. If they couldn't trust me, who could they trust?

No, they thought Freddy had somehow gotten Eaudelein to meet him at the shop and murdered her. My Freddy may have hated Eaudelein, but he would never have killed the mother of his daughter, no matter how evil she'd treated him.

Raydeen put the word out on the police radio she carried that we were looking for Freddy. Detective Mertis held a low-toned conference with Randy. Randy shot a few worried looks in my direction, then wrote a few more things in his notebook.

Around nine, Freddy and Hank came tearing up to the store in Hank's old pickup. Freddy rushed through the door. "Patsy, I just heard. Are you all right?" Surely, I thought, Detective Mertis could tell, just from meeting my Freddy, that he was no killer. But that wasn't the case.

"Fred, I'm afraid we're going to need to ask you to come down to the station with us," said Randy. He didn't say he was sorry or talk to Freddy like they'd known each other for years. He was Randall Vaughn, Wallace County sheriff. And Freddy was a prime suspect in a murder investigation.

They didn't tell me or Hank to come to the station. They just took Hank's prints and asked him where he'd been last night. When he said fishin', they didn't say anything about *him* coming down there. Of course, he hadn't been married to Eaudelein, but it was the principle of the thing.

As Randy was leading Freddy to the patrol car, Freddy stopped dead in his tracks and whirled around. "Oh my Lord," he cried. "What about Loretta? Does she know?" No one had thought to go to Freddy's daughter. "Babe, I hate to ask you, but would you find her? Someone's gonna have to tell her about her mama." I quickly figured out that the someone was me.

What else could I say but "Sure, hon, don't worry. I'll go get her and bring her back to our place."

Freddy and I weren't married. Yet. Freddy'd gotten taken in the divorce. Things were so tight financially that he just couldn't see getting married. He said he didn't want to marry me with so much debt hanging over his head. If you ask me, I think Eaudelein burned him so bad he was afraid of its happening again. So, against the town's better judgment, 'cause you know they judged everybody, I let Freddy move in.

He'd been such a pitiful wreck when we met. Although we both grew up in Barrow, he'd been a few years ahead of me in school and left to join the army as soon as he graduated. Freddy was a Baptist and I belonged to the Methodist church, so our paths never crossed until I stopped in the store to buy bait. Fishin' was gonna be my new hobby, and Freddy was only too happy to help me find a tackle box.

His divorce had only been final a few months, and he was bitter. He couldn't cook, didn't care to, and lived like a prisoner in his tiny apartment. When we began dating, all that changed.

We'd been living together for almost ten months, and in that time Freddy'd come around pretty well. He liked my fried chicken and creamed potatoes, and he'd put on about fifteen pounds. He'd made himself a little workshop in my shed out back and had even joined the softball league. But we didn't talk about marrying any more. I felt that was best left to time.

Loretta, his fifteen-year-old daughter, had been the one thorn in the side of our relationship. She was a dark-haired, sullen child who took after her mother in looks and attitude. Loretta saw me as the Other Woman, standing between her parents and reconciliation. No amount of talking on Freddy's part could persuade her otherwise. She tolerated me and rarely spent the night at our house. Of course, Eaudelein had a lot to do with that. She poisoned the child's mind. She told Loretta that Freddy had started seeing me long before he and Eaudelein separated. That was flat not true. Freddy was living on his own when I met him.

I was going to have trouble with Loretta, I just knew it.

When I pulled up in front of Eaudelein's house, there were cars parked in the driveway. Folks would have known that Loretta was alone, with no one to break the news to her. It wasn't their place, however, to come tromping over and interfere. It was just going to make my job harder.

As I walked up the path, I could hear Loretta wailing. She'd been close to her mother, but this was the wail of someone milking it for all it was worth.

Loretta's aunt, Minnie, Eaudelein's oldest sister, was sitting on the sofa, patting Loretta's hand. Tears streamed down both their faces, and a little group of busybodies stood around looking helpless.

They were not glad to see me, but Minnie was at least civil. She only asked "What are you doin' here?" instead of "What are you doin' here, bitch?"

"Freddy was worried about Loretta. He asked me to come over and make sure she was all right. He's down at the station, helping the police with the investigation." I was putting the best light on the situation for Loretta's sake.

"Loretta," I said, "your daddy wants me to bring you back to our place till he gets home. Then we can sort things out from there."

Loretta lifted her tear-swollen face and favored me with a malevolent glare. "You did this," she shrieked. "You killed my mama!"

Minnie broke in, "Now, Loretta, honey, Patsy wouldn't have killed your mama. And if she had," she continued, with a warning glance in my direction, "the cops would have her in jail." Minnie wasn't defending me. She just didn't want to end up with Loretta in her custody. Everybody knew that Loretta was trouble. Her mama'd been having a devil of a time trying to ride herd on her rebellious child.

Every time Freddy turned around, Eaudelein was on the phone whining about how Loretta had skipped school, missed curfew, or talked back. What was he going to do about it? Then, when Freddy tried to do something, Eaudelein and Loretta double-teamed him. Watching the two of them work Freddy over was like watching Roller Derby, only my Freddy was stuck in the middle.

"Loretta, honey," I said, trying again, "I know you feel awful. I can't imagine how terrible this is for you. Let's get a few of your things and go on back to my place. Your daddy needs you."

That did it; Freddy's baby girl was on her way to comfort her daddy. She tolerated me on the ride back across town. She sat hunched against the passenger-side car door, snuffling into a crumpled Kleenex. She was actually a very sad little girl, vulnerable in her grief, and not the hard case she led the rest of us to believe.

I didn't say much until we were inside. I offered her a Coke or something to eat, but she said no. "Where's my dad?" she asked after an hour had passed.

"I don't know, sugar." I was beginning to feel a little anxious myself. "Loretta, did your mama go out anyplace last night?" I figured Loretta might know something that would help Freddy out. The police would want to talk to her at some point, too.

"I don't know. I was over at Tammara's, spending the night. Mama said she might be going out later but that she wouldn't be gone long." Loretta was tugging at her long black hair and chewing her lip. I could tell that my asking her questions was only going to make her more nervous, so I quit.

The sound of a car door slamming had both of us up out of our seats and over to the front door. It was Randy, and he was alone. Where was Freddy?

He didn't look me in the eye the whole way up the path. When he got to the bottom porch step, he looked up at the two of us. "Patsy. Loretta, I'm sorry about your mama." His eyes were sad.

"Where's my daddy?" Loretta asked, ignoring Randy's solicitude.

"Let's go inside," I interjected. I didn't figure we should be talking about all this under the neighbors' watchful eyes. Randy seemed to jump at the idea, so we trooped into my tiny living room.

"Loretta, Patsy, I wanted to be the one to tell you this. Freddy has been arrested for the murder of Eaudelein."

"Randy, how could you?" I yelled over Loretta's howl of rage and grief. "You know better than that! You've fished with him. You know Freddy would never hurt anybody. It was all that Mertis's doing, wasn't it?"

Randy looked apologetically at Loretta. "Honey, I need to talk to Patsy alone. Would you excuse us?" Loretta favored him with one of her most evil glares, then flounced from the room. I figured she'd go just far enough to be out of sight yet still overhear our conversation.

Randy caught on and lowered his voice. "Patsy, his prints were all over the baseball bat used to bash in Eaudelein's head."

"Well, that don't mean nothing. Freddy kept that bat behind the counter, by the register. It stands to reason that his prints would be all over it."

"Freddy was out alone, without an alibi, at 4:00 A.M., the time of the murder. Everybody knows he and Eaudelein were at each other's throats. Somebody overheard the two of them fighting last week, and Freddy threatened to kill her then."

I knew the fight Randy meant. It had been all over town. Freddy had stopped to pick up Loretta at the house, and Eaudelein had come out to pick a fight. She threatened to keep Loretta away from Freddy. He'd freaked out and told her he'd see her dead before he let her take Loretta away from him.

He didn't actually mean he would kill Eaudelein. It was a remark made in anger. I had to admit I wasn't sure what would have happened if Eaudelein had somehow taken Loretta away from Freddy.

"Daddy wouldn't kill Mama." We hadn't heard Loretta creep down the hallway, hadn't seen her walk into the room.

"I'm sorry, Loretta." Randy nodded to me and walked out the front screen door. "Patsy?"

"What, Randall?" We were adversaries now.

"Get Freddy a lawyer. He ain't thinkin' too clear."

I started to ask him what that meant, but he was already opening his car door.

Loretta was pacing the floor when I returned. "Well, what are you going to do?" she asked.

"Loretta, I know this has been a horrible day for you," I began.

"Cut the sympathy crap. I got one parent left. I ain't gonna lose him, too."

"All right then," I said evenly, "I'm dealin' you in. You and I are going to have to work together on this."

For the next hour that's what we did. I called Sam Barfield and retained him as Freddy's attorney. I had Loretta write down everything she could remember about her mother's last twenty-four hours.

Loretta's list was scrawled in childish, loopy script across the paper I'd given her. She seemed to remember the details of Eaudelein's last day only as they pertained to herself. "Mama fixed me breakfast at 10:00 A.M. Mama told me to clean my room before I went to Tammara's. Mama was washing up the supper dishes when I left with Tammara. She said she might go out later. I asked her to pick up more Froot Loops."

Loretta's little world revolved around Loretta. She could tell me pretty much every detail of her day, when she put on her makeup, what she wore, when her boyfriend Eddie called. Her mother existed as cook, chauffeur, and banker to Loretta's adolescent needs. Oh well, no help there.

"Loretta, I need to leave you here and go see your daddy."

She didn't like that. "I'm comin', too. He's my daddy." And you're only his girlfriend. She left that part hanging unspoken between us.

"They won't let minors in," I said. I grabbed my purse and car keys and headed for the door. "There's sandwich meat in the fridge. Don't go anywhere. I'll be back in an hour." Loretta was looking like a thundercloud, but I continued on briskly. "If we're gonna prove that your daddy didn't kill your mama, we're gonna have to find out who did. Why don't you work on that list a bit more and see what you can remember. If your mama was going out last night, where was she going? Was she seein' anybody in particular?"

I left her sitting at the kitchen table, staring at the pad of paper with her mother's activities on it. When she didn't think I was looking, she allowed her grief to show through. Tears slid down her cheeks and hit the paper.

I got a bit nervous on the ride over to see Freddy. I'd never been inside the jail before. Everybody in town knew where it was—a mile outside of town, on State Route 138. It sat back from the road, a small, squat, concrete building with a barbed wire–enclosed exercise yard. Livin' around here, you drove past it on a regular basis, and like the cemetery, you didn't pay it much mind until you needed to.

Raydeen was working when I got there. We didn't know what to say to each other. If everyone thought Freddy was guilty, then what did they think about me? I didn't want to talk to Raydeen until I'd talked to Freddy and figured out where things were heading.

"I guess you wanna see Freddy, huh?" she asked.

"Well, yeah." It was all I could do not to scream at her, I was so anxious.

She led me back to the jail proper. Steve Asher, a young deputy just a few years older than Loretta, let me into the visitors' room. There was a bank of cubicles with brown wooden chairs in front of the counters that held the phones. Just like TV, I thought. I entered a cubicle and sat down. The visitors before me had scratched their initials into the hard Formica: *C.R. +J.D.—love forever. T.J. loves M.J.— I will wait forever.*

When Freddy was brought in, I realized just how serious our situation was. The man I loved was in jail for murder. Even my loser first husband Roy hadn't ever been in jail.

Freddy looked scared. We picked up the receivers and pressed them to our ears. "How ya doin', babe?" he asked with a weak smile.

"Don't worry about me," I said. "Loretta's okay, too. I got her back at our place. Minnie's gonna handle the funeral arrangements." Freddy nodded. "I called Sam Barfield and asked him to represent you. He's gonna come by tonight or first thing tomorrow." There was one brief moment when I found myself wondering, Freddy, you didn't do it, did you? Of course not. I couldn't doubt Freddy's innocence.

"Who could've killed her?" we both asked at the same instant.

"Patsy, don't take this wrong," Freddy began. "I'm sad about Eaudelein. Yesterday I could've told you that if her guts was on fire, I wouldn't a spit on her to put 'em out. But, hell, Patsy, I didn't want her to die. I keep thinkin' about when we first met, and when Loretta was little. I used to love her. She was Loretta's mama for Pete's sake." I listened, watching Freddy's face.

"They say I killed Eaudelein because she was gonna take Loretta away from me. They don't understand. Eaudelein would've come to her senses. I wouldn't have killed her, no matter what she did."

"Freddy," I broke in. "You don't have to explain it to me. I know you. We just gotta figure out who killed her. Do you have any idea?"

"Eaudelein had a habit of pissin' people off, but I don't know of anybody who hated her enough to kill her."

Freddy was thinking now, not feeling sorry for himself. That was good.

"Was she seein' anybody?"

"Well," he said slowly, "she'd been stranger than usual lately. She was real peculiar about when I picked up Loretta. She didn't want me just stopping by to see Loretta without asking. I figured she was seein' somebody and didn't want me to know. When she started talking about not letting me see Loretta, I started worrying that her new guy might live out of town. Maybe she was fixin' to move away with him or something."

The deputy, Steve, opened the door and said something to Freddy. "I gotta go now, babe. Hang in there."

Hang in there. That was my Freddy, worrying about me. I picked up my purse and headed home. At least I had something to go on now. Eaudelein had a new boyfriend. Loretta hadn't said a word about that.

It was the first thing I asked her about when I got home. She had been on the phone when I got there but hung up quickly as I walked through the front door. She'd been crying again. I sat down next to her on the couch. I wanted to reach over and put my arms around her, but she was such a prickly pear. She didn't like me, so I wasn't going to push myself on her.

"I stopped at the Kentucky Fried and grabbed us a bucket of extra crispy. Let's go eat."

"I'm not hungry."

"Honey, you got to eat." Loretta was no match for me. She might have had the rest of the adults in Barrow scared of her, but I drove a schoolbus. I ate kids like her for lunch, sack and all.

"Sweetie," I went on, ignoring her attitude, "I know you don't feel like it, but we've got a lot to do. I can't have you fainting from lack of food. Eat. It'll make you feel better, and you'll be able to think better, too."

She followed me into the kitchen. We polished off the entire bucket between us and made big dents in the coleslaw and potatoes.

"Now," I said, clearing the plates away, "who was your mother seeing?"

Loretta looked uneasy. "Nobody," she said.

"Loretta," I said, daring her to lie again.

"She didn't want me to tell anybody." She was working it out. "It was Daddy's partner, Hank. Mama said Daddy'd freak if he knew. She and Hank wanted to keep it a secret till they figured out what to do."

Hank? That was so hard to believe. Hank and Freddy were best friends. They owned the Bait and Tackle Shop together. Hank had stuck by Freddy all through the divorce, siding with him, commiserating with him. Hank would never go near Eaudelein.

"Loretta, are you sure?" I asked.

"I'm sure," she said earnestly. "If she was going out last night, it would have been with him. She always went out when I was with Daddy or over at a friend's house."

"When did she start seeing Hank?"

"About three months ago. I didn't find out until about a month ago. I came home early from a friend's house just as he was leavin'. Hank was all freaked about it. Mama just laughed. She told me later that Hank didn't want Daddy to know and that we'd better keep it quiet, just till everything got sorted out and they could tell Daddy."

This was just great. Freddy's ex and his best friend. If Freddy'd been bitter before, he'd swear off matrimony forever now. What this was gonna do to his friendship with Hank, and their business, was beyond me. I'd be really pissed if I were him.

Then I started thinking. Hank didn't have an alibi for last night. Hank was the last person to see Eaudelein alive. Could he have killed her?

"Loretta, I gotta go see Hank." I was headed for the door before she could formulate a response.

"Wait," she yelled as I pushed open the door. "I'm coming, too."

"No, Loretta. You stay here by the phone. If your daddy calls, don't tell him where I am." Oh good, I thought, now I'm a liar, too.

Hank wasn't at the bait shop. The door had a sign, hastily scrawled, that read: "Closed due to death."

I headed on down to the lake where Hank had a double-wide. Hank was thirty-five and had never been married. He lived alone on the lake, where he kept his Ranger bass boat lovingly housed in a covered boat dock. The boathouse and bass boat had cost Hank more than his lake property and the double-wide. Hank lived to fish. He was a tall, quiet man who had always seemed a bit awkward around women. I'd seen him many a time, chatting it up with a male customer about fish or what bait to use. As soon as a woman so much as pulled up to the gas pumps outside, he'd clam up. He was only a little less bashful around me.

He was walking up the hill from the dock when I got out of my car. His head was down, and he carried his tackle box with him. I waited till he got closer, then called out, "What's the matter, fish not bitin'?" Hank was startled and turned a bright red.

"Aw, I just thought fishing might take my mind off things. You know how that goes, I guess."

"No, Hank, I don't. I've been forced to stay right here dealin' with Loretta and gettin' your buddy Freddy a lawyer."

Hank's blush crept down his neck, below his bushy black beard. His ears were burning, too. I was angry, but I didn't want to blow any chance of getting information from him by losing it.

"Loretta told me you've been seein' Eaudelein. She said you saw her last night." I just laid it there between us and waited.

"Oh, Patsy. Gawd dawg." Hank sighed and wiped his hand over his face. "Yeah, it's true. Gawd, I feel like such a heel. I didn't mean no-body any pain. Eaudelein, she just kept comin' around and comin' around, talkin' and flirtin' with me." He paused and fiddled with the latch on his tackle box.

"She told me she liked me. She wanted us to go out. I told her no at first, but she had such a way about her." When Eaudelein wanted something, she got it all right. Hank, with his lack of experience with women, would have been no match for Eaudelein. I waited for him to go on.

"I never had a woman do that to me before." He looked like a stupid schoolboy. He'd fallen in love. "I didn't know what to do about it. It was killin' me. I felt like dirt every time I was around Freddy. I wanted to tell him, but I never could find the right time."

"Were you with her last night?"

Hank looked miserable. "No, er, aw hell, yeah. I was with her. But honest to Gawd, I had her back to her place by one. She didn't want to stay over 'cause Loretta was comin' home first thing in the morning. We hung around here, then I took her back to her place."

"Did you see her go inside?" Hank nodded yes. "Then what happened?"

"Well, I came back here and decided to go fishin'. I'd told Freddy I'd meet him out on the lake by daybreak. I figured I'd just hook up with him earlier. I wasn't really sleepy, and I did need to get some time in before the tournament."

"Well, good, then," I said, relieved. "You and Freddy are each other's alibis for the time of the murder."

Hank looked down, scuffing at a patch of grass with his boot. "Patsy, I didn't find Freddy till around five. He wasn't in any of our usual places. I looked everywhere. I finally caught up to him at the gas docks. I don't know where he was."

This was not good. I left Hank's feeling more confused than before. Where had Freddy been? Was Hank telling the truth? I was inclined to think so. Freddy was gonna be devastated when he found out Hank had been lying to him for months. How could he ever trust anyone again? We'd never get married at this rate.

It was best not to dwell on that right now. I was gonna have enough trouble springing Freddy from jail. Maybe Loretta had remembered some helpful detail from Eaudelein's life that could help us figure out just who had done her in. But I wasn't feeling hopeful when I got back home.

Loretta's boyfriend Eddie had come over. She'd known better than to let him in, so they were sitting on the porch swing together. Loretta was crying, and Eddie had his arm around her shoulders.

She wiped her eyes and jumped up to greet me as I started up the path. "Well," she said impatiently, "what did he say? Was he with her?"

"He was with her," I answered, "but he dropped her back at the house around 1:00 A.M."

"Bullsh . . ." Loretta broke off abruptly and clammed up.

"Loretta? Do you know something else? Have you remembered something else?"

"No. You didn't believe him, did you?"

"I don't know, Loretta. I was kinda hoping he would tell us something that would let your father off the hook, but if anything, he made it more confusing. He said after he dropped your mama off, he went looking for your daddy out on the lake but didn't find him till five."

Loretta was scowling. Eddie must have sensed that another storm was brewing because he said he had to get on home. Loretta let him kiss her on the cheek, then watched him climb into his old clunker and drive off.

I went inside, and Loretta followed me. "I'm gonna go off for a little while," she said.

"You can't go off now. It's getting dark." I didn't want her wandering across town alone, after dark.

"I wanta go see Tammara." Tears trembled on her lashes. "She's my best friend."

I sighed. Hell, the kid had lost her mama, and her daddy had been arrested, all in one day. If she wanted to talk to her best friend, then why not?

"All right, but I'll drive you over." That suited her. "And you can't stay too long. I'll run a couple of errands, then come back and pick you up." Loretta didn't say anything, just sat quietly for the short ride to Tammara's.

Tammara was waiting in the front yard. She was a cute, short cheerleader with an attitude. She wore combat boots and little round sunglasses and had her hair pulled back in a ponytail. When Loretta hopped out of the car, Tammara wrapped her in a tight hug and began to cry tears of sympathy.

I leaned out the window. "I'll be back to get you in an hour," I called. As I drove away, I saw the two girls sink into a huddle on the front lawn. I decided to go see Minnie, Eaudelein's sister, and let her know that I'd be keeping Loretta indefinitely. I needed to find out about the funeral arrangements, too.

Minnie's place wasn't hard to find. She and the rest of Eaudelein's family lived in a family compound that surrounded their grandfather's farm. Minnie was sitting on the front porch of her tiny house with a few other family members. They all stared as I pulled in the driveway and parked. "Hey, Minnie," I said as I walked up. I didn't wait for her to respond. "I just came by to let you know we'd be keeping Loretta."

"For how long?" she asked. Everyone else just stared.

"We'll figure out the details when Freddy gets out."

Minnie snorted. "Freddy Buck Owens murdered my sister. He'll never see the outside of a prison if I have anything to do with it." She was daring me to get into it with her.

I ignored the bait. "Did you know she was seeing Hank?" I asked.

"Me and just about everybody else in town but you and Freddy." The group on the porch snickered. This was going nowhere. I could call the town's one funeral parlor to find out about the funeral. In the meantime, I needed to get to the Piggly Wiggly and buy Froot Loops for Loretta.

It had been exactly an hour when I returned to Tammara's house. The girls had disappeared from the front yard, so I went up to the front door and rang the bell. Tammara's mother came to the door looking politely confused. I explained that I'd come to pick up Loretta.

"Oh, well, they're not here. Tammara left to drive Loretta home. She said they were supposed to meet you there."

"Maybe we miscommunicated," I said. "I'll meet them there." I turned to leave, then turned around. "Can I ask you one more question?"

"Sure." Tammara's mother waited.

"When did Loretta leave to go home this morning?"

"I'm not sure I understand," Tammara's mother said. "Loretta wasn't here this morning."

"She didn't spend the night?"

"No, absolutely not. Tammara's been on restriction all week. She hasn't been allowed to have company. I only made an exception today because of Loretta's mother."

Loretta had lied.

I didn't know what was going on, but I was beginning to get a picture. I couldn't wait to get to that girl, but when I got to my place, Loretta wasn't there.

Maybe Tammara had driven Loretta to see Eddie. I knew his parents, so it wasn't hard to find his phone number in the book. Eddie answered. No, he hadn't seen or heard from Loretta. Just as well; I'd thought of a few questions I wanted to ask him without Loretta around to coach him. I grabbed my chance. "Eddie, where did you and Loretta go last night?"

"We went to, uh, well, we were just riding around the square. Then . . ." Eddie caught up with himself and clammed up. Bingo. The next question I wanted to ask in person.

I raced across town and was in luck. Eddie answered the door. He was startled to see me and frightened. "Come out here on the porch," I hissed. He hesitated, looking back over his shoulder into the living room where his parents sat.

"Who is it, Eddie?" his father called.

"Just a friend, Dad." Eddie quickly pulled the door shut behind him and stepped outside. "I told you, she's not here," he said.

"I know, Eddie. I just had one more question. Where did you two spend the night?"

Eddie was flustered. "What do you mean? We didn't . . ."

I didn't have time to waste on whatever story he was trying to manufacture. I had a feeling that Loretta was in danger. "Cut to the chase, Eddie. I know you and Loretta spent the night together. Now, was it at her house or where?"

Eddie gave up. "Yeah, we were at her place. Her mama was spending the night out with her boyfriend."

"Did she tell Loretta that?"

"No, but that's what she always did when Loretta wasn't home. That's why we knew it would be cool at her place."

That was all I needed to hear. I turned and raced for the car. I yelled back over my shoulder, "Eddie, call the sheriff, ask for Randy Vaughn. Tell him Patsy said to get out to Hank Starr's and bring some deputies with him." Eddie seemed hesitant. "Do it, Eddie!"

He had turned and was going inside when I drove off. I had to hurry. My car, an older Cavalier, wasn't used to fast speeds. I drove defensively, prided myself on that; now I hurtled out of town like a maniac.

When I hit the dirt road to Hank's place, I had to stand on the brakes to keep from plowing into the rear of Tammara's vw. Tammara was leaning against the side, smoking a cigarette. She looked scared.

"Oh man, I'm really glad you're here. Loretta told me to wait here and if she wasn't back in a half hour, call you." She twisted her watch around on her wrist and stared at it. "It's been twenty-seven minutes."

Loretta had been a very foolish girl. "Tammara, here's what you do, honey. Get yourself up the road to the Quick Stop and use their phone to call 911. Tell them to get ahold of Randy, and give him directions here. Tell him to hurry." I wanted to cover myself in case Eddie hadn't called.

Then I took off running for Hank's place. I didn't want him to hear me coming and do anything foolish. It was quite dark now; the light in Hank's boathouse was the only thing to guide me. I crept past the house, headed for the dock.

The sound of voices carried up from the water. Hank's was a low monotone, Loretta's an angry tornado. "You can't get away with this," she yelled. "They'll know it was you." I slipped silently up to the boathouse. Hank was unhitching the bow lines and preparing to cast off. Loretta lay on the floor of the boat, her arms and legs bound with rope.

"Loretta," Hank said as he moved to untie the stern lines, "this carryin' on won't do you no good. Cain't nobody hear you. I wouldn't be havin' to do this if you'd been doin' what yore mama told you to do last night." Hank moved to the driver's seat and inserted the key in the ignition. He was fixin' to pull out of the boathouse and take Loretta. I couldn't let that happen.

"My daddy'll come after you, Hank," Loretta screamed. "They'll fry your ass if you kill me. I'm a minor." Oh nice goin', Loretta, I thought.

Hank stayed cool. "No they won't, Loretta. When you don't show up, they'll figure you lured your mama down to your daddy's shop and killed her. They'll think you wanted to frame your daddy so's you could get the insurance money. Just like them brothers out in California done. Kids are runnin' wild these days."

Loretta's response was lost as Hank cranked the engine. It was now or never. I made my move. I took a flying leap from the dock and hit the bow of the boat just as it moved out of the slip into the open channel.

Loretta's eyes widened, and Hank looked as if he couldn't believe it was me. When he came for me, I tried to be ready. All those classes at Mr. Chu's Tae Kwan Do studio were going to come in handy, I thought. Where were the police?

"Hank Starr, you take this boat back to shore!" I screamed. "I'm placing you under a citizen's arrest!" His beefy hands wrapped around my throat like a vise. This was not like any practice I'd ever done at Mr. Chu's. Spots danced before my eyes and as it grew impossible to breathe, I saw Freddy's face. He was lookin' real sad, and I started feelin' sad. We were never gonna get married. Then I started getting mad. Hell fire, it was always something.

Mr. Chu's face floated up then. What was he saying? Oh, yeah, I could hear his voice. "Find your rage," he said. "Break his hold. Hit him where it hurts. Predators look for the weak."

I had found my rage. No Hank Starr was gonna keep me from the altar. I summoned up one last burst of energy and threw my arms up through Hank's. I brought my knee up and rammed it into his groin. I had lost control and was going to kill him. I shattered his kneecap with a swift kick and would have crushed his windpipe had Randy not arrived.

Apparently he'd been screaming at me from the shore, but I hadn't heard. As the boat had drifted back toward the dock, Randy had leapt on board.

He grabbed my shoulders and shook me. "Patsy, stop. It's Randy. Stop, you're okay now." I was shaking with the adrenaline and fear. "It's okay now, honey," he said, pulling me closer to him.

The dock was overrun with deputies. Raydeen was bustling around, issuing orders. Randy told me later that both Eddie and Tammara had called 911, leaving desperate messages. Randy had arrived with all the backup available in Wallace County.

Hank told everything once he was faced with the reality of his arrest. He and Eaudelein had been at the bait shop around 3:00 A.M. Hank was preparing to go fishing and needed to pick up some bait. He and Eaudelein had been out drinking all night, celebrating because Eaudelein had agreed to marry Hank. While Hank was scooping out minnows, Eaudelein started going on about how, when they were married, she'd have control over the Bait Shop. She was crowing about how she'd make Freddy's life miserable. Hank realized that Eaudelein never really loved him; she'd merely wanted to use him to torture her ex-husband.

Hank, about to lose the one love of his life, lost control. He grabbed the baseball bat and beat Eaudelein to death. He was getting ready to take her out to the middle of the lake and dump her when some fishermen pulled up to the shop.

They saw Hank's pickup, figured someone was there, and began knocking on the door. Hank panicked and dumped Eaudelein in the tank. Then he gave the men bait and sent them on their way. Even though the men weren't locals, Randy figured they'd be easy enough to track down, if need be.

"The way things look now," Randy said, "Hank's gonna plead guilty. Says he was temporarily insane."

"Hell," said Freddy as Randy returned his personal belongings and signed the release papers, "I guess that explains my whole marriage to Eaudelein. Too bad I couldn't plead that during the divorce."

Freddy stuck close by me the whole ride home. "Babe, you sure he didn't hurt you?"

"Freddy, I'm fine," I insisted. If the truth be known, I was enjoying myself.

"Babe, I just don't know how I can ever repay you," he said for the umpteenth time.

"Aw, Freddy," I said, patting his knee, "we'll think of something." I was thinking a June weddin' would be nice. We'd hitch a knot in the tail of matrimony yet.

NANCY BARTHOLOMEW, a transplanted Yankee, maintains a private psychotherapy practice in Greensboro, but that doesn't stop her from satisfying her inner writer. Her funny, spicy work features exotic dancers, country singers, bikers, and cops. She is author of eight books in three series and counting, including *Drag Strip* and *Stand By Your Man*.

A STAR FOR A WARRIOR

Manly Wade Wellman

Young David Return half-ran across the sunbright plaza of the Tsichah Agency. He was slim everywhere except across his shoulders, his tawny brow, his jaw. For this occasion he had put on his best blue flannel shirt, a maroon scarf, cowboy dungarees, and, on his slim toed-in feet, beaded moccasins. Behind his right hip rode a sheath-knife. His left hand carried his sombrero, and his thick black hair reflected momentary blue lights in the hot morning. Once he lifted the hat and slapped his thigh with it, in exultation too great for even an Indian to dissemble. He opened the door of the whitewashed cabin that housed the agency police detail and fairly bounded in.

"*Ahi!*" he spoke a greeting in Tsichah to the man in the cowskin vest who glanced up at him from a paper-littered table. "A writing from the white chiefs, Grandfather. I can now wear the silver star."

The other man lifted a brown face as lean, keen, and grim as the blade of a tomahawk. Tough Feather, senior lieutenant of the agency police, was the sort of old Indian that Frederic Remington loved to paint. He replied in English. "Reports here," he said austerely, "are made in white man's language."

David Return blinked. He was a well-bred young Tsichah and did his best not to show embarrassment. "I mean," he began again, also in English, "that they've confirmed my appointment to the agency police detail, and—"

"Suppose," interrupted Tough Feather, "that you go outside, and come in again—properly."

Some of the young man's boisterous happiness drained out of him. Obediently he stepped backward and out, pulling the door shut. He waited soberly for a moment, then re-entered and stood at attention.

"Agency Policeman David Return," he announced dutifully, "reporting for assignment as directed."

Tough Feather's thin mouth permitted a smile to soften one of its corners. Tough Feather's deep-set black eyes glowed a degree more warmly. "Your report of completed study came in the mail an hour ago," he told David, and he picked up a paper. "They marked you 'Excellent' everywhere, except in discipline. There you're 'Qualified.' That's good, but no more than good enough."

David shrugged. "The instructors were white men. But you'll not have any trouble with me. You're my grandfather and a born chief of the Tsichah."

"So are you a born chief," Tough Feather reminded him, "and don't forget it. This police work isn't a white man's plaything. We serve the government, to make things better for all Indians. *Ahi*, son of my son," and forgetting his own admonition Tough Feather himself lapsed into Tsichah, "for this I taught you as a child and saw that you went to school and to the police college. We work together from this day."

"*Nunway*," intoned David, as at a tribal ceremony. "Amen. That is my prayer."

From a pocket of the cowskin vest Tough Feather drew a black stone pipe, curiously and anciently carved. His brown fingers stuffed in flakes of tobacco. He produced a match and struck a light. Inhaling deeply, he blew a curl of slate-colored smoke, another and another and others, one to each of the six holy directions—north, west, south, east, upward, and downward. Then he offered the pipe to David.

"Smoke," he invited deeply. "You are my brother warrior."

It was David Return's coming-of-age. He inhaled and puffed in turn, and while the smoke clouds signalized the directions, he prayed silently to the Shining Lodge for strength and wisdom. When he had finished the six ritualistic puffs he handed the pipe back to Tough Feather, who shook out the ashes and stowed it in his pocket. Then from the upper drawer of the desk Tough Feather produced something that shone like all the high hopes of all young warriors. He held it out, the silver-plated star of an agency policeman.

Eagerly David pinned it to his left shirt pocket, then drew himself once more to attention. "I'm ready to start duty, Grandfather," he said.

"Good." Tough Feather was consulting a bit of paper with hastily scribbled notes. "David, do you remember an Indian girl named Rhoda Pleasant who came to the agent last week with letters of introduction?"

"I remember that one," nodded David. "Not a Tsichah girl. A Piekan, going to some university up north. She's pleasant, all right," and he smiled, for Indians relish puns as much as any race in the world.

"Not pleasant in every way," growled Tough Feather, not amused. "She's been here too long, and talked too much, for a stranger woman. Plenty of young Tsichah men like her even better than you do. They might finish up by not liking each other."

"Then she's still here on the reservation? I met her only the one time, and the next day she was gone."

"But not gone away," Tough Feather told him. "Gone in. She borrowed a horse and some things to camp with. You know why, don't you? She wants to learn our secret Tsichah songs." The hard-cut old profile shook itself in conservative disapproval.

"*Ahi*, yes," said David. "She talked about that. Said she was getting her master's degree in anthropology, and she's hoping for a career as a scholar and an Indian folklore expert. She told me she'd picked up songs that Lieurance and Cadman would have given ten years of their life to hear and get down on paper. But I couldn't tell her about our songs if I wanted to. We hear them only two or three times a year, at councils and ceremonies."

"The songs are like the chieftainships, passed from father to son in one or two families," reminded Tough Feather. "Right now only three men really know them—"

"And they're mighty brash about it," broke in David, with less than his usual courtesy. "I know them. Dolf Buckskin, Stacey Weed, and John Horse Child. All of them young, and all of them acting a hundred years old and a thousand years smart, out there in their brush camp with a drum—the kind with a pebble-headed stick—and a flute. They think we others ought to respect and honor them."

"And you should," Tough Feather replied stiffly. "They're young, but their fathers and grandfathers taught them songs and secrets that come down from our First People. Those three young men are important to the whole Tsichah nation. Too important to be set against each other by Rhoda Pleasant."

"You mean she's out there seeing them?" David was suddenly grave, too. "I see what you're worried about. They'd not pay any attention to a man who asked rude questions, but a young woman as pretty as that Piekan—*ahi!* She'd give anybody squaw fever."

"Go to their camp," commanded Tough Feather. "It's off all the main trails, so you'll have to ride a pony instead of driving a car. Tell the girl she must report back here and then go somewhere else."

David frowned. This was not his dream of a brilliant first case for his record. Then he smiled, for he reflected that the ride back from the camp of the singers would be interesting with a companion like Rhoda Pleasant. "Where is that camp, Grandfather?"

Tough Feather pointed with the heel of his hand. "Southwest. Take the Lodge Pole Ridge trail, and turn at the dry stream by the cabins of old Gopher Paw and his son. There's no trail across their land, but you'll pick one up beyond, among the knolls and bluffs. That branches in a few miles, and the right branch leads to where the singers are camped. Take whatever pony you want from the agency stable."

"The paint pony?" asked David eagerly.

"He's not the best one," and Tough Feather eyed his grandson calculatingly. "Not the best traveler, anyway."

"Now about a saddle," went on David, "will you lend me the silver-mounted one that Major Lillie gave you ten years ago?"

Tough Feather smiled, perhaps his first real smile in twenty or thirty days. "All right, take it and take the prettiest bridle, too. You're probably right, David. You'll have less trouble bringing that girl back if you and your pony are good to look at."

The paint pony was not the best in the agency stables, but he was competent on the narrow rough trail that David had to take. His light-shod feet picked a nimble way through the roughest part of the reservation, over ground even less fit for farming than the poor soil of prairie and creek bottoms. It was rolling and stony, grown up here and there with cottonwood scrub and occasional clumps of willow or Osage orange.

Once or twice rabbits fled from the sound of the hooves, but not too frantically: animals felt safe in the half-cover of this section; long ago they had escaped here from the incessant hunting enthusiasm of Tsichah boys with arrows or cheap old rifles.

David followed the right branch of the trail that his grandfather had described and went down a little slope, across an awkward gully where he had to dismount and lead the pony, and beyond among scattered boulders.

He felt that he was getting near his work, and in his mind he rehearsed the words, half lofty and half bantering, with which he would explain to Rhoda Pleasant that she must cease her troublesome researches and head back with him. She was a ready smiler, he remembered, both bolder and warmer in manner than any Tsichah girl he knew. And she wore her riding things with considerable knowledge and style, like a white society girl.

Suppose she elected to be charmingly stubborn, to question his authority? He decided to stand for no nonsense and to admit no dazzlement from her smile and her bright eyes. He would be like the old warriors who had no sense of female romance or glamour, who took sex, like all important things, in their dignified stride.

Then he rode around a little tuft of thorn bushes and saw that Rhoda Pleasant was beyond hearing arguments or considering authorities.

Here by the trailside was her little waterproofed tent, with a canvas ground cloth and a mosquito bar. Near it was picketed the bay horse she had borrowed at the agency. A fire had burned to ashes, and a few cooking utensils lay beside it. On the trail itself lay Rhoda Pleasant, grotesquely and limply sprawled with her face upward.

Her riding habit was rumpled, her smooth-combed black hair gleamed in the sunlight like polished black stone. She looked like a rag doll that some giant child had played with and dropped on tiring of it. Thrown away, that was how she looked. David Return knew death when he saw it.

He got off his pony and threw the reins over its head, then squatted on his heels beside the body. Rhoda Pleasant's neck-scarf had been white. Now it was spotted with stale blood, dark and sticky. David prodded her cool cheek with a forefinger. Her head did not stir on her neck. That was *rigor mortis*. She had been dead for hours, probably since before dawn. Fully dressed as she was, she might have died before bedtime the night before.

David studied her clay-pale face. The dimmed eyes were open, the lips slack, the expression—she had no expression, only the blank look he had been taught to recognize as that of the unexpectedly and instantly stricken.

Gingerly he drew aside the scarf. The throat wound was blackened with powder but looked ragged, as if a bullet and a stab had struck the same mark. Someone had shot Rhoda Pleasant, decided David, then had thrust a narrow, sharp weapon into the bullet hole.

Rising, David turned his attention to the trail. Its earth was hard, but not too hard to show the tracks of moccasins all round the body, moccasins larger than David's. More tracks were plain nearer the tent and the fire, of the large moccasins and of a companion pair, long and lean. Here and there were a third set of moccasin prints, this time of feet almost as small as Rhoda Pleasant's riding boots.

Three men had been there, apparently all together. And there were three tribal singers camped not far away.

David broke bushes across the trail on either side of the body and from the tent brought a quilt to spread over the blank, dead face. Mounting again, he forced the paint pony off the trail and through thickets where it would disturb no clues. When he came to the trail beyond, he rolled a cigarette and snapped a match alight. Before he had finished smoking he came to another and larger camp.

In a sizable clearing among the brush clumps, by a little stream undried by the summer heat, stood an ancient Sibley tent like a square-bottomed teepee. Behind it was a smaller shelter, of bent sticks covered thickly with old blankets in the shape of a pioneer wagon cover. It was big enough for a single occupant's crouching or lying body, and entrances before and behind were tightly lapped over. Near one end burned a small, hot fire, with stones visible among its coals. As David watched, a hand poked out with rough tongs made of green twigs, lifted a stone, and dragged it inside. Strings of steamy vapor crept briefly forth.

"Sweat lodge," said David aloud. The old Tsichah had built and used sweat lodges frequently, but he himself had seen only a few and had been in one just once in his life, as part of the ceremony of joining the Fox Soldier society two years back. He called in Tsichah: "*Ahi*, you singing Indians! Someone has come to see you!"

From the Sibley tent came Stacey Weed. He was taller than David and leaner, with hair cut long for a young Indian. All that he wore was a breechclout and moccasins. In one hand he carried a canvas bucket, and he turned at first toward where the camp's three horses were tethered on long lariats downstream from the tent. Then he pretended to notice David and lifted a hand in a careless gesture of greeting. "*Ahi*, nephew," he said, also in Tsichah.

To be called nephew by a Tsichah can be pleasant or unpleasant. An older man means it in friendly informality; a contemporary seeks to patronize or to snub or to insult, depending on the tone of his voice. Stacey Weed was perhaps two years older than David, not enough seniority to make for kindliness in the salutation.

"John," called Stacey back into the tent, "we must be important. A boy with a new police star has ridden in."

John Horse Child followed Stacey into the open. He too was almost naked, powerfully built, and just under six feet tall. His smile was broad but tight. "I heard that David Return had joined the police," he remarked to Stacey, as though discussing someone a hundred miles away.

David kept his temper. He spoke in English, as he judged his grandfather would do. "I suppose," he ventured, "that Dolf Buckskin's in the sweat lodge."

John and Stacey gazed at each other. Their eyes twinkled with elaborate mockery. "They say that policemen get great wisdom with those stars they wear," said John, carefully choosing the Tsichah words. "They can tell who's in a sweat lodge and who is not. It's a strong medicine. They learn things without being told."

"Then why tell them things?" inquired Stacey brightly.

The two squatted on the earth, knees to chin. John began to light a stone pipe, older and bigger and more ornate than the one Tough Feather had shared with David earlier that morning. It was part of the ceremonial gear these tribal singers used in the rites they knew. John smoked a few puffs, passed it to Stacey, who smoked in turn, then handed the pipe back. Neither glanced at David, who got quickly out of his saddle and tramped toward them. He still spoke in English, which he knew they understood, but he used the deep, cold voice of unfriendly formality.

"I'm as good a Tsichah as either of you ever dared to be," he told them. "I'm a good American citizen too, and whether you like it or not this ground is part of a government reservation, under police authority. If we're going to have trouble it will be of your starting. I want to ask—"

A wild yell rang from the sweat lodge. Out scuttled Dolf Buckskin, slimmer and shorter and nuder than either of his friends. He shone with the perspiration of the lodge's steamy, hot interior. Even as David turned toward him, Dolf threw himself full length into the widest part of the stream and yelled even louder as the cold water shocked his heated skin. He rolled over and over, then sat up and slapped the water out of his shaggy hair.

"Come here, Dolf," called David, and Dolf pushed his slim feet into moccasins, tied a clout about his hips, and stalked over, with a grin as maddening as Stacey's and John's.

"Rhoda Pleasant," began David, "came and camped nearby, with the idea of tricking you into teaching her our tribal songs."

"We know that," said Dolf.

David decided to go back to the Tsichah tongue, since they refused to drop it. "She made eyes and smiles at the three of you," he went on. "She half promised all sorts of things if you would tell her your secrets."

"We know that," Stacey echoed Dolf, and the three of them looked at each other knowingly, like big boys teasing a little one.

Dolf sat down with his friends, and David stood looking down at them. He pointed trailward with his lifted palm.

"Rhoda Pleasant lies dead back there," he went on, "within a little walk from here."

Then he reflected silently that it is not good to stretch your face with a mocking grin, because when something takes the grin away you look blank, almost as blank as somebody who has been suddenly killed. The three singers betrayed no fear or shock, for they were Indians and steeped from boyhood in the tradition of the stoic; but they succeeded only by turning themselves stupidly expressionless.

John Horse Child broke the silence finally. "We know that, too," he said.

Stacey offered David the ceremonial pipe. It was still alight.

"Smoke," urged Stacey. "We will joke with you no more."

David squatted down with the three, puffing as gravely as when he had smoked with Tough Feather. Then he handed back the pipe and spoke in Tsichah.

"First, let me tell what I know already. You're all tribal singers, medicine men, and when you think your knowledge is big and your position strong, you think the truth. Nobody among the Tsichah can replace any one of you very well. You are keepers of knowledge that should live among the people. You," he tilted his chin at John Horse Child, "play the flute. You," and he indicated Dolf Buckskin, "beat the drum with the pebble-headed drumstick. And Stacey, you are the singer and dancer. Without one, the other two are not complete. Besides, you are close friends, like three brothers."

"*Yuh*," assented Stacey. "That is true."

"I know things about the girl too. A small bullet was fired into her throat, and then a thin knife was stabbed into the same place. She died, I think, not too late last night. And all three of you have been at her camp."

"All three of us have been there several times," said John quietly. "Do you think, David, that all three of us killed her?"

"I think one went alone to her and killed her and made both the wounds," replied David. "I think that one hid his tracks and that you went together and found her dead this morning. I think the killer has not told his two good friends what he did.

"If these things are true we can believe more things. Of you three, one knows who killed Rhoda Pleasant because he is the killer. Of the other two, each knows that one of his two friends killed her, and he wants to help whichever of the two it may be. I can see that much, because I know who you are and what you do and what Rhoda Pleasant was trying to do here."

"She came smiling and flattering and asking for our songs," Dolf Buckskin admitted.

"*Ahi*," went on David, "she was a pretty girl, prettier than any on this reservation. Three men, living alone together, find it easy to look at that sort of girl and to like her. Now I come to the place where I am not sure what to think. I cannot say surely which of several reasons the killer had to do that thing."

"Every killer has a reason," said John weightily, handing the pipe along to Stacey.

"It was about the songs, anyway," David ventured.

Stacey smoked the pipe to its last puff, tapped out the ashes, and began to refill it. "Perhaps it was none of us, David. Perhaps some other man, someone who wanted to steal from her."

"No," said David emphatically. "Her face showed no fear or wonder. She had no trouble with the one who came to kill her, and she must have seen him, for the wounds were in front. Nobody else lives near here, anyway. I think the killer is right here."

John's grin of mockery found its way back. "Why don't you arrest the guilty man?" he challenged. "Nobody will stop you."

"But," added Stacey, rekindling the pipe, "you can't take the wrong man. The government courts would set him free and pay damage money for false arrest. Probably, the policeman who guessed so foolishly would be discharged."

"I'll get the right one," promised David. "The two innocent men won't be bothered."

"*Ahoh*—thanks," said Stacey deeply, and he passed the pipe to Dolf.

"*Ahoh* from me, too," echoed Dolf.

"And from me *ahoh*," chimed in John. The pipe traveled around the circle again, David smoking last. Finally he rose to his feet.

"If you don't hinder me I want to search the tent," he said.

"What you wish," granted Stacey, receiving the pipe from him.

David went to the tent and inside. Sunlight filtered brownly through the canvas. Three pallets, made up of blankets spread over heaps of springy brush, lay against the walls. David examined with respectful care a stack of ceremonial costumes, bonnets, and parcels in a corner, then turned to the personal property of the three singers.

John's bed could be identified by three flutes in a quiverlike buckskin container, slung to the wall of the tent. David pulled out the flutes one by one. Each was made of two wooden halves, cunningly hollowed out and fitted together in tight bindings of snakeskin.

Each had five finger holes and a skillfully shaped mouthpiece. At the head of the pallet lay John's carving tool. David slid it from its scabbard—an old, old knife, its steel worn away by years of sharpening to the delicate slenderness of an edged awl. It showed brightly clean, as from many thrustings into gritty soil. Someone had scoured it clean of Rhoda Pleasant's blood.

On another cot lay Dolf's ceremonial drum of tight-cured raw buckskin laced over a great wooden hoop and painted with berry juices in the long ago—strange symbols in ocher and vermilion. David looked for the drumstick that he had often seen at public singings, a thing like a little war club with an egg-sized pebble bound in the split end of the stick. It was not in sight, and he fumbled in the bedclothes.

His fingers touched something hard, and he brought it to light— not the drumstick but an old-fashioned pocket pistol barely longer than his forefinger. David broke it and glanced down the barrel, which was bright and clean and recently oiled.

His exploration of Stacey Weed's sleeping quarters turned up a broad sheath-knife but no gun. He emerged from the tent with John's slender carving tool and Dolf's pistol.

"You found them," said Stacey, hoisting his rangy body from its squat. "Which killed her?"

"Both," volunteered John, but David shook his head.

"Either wound would have been fatal," he said, "but the bullet went in first, and the knife followed. That changed the shape of the round bullet hole. As I say, she was struck down from in front, and she knew her killer and had not feared or suspected him."

"That bullet must have struck through her spine at the back of the neck," said Stacey at once, "or she would have looked surprised, at least, before she died."

"*Ahoh*, Stacey," David thanked him. "That is a helpful thought. Now, Rhoda Pleasant smiled on you all, but who did she like best?"

"She wanted only the songs," replied Dolf.

"And did she get any of them?" demanded David quickly.

Stacey shook his head. "I don't think so, David. We sang when she first came, but when we saw her writing on that paper lined out to make music-signs on, Dolf said to stop singing. That was the first day she visited us and cooked our noon dinner."

David tried from those words to picture the visit. Rhoda Pleasant had tried to charm and reassure the three by flattery and food. She had almost succeeded; they had begun to perform. When they grew suspicious and fell silent, had she concealed her disappointment and tried something else? He hazarded a guess, though guessing had been discouraged by his instructors.

"Then she tried paying attention to one of you alone. Which?" He waited for an answer, and none came. "Was it you, John, because you could play the songs on the flute?"

John shook his head, and Stacey spoke for him. "It was I. She wanted both words and music, and I knew them. She whispered for me to visit her camp. That was two days ago.

"I went," Stacey continued, "but she tricked no songs out of me. She tried to get me off guard by singing songs she had heard on other reservations, and the best of them was not as good as our worst. I sang nothing in exchange. Yesterday she came back and tried her tricks on John instead."

"We went riding together," said John. "She talked about songs to me, too, but I only said I had forgotten to bring my flute."

"Then she hunted out Dolf?"

"*Wagh!*" Dolf grunted out the Tsichah negative like an ancient blanket Indian and scowled more blackly still. "Why should she pay attention to me? I am a drummer, and drum music is easy. The one time she heard us all together was enough to teach her what she wanted to know about my drum."

More silence, and David examined these new grudging admissions. Rhoda Pleasant had, very practically, concentrated on the two singers whose secrets were hardest to learn. On their own showing, John and Stacey had kept those secrets loyally. "This brings us to last night," said David at last.

"I will say something," John spoke slowly. "You think the pistol killed her, and it's Dolf's pistol. But perhaps he didn't use it. Perhaps Stacey did, or I, to make it look like Dolf."

"Perhaps," granted David. "Perhaps not. I think the stab in the wound was to change the shape of the bullet hole. It covered the killer's trail, as the scratching away of the tracks at her camp did."

"But it hid nothing," reminded John.

"Perhaps it *pretended* to hide something," pursued David. "The

killer might have thought that he would give the wound a disguise—
but one easy to see through."

"*Ahi*," replied Stacey gravely. "You mean that the bullet hole would
mean Dolf's pistol and make him guilty—because the knife is John's
and the pistol is Dolf's. Perhaps you want to say that I stole them
both and killed Rhoda Pleasant."

"Perhaps he wants to say that I used my own pistol to kill," threw
in Dolf, "and did the other things to make the pistol wound look like
a false trail."

"There is a way to show who fired the shots," David informed
them. "A white man's laboratory trick, with wax on the gun hand and
then acid dripped on to show if there was a fleck of powder left on
the hand from the gun going off."

"My hand would show flecks like that," Dolf said readily. "I fired
the gun for practice yesterday."

"I saw him," seconded John. "Anyway, David, you promised that
you would take only the guilty man. That means you must find him
here and now, without going to the agency for wax and acid."

"It was a promise," David agreed, "and the Tsichah do not break
their promises to each other." He held out the thin-ground knife.
"This was bloody, and now it is clean. Who cleaned it?"

"Whoever used it," said Stacey.

David put the knife on the ground. "You were telling me a story,
John. You stopped where you and Rhoda Pleasant went out riding
and came back yesterday."

"She left me here at camp and rode on alone," John took up the account. "Dolf and Stacey saw her go away. We three were here together
for supper, and together we went to sleep early. Then—"

"Then, this morning, I went to her camp alone," said Stacey. "Last
night, when she came back past here with John, she made me a sign,
like this." He demonstrated, a scooping inward to beckon Indian
fashion, then a gesture eastward. "Come after sunrise, she told me
by that sign. I thought she would beg again for the music. I would
let her beg, then laugh at her and say she was wasting her time with
us. But I found her lying face up in the trail."

"As I found her," finished David for him. "Well, you probably are
telling the truth. If you were questioned long in this way, any lies
in your stories would trip each other up. This much is plain as your

tracks at her camp: the killer went to her alone, with the knife and the pistol. He did not want his friends to know—"

"His friends do not ask to know," said Dolf, with an air of finality.

"Because," amplified John, hugging his thick knees as he squatted, "his friends know, like him, that Rhoda Pleasant was a thief of secrets. Nobody here is sorry she died, though we would be sorry if one of us suffered for killing her."

"Nobody is sorry she died?" repeated David, and he tried to study all three of their faces at once. They stared back calmly.

"But all three went to her camp," said David again. "Not Stacey alone."

"I came and got them to see her," Stacey told him. "We had to decide what to do. We saw everything there you saw. We talked as we waited there. Finally we agreed we must carry the news, after we all took sweat baths."

"Sweat baths?" echoed David. "Why?"

"We are medicine men, and we had all touched a dead body," John answered him coldly. "Sweat baths are purification; or have you forgotten the Tsichah way since you learned the policeman's way?"

"I have forgotten neither way," was David's equally cold response. "Who said to carry the news, and who said to take the sweat bath?"

"I thought of both those things," Dolf volunteered.

"No, I think I did," argued Stacey. "I built the fire anyway and gathered the rocks to heat."

"But I took the first bath," insisted John, "for I touched her first when we saw her together. Then Stacey took his, and then Dolf, who had not finished when you first came."

David pointed to the slim knife he had brought from the sleeping tent. "This went to the lodge with you, John?"

"If you expect to find prints of guilty fingers, you will not," said John. "Yes, I took the knife into the sweat lodge—to purify it from the touch of that dead Piekan squaw, *ahi*," and he put out his palm and made a horizontal slicing motion. "I finish. That is the end of what I will say."

There was silence all around. David stooped and took the knife, wedging it into the sheath with his own, then put Dolf's pistol into his hip pocket.

"Something here I have not yet found," he announced. "And I have wondered about it all the time we were talking. I think I know where it is now. I, too, am going into your sweat lodge. Can any of you say why I should not?"

They stared, neither granting nor denying permission. David walked past the Sibley tent to the close-blanketed little structure, pulled away the blanket that sealed the door, and peered in through the steam that clung inside. It billowed out, grew somewhat thinner, and he could see dimly. Under his breath he said a respectful prayer to the spirit people, lest he be thought sacrilegious in hunting there for what he hoped to find. Then he dropped to all fours and crawled in.

On the floor stood an old iron pot of water, still warm. In it were a dozen of the stones that had been dropped in at their hottest to create the purifying steam. David twitched up his sleeve and pulled out one stone, then another and another. They were like any stones one might find in that part of the reservation. He studied the ground, which was as bare and hard as baked clay, then rose from all fours and squatted on his heels. His hands patted and probed here and there along the inner surface of blankets until he found what he was looking for.

He seized its little loop of leather cord and pulled it from where it had been stuck between the blankets and one of the curved poles of the framework. A single touch assured him, and he edged into the open for a clear examination of it.

The thing was like a tiny war club of ancient fashion. A slender foot-long twig of tough wood had been split at the end, and the two split pieces curved to fit around a smooth pebble the size of an egg. Rawhide lashings held the stone rigidly in place. It was the ceremonial drumstick he had missed when searching Dolf Buckskin's bed in the tent, the absence of which he had been trying to fit into the story of Rhoda Pleasant's death. He balanced it experimentally, swung it against his open hand, carefully bent the springy wooden handle.

Then he thrust it inside his shirt, standing so that the three watching singers could be sure of what he handled and what he did with it. He walked over to where his pony cropped at some grass.

"I'm going to look at Rhoda Pleasant once more," he announced. "That look will be all I need to tell me everything."

Mounting, he rode slowly up the trail to the silent camp of the dead girl. He dismounted once again and took the cover from the expressionless face.

Again he put out a finger to touch, this time at the side of the head, where Rhoda Pleasant's hair was combed smoothly over the temple. He felt the other temple, and this time his finger encountered a yielding softness.

"*Ahi*," he grunted, as if to confirm everything. "The thin bone was broken."

He returned to his horse and lounged with his arm across the saddle, quietly waiting.

Hoofbeats sounded among the brush in the direction of the singers' camp. After a moment Dolf Buckskin rode into sight. He had pulled on trousers and a shirt, as though for a trip to the agency.

"I am waiting for you," called David to him.

"I knew you would be," replied Dolf, riding near. "Maybe I should have told you all about it when you brought my drumstick out of the sweat lodge, but it was hard to speak in front of my two friends who were trying to help me."

"You need not tell me much," David assured him, as gently as he could speak. "I knew the answer when John told of purifying his carving knife in the sweat lodge because it had touched the dead body of Rhoda Pleasant. Your drumstick was missing. I reasoned that if the drumstick was also in the sweat lodge, all was clear. And it was. Why should you have taken the drumstick into the lodge? Only to purify it, as you yourself must be purified. Why should it need purifying? Only if the drumstick too had touched the dead body. Why should it have touched the dead body? Only if the drumstick were the true weapon."

David paused. "You're a good drummer, Dolf. By long practice you can strike to the smallest mark—even the thin bone of the temple—swiftly and accurately, with exactly the strength you choose. That pebble-head is solid, the handle is springy. It was a good weapon, Dolf, and easier to your hand than any other."

"She did not even hear me as I came up behind her," Dolf said with something like sorrowful pride. "You were wrong about her seeing the killer and not fearing him. She never knew."

"You used your own gun and John's knife to hide the real way of killing. They were the false trails. But you could not break the old ceremonial rites. The true weapon had to be purified—and so I knew the truth."

Dolf raised his head and looked at the still form. "It's strange to think of what I did. I wanted her so much."

"*Yuh*," and David nodded. "You wanted her. She would not look at you, only at John and Stacey. You were left out, and your heart was bad. Perhaps if you explain to the court that for a time your mind was not right, you will not be killed, only put in jail."

"I don't think I want to live," said Dolf slowly. "Not in jail, anyway. Shall I help you lift her and tie her on her horse's back?"

"*Ahoh*," said David. "Thank you."

When the three horses started on the trail back, David glanced down at his silver-plated star. It was dull and filmy—from the steam of the sweat lodge. An agency policeman's star should not be dull at the end of his first successful case. It should shine like all the high hopes of all young warriors. Proudly David burnished the metal with his sleeve—until it shone with the wisdom of the Shining Lodge and the strength of the white man's star.

MANLY WADE WELLMAN (1903–86) is one of North Carolina's most beloved storytellers, writing books and short stories in many genres, including history, folklore, mystery, science fiction, and travel. In 1955 he won the Edgar Allan Poe Award for nonfiction from the Mystery Writers in America, and in 1978 he received the North Carolina Award for Literature.

In 1946 Wellman won the Ellery Queen Mystery Magazine Award over William Faulkner for the short story included here, "A Star for a Warrior." Faulkner, incensed, fired off an angry protest to the magazine's editors, but they were firm. Wellman's story won for two reasons, the editors said: it introduced a new type of detective character, and it set his story against a background not previously used in the detective field.

THE DISSIPATED JEWELER

O. Henry

You will not find the name of Thomas Keeling in the Houston city directory. It might have been there by this time if Mr. Keeling had not discontinued his business a month or so ago and moved to other parts. Mr. Keeling came to Houston about that time and opened up a small detective bureau. He offered his services to the public as a detective in rather a modest way. He did not aspire to be a rival of the Pinkerton agency but preferred to work along less risky lines.

If an employer wanted the habits of a clerk looked into, or a lady wanted an eye kept upon a somewhat too gay husband, Mr. Keeling was the man to take the job. He was a quiet, studious man with theories. He read Gaboriau and Conan Doyle and hoped some day to take a higher place in his profession. He had held a subordinate place in a large detective bureau in the East, but as promotion was slow, he decided to come West, where the field was not so well covered.

Mr. Keeling had saved during several years the sum of $900, which he deposited in the safe of a businessman in Houston to whom he had letters of introduction from a common friend. He rented a small upstairs office on an obscure street, hung out a sign stating his business, and, burying himself in one of Doyle's Sherlock Holmes stories, waited for customers.

Three days after he opened his bureau, which consisted of himself, a client called to see him.

It was a young lady, apparently about twenty-six years of age. She was slender and rather tall and neatly dressed. She wore a thin veil, which she threw back upon her black straw hat after she had taken the chair Mr. Keeling offered her. She had a delicate, refined face, with rather quick gray eyes, and a slightly nervous manner.

"I came to see you, sir," she said in a sweet, but somewhat sad, contralto voice, "because you are comparatively a stranger, and I could not bear to discuss my private affairs with any of my friends. I desire to employ you to watch the movements of my husband. Humiliating as the confession is to me, I fear that his affections are no longer mine. Before I married him he was infatuated with a young woman connected with a family with whom he boarded. We have been married five years, and very happily, but this young woman has recently moved to Houston, and I have reasons to suspect that he is paying her attentions. I want you to watch his movements as closely as possible and report to me. I will call here at your office every other day at a given time to learn what you have discovered. My name is Mrs. R——, and my husband is well known. He keeps a small jewelry store on —— Street. I will pay you well for your services, and here is $20 to begin with."

The lady handed Mr. Keeling the bill, and he took it carelessly as if such things were very, very common in his business.

He assured her that he would carry out her wishes faithfully and asked her to call again the afternoon after the next at four o'clock, for the first report.

The next day Mr. Keeling made the necessary inquiries toward beginning operations. He found the jewelry store and went inside ostensibly to have the crystal of his watch tightened. The jeweler, Mr. R——, was a man apparently thirty-five years of age, of very quiet manners and industrious ways. His store was small but contained a nice selection of goods and quite a large assortment of diamonds, jewelry, and watches. Further inquiry elicited the information that Mr. R—— was a man of excellent habits, never drank and was always at work at his jeweler's bench.

Mr. Keeling loafed around near the door of the jewelry store for several hours that day and was finally rewarded by seeing a flashily dressed young woman with black hair and eyes enter the store. Mr. Keeling sauntered nearer the door, where he could see what took place inside. The young woman walked confidently to the rear of the store, leaned over the counter, and spoke familiarly to Mr. R——. He rose from his bench, and they talked in low tones for a few minutes. Finally, the jeweler handed her some coins, which Mr. Keeling heard clinking as they passed into her hands. The woman then came out and walked rapidly down the street.

Mr. Keeling's client was at his office promptly at the time agreed upon. She was anxious to know if he had seen anything to corroborate her suspicions. The detective told her what he had seen.

"That is she," said the lady, when he had described the young woman who had entered the store. "The brazen, bold thing! And so Charles is giving her money. To think that things should come to this pass."

The lady pressed her handkerchief to her eyes in an agitated way.

"Mrs. R——," said the detective, "what is your desire in this matter? To what point do you wish me to prosecute inquiries?"

"I want to see with my own eyes enough to convince me of what I suspect. I also want witnesses, so I can instigate suit for divorce. I will not lead the life I am now living any longer."

She then handed the detective a $10 bill.

On the day following the next, when she came to Mr. Keeling's office to hear his report, he said:

"I dropped into the store this afternoon on some trifling pretext. This young woman was already there, but she did not remain long. Before she left, she said: 'Charlie, we will have a jolly little supper tonight as you suggest; then we will come around to the store and have a nice chat while you finish that setting for the diamond broach with no one to interrupt us.' Tonight, Mrs. R——, I think, will be a good time for you to witness the meeting between your husband and the object of his infatuation and satisfy your mind how matters stand."

"The wretch," cried the lady with flashing eyes. "He told me at dinner that he would be detained late tonight with some important work. And this is the way he spends his time away from me!"

"I suggest," said the detective, "that you conceal yourself in the store, so you can hear what they say, and when you have heard enough you can summon witnesses and confront your husband before them."

"The very thing," said the lady. "I believe there is a policeman whose beat is along the street the store is on who is acquainted with our family. His duties will lead him to be in the vicinity of the store after dark. Why not see him, explain the whole matter to him, and when I have heard enough, let you and him appear as witnesses?"

"I will speak with him," said the detective, "and persuade him to assist us, and you will please come to my office a little before dark tonight, so we can arrange to trap them."

The detective hunted up the policeman and explained the situation.

"That's funny," said the guardian of the peace. "I didn't know R—— was a gay boy at all. But, then, you can never tell about anybody. So his wife wants to catch him tonight. Let's see, she wants to hide herself inside the store and hear what they say. There's a little room in the back of the store where R—— keeps his coal and old boxes. The door between is locked, of course, but if you can get her through that into the store she can hide somewhere. I don't like to mix up in these affairs, but I sympathize with the lady. I've known her ever since we were children and don't mind helping her to do what she wants."

About dusk that evening the detective's client came hurriedly to his office. She was dressed plainly in black and wore a dark round hat and her face was covered with a veil.

"If Charlie should see me he will not recognize me," she said.

Mr. Keeling and the lady strolled down the street opposite the jewelry store, and about eight o'clock the young woman they were watching for entered the store. Immediately afterward she came out with Mr. R——, took his arm, and they hurried away, presumably to their supper.

The detective felt the arm of the lady tremble.

"The wretch," she said bitterly. "He thinks me at home innocently waiting for him while he is out carousing with that artful, designing minx. Oh, the perfidy of man."

Mr. Keeling took the lady through an open hallway that led into the backyard of the store. The outer door of the back room was unlocked, and they entered.

"In the store," said Mrs. R——, "near the bench where my husband works is a large table, the cover of which hangs to the floor. If I could get under that I could hear every word that was said."

Mr. Keeling took a big bunch of skeleton keys from his pocket and in a few minutes found one that opened the door into the jewelry store. The gas was burning from one jet turned very low.

The lady stepped into the store and said: "I will bolt this door from the inside, and I want you to follow my husband and that woman. See if they are at supper, and if they are, when they start back, you must come back to this room and let me know by tapping thrice on the door. After I listen to their conversation long enough I will unbolt the door, and we will confront the guilty pair together. I may need you to protect me, for I do not know what they might attempt to do to me."

The detective made his way softly out and followed the jeweler and the woman. He soon discovered that they had taken a private room in a little out-of-the-way restaurant and had ordered supper. He lingered about until they came out and then hurried back to the store and, entering the back room, tapped three times on the door.

In a few minutes the jeweler entered with the woman, and the detective saw the light shine more brightly through a crack in the door. He could hear the man and woman conversing familiarly and constantly but could not distinguish their words. He slipped around again to the street and, looking through the window, could see Mr. R—— working away at his jeweler's bench while the black-haired woman sat close to his side and talked.

"I'll give them a little time," thought Mr. Keeling, and he strolled down the street.

The policeman was standing on the corner.

The detective told him that Mrs. R—— was concealed in the store and that the scheme was working nicely.

"I'll drop back behind now," said Mr. Keeling, "so as to be ready when the lady springs her trap."

The policeman walked back with him and took a look through the window.

"They seem to have made up all right," said he. "Where's the other woman gotten to?"

"Why, there she is sitting by him," said the detective.

"I'm talking about the girl R—— had out to supper."

"So am I," said the detective.

"You seem to be mixed up," said the policeman. "Do you know that lady with R——?"

"That's the woman he was out with."

"That's R——'s wife," said the policeman. "I've known her for fifteen years."

"Then, who—?" gasped the detective. "Lord A'mighty, then who's under the table?"

Mr. Keeling began to kick at the door of the store.

Mr. R—— came forward and opened it. The policeman and the detective entered.

"Look under that table, quick," yelled the detective. The policeman raised the cover and dragged out a black dress, a black veil, and a woman's wig of black hair.

"Is this lady your w-w-wife?" asked Mr. Keeling excitedly, pointing out the dark-eyed young woman, who was regarding them in great surprise.

"Certainly," said the jeweler. "Now what the thunder are you looking under my tables and kicking down my door for, if you please?"

"Look in your showcases," said the policeman, who began to size up the situation.

The diamond rings and watches that were missing amounted to $800, and the next day the detective settled the bill.

Explanations were made to the jeweler that night, and an hour later Mr. Keeling sat in his office busily engaged in looking over his albums of crooks' photos.

At last he found one, and he stopped turning over the leaves and tore his hair. Under the picture of a smooth-faced young man with delicate features was the following description:

"JAMES H. MIGGLES, alias Slick Simon, alias The Weeping Widow, alias Bunco Kate, alias Jimmy the Sneak, General confidence man and burglar. Works generally in female disguises. Very plausible and dangerous. Wanted in Kansas City, Oshkosh, New Orleans, and Milwaukee."

This is why Mr. Thomas Keeling did not continue his detective business in Houston.

O. HENRY'S (1862–1910) distinguished career as a short-story writer began in less than distinguished circumstances—a prison cell, where he was jailed for embezzlement. Henry's wife had died, and he began to write short stories from prison to support his daughter, Margaret, who lived with a relative. After leaving prison, he moved to New York City, where he became very successful. During his lifetime Henry published ten collections and wrote over 600 short stories, including the famous "The Gift of the Magi," "The Ransom of Red Chief," and "The Furnished Room." O. Henry was a pseudonym assumed by William Sydney Porter, who was born in Greensboro.

First printed in the *Houston Post*, May 17, 1896.

MURCHISON PASSES A TEST

Toni L. P. *Kelner*

I am Abram Murchison, and even though I don't know Freud or Jung, after almost fifty years of running a store, I know people. So maybe you can learn psychology without going to college.

Not that I've got anything against going to college. Would I put a convenience store across the street from North Carolina State University if I didn't want educated people around? The students are like any kids—they buy potato chips and Coca-Cola and get embarrassed when they need sanitary items or men's protections. The professors aren't so different from the other people in the neighborhood. In the morning they buy coffee and sweet rolls, and in the evening they buy milk and bread so they don't have to go to one of those supermarkets that takes up an entire city block.

Some of the professors act as if they're better than a man who runs a store, but most of them are polite. A few even take a minute to pass the time of day. I talk to them the same way I do to people who don't have half a dozen letters after their names. By me, I think they're glad to talk about normal things, like the weather and basketball, instead of Milton and statistical variance and isosceles triangles.

Being across the street makes it convenient for my son David when he's ready to go to college. He walks to class and then comes to the store in the afternoon, because college or no college, David still has to do his share at the store, so I'm not too surprised when he bursts through the front door one day in May, only a little because he's early.

"Pop, you're not going to believe this! You've got to do something!" he says.

"What is it I'm not going to believe?" I say, wondering how upset I should get. I can tell from David's face that he's upset plenty.

"That son of a bitch—"

"Watch your language. This is a business, not a locker room."

There's nobody in the store but the two of us, but I don't want him to get in the habit of swearing where people can hear. I expect him to argue that I'm living in the past, but he just keeps going, which tells me he's even more upset than I thought.

"That idiot is flunking my entire class!"

I don't know what to say, I'm so shocked. If this had been David's freshman year, it would have been bad, but this is the final semester of his senior year, which makes it worse. "You're not going to graduate?"

"No, I'll still graduate," he says, as if that's not the point. Never mind the cap and gown we've bought him, and the invitations we've sent to our family, and the big party his mother has been getting ready for all month. Not to mention the gold class ring hidden in my sock drawer.

He says, "But it's going to mess up my G.P.A. I won't graduate Cum Laude."

"What do you mean, Cum Laude?"

"It's Latin for 'with honors.'"

"I know what it means. Since when are you graduating with honors?"

He looks embarrassed, which he almost never does. "It was going to be a surprise for you and Mom. I figured out at the end of junior year that I might make it. That's why I took Intro Psych in the first place. I heard it was an easy A, and I wanted to boost my average."

He tries to make it sound as if he was doing me a favor by taking an easy class. I know better, but now isn't the time to discuss it.

David says, "I only needed a B, which meant I only needed a 75 on the final exam."

I think kids learn more arithmetic by figuring out what scores they need to get by than they do by studying. "And you didn't get a 75?"

"I don't know what I would have gotten, but what I've got now is 0. Professor Spratlin found out that somebody cheated, and he got so mad when nobody would confess that he's flunking us all. He won't even tell us how we really did on the exam."

"Spratlin," I say, thinking that this explains a lot. He's one of the good professors, the ones who talk to me, but the man always fidgets. N.C. State is a big engineering and agriculture school, and he thinks they don't take psychology professors seriously.

This worries him, which makes him fidget, which means people don't take him seriously, which is why my son only took his course to get an easy A. "But you're still going to graduate?"

David nodded. "I'm one of the lucky ones. Some of the others are going to have to go to summer school if he doesn't change his mind."

I think about the other parents, and the caps and gowns they bought, and the invitations they've sent, and the parties they've planned. "It's not right that he should do this."

"I know, but he won't listen to us. Pop," he starts to say, and I think I know what he's going to ask, "do you think Mom would go talk to him?"

Okay, I didn't know what he was going to ask, but I understand.

My wife smiles most of the time and still giggles like she did when she was a girl. Some people think this means she's easy to push around, but they don't think that for long. "Of course. Or I could talk to Spratlin right now."

David thinks his mother would be better but doesn't want to say so, so he says, "I don't want you to have to close the store early."

"Who said anything about closing the store? He's coming this way."

"What?" David jerks around and looks through the window to see Spratlin crossing the street.

Professor Spratlin is a tall, thin man, and more of his bones show than with most people. He's got an Adam's apple that makes you believe that it was him who ate something he shouldn't have, not Adam. And like I said before, he fidgets. Never had I seen him when his hands weren't reaching into his pockets to come out with nothing and when his feet weren't moving around as if he needs to use the restroom that we don't let customers use because of what drunken college students can do to a restroom.

Before Spratlin can get into the store, David is halfway to the back room. "You talk to him, Pop. I'm afraid of what I might say."

Why he thinks he'd say anything worse than what I'm thinking, I don't know, but he's gone before I can argue with him, and Spratlin opens the door.

I nod at him to say hello. Spratlin nods back and reaches for a shopping basket, which I know he's going to bang into two or three shelves before he gets what he needs. Only he must be even more nervous than usual because I hear five thumps before he puts the basket on the counter in front of me. Of course, he knows David is my son, and even if he didn't see David hide in the back room, he must be wondering if I know what he's done.

I pick up the carton of milk as if I don't already know the price and say, "How are you today?"

He takes a second to answer. "Well, it's been a disturbing day." He nods, shuffles his feet, and nods some more.

I punch in the price of the milk, then pick up the frozen chicken dinner. "David told me about what happened."

"I trust he explained why I had to take that action."

"He tried," I say, "but he doesn't really understand it himself. He told me you found out that somebody had cheated, but nobody would say who it was."

"That's correct," he says, nodding.

"What he didn't tell me was how you knew somebody cheated if you didn't see it."

He fidgets faster, and I know he doesn't want to talk about it, but since I've still got his chicken dinner, he can't leave. So he says, "Does it matter how I knew?"

I don't answer him, but I don't ring up his chicken dinner, either.

"It wasn't hard to determine," he says. "Two students handed in papers with the exact same answers to every problem."

"You mean they got the same problems right and the same ones wrong?"

"Actually, both of them answered every problem correctly."

I punch in the price of the chicken dinner and reach for a frozen lasagna. "How do you know they didn't know the right answers?"

"From their previous history. Neither of them had participated in class discussions, both had done poorly on the midterm, and both had handed in poor term papers. It doesn't seem reasonable that either of them would suddenly grasp the material."

"Then I can understand why you think those two students cheated. What I don't understand is why you are making the whole class pay for their wrongdoing."

"Since the two students in question refused to confess, I prevailed upon the other students to tell me what they knew. None of them would."

"How would they know?"

"Somebody must know. I cannot conceive of a way those two students could have cheated to that extent without another student witnessing it."

"Were you there when they took the test?"

"Of course. I was in the front of the class, and my assistant was in the back. Admittedly Jordan was tired that morning from staying up to study for his own exams, but I've been teaching long enough to know the importance of staying alert."

"But neither of you saw how they did it?"

"Obviously, the cheaters were resourceful enough to hide their actions from me. Still, there were twenty other students in that classroom, and I can't believe that none of them saw anything. It's just not possible." For a few seconds he stops fidgeting and holds his mouth tight.

Now I understand. The cheating made him mad, but what really got to him was not being able to figure out how they did it. So he decided the whole class must be in on it, and he was going to punish them all. I ring up the lasagna and pick up a frozen Salisbury steak. "You say you've been a teacher a long time?"

"Over twenty years."

"Then you must know the ways kids cheat. I haven't taken a test other than my driving test since I left high school, but I remember. One way is to copy off another student's paper. You would have seen that, wouldn't you?"

"Of course, but the two students weren't sitting anywhere near each other, and besides, one copying from the other wouldn't explain how the first one got every problem right."

"Then there's writing the answers on a hand or a leg or on a piece of paper."

"Neither of those are nearly as easy as they sound, especially not when the students are being watched. I'd have noticed the contortions if they had something written on their persons, and I don't allow them to carry anything other than two pencils and the exam into the testing room, which limits their ability to hide a crib sheet."

"There's hiding the answers in the classroom before the test."

"I don't give the exam in our regular classroom, and I didn't announce which room we'd be using until that morning. Besides, those possibilities imply that they knew what was going to be on the test. We covered a great deal of material—they didn't know what I was going to ask."

"What if they stole the test paper beforehand?"

"I didn't make up the exam until the day before." Then, not letting me ask my next question, he says, "Nobody could have hacked into my computer to get the test, either. My system is completely secure."

From the way I've heard computer science majors talk in the store, I bet it wasn't as protected as he thought, but it would probably have taken more than one night to get the test. I think of something else, too, but don't bother to ask him about it when he's so sure of himself.

Spratlin looks as if he's sorry as he says, "Up until I graded the tests last night, I wouldn't have thought there was any method of cheating I hadn't seen." He looks down at the frozen Salisbury steak, which isn't going to be frozen much longer if I keep him there.

I ring it up and try to go slow while I ring up his loaf of bread, package of cheese slices, and jar of mayonnaise. I don't know what else I can say to convince him, but I don't want him to leave while David still has a 0 on his test. It's while I'm holding that jar of mayonnaise, which is the smallest size jar of mayonnaise that I sell, that I think of something.

I say, "You know, you would be surprised to learn how much I know about the people who shop here, just from what they buy."

His fidgeting gets worse, then better, then worse, as he tries to figure out why I'm changing the subject. "Is that so?"

"It is so," I say. "Take what you've got here. Three frozen dinners, all different. That shows me that you don't cook very much and you eat alone."

"The cooking is obvious, but how do you know I don't have a wife who likes frozen dinners?"

"Because there's three, not two, and they're different kinds."

Before he can argue that his imaginary wife has a hard time making up her mind, I say, "And this mayonnaise. To buy such a small jar means that you're the only one who uses it. My uncle who lived alone bought small jars like this because a big jar would spoil before he finished it." My uncle also was on a low-fat diet, but I don't want to spoil my own argument. "Students come here, too, and if I were a betting man, I would bet that I could tell you things about them that you don't know."

He realizes where I'm going, but he keeps listening. "Like what?"

"Give me the names of some of your students, and I'll tell you. Maybe the ones in the class with David."

He's got a little smile, and I think that even though he flunked everybody because he was mad, he knows it wasn't a good thing to do, which means that I might be able to talk him out of it. He names three names, but luck isn't with me, because I don't recognize any of them. Then he names Leigh, a girl I do know. "There's one thing that Leigh buys, but not when my son is here. She won't buy it if there's anybody else she knows, either."

"Oh?"

I nod solemnly. "Every week she comes in and buys a soap opera magazine."

He laughs and tells me Leigh is studying literature, which is why she keeps the soap opera magazines a secret. Then he names more names.

I tell him that Leo must be diabetic from what he buys, and Jim has jock itch, which I could tell as much from how he walks as from what he buys. I know his assistant Jordan, too, from the Stridex and science fiction magazines he buys. One time last week he must have finally gotten lucky because he bought men's protections for the first time all semester. Tiffany works too hard, so she gets sick a lot and buys cough medicine, but Cindy must be a hypochondriac because nobody could need all the medicines she buys. I even tell him that I'm worried that Mary Ann is one of those who makes herself throw up because she buys so much junk food and stays so skinny. Spratlin looks concerned, and I wonder if he's going to try to help her.

Then finally he names Chris, a boy David knows, and from the way he hesitates, Chris must be one of the students he thinks cheated.

"Chris must go to parties more than he goes to class," I say. "He buys beer and pretzels and then has to come in for coffee before class to wake himself up. Since your class is a morning class, he must have missed it many times."

Spratlin nods, which shows I'm not telling him anything new, but the next part he doesn't know.

I say, "One thing about Chris. He's smarter than he acts. Every semester, a week or two before exams, he quits going to parties. He comes by at night to get Coca-Cola and coffee, and he doesn't smell like beer. When he comes by in the morning, even though he looks tired, he doesn't look as if he's suffering from the night before. That's when he hits the books and learns what he should have been learning all semester."

Spratlin stops fidgeting, and I know he's thinking that maybe he made a mistake.

"Last week, Chris came in and bought two big bottles of Coke and said he was pulling an all-nighter to study. I was working that night because David was studying, too. In fact, he was studying for your exam." I finally finish ringing up Spratlin's things and put them in a bag to give him a chance to think.

Finally he says, "What about Deborah? Does she come in here?"

"Sometimes," I say, knowing that she must be the other one who cheated. "She doesn't talk much to me, not since I told her she has to pay with money, not a debit card. Since then she always pays with big bills, and I don't think she likes the way I check her bills. Not that I've ever had a problem with her money, but you can't be too careful. She came in that same night as Chris, but I guess she didn't need to study. Maybe she was going to pull an all-nighter, but not with books. She bought a box of men's protections." In case Spratlin doesn't know what I mean, I say, "Condoms."

"I see." Spratlin hands me money and reaches for his bag. "This has been quite illuminating, but I should be going."

I know I've convinced Spratlin that Chris may be honest, but he thinks Deborah isn't, so he won't change his mind because he still doesn't know how she cheated without someone seeing it. I decide it's time for David to join us. "David," I call.

David comes out. "Did you call me, Pop?"

"Professor Spratlin and I have a couple of questions for you."

Actually, Spratlin wants to go, but now that I've said that, he can't do anything except fidget. "It's about one of your classmates."

"I don't know who cheated," he says, and he glares at both of us. "And I wouldn't tell if I did."

"I know, it's against the code to rat on another student, even if it means you get a 0 on an exam."

"That attitude is common among subgroups, usually known as honor among thieves," Spratlin says, as if he's teaching a class. "Actually, professional criminals have no compunctions about turning in a fellow criminal if it's expedient."

Before David can argue about that, I say, "But since I'm not asking who cheated, it doesn't matter. What I want to ask is whether or not your classmate Deborah has a boyfriend?"

David looks at Spratlin, who looks at him, and I know they're both wondering why I care about Deborah's boyfriends.

David says, "She says she's dating some rich guy up at Yale, and she wanted to go to school up North to be near him, but her father made her come here. I think she came here because she couldn't get into anyplace else with her grades, but her dad is an alum and has pull here."

"Is her boyfriend visiting?"

"I don't think so. All she's been talking about is the trip to Paris their parents are giving them for graduation, and how they're going to meet at the Eiffel Tower, and how romantic it's going to be. Only I don't think she's going to graduate now." He glares at Spratlin again, who looks down at his shuffling feet.

"Deborah is a pretty girl, isn't she?" I say.

"If you like that type," David says, as if I don't know how much he likes blondes and as if I haven't seen him watching her. Maybe Deborah's blonde hair comes from a bottle, but it looks good.

"So Deborah, who doesn't get good grades and whose boyfriend is in Connecticut, buys condoms. Of course, she could have been getting ready for her trip, but most people don't pack the night before an exam." Then I ask, "What about Jordan? Does he have a girlfriend?"

"Jordan?" David laughs. "No way."

Spratlin is catching on. Now I ask him about what I thought of before but didn't ask. "Professor Spratlin, you said nobody could have stolen the test because you only wrote it out the day before. Did you make copies for the students yourself?"

"No," he says. "My assistant Jordan made the copies." Then he nods slowly.

There's no need for me to say more. Spratlin knows what I know, that even an honest assistant might be tempted by a pretty girl when he doesn't have a girlfriend of his own. The only question is what Spratlin is going to do about it.

After a minute, Spratlin says, "David, I'm scheduling a meeting for the students in your class tomorrow afternoon. It's going to be posted, but I'd appreciate it if you'd spread the word."

"Yes, sir," David says with a grin.

Spratlin starts to leave but turns back to say, "By the way, you got a 95 on the exam."

So David wears his cap and gown and his new class ring to graduate Cum Laude, and since we don't tell his mother beforehand, I get to hear her squeal and giggle when it's announced. Then I get to explain to our relatives that this means David has graduated with honors, which is an honor for me.

Chris graduates, too, but not with honors. As for Deborah, her name is in the program, which was printed early, but when it's her turn to get a diploma, they skip over her. I think her boyfriend is going to be lonely in Paris.

When we're standing around after the ceremony to take pictures of David and his diploma, Spratlin comes by to shake my hand and tell me how much he appreciates the psychology lesson. I tell him that maybe engineering is good for engineers and agriculture is good for farmers, but psychology is good for everyone. I say this in a loud voice, so other students and parents and professors can hear it. Spratlin smiles, and when he walks away, he isn't fidgeting so much.

TONI L. P. KELNER has been living in Massachusetts for a few years now, but her heart belongs in North Carolina, where she grew up and graduated from the University of North Carolina at Charlotte. Her mystery series, which features computer programmer Laura Fleming, takes place in Byerly, North Carolina, which, Kelner says, if it existed, would be located near Hickory and have its own exit off NC 321. Two of Kelner's short stories have been nominated for an Agatha, a Macavity, and an Anthony between them.

sarah R. shaber

"ecil Petty is dead," the voice on the other end of the phone line crowed. "Is that great or what?"

"That is good news," Simon said. He was out of bed by now, drawing up his bedroom window shades, staring at the house across the street where Petty had lived for years.

"Do you think his daughter will move in, or will she sell the house?"

Simon's caller was Mack Smith, a realtor who lived a couple of streets over, hence his obsession with the future of Petty's house. He once told Simon that he started each day reading the obituaries, scanning for desirable addresses.

In Simon's historic neighborhood residents were known by their homes as much as by their names. Mack owned a stucco mission home that would be ugly if it wasn't so unusual. Simon lived in a Craftsman bungalow.

Petty's cottage, the Hawthorne from the 1918 Sears mail-order catalog, was easily worth $400,000 today. Not bad appreciation for a one-bathroom shingled home that had arrived at its narrow lot in numbered pieces after a cross-country journey by rail.

"Do we know what Professor Petty died of?" Simon asked Mack. "Can't have been his heart. He didn't have one."

Petty may not have met the precise definition of a sociopath, but he came mighty close. He left bags of garbage in front of his neighbors' houses on trash collection day. During election season he loitered around the neighborhood's streets until folks left for work, then he'd sneak onto their front porches and leave homophobic and racist literature clipped to their mailboxes. He was nasty to the itinerant laborers who canvassed the neighborhood looking for odd jobs, calling the police on them whenever the spirit moved him. Girl Scouts and high school band members selling cookies or fruit learned not to knock on Petty's door if they didn't want it slammed in their faces, preceded by an obscenity or two. He opposed every initiative the neighborhood association favored. He made life miserable for his graduate students. Simon couldn't think of a single person who would care to attend his funeral.

"There's just one thing," Mack said. "His front lawn is crawling with cops. Why do you suppose that is?"

Simon saw that it was indeed crawling with cops. And an ambulance, a City/County Bureau of Investigation van, and a couple of police cruisers lined the curb in front of Petty's house. Simon recognized Petty's son-in-law's car, a sun-faded blue Volvo station wagon, parked in the driveway behind Petty's Cadillac.

"You don't suppose he's been murdered, do you?" Mack said, joking. "Think of the suspects."

Simon didn't answer, but he watched the activity across the street with some disquiet.

"You're in with the police," Mack said. "Find out what's happened. I've got to go to work. Call me."

Simon was indeed "in" with the police. A tenured professor of history at Kenan College, a small liberal arts school nestled on a lovely campus nearby, Simon Shaw consulted with police departments on "cold cases"—murders so old his historian's skills proved essential to their solution. He was a brilliant scholar and a fine writer. His first book, developed from his doctoral thesis at the University of North Carolina at Chapel Hill, had won a Pulitzer Prize. He preferred teaching undergraduates to research and writing, though, which was why he stayed at Kenan.

Solving murders was Simon's avocation. After some initial resistance he assumed the label "forensic historian" bestowed on him by the *Raleigh News and Observer*. When a profile of him appeared in *People* magazine, he acquired minor celebrity status. People recognized him at the grocery store and asked for his autograph. His friends accused him of relishing the attention.

Simon looked too young to be a full professor. He was a small man who dressed in blue jeans, drove a Thunderbird, and listened to rock music. His black curly hair was a little long, and his dark looks echoed those of his mother, a Jewish woman who hailed from Queens. Simon was a native North Carolinian himself. His father's family had lived in the mountains of North Carolina for so long Simon joked that the first Shaw must have sprouted like a mushroom from the damp forest soil in Watauga County and built his log cabin on the spot. Simon grew up in Boone, where his father taught classics at Appalachian State University and his mother was a public health nurse.

Simon pulled on a T-shirt and jeans and joined the knot of neighbors gathered on the sidewalk opposite Petty's house. The bright sun forecast another hot July day.

"You can't guess, Simon," said a barefoot young mother, her tiny baby snug in a carrier on her chest. "A police detective questioned us. About Professor Petty."

"He got an earful, too," said the retired librarian who owned the gingerbread Victorian around the corner, "but he wouldn't tell us anything. It's suspicious, don't you think? If Petty had just up and died, would there be this much commotion? Petty's son-in-law found the body. I saw him let the police into the house. He looked like death himself."

"The detective who questioned you, what did he look like?" Simon asked.

"He was a big African American man," the librarian's wife said. "Middle-aged, short gray hair, handsome suit."

"Sergeant Otis Gates," Simon said.

"You know him?" the young mother said.

"Yeah," Simon said. "He's a homicide detective."

For a half a minute the group was silent, then they all started to talk at once. The librarian raised his hand to shush them.

"For God's sake, Simon, go over there and pump him for information," he said. "We need to know what's going on."

Simon went. He was curious himself, and worried, for that matter. No one wanted a murder on the street, even if the victim was as unpopular as Petty.

Of course, the uniformed policeman watching the street out in front of Petty's house wouldn't let him by.

"I'm a friend of Sergeant Gates," Simon said. "Could I speak to him? I live over there," he said, gesturing across the street. "The neighbors are anxious, as you can imagine."

"I recognize you, Professor Shaw," the officer said. "But I can't let you inside. You understand."

Just then Otis came out of Petty's house. He spotted Simon and raised his hand in greeting, then motioned Simon over to him. The policeman let him through the yellow tape barricade, and Simon joined Otis on the porch.

"Murder?" Simon asked him.

"Definitely," Otis answered. "And no shortage of suspects, I hear."

"He was an awful human being," Simon said. "But still."

"The 'still' part is my job," Otis said. "Speaking of which, I could use your help. Have you ever been in the house? In the study?"

"Yeah," Simon said. "several times."

"Come inside," Otis said.

Simon hesitated.

"Don't worry, the body is gone already."

Simon avoided corpses. Most of the victims in his cases had been dead a lot longer than Petty, and viewing their remains gave him a headache. He preferred to leave crime scenes and autopsies to the experts.

As he passed through the house, Simon noticed Petty's son-in-law slumped on the living room sofa, his head in his hands. A female paramedic sat at his side, a hand on his shoulder, speaking to him quietly.

Inside Petty's study a tarpaulin covered part of the floor, concealing the gruesome evidence of the murder. Otherwise the room was the picture of a scholar's den. Hundreds of books shared shelf space with Greek and Roman memorabilia, including plaster busts of Claudius and Pyrrhus and a rearing bronze warhorse missing its rider.

"Is this stuff worth anything?" Otis asked. "Could robbery be a motive?"

"Reproductions, all of them," Simon said. "And I don't see any-thing missing."

"And that," Otis said, gesturing toward the full-size Greek warrior that stood in a corner. "Fake, too?"

"Yeah," Simon said. "He ordered the stuff from a reenactment catalog." The Spartan mannequin was poised for war. A horsehair-crested leather helmet protected his head, while a wood and bronze shield painted with a ferocious face shielded his body. He wore a canvas cuirass across his chest and bronze greaves strapped around his calves. A short iron sword with bronze fittings hung from his shoulder by a baldric, but his outstretched hand was empty.

"Where's the spear"? Simon asked.

"Rammed through Professor Petty," Otis said. "Pinned him to the floor."

"Good God!"

"Yeah, and he didn't die right away either. Lived for an hour or so, according to the crime scene guys. Died around midnight, they think."

"Damn. No one deserves that."

"This is what I want you to see," Otis said, handing Simon a pair of latex gloves and stretching a pair over his own large hands. Gates withdrew a leather belt from a brown paper evidence bag and gave it to Simon, who inspected it carefully. It was an ordinary leather belt, with two exceptions: it was heavily stained with blood, and random letters, written in heavy black marker, ranged fully across its length. The letters were: A M Z Q L D M X Y O M S T E.

"While Petty was lying pinned to the floor bleeding to death, he took off his belt and wrote these letters on it. We found the marker on the floor next to the body."

"Hmmm."

"Hmmm, what?"

"Nothing, really." Simon said, giving the belt back to Gates and stripping off his gloves. "Could it be a code?"

"I thought of that. We'll send it off to the forensic cryptologists at the FBI. Most likely Petty was half-crazy with shock and pain, and the letters mean nothing."

Out on Petty's back porch Gates scribbled in his notebook. He was about the only person Simon knew who still used a pencil. Simon waited for him to finish, inhaling the rich sweet odor of the red trumpet vines and honeysuckle that climbed Petty's back fence, luring hummingbirds. Petty loved birds, which just went to show you that no one was all bad. The vine-laden fence divided Petty's backyard from a bank parking lot. In fact, banks lined the entire street, buffering the old neighborhood from the noise and traffic of Cameron Village, a tiny urban shopping center that was home to trendy boutiques and restaurants.

"Anyone else hate this guy besides the neighbors?" Otis asked.

"Every student he ever had. He was picky, contradictory, and just plain mean. He was an emeritus professor at State, so he still served on an occasional thesis committee." Simon knew of two former students of his who were struggling with Petty's scathing last-minute comments on their final drafts. He saw no need to volunteer their names to Gates. He'd find them out for himself when he interviewed Petty's colleagues at State.

"Petty had one married daughter," Gates said, consulting his notebook.

"Nice young woman," Simon said. "She has three children, I believe. Her husband runs the Italian bistro in Cameron Village."

"I've been there. Great calamari. He found the body, you know. The son-in-law, Mark Lozano. Dropped in on the old man this morning."

"I saw him in the house. He looked shell-shocked," Simon said.

Simon called Mack Smith at his office and reported what he had learned.

"You know what," Mack said. "When I got to work I heard that Petty's house was already for sale. One of our guys has the listing. He just hadn't put the sign out front yet. Petty told our agent he was moving to Italy. Had you heard anything about that?"

Simon hadn't, which was a surprise. The academic grapevine was usually swift and accurate. Petty must have kept his plans very quiet.

Simon wasn't teaching this summer; he was working on a new book on the coastal history of North Carolina, but he liked to drop by the history department to eat lunch with the few faculty who stayed in town to teach summer school.

Sophie Berelman, with her long dark hair wound into a thick braid and wearing her trademark cat's-eye-shaped glasses, was forking up salad, dieting after the birth of her first child. Simon's close friend Marcus Clegg, acting chair for the summer, was eating lunch with her. Clegg could pass as a refugee from the sixties, if he'd been old enough, with his shoulder-length brown hair, John Lennon glasses, and brown lunch bag of healthy sandwiches and fruit.

Simon joined them with his satchel of fast food. He stuck a straw in the super-sized Coke and drained half of it.

"We're listing suspects, Simon," Sophie said. "We're up to 157."

"That's not funny, Sophie," Marcus said, turning to Simon. "Your friend Otis Gates was on the phone to me this morning. Seems a couple of our former students are only too glad that Petty is dead. I think you taught both of them?"

Kenan didn't offer graduate degrees, but many of its graduates went on to study further at nearby universities. Simon knew exactly whom Marcus meant: Amber Marie Hardy, a doctoral candidate at State, and Rufus West, a master's candidate there. Both of them were desperate to finish their degrees, and both had been driven to distraction by Petty's criticisms of their theses.

"Sergeant Gates was surprised you hadn't mentioned them to him this morning," Marcus said.

"I figured he'd find out about them soon enough."

"I talked to a friend of mine at State this morning," Sophie said. "Petty's house was for sale and he was moving to Italy. Met an Italian woman there when he was on vacation last year."

Rufus West poked his head into the room.

"Hi, Rufus," Marcus said. "Come on in."

"I need to talk to Professor Shaw," Rufus said. He looked desperately at Simon. "In private," he added.

"Sure," Simon said. "Of course."

Rufus shut the door of Simon's office and slumped into a chair. He clumsily lit a cigarette.

"I haven't smoked in years," he said. "But it's this or major drugs. When I heard this morning that Petty was dead, you can't imagine how happy I was. The next thing I know, there's a giant police detective at the door, quizzing me, and I realize I'm a suspect!"

"Did he say so?" Simon said.

"Not in so many words. But he'd heard how Petty was screwing me over. I'm on the fifth draft of the damn thesis. Petty still hated it. I just wanted the degree so I could make a few thousand more a year teaching, maybe work up to principal one day. Can't do that without a master's anymore."

"Relax," Simon said. "Motive doesn't prove murder. You need opportunity, too."

"I'm trying to tell you," Rufus said. "I was at Petty's last night! Half the neighborhood was out walking their damn dogs when I pulled up to the house! I came to thrash it out with him. We had a huge argument. He said I had no academic talent at all and that he wasn't going to initial my thesis. Ever!"

"You didn't kill him, Rufus!"

Rufus dragged his hand through his hair, scattering cigarette ashes around his shoulders.

"No," he said. "Of course not. He was alive when I left, about 10:30, I think it was. I've got sort of an alibi, though. Amber pulled up to the house right after me. She was livid. She'd just got back what she thought was her final draft with Petty's comments. She said it would take another semester to rewrite. That job offer she got from Meredith College depends on her having her doctorate by the fall."

Amber was a single mother, struggling through graduate school after her young husband died in the Gulf War. She needed that job.

"You don't think Amber could have murdered him, do you? Is she strong enough?"

"Oh, she could have done it. She works out, and Petty was a little old man. . . . But I'm sure she didn't kill him. I mean, I hope she didn't."

Simon hoped so, too.

"She told the police that Petty was alive when she arrived and still alive when she left," Rufus said. "But, of course, we could have been in it together."

"Just tell the truth, both of you, and sit tight. Otis is a fine detective. He'll get to the truth."

"Can you help us, Simon? Amber and me, I mean. Isn't Sergeant Gates a friend of yours?"

"I don't know," Simon said. "I'll see what I can do."

Rufus left Simon's office, lighting another cigarette as he went.

Simon felt sick. He liked both Amber and Rufus. He thought of Rufus's wife, his three children, his broken-down minivan, and his love of teaching high school. Then he recalled Amber when she first arrived at Kenan, an older student out of place in a flowered Lilly shift and pink Pappagallo flats. She quickly adapted, changing to jeans and putting her toddler to bed on a pillow on the library floor so she could study at night.

Simon rooted around in his drawer, found a Goody's headache powder, and stirred it into his Coke. He wondered if it was likely that either Rufus or Amber, both normal, law-abiding people, could have murdered Cecil Petty.

Of course it was possible. It was more than possible. It seemed certain. Either Rufus killed Petty and Amber covered up for him, or Amber killed him herself. It would have been so easy to knock the old man down and ram the warrior's spear into him, solving so many problems. Of course Petty didn't lack enemies, but only Rufus and Amber had been seen at his house the night of the murder. Then there was the writing that Petty had left behind. Simon had no doubt it was a message of some kind. Petty had lived for an hour or so. He wouldn't have missed his chance to implicate his murderer. Simon wondered what the FBI would make of the random letters scrawled across Petty's belt.

"Rufus West has changed his story," Otis said.

"Really," Simon said, shifting the telephone receiver to his other hand so he could finish his peanut butter and peach jam sandwich.

"Now he says he waited for Amber outside Petty's house and that he saw Petty alive before she left, when he showed her to the door. Then, according to this fairy tale, he and Amber talked for a few minutes before they both drove off."

"What's his excuse for changing his story?"

"He says that at first he wanted to shift blame to Amber, to keep from being a suspect, then got an attack of conscience."

"It could be true."

"Baloney. One of those two, or both of them, killed Petty."

"You don't have any other options? What about the family? Aren't they always prime suspects?"

"Well, gossip is that Petty and his daughter and her husband didn't get along. According to the staff Petty would come eat at the restaurant, for free, and then criticize the food. But they're in the clear. Petty's daughter left the restaurant and got home right at six, according to the babysitter. Her baby had a temperature, and she's on record phoning the pediatrician on call several times during the evening. Her husband was at their restaurant until well past one. His routine was the same as always. The restaurant closes at eleven, and then he and another chef prep for the next day. The staff confirms it. Besides, you'd think they'd be happy Petty was selling up and moving to Italy where they'd be rid of him."

"What are you waiting for, then?"

"We don't have any direct evidence that Rufus or Amber is the murderer. I'm hoping that the report from the FBI cryptologist will clear things up. If those letters are a code revealing the murderer's name, the FBI will crack it. There are no unbreakable codes."

Finished with his sandwich, Simon jotted the letters of Petty's message on his napkin: A M Z Q L D M X Y O M S T E.

"Not true," he answered Gates.

"What?"

"It's not true that there're no unbreakable codes. There's the Voynich manuscript, 232 pages written over 400 years ago in a secret script. Never deciphered. And in 1897 the composer Edward Elgar sent an encrypted message to a friend. It's never been decoded. And don't forget the Zodiac killer ciphers, sent by a serial killer to the police from 1966 to 1974. The killer has never been caught."

"Enough. I guarantee you that the FBI can unravel a coded scribble written by a dying man."

Simon stared at the letters that ranged across his napkin.

"Otis, have you had this happen before? You know, when you have more sympathy for the murderer than the victim."

"Sure. Plenty of victims are creeps. That's why they've been murdered."

A couple of weeks later Gates showed up at Simon's door.

"Hey," he said, as Simon showed him in.

"Hey, yourself," Simon said. "You off duty?"

Gates wore crisp khakis and a polo shirt instead of his usual immaculate suit.

"Took a personal day," Gates said. "Had a dentist appointment, stuff like that. Thought I'd stop by and visit. You busy?"

"Not really." Simon led Gates onto his back porch, where the ceiling fan turned lazily overhead. His laptop computer and a stack of notecards, anchored by a couple of rocks against the breeze from the fan, lay abandoned on the glass coffee table.

"I'm interrupting you," Otis said.

"It's okay," Simon said. "I'm getting nowhere fast."

Otis settled into a wicker chair while Simon fetched him an iced tea.

"You look tired," Otis said to him, stirring his tea with the mint twig Simon had added to it. "Not sleeping well, are you?"

"No, I'm not," Simon said, with no explanation.

"The FBI sent back their report on the Petty case. They can't decipher the letters on the belt."

"You sent them the belt itself?"

"Of course not. It's still locked up in the evidence room. We typed out the letters on the belt and faxed it."

"You always said it wasn't a code."

"That was before I saw the look on your face after I expressed that particular opinion."

Simon wasn't a good liar. He allowed a worried expression to cross over his face before he subdued it.

"Look, Simon. I know it's difficult in a case like this, when you sympathize with the suspects. But wouldn't you rather the correct person got arrested for Petty's murder than the wrong one?"

"Without admitting anything, Otis, I'd like to say that solving this crime won't really be a victory, will it? I mean, Petty won't be missed, and his murderer, well, maybe it would be best if he wasn't caught."

"Best for whom? You? Because you want to avoid the responsibility of sending someone you sympathize with to jail?"

Simon didn't answer him.

"I know you," Otis said. "You have some arcane, otherwise useless piece of information that will help me solve this case. You've got to give it to me. Don't make me come back here once I'm back on duty and arrest you for withholding information. You won't like jail, believe me, and you'll tell me eventually."

Simon massaged his neck, hard, with both hands.

"What do you think will happen to the murderer, given that you can find him, if there are extenuating circumstances?" Simon asked.

"That's not my job," Otis said. "My job is to solve the murder. The jury's job is to convict or acquit. It's the judge's job to pass sentence, which is when those extenuating circumstances you refer to come into play. And it's your job to tell me everything you know. I know you can decipher Petty's message. I can see it in your face."

Simon quit rubbing the back of his neck and moved to massaging his temples.

"Okay," he said. "Whatever. I can't keep quiet any longer anyway."

"Thank God," Otis said. He handed Simon a single sheet of paper with the letters Petty had scrawled just before his death printed on it. "What is it?"

"It's a transposition cipher," Simon said.

"Just scrambled text?" Otis asked. "Surely the FBI could have figured that out."

"Not without the key," Simon said.

"So tell me what it is."

"It's in your evidence room."

Gates signed the register at the evidence desk, and a uniformed policeman ushered the two of them into the windowless room. The overhead fluorescent lights popped and buzzed as Gates unlocked one of dozens of wire cages that jammed the room, pulled out a plastic bag containing Petty's belt, and handed it to Simon.

"I need the spear, too," Simon said.

Gates removed the spear and unwrapped it from the brown paper that protected it. Bloodstains soaked the first eight inches or so of the spear shaft.

"I don't get it," Gates said. "Where's the key?"

"Right here," Simon said, indicating the spear. "It's a scytale. The world's first cipher. Invented by the Spartans. Say the commander of the Spartan army wanted to send a message back to his king in the city. He'd wrap a strip of goatskin around the shaft of a stick, write his message along one side, and unwind the strip of skin. Then he'd fill in the spaces between the letters of the message with random letters, which made the dispatch read like gibberish, and send a runner to deliver the strip of skin to Sparta. There the king would wrap the skin around a stick of the exact same diameter as the commander's and decipher the message."

Simon repressed a vision of Petty pinned to the floor, bleeding to death, pulling off his belt, wrapping it around the spear that impaled him, and scrawling the name of his murderer.

"I'll be damned," Gates said. "A scytale, you say?" He wrapped the belt around the spear and turned it over and over in his hands. "I still can't read it."

"Right here," Simon said, showing him. "MLXME. Mark Lozano killed me."

"The son-in-law."

"Exactly. Petty must have expected Lozano would 'discover' his body, so he needed to disguise his message."

"But Lozano's staff said he didn't leave the restaurant."

"I think, if you question them again, you'll find they didn't mean exactly that. Lozano didn't do anything different that evening. I'll bet he took the restaurant receipts to the night deposit at the bank, same as he did every night."

"The bank behind Petty's house. Lozano paid his father-in-law a quick visit. Why did he kill him?"

"It's up to you to find that out. You're the detective."

When Otis stopped by Simon's house a couple of days later, he found the young professor, in jeans and a Kenan College T-shirt, typing away on his porch.

"I thought you'd want to know," Gates said. "We arrested Lozano today."

Simon shut his laptop down.

"I'll have to testify at his trial, won't I?" Simon asked.

"'Fraid so."

"I was hoping the FBI would save me from that by decrypting the cipher," Simon said. "If you'd sent them the belt instead of the letters typed on a sheet of paper, the cryptologist might have recognized it as a scytale. So what was Lozano's motive?"

"Petty had suddenly taken it into his head to cash out everything and move to Italy to live for the rest of his life. Unfortunately, that included the $50,000 he'd lent his daughter and son-in-law to start the restaurant. They couldn't afford to give the money back to Petty and keep the business going."

"The jerk."

"Lozano tried to talk his father-in-law out of pulling his money out of the business. When Petty refused, Lozano lost his temper and killed him. He came back in the morning to 'discover' the murder, hoping that would distract our attention from him. The daughter wasn't involved, and she and the kids will be okay. They've got the restaurant and her inheritance from Petty. The best Lozano can hope for is first-degree manslaughter."

"I don't know about that," Simon said. "Maybe he'll get off. Everyone in the neighborhood is contributing to a defense fund. This is still the South. Home of the 'he needed killin' defense."

SARAH R. SHABER wasn't born in North Carolina, but she got here as soon as she could. She attended college at Duke University and graduate school at the University of North Carolina at Chapel Hill and has lived in Raleigh ever since. The first book in her series featuring historian and amateur sleuth Professor Simon Shaw, *Simon Said*, won the St. Martin's Press Best First Traditional Mystery Award.

MR. STRANG TAKES A PARTNER

William E. Brittain

"Would you be Mr. Strang, now?"

Mr. Strang looked up from the heap of chemical-stained glassware on the demonstration table at the front of his classroom. It was nearly 4:30, and he still had to wash the lab apparatus—"scrubbing the pots," he called it. This late in the day he didn't feel up to facing some overbearing parent bent on turning an offspring's C– into an A by dint of paternal persuasion.

A single glance at the figure in the doorway calmed his fears. The slender man who stood there might have been taken for a small boy but for a face seamed with creases which were accentuated by his broad smile. He was scarcely five feet tall, and his unruly shock of red hair was tinged here and there with wisps of gray. All in all, he put Mr. Strang in mind of a well-dressed leprechaun.

"I'm Mr. Strang." The science teacher wiped his damp hands on the lapels of his jacket.

The little man extended a hand. "Corcoran's the name—Wesley Corcoran."

"Oh? Patty's father?"

"Yes. Matter of fact, Patricia's the reason I came calling."

"But she's doing quite well in biology and—"

"Tush, tush! It's not Patricia's schooling I wanted to see you about."

"Then what—"

"Mr. Strang, did you not tell my daughter's class as how any problem can be solved if all the evidence is available, and it's approached in the proper manner?"

Mr. Strang felt his face start to redden. "Well, I—"

"And furthermore, I understand you're quite the one for figuring out things. Not just science stuff neither, but all kinds of puzzles and things."

"Mr. Corcoran, it's really quite late, and I must be—"

"Ah, you force my hand. I was saving this to show you at a more opportune time, but before you can get somebody's help, you first have to get his attention, as the woman said while bashing at her husband with a rolling pin."

Corcoran reached into a jacket pocket and brought out what appeared to be a folded sheet of paper from a legal pad. "Would you just take a few seconds to read this?"

The teacher unfolded the paper. The penciled words on it were written in a quavery hand. It appeared to be a poem of some kind.

WHY work at my conundrums, faithful Wes?
   To seek your fortune, no more and no less.
Now, having answered WHY, I leave to you
   To find the WHAT, the WHEN, the WHERE, and WHO.
All answers lie beneath my roofing tiles
   And in Alaska's literary isles.
The one you seek's a truly Nob'l man.
   Now solve my little word games—if you can.

"What say you, Mr. Strang?" Corcoran asked when the teacher had finished reading. "Should I go now and leave you in peace?"

A grin spread across Mr. Strang's face as he saw the impish gleam in Corcoran's eyes. "You old fraud!" the teacher exclaimed. "Patty told you I could never turn down a good puzzle. Now what's this all about? Nothing criminal, is it?"

Corcoran shook his head. "More in the financial field. And now it's your turn. What have you gathered from the poem? About the man who wrote it, I mean?"

"Hmm." The teacher ran gnarled fingers through his sparse crop of hair. "I can't make much sense of the poem itself. But the writer— that's something else again. He's quite wealthy but in rather poor health. He's also fairly intelligent, and either his background or interests—or both—run to the newspaper business."

"Ah, ha!" Corcoran gave Mr. Strang's back a congratulatory pat. "You're just the man for me, sir. But how'd you know all them things just from the few lines here?"

"Well," Mr. Strang replied, "the hand that wrote these lines trembled. I surmised it was because of illness. As to his wealth, not only does he mention a fortune, but he also refers to his roofing tiles. Yes, the word does make the line rhyme properly, but it's also suggestive of enough money to afford something better than the usual asphalt shingles. The newspaper business? Every cub reporter in the world soon learns that *who*, *what*, *when*, *where*, and *why* are the elements of a good news story. The intelligence is obvious. He wrote the poem, didn't he? And it's got us both mystified."

Mr. Strang sat down at his desk. "And now that I've told you what I got from the poem, it's back to you again, Mr. Corcoran. What's this all about? Who wrote it? And why?"

"It was done by Rutherford Pyle," answered Corcoran.

Mr. Strang immediately recognized the name. "But I read he'd died just last week. Right here in Aldershot. His heart, wasn't it? A pity, too. Pyle could do things with the English language that were incredible. One of the most persuasive writers I ever read."

A smile spread across Corcoran's face. "You know a bit about Mr. Pyle, then?"

"More than a bit. He was an Horatio Alger hero come to life. A newspaper delivery boy at twelve. Fifteen years later he owned a Midwest paper, and ten years after that he had four more. Ran them all himself, wrote a lot of the copy and editorials, said what he thought regardless of outside pressures, and the devil take the hindmost."

"Ah, that was a long time back," sighed Corcoran. "Those were the good days, Mr. Strang. And I was at his side through them all. My job was to kind of look after Mr. Pyle and do whatever little things he wanted of me. He said I was his good luck charm. But old age creeps up on us all. And when he had them two heart attacks—near five years ago, they were—he took the big house here in Aldershot to be near his daughter and her husband. Me and Patricia—my wife died long since, God rest her soul—lived there with him the whole time. The attacks weakened him something terrible. A short walk about the house once a day was the best he could manage. But I saw to it that the necessary chores got done, and in return, Mr. Pyle gave me an education like no other in the world."

"Education?" asked Mr. Strang. "What do you mean?"

"Mr. Pyle has—had—a library that takes up near half the main floor. Oh, he was weak of body, but his mind was as quick as ever. Having naught to occupy himself, he decided to educate me beyond the six years of public school I'd had as a boy. I resisted at first, but later on his problems got to be kind of fun."

"Problems?"

"Yes, sir. He'd pretend like I was a reporter and he was sending me out to get a story. Only the place I'd go to get it was downstairs to the library. And heaven help me if I didn't have the who, what, when, where, and why by the time I returned."

"Just how did that work?" Mr. Strang asked.

"Well, I remember one time when he set me the task of finding two words that sounded the same but had opposite meanings. To find 'em, I had to read the dictionary, learning new words by the score."

"And what were the two words?"

"There were quite a few. Take two of 'em, now—*raise* and *raze*, to build up and to tear down. Y'see, that was the cleverness of it. To find what Mr. Pyle asked, I had to do a tremendous amount of reading. I daresay there's few books even in that vast library of his what ain't got my thumb smudges in 'em. I'd have to find out everything there was to know about famous characters in literature—Uriah Heep, for instance—and bring in a story just like the character was a living person. Or there'd be a place I was to research, right down to knowing how much it would cost to fly there. And all the time I was learnin' and learnin', and me not even knowin' it. Because of Mr. Pyle's kindness, I'll vow there's many a college professor I could give a run for his money. It's because Mr. Pyle was so good to me that I know he wouldn't—he wouldn't—"

"He wouldn't what, Mr. Corcoran?"

"Mr. Pyle up and died, and now Patricia and me are out on our own, without enough money between us to buy a decent meal. That's not how he would have wanted it."

"But surely there's a will," said the teacher.

"There is. It leaves everything to his daughter. He died too fast, Mr. Strang. Too fast."

"Too fast, Mr. Corcoran? I don't understand."

"Well, sir, over the past few months Mr. Pyle began talking with me about how things was going to be after he died. His estate and all. He was beginning to have intimations of his own mortality, don't you see. I was not mentioned in the will, as he didn't want his daughter and me arguing over who gets what. But several weeks ago he told he'd put some money aside so me and Patricia would be taken care of after he'd passed away."

"I'm still puzzled. Why can't you just take that money and—"

"He didn't put the money in a bank or something like that. No, he concealed it somewhere in that house. And then he set me one more task. I was to be a reporter again and use the clues he gave me—leads, as he called 'em—to track down where the money was stashed away. If I couldn't find it inside a month, he promised to reveal the hiding place. Oh, it was foolish to do the thing that way, but he had so few things to occupy his mind. But before the month ended, he was—was—"

"Is that what this is all about?" asked Mr. Strang. "You mean hidden in that big house there's money which Rutherford Pyle meant you to have?"

"That's it, Mr. Strang," Corcoran replied. "Somewhere in the house—probably in the library itself—is the fortune mentioned in the poem. But before I could give the place a proper look, the lawyers for the estate told me I had to get out. The house is closed tight, and Patricia and I are living in a single room with barely enough ready cash to pay this week's rent."

"Umm." Mr. Strang toyed with his acid-stained necktie. "You know, Mr. Corcoran, legally you haven't a leg to stand on. If Pyle left everything to his daughter, you can't claim a dime based on some vague promise he made before he died."

"True. But the daughter—Laura Aikens is her married name— has left me a bit of hope. She knew the high regard her father had for me. She said if Mr. Pyle meant me to have something, I was to have it."

"Then why not just go back and search until the money shows up?"

"No, that won't do. I showed Mrs. Aikens the poem and the rest, but she wasn't convinced they were anything but the maunderings of an old man. The only way I could claim what was due me, she said, was to prove to her that the clues made some sense and then go into the house and head straight for the hiding place. She'd not allow any hunting expeditions, with me claimin' any cash I came upon."

"I see," said Mr. Strang. "That's the problem, then. You have to prove to Laura Aikens's satisfaction that a hiding place exists and then locate it without any margin for error."

"That's it indeed," replied Corcoran. "And it must be done within the next four days, as after that, Mr. and Mrs. Aikens are moving away, leaving only a caretaker and the house locked up tight. I despaired of having any chance at all until Patricia suggested you might be able to help."

Mr. Strang rubbed his hands together briskly. "Challenge accepted, Mr. Corcoran," he said. "The poem goes here." He spread the wrinkled yellow paper on his desk and then gestured to Corcoran.

"Let's have the rest of it," he said. "You've talked about clues—plural—as well as the poem 'and the rest.' What 'rest,' Mr. Corcoran? What other leads did Mr. Pyle give you?"

Again Corcoran reached into a pocket. He pulled out four small white cards. "I'm afraid you'll find these as confusing as the poem," he told the teacher.

There were words on each card in the same spidery handwriting as the poem. Mr. Strang peered through black-rimmed glasses at the top one.

Bobby writes to a rodent.
WHO have plans turned to dust at 39 and 40?

The next message was equally obscure:

Fight him for a nation!
WHAT are the fruits of Julie's labors?

The third didn't help much either:

Bill's Dicky Three emotes, beginning one and one.
WHEN is the season of low spirits?

And finally:

Public Enemy Number One begins to Nod.
WHERE is the marked man's newfound land?

Mr. Strang stared long and hard at the four cards. "Nothing," he said finally. "Let me see that poem again."

He tapped the yellow paper with a gnarled finger. "The WHY is given here," he said. " 'To seek your fortune, no more and no less.' WHAT and WHEN and WHERE and WHO have something to do with the clues on the white cards. But we must begin with the poem. I'm sure of it."

"Can you find nothing at all?" asked Corcoran anxiously.

"The first part of the poem's clear enough. You're to seek your fortune somewhere in the house — 'beneath my roofing tiles.' It's the next two lines that stump me. What are 'Alaska's literary isles'? And why make a contraction of the word 'noble,' to say nothing of capitalizing it?"

"As to the isles," murmured Corcoran, "the only ones I was able to think of up around Alaska are the Aleutians."

"Aleutians," replied Mr. Strang. "Yes, they're well enough known, and I don't think Pyle would give you something too obscure. But whoever heard of literary Aleutians?"

"I have!" called a chipper voice from the hallway outside the room.

"What!" cried Mr. Strang and Corcoran together.

A smiling woman's face appeared around the corner of the doorway. It was surmounted by gray hair tied with a large knot in the back. Several pencils were stuck into the knot like pins in a cushion.

"Maude Wiggins, get in here this instant!" bellowed Mr. Strang.

The woman entered the room, cocking her head like a somewhat aged sparrow. "Wesley Corcoran, Maude Wiggins," said Mr. Strang. "Maude's our head librarian."

"I'd just finished unpacking some reproductions of so-called art masterpieces," she said. "Masterpieces, my foot! Honestly, Leonard, how anybody can put a few daubs of paint on a canvas and sell it for thousands of dollars is beyond me. Anyway, I was just passing your room when I heard you say — "

"Literary Aleutians," Mr. Strang repeated. "What are they, Maude?"

"Literary allusions," she said, stressing the pronunciation, "are oblique references to — well, literature. For example, Leonard, if you were to tell me that 'age cannot wither me, nor custom stale my infinite variety,' I'd know you'd been reading Shakespeare's *Anthony and Cleopatra*, even as I fell swooning into your arms."

"Aleutians — allusions," mused Mr. Strang. "Nearly identical sounds. Hydrozoa, Maude, I think you've found it! That's just the kind of linguistic trick that Pyle loved to pull. And the last line of the poem even mentions 'word games.' We didn't catch on because we were reading, not listening. Maude, I love you. You're beautiful. Will you run away with me and live in sin in a thatched hut somewhere?" And he planted a big kiss on her cheek.

"Leonard Strang, you're an old fool!" she sputtered. "At your age, sinning means grabbing fifteen minutes of extra sleep in the morning."

"I'm only two years older than you, Maude."

She made a mock slap at his face. "And you're no gentleman, either."

By the desk, Corcoran shook his head in confusion. "I don't get it," he said. "What's happening here?"

"I was about to ask the same thing," said Maude.

"'All answers lie beneath my roofing tiles'—that is, in the house," explained Mr. Strang, his hands trembling with excitement. "'And in Alaska's literary isles'—in literary allusions. The WHAT, WHEN, WHERE, and WHO questions have their answers in the Pyle library. And when we find the answers, they'll lead us to the money, to the fortune."

"I don't know what this is all about," said Maude. "But if you need a library, mine's available. And this sounds a lot more exciting than going home and cleaning the oven. So I demand to join you, with full partnership privileges. After all, if it weren't for me, you two would still be freezing in Alaska."

"We're delighted to have you," said Mr. Strang gallantly. "Tell me, partner, do you think our beloved principal, Mr. Guthrey, would be annoyed if we spent a few hours in the library?"

"I think he'd have a fit," replied Maude. "Everybody's supposed to be out of the building by five o'clock. Oh, well, it's his blood pressure, not mine. Come on, I still have my key. Just my luck. The first time in twenty-five years a man—two men—want to spend an evening alone with me, and all we're going to do is look at books."

Once seated at one of the library's huge tables, Mr. Strang filled Maude in on Corcoran's problem. Then the three took turns staring at the four cards.

"Which one do you have now?" Mr. Strang asked Corcoran after thirty minutes of fruitless endeavor.

"The one about Public Enemy Number One," was the reply. "All that's in my mind is Edward G. Robinson in the movie." ·

"I'm working on 'Bill's Dicky,'" said Maude. "Isn't that just too cute for words? To my way of thinking, the person who invented diminutives of names should be drawn and quartered. 'Bill's Dicky' indeed. How would you like to be called Lenny Strang, Leonard? Why can't this be William's Rich—"

And then there was a silence as Maude and Mr. Strang stared at each other. This was followed by a wild scrambling as they both raced to the far end of the room.

Maude, being more familiar with the arrangement of the library, was the first to reach the proper place. She removed a book from the shelf, riffled through its pages for a few moments, then pointed to a line of type.

"Got it," murmured Mr. Strang. "Now we know the WHEN." And he jotted the line in a small notebook.

"Now that we've got the hang of it, Leonard, it shouldn't take long to figure out those other cards," said Maude. "Let me try my hand at WHO."

WHO came easily. WHAT and WHERE required a bit more thought, and there were several unproductive searches through the library's stacks. But in another hour both Mr. Strang and Maude Wiggins were sure they knew the identity of Rutherford Pyle's "Nob'l man." And they were reasonably certain of the location of Wesley Corcoran's fortune in the huge Pyle mansion.

Still, they put their theory to Corcoran himself with some misgivings. "We'll only get the one chance," Mr. Strang told him. "And if we're wrong, it's good-bye fortune."

"In for a penny, in for a pound," was Corcoran's blithe reply. "Your ideas sound fine to me. And if they don't work out, at least we had our try. I'll not hold hard luck against either of you. Now I guess it's time to make an appointment with Mrs. Aikens."

She was perhaps fifty years old. Her bearing was queenly as she approached the massive chair in the center of the room, and she carried a long cigarette holder in her right hand like a royal scepter. Before sitting down she turned in a full circle, looking intently at the shelves of books which covered all four walls from floor to ceiling.

The room in the Pyle mansion was huge, larger even than the Aldershot High School library.

It had to be huge, thought Mr. Strang, to contain a presence as commanding as that of Mrs. Laura Aikens.

"Mr. Corcoran, Mr. Strang, Miss Wiggins," she said, settling into the chair's depths with great aplomb, "welcome to my father's house. You tell me, Mr. Corcoran, that father wished you to have some token of gratitude for your years of service to him. It is my further understanding that Mr. Strang and Miss Wiggins are assisting you—your paladins, so to speak."

"Yes, Mrs. Aikens." Corcoran's voice was little more than a husky whisper.

"Very well," she went on. "I will not stand in the way of any wishes my late father had concerning the disposition of his estate, and I reject any petty legal arguments concerning the propriety of those wishes. Very simply, Mr. Corcoran, if father wished you to have something, you will have it.

"But I won't have any clever opportunist sullying my father's memory by trying to gain by trickery that which is not his. So the ground rules, if you will, are simple. You must convince me that the clues of which you spoke came from my father. You must further convince me that those clues lead to a specific spot in this house. And finally, you must go to that spot and find something of real or sentimental value to you. If these three conditions are met, I will give you that which you claim as soon as the will is probated. Is that understood?"

"Y-yes," sputtered Corcoran.

"Then you may begin."

Mr. Strang and Maude Wiggins whispered together for a few seconds. Then the librarian shook her head firmly and backed toward the far wall. Mr. Strang walked to the great chair, reached into his pocket, and removed the poem and the four white cards.

"It seems I've been elected to do the talking," he said. "First, I—we—ask you to look at these cards, Mrs. Aikens. Are they in your father's handwriting?"

She examined the cards intently. Finally she nodded. "Yes, my father wrote these."

"First condition met, then," the teacher stated. "For these are the clues he gave to Wesley Corcoran."

For the first time a bit of a smile played about Mrs. Aikens's lips. "Go on."

"Note the poem. Its fifth and sixth lines state that the fortune is in this house and also in 'Alaska's literary isles.' Mr. Corcoran and I took that to mean the Aleutians and, by extension, literary Aleutians. But we give Miss Wiggins full marks for discovering that your father was referring to literary *allusions*."

Mrs. Aikens's smile grew larger. "I will grant—reluctantly, Mr. Strang—that the pun in the phrase 'literary Aleutians' is one which my father was not only capable of but which he would have delighted in."

"Therefore," the teacher continued, "the WHAT, WHEN, WHERE, and WHO cards must be literary references."

"Must they? You'll have to convince me, Mr. Strang."

"I hope to. Now each card first makes a cryptic statement and then asks a question. This seems to indicate that the statement is a clue to answer the question. Wouldn't you agree?"

Mrs. Aikens remained impassive. "Go on."

"Our first break came on the 'Bill's Dicky' card when Maude— Miss Wiggins—objected to the diminutive names and substituted the full ones. When that was done, the line read: 'William's Richard Three emotes, beginning one and one.'"

"Oh!" Suddenly Laura Aikens clapped her hands together in delight. The childish gesture was so out of character that Mr. Strang stared in astonishment.

"William Shakespeare's *Richard III*!" she cried. "Of course."

The teacher breathed a sigh of relief. It seemed the second condition—that the woman be convinced that the cards indeed held clues—could be met more easily than he'd feared.

"And Scene *One* of Act *One*," he said, accenting the numbers, "begins with Richard saying, 'Now is the winter of our discontent made glorious summer of this sun of York.' So, Mrs. Aikens—'WHEN is the season of low spirits?'"

"The winter of our discontent."

"Good." Mr. Strang felt himself to be on firm ground now. Laura

Aikens seemed as pleased to give a correct answer as any giggling schoolgirl.

"Now let's try the WHO card," he went on.

"Bobby—Robert," mused Laura Aikens. "Let me see. That might be Robert Browning or Robert Burns or Robert Louis—"

"I was at a loss on that one," Mr. Strang interrupted, "until Maude bailed me out. It seems one of Robert Burns's best-known poems is titled *To a Mouse*. And line 39 of the poem, continuing on to 40, is," Mr. Strang consulted his notebook, "'The best laid schemes o' mice an' men gang aft a-gley.' So if 'a-gley' means wrong, WHO, then, 'have plans turned to dust?'"

"Mice and men, isn't it?" replied Laura Aikens.

"Right," said the teacher. "Third, let's consider Public Enemy Number One. This took us a bit longer. But it occurred to me that 'begins to' on the card might mean 'starts toward.' I also got to wondering whether 'Number One' might mean not the most dangerous but the first in time. Public enemies of importance are usually killers, Mrs. Aikens. And the Number One murderer, who was marked by the Lord for his crime, was—"

Laura Aikens arched her eyebrows. "You mean Cain?" she asked. "From the Bible?"

"I do," Mr. Strang assured her. "And note the capitalization of Nod. The Bible tells us, in Genesis 4:16, that: 'Cain went out from the presence of the Lord, and dwelt in the land of Nod—'"

"That's why it's capitalized!" Laura exclaimed.

"—'on the east of Eden!'" Mr. Strang concluded.

"Then the answer to WHERE is 'east of Eden.'" By now, Laura was enjoying herself hugely. "But there's still WHAT. 'Fight him for a nation!' That doesn't make sense. And who's Julie? Julius? Julian?"

"Maude, you figured this one out all by yourself," said Mr. Strang, turning to the librarian. "Do the honors, please."

"Well," Maude began with unaccustomed timidity, "I couldn't think of a pun for 'fight,' so I just started substituting words that meant about the same. 'War,' 'brawl,' 'quarrel,' and so forth. And then I hit on 'battle.'"

"Battle him for a nation," said Laura slowly. "I don't—yes, I do! Him and hymn—they sound the same, but they're different words. 'Fight him for a nation!' is 'The Battle Hymn of the Republic.'"

"Written by Julie Ward Howe," Mr. Strang chimed in. "And if you remember the first few lines, you'll get the 'fruits' of Julia's—or 'Julie's'—'labors.'"

Laura began humming softly. "Ta ta ta ta tata—where the grapes of wrath are stored." She paused. "The fruits—they're the grapes of wrath, aren't they?"

Mr. Strang nodded. "So now we have all four questions answered. WHO is 'mice and men.' WHAT is 'the grapes of wrath.' WHEN is 'the winter of our discontent.' And finally, WHERE is 'east of Eden.'"

Suddenly Laura Aikens seemed to change again before their eyes. Gone was the incredulous schoolgirl, happy in answering her teachers correctly. And again there sat in the huge chair the imperious queen of the Rutherford Pyle estate. "This has all been very interesting," she proclaimed. "But I scarcely see how the books you've mentioned lead to any kind of hiding place."

At that, Maude Wiggins marched up to the chair, her eyes flashing. "We don't want to see any of the books we mentioned," she snapped. "What we do want to look at is the shelf where your father kept the works of John Steinbeck."

"John Steinbeck? But—"

"Yes, Mrs. Aikens," said Mr. Strang gently. "John Steinbeck. The author of *Of Mice and Men*, *The Grapes of Wrath*, *The Winter of Our Discontent*, and *East of Eden*. Four titles by the same author—four literary allusions. And not very obscure titles, what with three of the books having been made into movies, to say nothing of numerous TV adaptations."

"But I always considered Steinbeck a rather earthy, rugged author. Why would father have referred to him in the poem as noble?"

"Not noble, Mrs. Aikens. Nob'l. Or, if we consider the capital N and put the missing vowel in its proper place—Nobel. Were you aware, Mrs. Aikens, that in 1962, John Steinbeck won the Nobel Prize for literature?"

Slowly Laura Aikens lowered her head. And then something shook her body. Once. Then again.

She was laughing.

"Father's wordplay," she giggled. "Even after death it goes on. There, Mr. Corcoran, on one of those shelves by the fireplace. There's where you'll find the Steinbeck books."

Corcoran approached the shelf. "There seem to be four Steinbeck books here," he said. "And the very titles you mentioned."

He drew one of the books from the shelf and peered closely at its cover. Then he sniffed it. "No first edition, this," he said. "It's too new. Worth perhaps $15 at most. I'm afraid we lose, Mr. Strang. Miss Wiggins, I'm sorry to have troubled you."

He held the book loosely by its spine, and Mr. Strang could see tears welling in his eyes. "He forgot me," Corcoran murmured sadly. "He forgot—"

Something appeared from between the pages of the book and fluttered to the floor. It was followed by a second fluttering. They appeared to be slips of paper.

Quickly Maude scooped up one from the floor, looked at both front and back, and uttered a loud gasp. "It's a $1,000 bill!"

But already Mr. Strang had snatched the book from Corcoran's hand and was shaking it vigorously. Bills dropped from between the pages like green snow. The second book revealed a similar cache. And the third. And the fourth.

A hundred such bills were found among the pages of the four Steinbeck volumes.

"One hundred thousand dollars!" Corcoran gasped, scarcely able to believe his own words. "Oh, thank you, Mr. Strang. And you, Miss Wiggins. And you, Mrs. Aikens."

"I won't be able to turn the money over to you until the will's probated," said Laura Aikens. "It's part of the estate now, and the lawyers will want to know about this. But as soon as everything is settled, I'll send you a check, Mr. Corcoran. And in the meantime, if you need a little something to tide you over, I'll be happy to—"

"Perhaps that won't be necessary," said Mr. Strang. "Once this story hits the newspapers, I'm sure Mr. Corcoran's credit will be excellent."

"One hundred thousand!" sighed Maude. "Leonard, on the strength of our success, I think you ought to take me out to dinner this evening. Ah, Le Chateau Brun. Or perhaps the Aldershot Inne."

"Dinner sounds fine," the teacher replied. "But Wesley Corcoran got the money, not I. And it's a week until payday. Will it be your place or mine?"

WILLIAM E. BRITTAIN is the author of many popular and critically ac-
claimed children's books, including *The Wish Giver*, *Shape-Changer*, and *Dr. Dredd's Wagon of Wonders*. His awards include a Newbury Honor in 1984. Among the mystery community he is best known for his "Mr. Strang" short stories, which starred his detective-teacher, the logical high school science teacher Leonard Strang. Brittain taught in North Carolina public schools and now lives in Asheville.

KILLER FUDGE

Kathy Hogan Trocheck

was busy touching up my mental image of the new Callahan Garrity: long sleek legs, nonexistent thighs, flat belly, firm shapely arms. My stomach growled angrily. I love the first day of a diet. The happy feeling of starvation, the power you feel over your gnawing appetite.

A shadow fell over the lawn chair where I was stretched out.

I opened one eye. A generously built black woman with a sad expression stood beside me, blocking out the sun that was to tone me, bake me, turn me into something out of a Coppertone ad.

"Callahan," she said tentatively. "Edna told me to come talk to you."

"Hello, Ruby," I said, with little enthusiasm. "If it's about that extra day you want to work, take it up with Edna. It's her day on the books. I'm taking the afternoon off for self-improvement."

Edna, my mother and business partner, was supposed to be handling the office while I recharged my batteries. It had been an awful week.

"No'm, it's not about work," Ruby said. "Well, it sort of is, but it's really about Darius."

"Darius," I said. "Is he one of your nephews?" Ruby has so many nieces and nephews, grandchildren and great-grandchildren, that I can never keep track of them all.

"Foster grandson," she prompted. "My Darius is in trouble, Callahan. I need you to see about it."

Seeing about other people's troubles is what I do in my nonexistent spare time. I bought The House Mouse shortly after quitting my job as a detective for the Atlanta Police Department. Some women take up tennis. I dabble in private investigation. Doesn't burn up near the calories, unfortunately.

I sat up slowly and looked down at my belly, slightly pink and flabby and oily from the suntan lotion. Not flat and brown. Oh well.

Ruby is a rock usually, one of those imperturbable women whose expressions stay calm in the face of untold troubles. She's a mainstay of The House Mouse, the cleaning business Edna and I run out of my house here in Atlanta. But today her lower lip was trembling, and she dabbed continually at her eyes with a crumpled hankie.

She perched at the edge of my lawn chair, smoothing her white cleaning smock down over her knees.

"You know Mr. Ragan, my Thursday morning job? Old gentleman lives alone over there off Hooper Avenue?"

I remembered the name.

"Mr. Ragan's dead," Ruby said. Tears spilled down her smooth round cheeks. "Murdered. And the police think my Darius did it. They come to the house this morning and took him away. Handcuffed him like you see on the TV news."

"Why would they suspect Darius?" I asked. "Does he even know Merritt Ragan?"

She nodded. "Darius been doing Mr. Ragan's yard work for a year. He liked that old man a lot. And Mr. Ragan liked him too. Paid Darius $25 to keep the yard nice. Darius wouldn't hurt that old man. He's a good boy. A good worker. So I want to know can you see about it? I'll pay. You can take the money out of my check every week."

She reached in her smock pocket and pulled out a crisp $100 bill and held it toward me. "This here's the down payment. Is that right?"

I stood up and pulled on the shorts I'd left on the ground, then straightened up to zip. They were definitely looser. "Keep the money, Ruby. Employees get a 50 percent discount on private investigation work."

Edna looked up from the bank deposit she'd been preparing and frowned. A stack of checks sat on the table next to a smaller stack of twenties. She took a deep drag on the extra-long filtered cigarette and exhaled slowly, letting the smoke halo her carefully coiffed white hair.

"You gonna help Ruby?"

"Yeah," I sighed. "Of course I'll help her. The woman's a saint. But that doesn't mean little Darius is. I guess I'll head down to homicide to see what the deal is with the charges. Can you hold the fort here?"

She glanced at the kitchen clock. "It's four now. The girls are done for the day. I'll put the answering machine on and come with you."

The last thing I needed was my mother along for the ride. "I may need you to do some phone work for me," I said tactfully. "Stay here and I'll call you after I know if they intend to keep him."

She pooched out her lower lip, took another drag on her cigarette, and regarded me through narrowed eyes. "I know a brush-off when I hear one."

As luck would have it, the only soul occupying the homicide detective's office was a friendly face, Bucky Deavers, an old friend from my days as a burglary detective.

We traded good-natured insults, then I got down to business.

"I'm looking for information on the Merritt Ragan homicide. I'm working for the kid you picked up and charged this morning."

Bucky leafed through some papers in a box of reports on his desk. "Oh yea. Merritt Ragan. He's the old dude over off of Hooper Avenue. Kid came in the house, saw all this money, bopped him on the head, took the money, and split."

I reached over and plucked the report from his hands. "I doubt the report says that."

He leaned back in the chair and folded his hands behind his neck. "Read it and weep," he said. "The kid did it, Callahan. His fingerprints are all over the kitchen and the murder weapon. Which was one of those heavy old-fashioned irons, by the way."

"He worked there," I said. "Yard man. And Ragan invited him in all the time. He probably saw the iron some other time and picked it up to ask about it."

"He's got a sheet," Bucky said. "Did time at the Youth Detention Center up in Alto for burglary and assault."

"Misspent youth," I said, scanning the report. "He's lived with his grandma for a year, cleaned up his act, works all the time, goes to church regular. He's a new kid."

"He's a rotten little killer," Bucky said. "We found the cash on him, 200 bucks. Had it stashed in his Air Jordans. He admitted he took it from Ragan."

"What?" I said, startled. "His grandmother doesn't know about any confession."

"Grannies don't know a lot of stuff," Bucky said, a touch too smugly. "Your friend Darius says he went to the house yesterday afternoon to see about getting paid early. He says he went in, saw a bunch of money laying around by the front door, and left."

"But he doesn't admit he killed the old man."

"Not yet," Bucky said. "But we know he did it, and he knows it too. Homicide in commission of another felony. Robbery. He's seventeen now, eighteen next month. We can try him as an adult. The DA's looking at the death penalty."

I sat up straight at the mention of Old Sparky, which is what they call Georgia's electric chair, the one they keep warmed up down at the state prison at Jackson. "Jesus, the kid's grandmother works for me. She swears he's been rehabilitated."

He was suddenly busy tidying things on his desktop. "I saw the grandmother this morning when we picked the kid up. Nice lady. She's lucky Darius didn't turn on her."

I stood up to leave. "She knows the kid and she says he didn't do it. That's enough for me. Can you get me in to see him?"

Darius Greene wasn't overjoyed to see me. He was slumped over in a chair when the guard escorted me into the visiting area. Long, blue-clad legs stretched out in front of him. He had one of those trick hair-cuts the kids were into lately, with the hair shaved to the scalp in the back, moderating to a wedge shape that angled sharply to the left.

"Darius, I'm Callahan. Your grandmother works for me. She thinks I can help you."

He cocked his head to the side and ran a practiced eye over me, then turned his attention back to the floor.

"You're the one who keep Grandmama washing toilets," he said tonelessly. "How're you gonna help me? Gimme some toilets to scrub?"

I felt my face flush hot with guilt. And then I got mad. "I'm the one who takes your grandmama to the hospital when her blood pressure goes up. I'm the one sees she gets paid a decent wage for her work, so she can buy fancy basketball shoes for some snot-nosed kid she loves. And I'm also a former cop and a private detective. I can help you if you let me. Did you know the DA is thinking of asking for the death penalty for Merritt Ragan's murder?"

"I heard," he mumbled. He didn't look worried.

I was losing patience. "Look, Darius. I've seen the police reports. This does not look good. Can you tell me anything at all about yesterday? Could anyone else have been in that house before you got there? Did you see Mr. Ragan when you went into the house? Had the door been forced?"

No answer.

"Did you kill him, Darius? Did you? Ruby says you're a good boy. What happened? Why'd you take the money and kill him? He was a helpless old man. Is that what you'd like to have happen to Ruby?"

He continued to stare at the floor. "Ain't tellin' you nothin'. I'm gettin' me a lawyer."

On the other side of the screened door, Caroline Ragan's lips set in a tight disapproving line when I told her who I was and what I wanted.

Somebody had told her that old-maid schoolteachers were supposed to be thin and humorless, and she'd taken their advice to heart. She had mouse-colored hair and close-set brown eyes, which she blinked continually.

"I'm sorry for Ruby's troubles. She kept this house immaculate. I guess it wouldn't hurt to let you come in and look around. The police said I could start cleaning things up today."

Merritt Ragan's gray saltbox house could have been an antique shop. Shelves lined the walls of every room, and each held a different collection. There were silver candlesticks, Steiff teddy bears, majolica, miniature snuffboxes, and blue and white porcelains. The wooden floor was dotted with jewel-toned Oriental rugs. The furniture was old too, and the mellow wood glowed in the late afternoon sunlight that poured through the windows.

"The kitchen's in there," Caroline said as we neared the back of the house. "That's where they found Daddy. Go ahead in. I . . . don't like to be there. Because of Daddy and all. The new cleaning service is supposed to take care of it tomorrow." She glared at me when she mentioned the new cleaning service.

Merritt Ragan's kitchen was one of the cheeriest murder scenes I've ever examined. White-painted cabinets lined the room, and a

fruit-motif wallpaper covered the walls. Crisply ruffled white curtains hung at the windows. The floor was gleaming yellow vinyl.
Spotless. I walked over to the back door and took a look. Fingerprint
powder stained the wall and the woodwork of the door. About the
door. The lock didn't look like it had been tampered with.

"The police cleaned up the blood," she said.

I turned around. Caroline stood in the doorway, her matchstick
arms crossed over her chest, as though she were chilled.

"Daddy must have let him in," she added. "I begged him to get a
lawn service. But he wouldn't hear of it. He was fascinated with that
Darius."

I got up and walked slowly around the room. The countertops
were those of a man who lived alone and liked things orderly. A
toaster, coffeemaker, and cordless phone were lined up in military
fashion. The stove held a copper teakettle and a small wooden file
box. Idly I flipped up the lid. A grease-spotted index card had a recipe
for tomato aspic written in purple ink in a tiny crabbed handwriting. I closed the box.

"Your father got on with Darius?"

"They were thick as thieves," she said, then laughed bitterly. "Lit-
erally, one might say."

"The police say they found quite a bit of cash on Darius. Two hundred dollars. Cash he admitted taking from the house. Was your
father in the habit of keeping that much cash around?"

She pulled nervously at the collar of her blouse.

"Cash? Daddy? I suppose he could have had that much around
the house. Usually he liked to pay for things by check or credit card.
It helped him with his record keeping."

I roamed the small room again, looking for something the police
might have missed. On a wooden chair pushed up to a small built-
in desk I spotted a cardboard box. The contents were a jumble of
odds and ends. A small blue and white platter. A sugar bowl with an
unusual hand-painted pattern of bluebirds and butterflies, a green
Depression-glass cake plate, and a pink tulip-shaped flower vase.
McCoy, probably.

"What's all this?" I asked.

She came over to look, and when she saw what was in the box,
she gave a small indignant snort.

"More of Daddy's trash. He went to estate sales every week and bought a lot of broken old junk. The good stuff he took to a flea market down by the airport and sold. It's so humiliating, having your own father paw through dead people's belongings. And actually selling them." She shuddered. "It's not as though he needed the money. Dad was retired from IBM."

I looked closer at Caroline Ragan. Her blouse was real silk, and the slacks she wore were well tailored. She wore a square-cut amethyst ring on her right hand, and a gold chain around her neck held a teardrop-shaped diamond pendant. Nice stuff for an old-maid schoolmarm.

"Are you the only heir?"

She stiffened. "I suppose. Stephen certainly couldn't inherit."

"Stephen?"

"My brother."

"Why not?"

She was annoyed with me. It happens. "He's institutionalized. At Atlanta Regional Hospital. He's been there for fifteen years. Since Mama died. They say he's schizophrenic."

"Was your brother violent?"

I saw a small muscle twitch in her cheek. "Not at all. He's very calm as long as he takes his medication."

I looked again at the back door. "That lock wasn't forced," I pointed out. "I looked at the front door briefly when you let me in. It didn't look tampered with either. That means your father probably let his murderer in here. Is there any chance Stephen could have gotten out of the hospital and come here?"

Her face flushed an ugly pink.

"That's impossible. I'd like you to leave now. Darius Greene killed my father. He's dangerous. An animal. My father's skull was crushed. Did you know that?"

I let myself out the back door because it was easier than walking past the wrathful Caroline Ragan.

The backyard was like the rest of the house: well groomed. The scent of new-mown grass hung in the warm afternoon air, and there were lawn mower tracks in the grass. Darius Greene had definitely been here.

A late-model white Buick was parked in the small detached garage. I had a sudden urge to snoop. After glancing around to see if Caroline was still glaring at me, I walked briskly up to the car and peeked in the passenger-side window.

Clean as a whistle. No Big Mac wrappers, Diet Coke cans, or spare pairs of sneakers. Not nothing. I looked around the garage. Hand tools were hung on pegs over a workbench. Rakes, shovels, and hedge clippers hung from nails along the rafters. I ran my fingers along the clipper blades. A couple of still-green leaves clung to my fingertips.

It wasn't going to be easy to tell Ruby that her precious grandson might be a murderer.

As I left the garage I glanced again at Ragan's car. This time my eye caught a flash of something sticking out from under the passenger's seat.

Quickly I opened the door and peered under the seat. It was a newspaper page, folded in precise quarters. It was the classified ad page from Thursday's newspaper. Thursday. The day Merritt Ragan had been killed. Four ads were circled in red ink. They were all for garage sales or estate sales. I dug in my purse, got out paper and pen, and copied down the addresses. Then I put the paper back where I'd found it.

I found a pay phone down the street from Ragan's house. Edna answered on the first ring. "House Mouse." She sounded bored.

"Mom? Call Atlanta Regional Hospital and ask about a patient named Stephen Ragan. Find out if there's any way he could have gotten out of there Thursday. Call me back at this number."

I'd pulled the van up close to the phone booth, so I got back in and studied the addresses I'd copied from Merritt Ragan's newspaper while I waited. The inside of the van was hot and stuffy. I got out and walked briskly several times up and down the block, keeping within earshot of the phone. The exercise was part of my new program.

After thirty minutes of pacing, my blouse was sweat-soaked and plastered to my back. A kid sat on the porch of a weather-beaten wooden house across the street. He was staring at me. I stared back. He pulled out a giant Snickers bar, tore off the wrapper, and began licking it, slowly and deliberately, like a cat with a dead mouse. He had chocolate smeared all over his face and hands. It was in his hair, between his toes probably. I could hear my own breathing go shallow. Feel the salivary juices trickling through my chocolate-deprived digestive tract. I wanted to vault across the street, snatch the Snickers from the kid, and inhale it all in one gooey chocolate-caramel-peanut-covered nanosecond. It took every ounce of moral fiber I possessed to go back to the phone booth and call the house again.

This time it was Ruby who answered the phone. "Edna had to, uh, go to the, uh, store," she stammered.

"Where is she really, Ruby?" I demanded. She was too saintly to be an effective liar. "Tell me."

"Lord have mercy, I don't know where she went," Ruby wailed. "I was sitting here when you called the last time. She got off the phone, looked up an address in the phone book, and took off out of here like a scalded dog."

"Never mind," I said. "I'll deal with her later."

"Callahan, wait," she said. "Did you talk to Darius?"

"I talked to him, but he wouldn't talk to me."

Silence.

"There's goodness in that boy. But don't nobody but me seem to know it. Can you do anything?"

I looked down at the scrap of paper with the estate sale addresses. "Maybe. What did Merritt Ragan look like? I only ever talked to him on the phone."

"Skinny little old fella. Reminded me of one of them bantam roosters. Had a full head of white hair. Little round bifocal glasses and one of them pointy little chin beards. What was the name of that man in the children's book? The man that made the princess spin gold all night till she guessed his name? He reminded me of him. Can't think of the name myself."

"Rumpelstiltskin?"

"That's the one," she said. "Mr. Ragan looked just that way."

My scrap of paper was looking like Darius Greene's last hope. "Go see him, Ruby," I urged. "Maybe he'll talk to you. Ask him where that money came from. And get him to tell the truth. It's the only thing that might save him."

"I'll see what I can do," she said wearily.

At the first house I had to elbow my way past a throng of people picking through stacks of old *National Geographic* magazines to get into the house. Right inside the front door I tripped over a metal and plastic contraption and nearly impaled myself on a set of brass fireplace tongs.

"That's why I'm selling the darned thing," said the woman who helped me to my feet. "The commercials make it look great; ski your way to a thinner you. They don't tell you it takes up a whole room in your house and you feel like throwing up after five minutes on it."

She'd said the magic word: thinner. I looked at the contraption with renewed interest. "Oh. A Nordic Ski-Track. How much? Does it work?"

"Twenty-five bucks," she said quickly. "I'll get my son to load it in the car for you."

I looked closer at the woman. She was two inches shorter and thirty pounds heavier than me. "I'll pass," I said. I described Merritt Ragan and asked her if she'd seen him.

"Oh, him," she said. "Cheapskate. He was here, talked me out of my grandmother's cake plate for two bucks."

An older woman wearing a large cotton duster over her dress was packing up boxes at the second address. "Oh yeah, I know Merritt," she said. "He comes to our sales all the time."

"I do this professionally," she said, before I could ask. "Run estate sales, that is. Merritt came by about ten Thursday. We had lots of books and coins and record albums. Nothing he buys. We chatted and he left."

She didn't seem curious about why I was asking, and I hated to tell her anyway.

The third house was in an older neighborhood of brick bungalows. An older man, maybe in his late sixties, said he'd been too busy to notice who'd been at his sale Thursday. He agreed to look through his cash box, but there was no check from Merritt Ragan.

Depressed, I nearly skipped the fourth house entirely after pulling up to the curb. Two young mothers had piled a load of playpens, baby strollers, toys, and other kid paraphernalia in the driveway. It was the exercise bike that caught my eye.

I got out of the van and circled it warily. Kicked the tire. Checked the odometer. It had twelve miles on it. One of the women noticed my interest.

"My husband gave me that last year for an anniversary gift," she said. "I kicked the bum out a week later. Let you have the bike for $30, and I'll throw in the Thigh Master for nothing."

"Don't think so," I said. It turned out that she hadn't seen anybody who looked like Rumpelstiltskin the day before.

A convenience store a couple blocks away looked like a good place to get a cold drink and use the phone. I left the drink cooler door open while I decided between Slim Fast and Ultra Slim Fast. I went with the Ultra. Then I called home again.

"House Mouse." My prodigal mother had returned.

"Where the hell were you?"

"You're dieting again, aren't you?" she snapped. "God help us all. If you must know, those old prunes over at the hospital wouldn't tell me diddly over the phone, so I went for a visit."

"You didn't," I said, knowing she had.

"Stephen Ragan hasn't been anywhere since Wednesday," she said. "He burned his hands in a craft class. Second-degree burns. He's in the infirmary and he's heavily sedated. I saw him with my own eyes."

I sighed. "Good work. I don't want to know how you got that information."

"I told 'em I was Sergeant Edna Bentley of the Atlanta PD," she said proudly.

When I pointed out that she'd committed a felony, impersonating a police officer, she made a rude noise. "Don't be late for supper," she said nastily. "It's fried chicken, buttermilk biscuits, and peach cobbler. Don't worry, though; since you're counting calories, I'll make unsweetened iced tea."

I hung up the phone and groaned.

That's when I noticed the cardboard sign tacked to a utility pole across the street. "Estate Sale. Thurs. Fri.," it said. There was an address and an arrow pointing down the nearest cross street.

The house was a two-story white frame affair. The lot was weedy, and the paint was peeling. I knocked at the screen door. When there was no answer, I poked my head in and hollered, "Anybody home?"

The woman who came bustling up the hall was in her early fifties probably. She was short, maybe 5'2", with gray hair cut in a Dutch boy, and her china blue eyes regarded me warily.

"Most everything's already sold," she said, wiping her hands on the rickrack-trimmed apron tied around her thick middle. "Just a few things left. Come in if you want. I'll be in the kitchen."

She hurried away down the hall. The house smelled of mothballs. She was right, there wasn't much left at all. The living room floors were stripped bare, and my footsteps echoed loudly in the high-ceilinged room. All that was left here was a lumpy brown armchair that faced an old rounded-edge television with aluminum-foil-wrapped antennas.

A large mahogany china cabinet looked forlorn in the dining room. There were light rectangles on the painted walls, where pictures had once hung. I peered inside the cabinet. There were some chipped crystal goblets and two solitary rose-patterned dinner plates. And a cracked cream pitcher with a familiar-looking design of bluebirds and butterflies. I picked it up. The handle had been broken and clumsily glued back together.

I wandered down the hallway toward the back of the house. The kitchen was an old-fashioned room, with worn green and white checkerboard linoleum, scarred wooden cabinets, and an immense old stove.

The room was thick with heat and a good, sugary smell. The woman was humming as she poured something chocolate into a square metal pan. She reached into a small white bowl and scattered nuts across the top, then moved to an ancient white Norge. She pulled the door open, put the pan inside, and pulled out another pan, setting it on a white-painted kitchen table.

"If you see anything you can't live without, make the check out to Barbara Jane Booker," she said. "That's me."

My stomach growled loudly. Embarrassed, I patted my tummy. "I'm dieting," I said apologetically.

"What a shame," she said. "I was going to offer you a piece of fudge. It's a new recipe I'm testing."

I held out the pitcher then. "Pretty, isn't it? And unusual too. It matches a sugar bowl I found at a dead man's house earlier today. It's cracked, see? I guess that's why he didn't buy it."

"I wouldn't know," she said. But she'd wrapped her hands in the apron and was nervously rolling and unrolling it.

"The man I'm referring to was murdered," I said, keeping my tone conversational. "Bludgeoned to death with an iron. The police think a seventeen-year-old kid did it."

While I was talking I was strolling around the kitchen. I stopped in front of the stove. It was still hot. She'd left the burner on. When I reached to turn it off, my hand brushed a small white card written on in purple ink. The card fluttered to the floor. I bent down to pick it up, and the last thing I remember was the sensation of cold metal meeting the side of my skull.

When I came to, I had a splitting headache. Something warm was oozing down the side of my face. I reached up gingerly to see how much blood there was. My fingers came back coated with chocolate and pecans.

"The fudge needed to set longer," Barbara Jane Booker said apologetically. "I guess I was too impatient to test it." She was kneeling over me with a roll of silver duct tape, which she was busily wrapping around my ankles. "When I get back from our little trip, I'll make a note to let it sit for at least four hours."

"Trip?" I said, wincing. My head hurt like hell.

"I can't leave you here," she said. "The house has been sold. We close tomorrow. Maybe six hours would be better. I hate runny fudge, don't you?"

"Uh-huh."

"So I thought, what about that big aluminum recycling bin over behind the high school? I've got bags and bags of cans in the trunk of my car that I was going to drop off anyway. I'm a firm believer in recycling. Aren't you? I'll just pop over there in your car, put you in, then dump the cans on top. To cover you up, you see. Monday is pickup day. I'm afraid I'll have to vandalize your car. To make it look like it was stolen by some of these teenage hoodlums who terrorize decent folks like me."

She was chattering away a mile a minute, wrapping that tape around and around my ankles.

"Mrs. Booker?"

She looked up. "I'm sorry. I didn't catch your name."

"Callahan. Callahan Garrity. I was just wondering how you were planning to dump me in one of those bins. I'm lots bigger than you, you know."

She smiled and flashed a dimple, then reached in the pocket of her apron and brought out a big rusty black revolver. "I thought this would persuade you to climb into the bin by yourself. I've got a touch of lumbago in my lower back. The doctor says absolutely no heavy lifting."

The gun was so big, she had to use both hands to hold it up. I folded my knees up against my chest, swiveled, and kicked her square in the chest, as hard as I could.

She fell backward, ass over teakettle, and the gun went clattering across that checkerboard floor. I scooted across the linoleum on my own butt, propelling myself forward with my bound ankles.

When I had the revolver, I trained it on her and managed, with difficulty, to stand up. Mrs. Booker, on the other hand, was howling with pain, screaming about her lumbago.

I cut myself free of the tape with a kitchen knife and held the gun on her with one hand while I dialed homicide with the other. While we waited for the cops to arrive, she told me what had happened. I fixed us both a glass of iced tea. Assault and battery is thirsty work.

"He got here around noon. I'd gone to get us some lunch. My husband sold him that box of recipes. You can imagine how I felt when I got back. Aunt Velma's recipes. Gone. I liked to have died. Aunt Velma's fudge recipe was in there. That was mine. Aunt Velma promised. My sisters and I are splitting the money from the house and the rest of the junk in here, but the fudge recipe was mine. Jerry, my husband, couldn't remember who'd bought what. Just like a man. But he did remember he'd taken mostly checks. I took the checks and drove to every address."

"And you ended up at a gray house off Hooper," I suggested.

"Nasty old bastard," she spat out. "He laughed when I asked for the recipe back. Said the box was full of money. No way would he give it back."

"Money?"

"Aunt Velma," she said, shaking her head fondly. "We found near $1,500 just in the kitchen. All tens and twenties. She grew up in the Depression, you know, and she never trusted banks. We found bills tucked under the shelf paper, in the pages of books, sewn into the hem of coats."

"And in the recipe box."

"I told him he could have the money," she said. "He laughed at me. So I pushed right past him. He was a runty little old thing. Came nipping and yapping at my heels, like one of those little lap dogs.

"'Get out or I'll call the police,' he was yelling. I just kept looking. Then I saw the box on the stove, with all the money in a pile around it. I offered him $20 for the fudge recipe card, but he wouldn't take it. 'This was the deal of the year,' he said. 'It's mine now. Get out.'

"When he tried to grab the box away, he hurt me. Broke one of my nails." She held up a plump pink digit to show me. The nail was ripped jaggedly. "I was so mad, I grabbed the nearest thing to hand. One of those old-timey sad irons."

She paused then and took a long sip of tea. "I grabbed that iron and hit him on the head as hard as I could. He dropped like a rock. I took the fudge recipe and left. I didn't care about any of the others. Aunt Velma wasn't really all that good of a cook. Except for fudge. I was going to take the money, but on the way out, I dropped it by the front door. It didn't seem right to take it with him dead and all."

Barbara Jane put down the tea glass then and leaned forward to tell me something in confidence, I thought. Instead, she reached out, ran a finger across my fudge-encrusted cheek, and licked it delicately.

"Mayonnaise," she said softly. "That was Aunt Velma's secret ingredient. Good old Blue Plate mayonnaise. I'd never have guessed in a million years."

KATHY HOGAN TROCHECK is a new arrival to North Carolina, but her southern mystery credentials are impeccable. A former reporter for the *Atlanta Journal-Constitution*, she began her career in Savannah, where she covered the real-life murder trials that were the basis for *Murder in the Garden of Good and Evil*. Her Callahan Garrity mysteries have been nominated for Agathas, Edgars, and Anthonys. She also writes under the name of Mary Kay Andrews.

SUSU AND THE 8:30 GHOST

Lilian Jackson Braun

hen my sister and I returned from vacation and learned that our eccentric neighbor in the wheelchair had been removed to a mental hospital, we were sorry but hardly surprised. He was a strange man, not easy to like, and no one in our apartment building seemed concerned about his departure—except our Siamese cat.

The friendship between SuSu and Mr. Van was so close it was alarming.

If it had not been for SuSu we would never have made the man's acquaintance, for we were not too friendly with our neighbors. The building was very large and full of odd characters who, we thought, were best ignored. On the other hand, our old apartment had advantages: large rooms, moderate rent, and a thrilling view of the river. There was also a small waterfront park at the foot of the street, and it was there that we first noticed Mr. Van.

One Sunday afternoon my sister Gertrude and I were walking SuSu in the park, which was barely more than a strip of grass alongside an old wharf. Barges and tugs sometimes docked there, and SuSu—wary of these monsters—preferred to stay away from the water's edge. It was one of the last nice days in November. Soon the river would freeze over, icy winds would blow, and the park would be deserted for the winter.

SuSu loved to chew grass, and she was chewing industriously when something diverted her attention and drew her toward the river. Tugging at her leash, she insisted on moving across the grass to the boardwalk, where a middle-aged man sat in a most unusual wheelchair.

It was made almost entirely of cast iron, like the base of an old-fashioned sewing machine, and it was upholstered in worn plush.

With its high back and elaborate ironwork, it looked like a mobile throne, and the man who occupied the regal wheelchair presided with the imperious air of a monarch. It conflicted absurdly with his shabby clothing.

To our surprise this was the attraction that lured SuSu. She chirped at the man, and he leaned over and stroked her fur.

"She recognizes me," he explained to us, speaking with a haughty accent that sounded vaguely Teutonic. "I was-s-s a cat myself in a former existence."

I rolled my eyes at Gertrude, but she accepted the man's statement without blinking.

He was far from attractive, having a sharply pointed chin, ears set too high on his head, and eyes that were mere slits, and when he smiled he was even less appealing. Nevertheless, SuSu found him irresistible. She rubbed against his ankles, and he scratched her in the right places. They made a most unlikely pair—SuSu with her luxurious blond fur, looking fastidious and expensive, and the man in the wheelchair, with his rusty coat and moth-eaten lap robe.

In the course of a fragmentary conversation with Mr. Van we learned that he and the companion who manipulated his wheelchair had just moved into a large apartment on our floor, and I wondered why the two of them needed so many rooms. As for the companion, it was hard to decide whether he was a mute or just unsociable. He was a short thick man with a round knob of a head screwed tight to his shoulders and a flicker of something unpleasant in his eyes. He stood behind the wheelchair in sullen silence.

On the way back to the apartment Gertrude said: "How do you like our new neighbor?"

"I prefer cats before they're reincarnated as people," I said.

"But he's rather interesting," said my sister in the gentle way that she had.

A few evenings later we were having coffee after dinner, and SuSu —having finished her own meal—was washing up in the downglow of a lamp. As we watched her graceful movements, we saw her hesitate with one paw in midair. She held it there and listened. Then a new and different sound came from her throat, like a melodic gurgling. A minute later she was trotting to our front door with intense purpose. There she sat, watching and waiting and listening, although we ourselves could hear nothing.

It was a full two minutes before our doorbell rang. I went to open the door and was somewhat unhappy to see Mr. Van sitting there in his lordly wheelchair.

SuSu leaped into his lap—an unprecedented overture for her to make—and after he had kneaded her ears and scratched her chin, he smiled a thin-lipped, slit-eyed smile at me and said: "*Goeden avond*. I was-s-s unpacking some crates, and I found something I would like to give you."

With a flourish he handed me a small framed picture, whereupon I was more or less obliged to invite him in. He wheeled his ponderous chair into the apartment with some difficulty, the rubber tires making deep gouges in the pile of the carpet.

"How do you manage that heavy chair alone?" I asked. "It must weigh a ton."

"But it is-s-s a work of art," said Mr. Van, rubbing appreciative hands over the plush upholstery and lacy ironwork and wheels.

Gertrude had jumped up and poured him a cup of coffee, and he said: "I wish you would teach that man of mine to make coffee. He makes the worst *zootje* I have ever tasted. In Holland we like our coffee *sterk* with a little chicory. But that fellow, he is-s-s a *smeerlap*. I would not put up with him for two minutes if I could get around by myself."

SuSu was rubbing her head on the Hollander's vest buttons, and he smiled with pleasure, showing small square teeth.

"Do you have this magnetic attraction for all cats?" I asked with a slight edge to my voice. SuSu was now in raptures because he was twisting the scruff of her neck.

"It is-s-s only natural," he said. "I can read their thoughts, and they read mine of course. Do you know that cats are mind readers? You walk to the refrigerator to get a beer, and the cat she will not budge, but walk to the refrigerator to get out her dinner, and what happens? Before you touch the handle of the door she will come bouncing into the kitchen from anyplace she happens to be. Your thought waves reached her even though she seemed to be asleep."

Gertrude agreed it was probably true.

"Of course it is-s-s true," said Mr. Van, sitting tall. "Everything I say is-s-s true. Cats know more than you suspect. They can not only read your mind; they can plant ideas in your head. And they can sense something that is-s-s about to happen."

My sister said: "You must be right. SuSu knew you were coming here tonight, long before you rang the bell."

"Of course I am right. I am always right," said Mr. Van. "My grandmother in Vlissingen had a tomcat called Zwartje just before she died, and for years after the funeral my grandmother came back to pet the cat. Every night Zwartje stood in front of the chair where Grootmoeder used to sit, and he would stretch and purr although there was-s-s no one there. Every night at half past eight."

After that visit with Mr. Van I referred to him as Grandmother's Ghost, for he too made a habit of appearing at 8:30 several times a week. (For Gertrude's coffee, I guessed.)

He would say: "I was-s-s feeling lonesome for my little sweetheart," and SuSu would make an extravagant fuss over the man. It pleased me that he never stayed long, although Gertrude usually encouraged him to linger.

The little framed picture he had given us was not exactly to my taste. It was a silhouette of three figures—a man in frock coat and top hat, a woman in hoopskirt and sunbonnet, and a cat carrying his tail like a lance. To satisfy my sister, however, I hung the picture, but only over the kitchen sink.

One evening Gertrude, who is a librarian, came home in great excitement. "There's a signature on that silhouette," she said, "and I looked it up at the library. Augustin Edouart was a famous artist, and our silhouette is over a hundred years old. It might be valuable."

"I doubt it," I said. "We used to cut silhouettes like that in the third grade."

Eventually, at my sister's urging, I took the object to an antique shop, and the dealer said it was a good one, probably worth several hundred dollars.

When Gertrude heard this, she said: "If the dealer quoted hundreds, it's probably worth thousands. I think we should give it back to Mr. Van. The poor man doesn't know what he's giving away."

I agreed he could probably sell it and buy himself a decent wheelchair.

At 8:30 that evening SuSu began to gurgle and prance.

"Here comes Grandmother's Ghost," I said, and shortly afterward the doorbell rang.

"Mr. Van," I said after Gertrude had poured the coffee, "remember that silhouette you gave us? I've found out it's valuable, and you must take it back."

"Of course it is-s-s valuable," he said. "Would I give it to you if it was-s-s nothing but *rommel*?"

"Do you know something about antiques?"

"My dear Mevrouw, I have a million dollars' worth of antiques in my apartment. Tomorrow evening you ladies must come and see my treasures. I will get rid of that *smeerlap*, and the three of us will enjoy a cup of coffee."

"By the way, what is a *smeerlap*?" I asked.

"It is-s-s not very nice," said Mr. Van. "If somebody called me a *smeerlap*, I would punch him in the nose. . . . Bring my little sweetheart when you come, ladies. She will find some fascinating objects to explore."

Our cat seemed to know what he was saying.

"SuSu will enjoy it," said Gertrude. "She's locked up in this apartment all winter."

"Knit her a sweater and take her to the park in winter," said the Hollander in the commanding tone that always irritated me. "I often bundle up in a blanket and go to the park in the evening. It is-s-s good for insomnia."

"SuSu is not troubled with insomnia," I informed him. "She sleeps twenty hours a day."

Mr. Van looked at me with scorn. "You are wrong. Cats never sleep. You think they are sleeping, but cats are the most wakeful creatures on earth. That is-s-s one of their secrets."

After he had gone, I said to Gertrude: "I know you like the fellow, but you must admit he's off his rocker."

"He's just a little eccentric."

"If he has a million dollars' worth of antiques, which I doubt, why is he living in this run-down building? And why doesn't he buy a wheelchair that's easier to operate?"

"Because he's a Dutchman, I suppose," was Gertrude's explanation.

"And how about all those ridiculous things he says about cats?"

"I'm beginning to think they're true."

"And who is the fellow who lives with him? Is he a servant, or a nurse, or a keeper, or what? I see him coming and going on the elevator, but he never speaks—not one word. He doesn't even seem to have a name, and Mr. Van treats him like a slave. I'm not sure we should go tomorrow night. The whole situation is too strange."

Nevertheless, we went. The Hollander's apartment was jammed with furniture and bric-a-brac, and he shouted at his companion: "Move that *rommel* so the ladies can sit down."

Sullenly the fellow removed some paintings and tapestries from the seat of a carved sofa.

"Now get out of here!" Mr. Van shouted at him. "Get yourself a beer," and he threw the man some money with less grace than one would throw a dog a bone.

While SuSu explored the premises we drank our coffee, and then Mr. Van showed us his treasures, propelling his wheelchair through a maze of furniture. He pointed out Chippendale-this and Affleck-that and Newport-something-else. They were treasures to him, but to me they were musty relics of a dead past.

"I am in the antique business," Mr. Van explained. "Before I was-s-s chained to this wheelchair, I had a shop and exhibited at the major shows. Then . . . I was-s-s in a bad auto accident, and now I sell from the apartment. By appointment only."

"Can you do that successfully?" Gertrude asked.

"And why not? The museum people know me, and collectors come here from all over the country. I buy. I sell. And my man Frank does the legwork. He is-s-s the perfect assistant for an antique dealer —strong in the back, weak in the head."

"Where did you find him?"

"On a junk heap. I have taught him enough to be useful to me, but not enough to be useful to himself. A smart arrangement, eh?" Mr. Van winked. "He is-s-s a *smeerlap*, but I am helpless without him. . . . Hoo! Look at my little sweetheart. She has-s-s found a prize!"

SuSu was sniffing at a silver bowl with two handles.

Mr. Van nodded approvingly. "It is a caudle cup made by Jeremiah Dummer of Boston in the late seventeenth century—for a certain lady in Salem. They said she was-s-s a witch. Look at my little sweetheart. She knows!"

I coughed and said: "Yes, indeed. You're lucky to have Frank."

"You think I do not know it?" Mr. Van said in a snappish tone. "That is-s-s why I keep him poor. If I gave him wages, he would get ideas. A *smeerlap* with ideas—there is-s-s nothing worse."

"How long ago was your accident?"

"Five years, and it was-s-s that idiot's fault. He did it! He did this to me!" The man's voice rose to a shout, and his face turned red as he pounded the arms of his wheelchair with his fist. Then SuSu rubbed against his ankles, and he stroked her and began to calm down. "Yes, five years in this miserable chair. We were driving to an antique show in the station wagon. Sixty miles an hour—and he went through a red light and hit a truck. A gravel truck!"

Gertrude put both hands to her face. "How terrible, Mr. Van!"

"I remember packing the wagon for that trip. I was-s-s complaining all the time about sore arches. Hah! What I would give for some sore arches today yet!"

"Wasn't Frank hurt?"

Mr. Van made an impatient gesture. "His-s-s head only. They picked Waterford crystal out of that blockhead for six hours. He has-s-s been *gek* ever since." He tapped his temple.

"Where did you find this unusual wheelchair?" I asked.

"My dear Mevrouw, never ask a dealer where he found something. It was-s-s made for a railroad millionaire in 1872. It has-s-s the original plush. If you must spend your life in a wheelchair, have one that gives some pleasure. And now we come to the purpose of tonight's visit. Ladies, I want you to do something for me."

He wheeled himself to a desk, and Gertrude and I exchanged anxious glances.

"Here in this desk is-s-s a new will I have written, and I need witnesses. I am leaving a few choice items to museums. Everything else is-s-s to be sold and the proceeds used to establish a foundation."

"What about Frank?" asked Gertrude, who is always genuinely concerned about others.

"Bah! Nothing for that *smeerlap*! . . . But before you ladies sign the papers, there is-s-s one thing I must write down. What is-s-s the full name of my little sweetheart?"

We both hesitated, and finally I said: "Her registered name is Superior Suda of Siam."

"Good! I will make it the Superior Suda Foundation. That gives me pleasure. Making a will is-s-s a dismal business, like a wheelchair, so give yourself some pleasure."

"What—ah—will be the purpose of the foundation?" I asked.

Mr. Van blessed us with one of his ambiguous smiles. "It will sponsor research," he said. "I want universities to study the highly developed mental perception of the domestic feline and apply the knowledge to the improvement of the human mind. Ladies, there is-s-s nothing better I could do with my fortune. Man is-s-s eons behind the smallest fireside grimalkin." He gave us a canny look, and his eyes narrowed. "I am in a position to know."

We witnessed the man's signature. What else could we do? A few days later we left on vacation and never saw Mr. Van again.

Gertrude and I always went south for three weeks in winter, taking SuSu with us. When we returned, the sorry news about our eccentric neighbor was thrown at us without ceremony.

We met Frank on the elevator as we were taking our luggage upstairs, and for the first time he spoke. That in itself was a shock.

He said simply, without any polite preliminaries: "They took him away."

"What's that? What did you say?" we both clamored at once.

"They took him away." It was surprising to find that the voice of this muscular man was high-pitched and rasping.

"What happened to Mr. Van?" my sister demanded.

"He cracked up. His folks came from Pennsylvania and took him back home. He's in a nut hospital."

I saw Gertrude wince, and she said: "Is it serious?"

Frank shrugged.

"What will happen to all his antiques?"

"His folks told me to dump the junk."

"But they're valuable things, aren't they?"

"Nah. Junk. He give everybody that guff about museums and all." Frank shrugged again and tapped his head. "He was *gek*."

In stunned wonderment my sister and I reached our apartment, and I could hardly wait to say it: "I told you your Dutchman was unbalanced."

"Such a pity," she murmured.

"What do you think of the sudden change in Frank? He acts like a free man. It must have been terrible living with that old Scrooge."

"I'll miss Mr. Van," Gertrude said softly. "He was very interesting. SuSu will miss him, too."

But SuSu, we observed later that evening, was not willing to relinquish her friend in the wheelchair as easily as we had done.

We were unpacking the vacation luggage after dinner when SuSu staged her demonstration. She started to gurgle and prance, exactly as she had done all winter whenever Mr. Van was approaching our door. Gertrude and I watched her, waiting for the bell to ring. When SuSu trotted expectantly to the door, we followed. She was behaving in an extraordinary manner. She craned her neck, made weaving motions with her head, rolled over on her back, and stretched luxuriously, all the while purring her heart out; but the doorbell never rang.

Looking at my watch, I said: "It's 8:30. SuSu remembers."

"It's quite touching, isn't it?" Gertrude remarked.

That was not the end of SuSu's demonstrations. Almost every night at half past eight she performed the same ritual.

I recalled how SuSu had continued to sleep in the guest room long after we had moved her bed to another place. "Cats hate to give up a habit. But she'll forget Mr. Van's visits after a while."

SuSu did not forget. A few weeks passed. Then we had a foretaste of spring and a sudden thaw. People went without coats prematurely, convertibles cruised with the tops down, and a few hopeful fishermen appeared on the wharf at the foot of our street, although the river was still patched with ice.

On one of these warm evenings we walked SuSu down to the park for her first spring outing, expecting her to go after last year's dried weeds with snapping jaws. Instead, she tugged at her leash, pulling toward the boardwalk. Out of curiosity we let her have her way, and there on the edge of the wharf she staged her weird performance once more—gurgling, arching her back, craning her neck with joy.

"She's doing it again," I said. "I wonder what the reason could be."

Gertrude said, almost in a whisper: "Remember what Mr. Van said about cats and ghosts?"

"Look at that animal! You'd swear she was rubbing against someone's ankles. I wish she'd stop. It makes me uneasy."

"I wonder," said my sister very slowly, "if Mr. Van is really in a mental hospital."

"What do you mean?"

"Or is he—down there?" Gertrude pointed uncertainly over the edge of the wharf. "I think Mr. Van is dead, and SuSu knows."

"That's too fantastic," I said. "*Really*, Gertrude!"

"I think Frank pushed the poor man off the wharf, wheelchair and all—perhaps one dark night when Mr. Van couldn't sleep and insisted on being wheeled to the park."

"You're not serious, Gertrude."

"Can't you see it? . . . A cold night. The riverfront deserted. Mr. Van trussed in his wheelchair with a blanket. Why, that chair would sink like lead! What a terrible thing! That icy water. That poor helpless man."

"I just can't—"

"Now Frank is free, and he has all those antiques, and nobody cares enough to ask questions. He can sell them and be set up for life."

"And he tears up the will," I suggested, succumbing to Gertrude's fantasy.

"Do you know what a Newport blockfront is worth? I've been looking it up in the library. A chest like the one we saw in Mr. Van's apartment was sold for hundreds of thousands at an auction on the East Coast."

"But what about the relatives in Pennsylvania?"

"I'm sure Mr. Van had no relatives—in Pennsylvania or anywhere else."

"Well, what do you propose we should do?" I said in exasperation. "Report it to the manager of the building? Notify the police? Tell them we think the man has been murdered because our cat sees his ghost every night at 8:30? We'd look like a couple of middle-aged ladies who are getting a little *gek*."

As a matter of fact, I was beginning to worry about Gertrude's obsession—that is, until I read the morning paper a few days later.

I skimmed through it at the breakfast table, and there—at the bottom of page 7—one small item leaped off the paper at me. Could I believe my eyes?

"Listen to this," I said to my sister. "The body of an unidentified man has been washed up on a downriver island. Police say the body

had apparently been held underwater for several weeks by the ice.
. . . About fifty-five years old and crippled. . . . No one fitting that description has been reported to the Missing Persons Bureau."

For a moment my sister stared at the coffeepot. Then she left the
breakfast table and went to the telephone.

"Now all the police have to do," she said with a quiver in her voice,
"is to look for an antique wheelchair in the river at the foot of the
street. Cast iron. With the original plush." She blinked at the phone
several times. "Would you dial?" she asked me. "I can't see the numbers."

The grande dame of cat mysteries, LILIAN JACKSON BRAUN became a
North Carolinian when she moved to the mountains outside Tryon in 1989.
Her day job was at the *Detroit Free Press*, where she worked for thirty years,
eventually becoming a department editor. Her first cat story was "The Sin
of Madame Phloi," written in 1966, inspired by the death of her own Siamese cat, who fell from a tenth-story window, a victim of foul play, Braun
believed. So began one of the most successful mystery series ever written,
now at twenty-five novels, many short stories, and counting.

DOGWALKER

orson scott card

was an innocent pedestrian. Only reason I got in this in the first place was I got a vertical way of thinking and Dog-walker thought I might be useful, which was true, and also he said I might enjoy myself, which was a prefabrication, since people done a lot more enjoying on me than I done on them.

When I say I think vertical, I mean to say I'm metaphysical, that is, simular, which is to say, I'm dead but my brain don't know it yet and my feet still move. I got popped at age nine just lying in my own bed when the goat next door shot at his lady and it went through the wall and into my head. Everybody went to look at them cause they made all the noise, so I was a quart low before nobody noticed I been poked.

They packed my head with supergoo and light pipe, but they didn't know which neutron was supposed to butt into the next so my alchemical brain got turned from rust to diamond. Goo Boy. The Crystal Kid.

From that bright electrical day I never grew another inch, any-where. Bullet went nowhere near my gonadicals. Just turned off the puberty switch in my head. Saint Paul said he was a eunuch for Jesus, but who am I a eunuch for?

Worst thing about it is here I am near thirty and I still have to take barkeepers to court before they'll sell me beer. And it ain't hardly worth it even though the judge prints out in my favor and the bar-keep has to pay costs, because my corpse is so little I get toxed on six ounces and pass out pissing after twelve. I'm a lousy drinking buddy. Besides, anybody hangs out with me looks like a pederast.

No, I'm not trying to make you drippy-drop for me—I'm used to it, okay? Maybe the homecoming queen never showed me True Love in a four-point spread, but I got this knack that certain people find real handy and so I always made out. I dress good and I ride the worm and I don't pay much income tax. Because I am the Password Man. Give me five minutes with anybody's curriculum vitae, which is to say their autopsychoscopy, and nine times out of ten I'll spit out their password and get you into their most nasty sticky sweet secret files. Actually it's usually more like three times out of ten, but that's still a lot better odds than having a computer spend a year trying to push out fifteen characters to make just the right P-word, specially since after the third wrong try they string your phone number, freeze the target files, and call the dongs.

Oh, do I make you sick? A cute little boy like me, engaged in critical unspecified dispopulative behaviors? I may be half glass and four feet high, but I can simulate you better than your own mama, and the better I know you, the deeper my hooks. I not only know your password *now*; I can write a word on a paper, seal it up, and then you go home and *change* your password and then open up what I wrote and there it'll be, your *new* password, three times out of ten. I am *vertical*, and Dogwalker knowed it. Ten percent more supergoo and I wouldn't even be legally human, but I'm still under the line, which is more than I can say for a lot of people who are a hundred percent zoo inside their head.

Dogwalker comes to me one day at Carolina Circle, where I'm playing pinball standing on a stool. He didn't say nothing, just gave me a shove, so naturally he got my elbow in his balls. I get a lot of twelve-year-olds trying to shove me around at the arcades, so I'm used to teaching them lessons. Jack the Giant Killer. Hero of the fourth graders. I usually go for the stomach, only Dogwalker wasn't a twelve-year-old, so my elbow hit low.

I knew the second I hit him that this wasn't no kid. I didn't know Dogwalker from God, but he gots the look, you know, like he been hungry before, and he don't care what he eats these days.

Only he got no ice and he got no slice, just sits there on the floor with his back up against the Eat Shi'ite game, holding his boodle and looking at me like I was a baby he had to diaper. "I hope you're Goo Boy," he says, "cause if you ain't, I'm gonna give you back to your mama in three little tupperware bowls." He doesn't sound like he's making a threat, though. He sounds like he's chief weeper at his own funeral.

"You want to do business, use your mouth, not your hands," I says. Only I say it real apoplectic, which is the same as apologetic except you are also still pissed.

"Come with me," he says. "I got to go buy me a truss. You pay the tax out of your allowance."

So we went to Ivey's and stood around in children's wear while he made his pitch. "One P-word," he says, "only there can't be no mistake. If there's a mistake, a guy loses his job and maybe goes to jail."

So I told him no. Three chances in ten, that's the best I can do. No guarantees. My record speaks for itself, but nobody's perfect, and I ain't even close.

"Come on," he says, "you got to have ways to make sure, right? If you can do three times out of ten, what if you find out more about the guy? What if you meet him?"

"Okay, maybe fifty-fifty."

"Look, we can't go back for seconds. So maybe you can't get it. But do you *know* when you ain't got it?"

"Maybe half the time when I'm wrong, I know I'm wrong."

"So we got three out of four that you'll know whether you got it?"

"No," says I. "Cause half the time when I'm right, I don't know I'm right."

"Shee-it," he says. "This is like doing business with my baby brother."

"You can't afford me anyway," I says. "I pull two dimes minimum, and you barely got breakfast on your gold card."

"I'm offering a cut."

"I don't want a cut. I want cash."

"Sure thing," he says. He looks around, real careful. As if they wired the sign that said "Boys' Briefs Sizes 10–12." "I got an inside man at Federal Coding," he says.

"That's nothing," I says. "I got a bug up the First Lady's ass, and forty hours on tape of her breaking wind."

I got a mouth. I know I got a mouth. I especially know it when he jams my face into a pile of shorts and says, "Suck on this, Goo Boy."

I hate it when people push me around. And I know ways to make them stop. This time all I had to do was cry. Real loud, like he was hurting me. Everybody looks when a kid starts crying. "I'll be good." I kept saying it. "Don't hurt me no more! I'll be good."

"Shut up," he says. "Everybody's looking."

"Don't you ever shove me around again," I says. "I'm at least ten years older than you, and a hell of a lot more than ten years smarter. Now I'm leaving this store, and if I see you coming after me, I'll start screaming about how you zipped down and showed me the pope, and you'll get yourself a child-molesting tag so they pick you up every time some kid gets jollied within a hundred miles of Greensboro." I've done it before, and it works, and Dogwalker was no dummy. Last thing he needed was extra reasons for the dongs to bring him in for questioning. So I figured he'd tell me to get poked and that'd be the last of it.

Instead he says, "Goo Boy, I'm sorry. I'm too quick with my hands."

Even the goat who shot me never said he was sorry. My first thought was, what kind of sister is he, abjectifying right out like that. Then I reckoned I'd stick around and see what kind of man it is who emulsifies himself in front of a nine-year-old-looking kid. Not that I figured him to be purely sorrowful. He still just wanted me to get the P-word for him, and he knew there wasn't nobody else to do it. But most street pugs aren't smart enough to tell the right lie under pressure. Right away I knew he wasn't your ordinary street hood or low arm, pugging cause they don't have the sense to stick with any kind of job. He had a deep face, which is to say his head was more than a hairball, by which I mean he had brains enough to put his hands in his pockets without seeking an audience with the pope. Right then was when I decided he was my kind of no-good lying son-of-a-bitch.

"What are you after at Federal Coding?" I asked him. "A record wipe?"

"Ten clean greens," he says. "Coded for unlimited international travel. The whole i.d., just like a real person."

"The president has a green card," I says. "The Joint Chiefs have clean greens. But that's all. The U.S. vice president isn't even cleared for unlimited international travel."

"Yes he is," he says.

"Oh, yeah, you know everything."

"I need a P. My guy could do us reds and blues, but a clean green has to be done by a burr-oak rat two levels up. My guy knows how it's done."

"They won't just have it with a P-word," I says. "A guy who can make green cards, they're going to have his finger on it."

"I know how to get the finger," he says. "It takes the finger and the password."

"You take a guy's finger, he might report it. And even if you persuade him not to, somebody's gonna notice that it's gone."

"Latex," he says. "We'll get a mold. And don't start telling me how to do my part of the job. You get P-words, I get fingers. You in?"

"Cash," I says.

"Twenty percent," says he.

"Twenty percent of pus."

"The inside guy gets twenty, the girl who brings me the finger, she gets twenty, and I damn well get forty."

"You can't just sell these things on the street, you know."

"They're worth a meg apiece," says he, "to certain buyers." By which he meant Orkish Crime, of course. Sell ten, and my 20 percent grows up to be two megs. Not enough to be rich, but enough to retire from public life and maybe even pay for some high-level medicals to sprout hair on my face. I got to admit that sounded good to me.

So we went into business. For a few hours he tried to do it without telling me the baroque rat's name, just giving me data he got from his guy at Federal Coding. But that was real stupid, giving me secondhand face like that, considering he needed me to be a hundred percent sure, and pretty soon he realized that and brought me in all the way. He hated telling me anything because he couldn't stand to let go. Once I knew stuff on my own, what was to stop me from trying to go into business for myself? But unless he had another way to get the P-word, he had to get it from me, and for me to do it right, I had to know everything I could. Dogwalker's got a brain in his head, even if it is all biodegradable, and so he knows there's times when you got no choice but to trust somebody. When you just got to figure they'll do their best even when they're out of your sight.

He took me to his cheap condo on the old Guilford College campus, near the worm, which was real congenital for getting to Charlotte or Winston or Raleigh with no fuss. He didn't have no soft floor, just a bed, but it was a big one, so I didn't reckon he suffered. Maybe he bought it back in his old pimping days, I figured, back when he got his name, running a string of bitches with names like Spike and

Bowser and Prince, real hydrant leg-lifters for the tweeze trade. I could see that he used to have money, and he didn't anymore. Lots of great clothes, tailor-tight fit, but shabby, out of sync. The really old ones, he tore all the wiring out, but you could still see where the diodes used to light up. We're talking neanderthal.

"Vanity, vanity, all is profanity," says I, while I'm holding out the sleeve of a camisa that used to light up like an airplane coming in for a landing.

"They're too comfortable to get rid of," he says. But there's a twist in his voice so I know he don't plan to fool nobody.

"Let this be a lesson to you," says I. "This is what happens when a walker don't walk."

"Walkers do steady work," says he. "But me, when business was good, it felt bad, and when business was bad, it felt good. You walk cats, maybe you can take some pride in it. But you walk dogs, and you know they're getting hurt every time—"

"They got a built-in switch, they don't feel a thing. That's why the dongs don't touch you, walking dogs, cause nobody gets hurts."

"Yeah, so tell me, which is worse, somebody getting tweezed till they scream so some old honk can pop his pimple, or somebody getting half their brain replaced so when the old honk tweezes her she can't feel a thing? I had these women's bodies around me, and I knew that they used to be people."

"You can be glass," says I, "and still be people."

He saw I was taking it personally. "Oh hey," says he, "you're under the line."

"So are dogs," says I.

"Yeah well," says he. "You watch a girl come back and tell about some of the things they done to her, and she's *laughing*, you draw your own line."

I look around his shabby place. "Your choice," says I.

"I wanted to feel clean," says he. "That don't mean I got to stay poor."

"So you're setting up this grope so you can return to the old days of peace and propensity."

"Propensity," says he. "What the hell kind of word is that? Why do you keep using words like that?"

"Cause I know them," says I.

"Well you *don't* know them," says he, "because half the time you get them wrong."

I showed him my best little-boy grin. "I know," says I. What I don't tell him is that the fun comes from the fact that almost nobody ever *knows* I'm using them wrong. Dogwalker's no ordinary pimp. But then the ordinary pimp doesn't bench himself halfway through the game because of a sprained moral qualm, by which I mean that Dogwalker had some stray diagonals in his head, and I began to think it might be fun to see where they all hooked up.

Anyway we got down to business. The target's name was Jesse H. Hunt, and I did a real job on him. The Crystal Kid really plugged in on this one. Dogwalker had about two pages of stuff—date of birth, place of birth, sex at birth (no changes since), education, employment history. It was like getting an armload of empty boxes. I just laughed at it. "You got a jack to the city library?" I asked him, and he shows me the wall outlet. I plugged right in, visual onto my pocket Sony, with my own little crystal head for ee-i-ee-i-oh. Not every goo-head can think clear enough to do this, you know, put out clean type just by thinking the right stuff out my left ear interface port.

I showed Dogwalker a little bit about research. Took me ten minutes. I know my way right through the Greensboro Public Library. I have P-words for every single librarian, and I'm so ept that they don't even guess I'm stepping upstream through their access channels. From the Public Library you can get all the way into the North Carolina Records Division in Raleigh, and from there you can jumble into federal personnel records anywhere in the country. Which meant that by nightfall on that most portentous day we had hard copy of every document in Jesse H. Hunt's whole life, from his birth certificate and first-grade report card to his medical history and security clearance reports when he first worked for the feds.

Dogwalker knew enough to be impressed. "If you can do all that," he says, "you might as well pug his P-word straight out."

"No puedo, putz," says I as cheerful as can be. "Think of the fed as a castle. Personnel files are floating in the moat—there's a few alligators, but I swim real good. Hot data is deep in the dungeon. You can get in there, but you can't get out clean. And P-words—P-words are kept up the queen's ass."

"No system is unbeatable," he says.

"Where'd you learn that, from graffiti in a toilet stall? If the P-word system was even a little bit breakable, Dogwalker, the gentlemen you plan to sell these cards to would already be inside looking out at us, and they wouldn't need to spend a meg to get clean greens from a street pug."

Trouble was that after impressing Dogwalker with all the stuff I could find out about Jesse H., I didn't know that much more than before. Oh, I could guess at some P-words, but that was all it was — guessing. I couldn't even pick a P most likely to succeed. Jesse was one ordinary dull rat. Regulation good grades in school, regulation good evaluations on the job, probably gave his wife regulation lube jobs on a weekly schedule.

"You don't really think your girl's going to get his finger," says I with sickening scorn.

"You don't know the girl," says he. "If we needed his flipper she'd get molds in five sizes."

"You don't know this guy," says I. "This is the straightest opie in Mayberry. I don't see him cheating on his wife."

"Trust me," says Dogwalker. "She'll get his finger so smooth he won't even know she took the mold."

I didn't believe him. I got a knack for knowing things about people, and Jesse H. wasn't faking. Unless he started faking when he was five, which is pretty unpopulated. He wasn't going to bounce the first pretty girl who made his zipper tight. Besides which he was smart. His career path showed that he was always in the right place. The right people always seemed to know his name. Which is to say he isn't the kind whose brain can't run if his jeans get hot. I said so.

"You're really a marching band," says Dogwalker. "You can't tell me his P-word, but you're obliquely sure that he's a limp or a wimp."

"Neither one," says I. "He's hard and straight. But a girl starts rubbing up to him, he isn't going to think it's because she heard that his crotch is cantilevered. He's going to figure she wants something, and he'll give her string till he finds out what."

He just grinned at me. "I got me the best Password Man in the Triass, didn't I? I got me a miracle worker named Goo Boy, didn't I? The ice-brain they call Crystal Kid. I got him, didn't I?"

"Maybe," says I.

"I got him or I kill him," he says, showing more teeth than a primate's supposed to have.

"You got me," says I. "But don't go thinking you can kill me."

He just laughs. "I got you and you're so good, you can bet I got me a girl who's at least as good at what she does."

"No such," says I.

"Tell me his P-word and then I'll be impressed."

"You want quick results? Then go ask him to give you his password himself."

Dogwalker isn't one of those guys who can hide it when he's mad. "I want quick results," he says. "And if I start thinking you can't deliver, I'll pull your tongue out of your head. Through your nose."

"Oh, that's good," says I. "I always do my best thinking when I'm being physically threatened by a client. You really know how to bring out the best in me."

"I don't want to bring out the best," he says. "I just want to bring out his password."

"I got to meet him first," says I.

He leans over me so I can smell his musk, which is to say I'm very olfactory and so I can tell you he reeked of testosterone, by which I mean ladies could fill up with babies just from sniffing his sweat. "Meet him?" he asks me. "Why don't we just ask him to fill out a job application?"

"I've read all his job applications," says I.

"How's a glass-head like you going to meet Mr. Fed?" says he. "I bet you're always getting invitations to the same parties as guys like him."

"I don't get invited to *grown-up* parties," says I. "But on the other hand, grown-ups don't pay much attention to sweet little kids like me."

He sighed. "You really have to meet him?"

"Unless fifty-fifty on a P-word is good enough odds for you."

All of a sudden he goes nova. Slaps a glass off the table and it breaks against the wall, and then he kicks the table over, and all the time I'm thinking about ways to get out of there unkilled. But it's me he's doing the show for, so there's no way I'm leaving, and he leans in close to me and screams in my face. "That's the last of your fifty-

fifty and sixty-forty and three times in ten I want to hear about, Goo Boy, you hear me?"

And I'm talking real meek and sweet, cause this boy's twice my size and three times my weight and I don't exactly have no leverage. So I says to him, "I can't help talking in odds and percentages, Dog-walker, I'm vertical, remember? I've got glass channels in here; they spit out percentages as easy as other people sweat."

He slapped his hand against his own head. "This ain't exactly a sausage biscuit, either, but you know and I know that when you give me all them exact numbers it's all guesswork anyhow. You don't know the odds on this beak-rat anymore than I do."

"I don't know the odds on *him*, Walker, but I know the odds on *me*. I'm sorry you don't like the way I sound so precise, but my crystal memory has every P-word I ever plumbed, which is to say I can give you exact to the third decimal percentages on when I hit it right on the first try after meeting the subject, and how many times I hit it right on the first try just from his curriculum vitae, and right now if I don't meet him and I go on just what I've got here you have a 48.838 percent chance I'll be right on my P-word first time and a 66.667 chance I'll be right with one out of three."

Well that took him down, which was fine I must say because he loosened up my sphincters with that glass-smashing table-tossing hot-breath-in-my-face routine he did. He stepped back and put his hands in his pockets and leaned against the wall. "Well I chose the right P-man, then, didn't I," he says, but he doesn't smile, no, he *says* the back-down words, but his eyes don't back down, his eyes say don't try to flash my face because I see through you, I got most excellent inward shades all polarized to keep out your glitz and see you straight and clear. I never saw eyes like that before. Like he knew me. Nobody ever knew me, and I didn't think he *really* knew me either, but I didn't like him looking at me as if he *thought* he knew me cause the fact is *I* didn't know me all that well and it worried me to think he might know me better than I did, if you catch my drift.

"All I have to do is be a little lost boy in a store," I says.

"What if he isn't the kind who helps little lost boys?"

"Is he the kind who lets them cry?"

"I don't know. What if he is? What then? Think you can get away with meeting him a second time?"

"So the lost boy in the store won't work. I can crash my bicycle on his front lawn. I can try to sell him cable magazines."

But he was ahead of me already. "For the cable magazines he slams the door in your face, if he even comes to the door at all. For the bicycle crash, you're out of your little glass brain. I got my inside girl working on him right now, very complicated, because he's not the playing around kind, so she has to make this a real emotional come-on, like she's breaking up with a boyfriend and he's the only shoulder she can cry on, and his wife is so lucky to have a man like him. This much he can believe. But then suddenly he has this little boy crashing in his yard, and because he's paranoid, he begins to wonder if some weird rain isn't falling, right? I know he's paranoid because you don't get to his level in the fed without you know how to watch behind you and kill the enemy even before *they* know they're out to get you. So he even suspects for one instant that somebody's setting him up for something, and what does he do?"

I knew what Dogwalker was getting at now, and he was right, and so I let him have his victory and I let the words he wanted march out all in a row. "He changes all his passwords, all his habits, and watches over his shoulder all the time."

"And my little project turns into compost. No clean greens."

So I saw for the first time why this street boy, this ex-pimp, why he was the one to do this job. He wasn't vertical like me, and he didn't have the inside hook like his fed boy, and he didn't have bumps in his sweater so he couldn't do the girl part, but he had eyes in his elbows, ears in his knees, by which I mean he noticed everything there was to notice and then he thought of new things that weren't even noticeable yet and noticed them. He earned his 40 percent. And he earned part of my 20, too.

Now while we waited around for the girl to fill Jesse's empty aching arms and get a finger off him, and while we were still working on how to get me to meet him slow and easy and sure, I spent a lot of time with Dogwalker. Not that he ever asked me, but I found myself looping his bus route every morning till he picked me up, or I'd be eating at Bojangle's when he came in to throw cajun chickens down into his ulcerated organs. I watched to make sure he didn't mind, cause I didn't want to piss this boy, having once beheld the majesty of his wrath, but if he wanted to shiver me he gave me no shiv.

Even after a few days, when the ghosts of the cold hard street started haunting us, he didn't shake me, and that includes when Bellbottom says to him, "Looks like you stopped walking dogs. Now you pimping little boys, right? Little catamites, we call you Catwalker now, that so? Or maybe you just keep him for private use, is that it? You be Boypoker now?" Well like I always said, someday somebody's going to kill Bellbottom just to flay him and use his skin for a convertible roof, but Dogwalker just waved and walked on by while I made little pissy bumps at Bell. Most people shake me right off when they start getting splashed on about liking little boys, but Doggy, he didn't say we were friends or nothing, but he didn't give me no Miami howdy, neither, which is to say I didn't find myself floating in the Bermuda Triangle with my ass pulled down around my ankles, by which I mean he wasn't ashamed to be seen with me on the street, which don't sound like a six-minute orgasm to you but to me it was like a breeze in August; I didn't ask for it and I don't trust it to last, but as long as it's there I'm going to like it.

How I finally got to meet Jesse H. was dervish, the best I ever thought of. Which made me wonder why I never thought of it before, except that I never before had Dogwalker like a parrot saying "stupid idea" every time I thought of something. By the time I finally got a plan that he didn't say "stupid idea," I was almost drowned in the deepest lightholes of my lucidity. I mean I was going at a hundred watts by the time I satisfied him.

First we found out who did babysitting for them when Jesse H. and Mrs. Jesse went out on the town (which for Nice People in G-boro means walking around the mall wishing there was something to do and then taking a piss in the public john). They had two regular teenage girls who usually came over and ignored their children for a fee, but when these darlettes were otherwise engaged, which meant they had a contract to get squeezed and poked by some half-zipped boy in exchange for a humbuger and a vid, they called upon Mother Hubbard's Homecare Hotline. So I most carefully assinuated myself into Mother Hubbard's estimable organization by passing myself off as a lamentably prepubic fourteen-year-old, specializing in the northwest section of town and on into the county. All this took a week, but Walker was in no hurry. Take the time to do it right, he said; if we hurry somebody's going to notice the blur of motion and look our way, and just by looking at us they'll undo us. A horizontal mind that boy had.

Came a most delicious night when the Hunts went out to play, and both their diddle-girls were busy being squeezed most delectably (and didn't we have a lovely time persuading two toddle-boys to do the squeezing that very night). This news came to Mr. and Mrs. Jesse at the very last minute, and they had no choice but to call Mother Hubbard's, and isn't it lovely that just a half hour before, sweet little Stevie Queen, being moi, called in and said that he was available for baby-stomping after all. Ein and ein made zwei, and there I was being dropped off by a Mother Hubbard driver at the door of the Jesse Hunt house, whereupon I not only got to look upon the beatific face of Mr. Fed himself, I also got to have my dear head patted by Mrs. Fed, and then had the privilege of preparing little snacks for fussy Fed Jr. and foul-mouthed Fedene, the five-year-old and the three-year-old, while Microfed, the one-year-old (not yet human and, if I am any judge of character, not likely to live long enough to become such), sprayed uric acid in my face while I was diapering him. A good time was had by all.

Because of my heroic efforts, the small creatures were in their truckle beds quite early, and being a most fastidious baby-tucker, I browsed the house looking for burglars and stumbling, quite by chance, upon the most useful information about the beak-rat whose secret self-chosen name I was trying to learn. For one thing, he had set a watchful hair upon each of his bureau drawers, so that if I had been inclined to steal, he would know that unlawful access of his drawers had been attempted. I learned that he and his wife had separate containers of everything in the bathroom, even when they used the same brand of toothpaste, and it was he, not she, who took care of all their prophylactic activities (and not a moment too soon, thought I, for I had come to know their children). He was not the sort to use lubrificants or little pleasure-giving ribs, either. Only the regulation government-issue hard-as-concrete rubber rafts for him, which suggested to my most pernicious mind that he had almost as much fun between the sheets as me.

I learned all kinds of joyful information, all of it trivial, all of it vital. I never know which of the threads I grasp are going to make connections deep within the lumens of my brightest caves. But I never before had the chance to wander unmolested through a person's own house when searching for his P-word. I saw the notes his children brought home from school, the magazines his family received, and more and more I began to see that Jesse H. Hunt barely touched his family at any point. He stood like a waterbug on the surface of life, without ever getting his feet wet. He could die, and if nobody tripped over the corpse it would be weeks before they noticed. And yet this was not because he did not care. It was because he was so very very careful. He examined everything, but through the wrong end of the microscope, so that it all became very small and far away. I was a sad little boy by the end of that night, and I whispered to Microfed that he should practice pissing in male faces, because that's the only way he would ever sink a hook into his daddy's face.

"What if he wants to take you home?" Dogwalker asked me, and I said, "No way he would, nobody does that," but Dogwalker made sure I had a place to go all the same, and sure enough, it was Doggy who got voltage and me who went limp. I ended up riding in a beakrat buggy, a genuine made-in-America rattletrap station wagon, and he took me to the for-sale house where Mama Pimple was waiting crossly for me and made Mr. Hunt go away because he kept me out too late. Then when the door was closed Mama Pimple giggled her gig and chuckled her chuck, and Walker himself wandered out of the back room and said, "That's one less favor you owe me, Mama Pimple," and she said, "No, my dear boyoh, that's one more favor *you* owe *me*," and then they kissed a deep passionate kiss if you can believe it. Did you imagine anybody ever kissed Mama Pimple that way? Dogwalker is a boyful of shocks.

"Did you get all you needed?" he asks me.

"I have P-words dancing upward," says I, "and I'll have a name for you tomorrow in my sleep."

"Hold onto it and don't tell me," says Dogwalker. "I don't want to hear a name until after we have his finger."

That magical day was only hours away, because the girl—whose name I never knew and whose face I never saw—was to cast her spell over Mr. Fed the very next day. As Dogwalker said, this was no job for lingeree. The girl did not dress pretty and pretended to be lacking in the social graces, but she was a good little clerical who was going through a most distressing period in her private life because she had undergone a premature hysterectomy, poor lass, or so she told Mr. Fed, and here she was losing her womanhood and she had never really felt like a woman at all. But he was so kind to her, for weeks he had been so kind, and Dogwalker told me afterward how he locked the door of his office for just a few minutes and held her and kissed her to make her feel womanly, and once his fingers had all made their little impressions on the thin electrified plastic microcoating all over her lovely naked back and breasts, she began to cry and most gratefully informed him that she did not want him to be unfaithful to his wife for her sake, that he had already given her such a much of a lovely gift by being so kind and understanding, and she felt better thinking that a man like him could bear to touch her knowing she was defemmed inside, and now she thought she had the confidence to go on. A very convincing act, and one calculated to get his hot naked handprints without giving him a crisis of conscience that might change his face and give him a whole new set of possible Ps.

The microsheet got all his fingers from several angles, and so Walker was able to dummy out a finger mask for our inside man within a single night. Right index. I looked at it most skeptically, I fear, because I had my doubts already dancing in the little light-points of my inmost mind. "Just one finger?"

"All we get is one shot," said Dogwalker. "One single try."

"But if he makes a mistake, if my first password isn't right, then he could use the middle finger on the second try."

"Tell me, my vertical pricket, whether you think Jesse H. Hunt is the sort of burr-oak rat who makes mistakes?"

To which I had to answer that he was not, and yet I had my misgivings and my misgivings all had to do with needing a second finger, and yet I am vertical, not horizontal, which means that I can see the present as deep as you please but the future's not mine to see, que sera, sera.

From what Doggy told me, I tried to imagine Mr. Fed's reaction to this nubile flesh that he had pressed. If he had poked as well as peeked, I think it would have changed his P-word, but when she told him that she would not want to compromise his uncompromising virtue, it reinforced him as a most regular or even regulation fellow and his name remained pronouncedly the same, and his P-word also did not change. "Invictus-xyzrwr," quoth I to Dogwalker, for that was his veritable password; I knew it with more certainty than I had ever had before.

"Where in hell did you come up with that?" says he.

"If I knew how I did it, Walker, I'd never miss at all," says I. "I don't even know if it's in the goo or in the zoo. All the facts go down, and it all gets mixed around, and up come all these dancing P-words, little pieces of P."

"Yeah but you don't just make it up; what does it mean?"

"Invictus is an old poem in a frame stuck in his bureau drawer, which his mama gave him when he was still a little fed-to-be. xyz is his idea of randomizing, and rwr is the first U.S. president that he admired. I don't know why he chose these words now. Six weeks ago he was using a different P-word with a lot of numbers in it, and six weeks from now he'll change again, but right now—"

"Sixty percent sure?" asked Doggy.

"I give no percents this time," says I. "I've never roamed through the bathroom of my subject before. But this or give me an assectomy, I've never been more sure."

Now that he had the P-word, the inside guy began to wear his magic finger every day, looking for a chance to be alone in Mr. Fed's office. He had already created the preliminary files, like any routine green card requests, and buried them within his work area. All he needed was to go in, sign on as Mr. Fed, and then if the system accepted his name and P-word and finger, he could call up the files, approve them, and be gone within a minute. But he had to have that minute.

And on that wonderful magical day he had it. Mr. Fed had a meeting and his secretary sprung a leak a day early, and in went Inside Man with a perfectly legitimate note to leave for Hunt. He sat before the terminal, typed name and P-word and laid down his phony finger, and the machine spread wide its lovely legs and bid him enter. He had the files processed in forty seconds, laying down his finger for each green, then signed off and went on out. No sign, no sound that anything was wrong. As sweet as summertime, as smooth as ice, and all we had to do was sit and wait for green cards to come in the mail.

"Who you going to sell them to?" says I.

"I offer them to no one till I have clean greens in my hand," says he. Because Dogwalker is careful. What happened was not because he was not careful.

Every day we walked to the ten places where the envelopes were supposed to come. We knew they wouldn't be there for a week — the wheels of government grind exceeding slow, for good or ill. Every day we checked with Inside Man, whose name and face I have already given you, much good it will do, since both are no doubt different by now. He told us every time that all was the same, nothing was changed, and he was telling the truth, for the fed was most lugubrious and palatial and gave no leaks that anything was wrong. Even Mr. Hunt himself did not know that aught was amiss in his little kingdom.

Yet even with no sign that I could name, I was jumpy every morning and sleepless every night. "You walk like you got to use the toilet," says Walker to me, and it is verily so. Something is wrong, I say to myself, something is most deeply wrong, but I cannot find the name for it even though I know, and so I say nothing, or I lie to myself and try to invent a reason for my fear. "It's my big chance," says I. "To be 20 percent of rich."

"Rich," says he, "not just a fifth."

"Then you'll be double rich."

And he just grins at me, being the strong and silent type.

"But then why don't you sell nine," says I, "and keep the other green? Then you'll have the money to pay for it and the green to go where you want in all the world."

But he just laughs at me and says, "Silly boy, my dear sweet pinheaded lightbrained little friend. If someone sees a pimp like me passing a green, he'll tell a fed because he'll know there's been a mistake. Greens don't go to boys like me."

"But you won't be dressed like a pimp," says I, "and you won't stay in pimp hotels."

"I'm a low-class pimp," he says again, "and so however I dress that day, that's just the way pimps dress. And whatever hotel I go to, that's a low-class pimp hotel until I leave."

"Pimping isn't some disease," says I. "It isn't in your gonads and it isn't in your genes. If your daddy was a Kroc and your mama was an Iacocca, you wouldn't be a pimp."

"The hell I wouldn't," says he. "I'd just be a high-class pimp, like my mama and my daddy. Who do you think gets green cards? You can't sell no virgins on the street."

I thought that he was wrong and I still do. If anybody could go from low to high in a week, it's Dogwalker. He could be anything and do anything, and that's the truth. Or almost anything. If he could do *anything* then his story would have a different ending. But it was not his fault. Unless you blame pigs because they can't fly. I was the vertical one, wasn't I? I should have named my suspicions, and we wouldn't have passed those greens.

I held them in my hands, there in his little room, all ten of them when he spilled them on the bed. To celebrate he jumped up so high he smacked his head on the ceiling again and again, which made them ceiling tiles dance and flip over and spill dust all over the room. "I flashed just one, a single one," says he, "and a cool million was what he said, and then I said what if ten? And he laughs and says fill in the check yourself."

"We should test them," says I.

"We can't test them," he says. "The only way to test it is to use it, and if you use it then your print and face are in its memory forever and so we could never sell it."

"Then sell one, and make sure it's clean."

"A package deal," he says. "If I sell one and they think I got more but I'm holding out to raise the price, then I may not live to collect for the other nine because I might have an accident and lose these little babies. I sell all ten tonight at once, and then I'm out of the green card business for life."

But more than ever that night I am afraid; he's out selling those greens to those sweet gentlebodies who are commonly referred to as Organic Crime, and there I am on his bed, shivering and dreaming because I know that something will go most deeply wrong but I still don't know what and I still don't know why. I keep telling myself, You're only afraid because nothing could ever make you rich and safe. I say this stuff so much that I believe that I believe it, but I don't really, not down deep, and so I shiver again and finally I cry, because after all my body still believes I'm nine, and nine-year-olds have tear ducts very easy of access, no password required. Well he comes in late that night, and I'm asleep he thinks, and so he walks quiet instead of dancing, but I can hear the dancing in his little sounds, I know he has the money all safely in the bank, and so when he leans over to make sure if I'm asleep, I say, "Could I borrow a hundred thou?"

So he slaps me and he laughs and dances and sings, and I try to go along, you bet I do, I know I should be happy, but then at the end he says, "You just can't take it, can you? You just can't handle it," and then I cry all over again, and he just puts his arm around me like a movie dad and gives me play-punches on the head and says, "I'm gonna marry me a wife, I am, maybe even Mama Pimple herself, and we'll adopt you and have a little spielberg family in Summerfield, with a riding mower on a real grass lawn."

"I'm older than you *or* Mama Pimple," says I, but he just laughs. Laughs and hugs me until he thinks that I'm all right. Don't go home, he says to me that night, but home I got to go, because I know I'll cry again, from fear or something, anyway, and I don't want him to think his cure wasn't permanent. "No thanks," says I, but he just laughs at me. "Stay here and cry all you want to, Goo Boy, but don't go home tonight. I don't want to be alone tonight, and sure as hell you don't either." And so I slept between his sheets, like with a brother, him punching and tickling and pinching and telling dirty jokes about his whores, the most good and natural night I spent in all my life, with a true friend, which I know you don't believe, snickering and nickering and ickering your filthy little thoughts; there was no holes plugged that night because nobody was out to take pleasure from nobody else, just Dogwalker being happy and wanting me not to be so sad.

And after he was asleep, I wanted so bad to know who it was he sold them to, so I could call them up and say, "Don't use those greens, cause they aren't clean. I don't know how, I don't know why, but the feds are onto this, I know they are, and if you use those cards they'll nail your fingers to your face." But if I called would they believe me? They were careful too. Why else did it take a week? They had one of their nothing goons use a card to make sure it had no squeaks or leaks, and it came up clean. Only then did they give the cards to seven big boys, with two held in reserve. Even Organic Crime, the All-Seeing Eye, passed those cards same as we did.

I think maybe Dogwalker was a little bit vertical too. I think he knew same as me that something was wrong with this. That's why he kept checking back with the inside man, cause he didn't trust how good it was. That's why he didn't spend any of his share. We'd sit there eating the same old schlock, out of his cut from some leg job or my piece from a data wipe, and every now and then he'd say, "Rich man's food sure tastes good." Or maybe even though he wasn't vertical he still thought maybe I was right when I thought something was wrong. Whatever he thought, though, it just kept getting worse and worse for me, until the morning when we went to see the inside man and the inside man was gone.

Gone clean. Gone like he never existed. His apartment for rent, cleaned out floor to ceiling. A phone call to the fed, and he was on vacation, which meant they had him, he wasn't just moved to another house with his newfound wealth. We stood there in his empty place, his shabby empty hovel that was ten times better than anywhere we ever lived, and Doggy says to me, real quiet, he says, "What was it? What did I do wrong? I thought I was like Hunt, I thought I never made a single mistake in this job, in this one job."

And that was it, right then I knew. Not a week before, not when it would do any good. Right then I finally knew it all, knew what Hunt had done. Jesse Hunt never made *mistakes*. But he was also so paranoid that he haired his bureau to see if the babysitter stole from him. So even though he would never *accidentally* enter the wrong P-word, he was just the kind who would do it *on purpose*. "He doublefingered every time," I says to Dog. "He's so damn careful he does his password wrong the first time every time and then comes in on his second finger."

"So one time he comes in on the first try, so what?" He says this because he doesn't know computers like I do, being half glass myself.

"The system knew the pattern, that's what. Jesse H. is so precise he never changed a bit, so when *we* came in on the first try, that set off alarms. It's my fault, Dog; I knew how crazy paranoidical he is, I knew that something was wrong, but not till this minute I didn't know what it was. I should have known it when I got his password, I should have known, I'm sorry, you never should have gotten me into this, I'm sorry, you should have listened to me when I told you something was wrong, I should have known, I'm sorry."

What I done to Doggy that I never meant to do. What I done to him! Anytime, I could have thought of it, it was all there inside my glassy little head, but no, I didn't think of it till after it was way too late. And maybe it's because I didn't want to think of it, maybe it's because I really wanted to be wrong about the green cards, but however it flew, I did what I do, which is to say I'm not the pontiff in his fancy chair, by which I mean I can't be smarter than myself.

Right away he called the gentlebens of Ossified Crime to warn them, but I was already plugged into the library sucking news as fast as I could and so I knew it wouldn't do no good, cause they got all seven of the big boys and their nitwit taster, too, locked up good and tight for card fraud.

And what they said on the phone to Dogwalker made things real clear. "We're dead," says Doggy.

"Give them time to cool," says I.

"They'll never cool," says he. "There's no chance, they'll never forgive this even if they know the whole truth because look at the names they gave the cards to; it's like they got them for their biggest boys on the borderline, the habibs who bribe presidents of little countries and rake off cash from octopods like Shell and ITT and every now and then kill somebody and walk away clean. Now they're sitting there in jail with the whole life story of the organization in their brains, so they don't care if we meant to do it or not. They're hurting, and the only way they know to make the hurt go away is to pass it on to somebody else. And that's us. They want to make us hurt, and hurt real bad, and for a long long time."

I never saw Dog so scared. That's the only reason we went to the feds ourselves. We didn't ever want to stool, but we needed their protection plan; it was our only hope. So we offered to testify how we did it, not even for immunity, just so they'd change our faces and put us in a safe jail somewhere to work off the sentence and come out alive, you know? That's all we wanted.

But the feds, they laughed at us. They had the inside guy, see, and he was going to get immunity for testifying. "We don't need you," they says to us, "and we don't care if you go to jail or not. It was the big guys we wanted."

"If you let us walk," says Doggy, "then they'll think we set them up."

"Make us laugh," says the feds. "Us work with street poots like you? They know that we don't stoop so low."

"They bought from us," says Doggy. "If we're big enough for them, we're big enough for the dongs."

"Do you believe this?" says one fed to his identical junior officer. "These jollies are begging us to take them into jail. Well listen tight, my jolly boys, maybe we don't want to add you to the taxpayers' expense account, did you think of that? Besides, all we'd give you is time, but on the street, those boys will give you time and a half, and it won't cost us a dime."

So what could we do? Doggy just looks like somebody sucked out six pints, he's so white. On the way out of the fedhouse, he says, "Now we're going to find out what it's like to die."

And I says to him, "Walker, they stuck no gun in your mouth yet, they shove no shiv in your eye. We still breathing, we got legs, so let's *walk* out of here."

"Walk!" he says. "You walk out of G-boro, glasshead, and you bump into trees."

"So what?" says I. "I can plug in and pull out all the data we want about how to live in the woods. Lots of empty land out there. Where do you think the marijuana grows?"

"I'm a city boy," he says. "I'm a city boy." Now we're standing out in front, and he's looking around. "In the city I got a chance, I know the city."

"Maybe in New York or Dallas," says I, "but G-boro's just too small, not even half a million people, you can't lose yourself deep enough here."

"Yeah well," he says, still looking around. "It's none of your business now anyway, Goo Boy. They aren't blaming *you*, they're blaming *me*."

"But it's my fault," says I, "and I'm staying with you to tell them so."

"You think they're going to stop and listen?" says he.

"I'll let them shoot me up with speakeasy so they know I'm telling the truth."

"It's nobody's fault," says he. "And I don't give a twelve-inch poker whose fault it is anyway. You're clean, but if you stay with me you'll get all muddy, too. I don't need you around, and you sure as hell don't need me. Job's over. Done. Get lost."

But I couldn't do that. The same way he couldn't go on walking dogs, I couldn't just run off and leave him to eat my mistake. "They know I was your P-word man," says I. "They'll be after me, too."

"Maybe for a while, Goo Boy. But you transfer your 20 percent into Bobby Joe's Face Shop, so they aren't looking for you to get a refund, and then stay quiet for a week and they'll forget all about you."

He's right but I don't care. "I was in for 20 percent of rich," says I. "So I'm in for 50 percent of trouble."

All of a sudden he sees what he's looking for. "There they are, Goo Boy, the dorks they sent to hit me. In that Mercedes." I look but all I see are electrics. Then his hand is on my back and he gives me a shove that takes me right off the portico and into the bushes, and by the time I crawl out, Doggy's nowhere in sight. For about a minute I'm pissed about getting scratched up in the plants, until I realize he was getting me out of the way so I wouldn't get shot down or hacked up or lased out, whatever it is they planned to do to him to get even.

I was safe enough, right? I should've walked away, I should've ducked right out of the city. I didn't even have to refund the money. I had enough to go clear out of the country and live the rest of my life where even Occipital Crime couldn't find me.

And I thought about it. I stayed the night in Mama Pimple's flop-house because I knew somebody would be watching my own place. All that night I thought about places I could go. Australia. New Zealand. Or even a foreign place. I could afford a good vocabulary crystal so picking up a new language would be easy.

But in the morning I couldn't do it. Mama Pimple didn't exactly ask me but she looked so worried and all I could say was, "He pushed me into the bushes, and I don't know where he is."

And she just nods at me and goes back to fixing breakfast. Her hands are shaking she's so upset. Because she knows that Dog-walker doesn't stand a chance against Orphan Crime.

"I'm sorry," says I.

"What can you do?" she says. "When they want you, they get you. If the feds don't give you a new face, you can't hide."

"What if they didn't want him?" says I.

She laughs at me. "The story's all over the street. The arrests were in the news, and now everybody knows the big boys are looking for Walker. They want him so bad the whole street can smell it."

"What if they knew it wasn't his fault?" says I. "What if they knew it was an accident? A mistake?"

Then Mama Pimple squints at me—not many people can tell when she's squinting, but I can—and she says, "Only one boy can tell them that so they'll believe it."

"Sure, I know," says I.

"And if that boy walks in and says, Let me tell you why you don't want to hurt my friend Dogwalker—"

"Nobody said life was safe," I says. "Besides, what could they do to me that's worse than what already happened to me when I was nine?"

She comes over and just puts her hand on my head, just lets her hand lie there for a few minutes, and I know what I've got to do.

So I did it. Went to Fat Jack's and told him I wanted to talk to Junior Mint about Dogwalker; and it wasn't thirty seconds before I was hustled on out into the alley and driven somewhere with my face mashed into the floor of the car so I couldn't tell where it was. Idiots didn't know that somebody as vertical as me can tell the number of wheel revolutions and the exact trajectory of every curve. I could've drawn a freehand map of where they took me. But if I let them know that, I'd never come home, and since there was a good chance I'd end up dosed with speakeasy, I went ahead and erased the memory. Good thing I did—that was the first thing they asked me as soon as they had the drug in me.

Gave me a grown-up dose, they did, so I practically told them my whole life story and my opinion of them and everybody and everything else, so the whole session took hours, felt like forever, but at the end they knew, they absolutely knew that Dogwalker was straight with them, and when it was over and I was coming up so I had some control over what I said, I asked them, I begged them, Let Dogwalker live. Just let him go. He'll give back the money, and I'll give back mine, just let him go.

"Okay," says the guy.

I didn't believe it.

"No, you can believe me, we'll let him go."

"You got him?"

"Picked him up before you even came in. It wasn't hard."

"And you didn't kill him?"

"Kill him? We had to get the money back first, didn't we, so we needed him alive till morning, and then you came in, and your little story changed our minds, it really did, you made us feel all sloppy and sorry for that poor old pimp."

For a few seconds there I actually believed that it was going to be all right. But then I knew from the way they looked, from the way they acted, I knew the same way I know about passwords.

They brought in Dogwalker and handed me a book. Dogwalker was very quiet and stiff, and he didn't look like he recognized me at all. I didn't even have to look at the book to know what it was. They scooped out his brain and replaced it with glass, like me only way over the line, way way over; there was nothing of Dogwalker left inside his head, just glass pipe and goo. The book was a User's Manual, with all the instructions about how to program him and control him.

I looked at him and he was Dogwalker, the same face, the same hair, everything. Then he moved or talked and he was dead, he was somebody else living in Dogwalker's body. And I says to them, "Why? Why didn't you just kill him, if you were going to do this?"

"This one was too big," says the guy. "Everybody in G-boro knew what happened, everybody in the whole country, everybody in the world. Even if it was a mistake, we couldn't let it go. No hard feelings, Goo Boy. He *is* alive. And so are you. And you both stay that way, as long as you follow a few simple rules. Since he's over the line, he has to have an owner, and you're it. You can use him however you want—rent out data storage, pimp him as a jig or a jaw—but he stays with you always. Every day, he's on the street here in G-boro, so we can bring people here and show them what happens to boys who make mistakes. You can even keep your cut from the job, so you don't have to scramble at all if you don't want to. That's how much we like you, Goo Boy. But if he leaves this town or doesn't come out, even one single solitary day, you'll be very sorry for the last six hours of your life. Do you understand?"

I understood. I took him with me. I bought this place, these clothes, and that's how it's been ever since. That's why we go out on the street every day. I read the whole manual, and I figure there's maybe 10 percent of Dogwalker left inside. The part that's Dogwalker can't ever get to the surface, can't ever talk or move or anything like that, can't ever remember or even consciously think. But maybe he can still wander around inside what used to be his head, maybe he can sample the data stored in all that goo. Maybe someday he'll even run across this story and he'll know what happened to him, and he'll know that I tried to save him.

In the meantime this is my last will and testament. See, I have us doing all kinds of research on Orgasmic Crime, so that someday I'll know enough to reach inside the system and unplug it. Unplug it all, and make those bastards lose everything, the way they took everything away from Dogwalker. Trouble is, some places there ain't no way to look without leaving tracks. Goo is as goo doo, I always say. I'll find out I'm not as good as I think I am when somebody comes along and puts a hot steel putz in my face. Knock my brains out when it comes. But there's this, lying in a few hundred places in the system. Three days after I don't lay down my code in a certain program in a certain place, this story pops into view. The fact you're reading this means I'm dead.

Or it means I paid them back, and so I quit suppressing this cause I don't care anymore. So maybe this is my swan song, and maybe this is my victory song. You'll never know, will you, mate?

But you'll wonder. I like that. You wondering about us, whoever you are, you thinking about old Goo Boy and Dogwalker, you guessing whether the fangs who scooped Doggy's skull and turned him into self-propelled property paid for it down to the very last delicious little drop.

And in the meantime, I've got this goo machine to take care of. Only 10 percent a man, he is, but then I'm only 40 percent myself. All added up together we make only half a man. But that's the half that counts. That's the half that still wants things. The goo in me and the goo in him is all just light pipes and electricity. Data without desire. Light-speed trash. But I have some desires left, just a few, and maybe so does Dogwalker, even fewer. And we'll get what we want. We'll get it all. Every speck. Every sparkle. Believe it.

No one had ever won the Hugo and Nebula awards for best science fiction novel two years in a row until ORSON SCOTT CARD received them for *Ender's Game* and its sequel, *Speaker for the Dead*, in 1986 and 1987. Card, who lives in Greensboro, is the prolific writer of dozens of books, plays, short stories, poems, and film and television scripts in every genre. Card has taught writing at several universities and written two books on writing, one of which won yet another Hugo award. His inventive and groundbreaking works have received acclaim—and best-seller sales—all over the world.

THE CORN THIEF

Guy Owen

hadn't used up but one week of my month on Grandpa Eller's farm when the corn thief came for the first time. I was the first one to find it out, too. That morning I got up early and put on my blue jeans and new chambray shirt. Already I heard the catbirds and mockers fussing in the chinaberry tree, and somewhere in the pasture toward the old sawmill site a mourning dove was calling.

I slept on a cot in Grandpa's room, so I moved about easy and slipped out to the backyard barefooted. I was twelve years old, and nothing in the world pleased me more than having my grandfather brag on me.

But when I went to the corncrib to shell the corn for the domineckers in the chicken run, I let out a whoop that must have waked up all of Cape Fear County. The lock had been pried off the facing, and the door was flung wide open. Wolf, the old one-eyed German shepherd that always smelled of mange medicine, was sniffing about the crib door, whining.

"Grandpa," I hollered, "come quick. We've purely been robbed!"

"What's come over you, Joel?" He was already hurrying across the backyard, stopping under the worm-eaten catalpa tree to hitch the galluses on his blue overalls. Without his felt hat on, his thin hair was white as snow in the morning sunlight. His face was seamed and old—all except his periwinkle eyes—and his short legs moved like a beagle's. I remembered then what Mama had said about him being too old to look after me, especially since he'd already had a stroke.

Ransom Martin, the new hired man, came scurrying out from the packhouse behind Grandpa, stretching his long legs. "What's all the commotion about?"

When Grandpa leaned in the crib door, he wasn't much taller than me. His sleepy eyes squinted, studying the pile of unshucked corn. "He didn't take much," he said, "whoever he was. Not more than a sackful he could tote on his back." His voice was matter-of-fact, and he didn't seem excited at all.

"Let's call Sheriff Slade, Grandpa," I suggested. "If he can't come he'd be sure to send a deputy."

"Shoot, boy," Ranse spoke up quick. "Make him drive all the way from Queen City for one sack of weevily corn?"

Grandpa agreed that it wouldn't be necessary to call the sheriff from the county seat.

"What you aim to do, Cap'n Jim?" Ranse asked, cornering his greenish eyes at my grandfather.

"First thing I figger to do," Grandpa said, calmly looking at the tall hired hand, "is get me a brand-new lock. A big one. And I reckon I'll tie old Wolf someplace close by tonight."

"I could stand guard with my new .22," I volunteered.

But they didn't pay me any mind, Ranse and Grandpa.

"That old dog," Ranse said, "he ain't no 'count." He spat tobacco juice toward the scalding barrel where a few chickens were scratching in last season's hog hairs and new mule-hoof parings. "He ought to be shot and put out of his misery."

When I turned around, Grandpa's housekeeper was standing by Ranse. Myrtle's face was puffy, and she acted as if she was mad from being waked up by all the hollering and whooping. Ranse told her about the stolen corn.

"I'm not surprised a bit in this world," she said. "I heard something. I kept hearing something the whole enduring night." Then she looked at Wolf and made a face. "He's too old to keep any thieves away. He's not fit for anything but to eat biscuits and carry fleas."

Grandpa stooped to pat Wolf. "You live long enough, you'll be old too one day," he said to Myrtle in a low voice. "Just because something's old don't mean it's worthless."

"I brought my rifle, Grandpa," I broke in. "I could stand guard on the back porch tonight."

"We'll wait and see, Joel."

Before we turned away, Ranse said, "I know a way to stop that thief."

"How's that, Mr. Martin?" I asked. For some reason I didn't like to call him "Mister." I'd seen the way he had of rubbing against the housekeeper when he thought they were alone.

But Grandpa was walking away. "I reckon me and Joel here'll get that lock."

Which is what we did. That evening, after we finished grading tobacco in the packhouse, we rode to the store at Eller's Bend in Grandpa's rattletrap Studebaker and bought the biggest lock that Uncle Sam Eller had in stock.

"Jim, you trying to keep something in or out with that all-fired lock?"

Since there were a few customers in the store, Grandpa didn't say anything, just sort of smiled. He bought me a nickel sack of peppermint sticks and a box of shells for my .22. Then we drove on back, and I helped him nail the new lock on the crib door.

For all the good it did. Because next morning we saw that the corn thief had come again and made off with another sack of corn. And Wolf, who was tied close by, hadn't barked once. It was puzzling. I knew the German shepherd was getting blind; maybe he was almost deaf, too.

"What'd I tell you, Cap'n Jim?" Ranse said with a knowing grin. "If that sorry no-'count dog was mine I'd shoot him, sure."

That night I slept in the barn loft with Grandpa, waiting for the corn thief to return. Lying awake on the sweet-smelling oats, I did a lot of thinking. One thing I decided, quick enough, was this: I wouldn't write Mama about the thief that plagued us, slipping about the farm so quiet in the night that Wolf wouldn't even bark at him. I wouldn't tell her because she didn't want me to spend July with Grandpa in the first place, since Grandma had died and Grandpa had been in the hospital and had to hire Myrtle for his housekeeper. But I reasoned that Grandpa needed me more than ever, and in the end I convinced her.

It wasn't Grandpa's idea to sleep in the barn loft; it was Myrtle's notion. She kept pestering him about it, in that scratchy voice of hers, until he gave in, maybe just to get some peace. And, of course, I went along. The truth of the matter is, I sort of sided with Myrtle— though I didn't like her at all, even if she was Mama's second cousin once removed. She was too bossy and sulky, and she never kept tea cakes in the stove warmer the way Grandma used to do. Not to mention coconut pies and pound cake in the food safe.

But Ranse Martin, the hired hand that slept on a cot in the pack-

house, had his own plan. "You listen to me now, Cap'n Jim. I'll fix a
trap with that double-barrel twelve-gauge of yours that'll take care
of the lowdown thief."

The housekeeper was clearing away the supper dishes. "You
might pay Ranse some mind now, Jim Eller," she said. She was a
short woman, with frizzly hair dyed the color of cornsilk, except
for the dark roots. Like Grandma, she dipped snuff, but she wasn't
clean with it. Sometimes her lips and teeth were stained with Sweet
Society snuff.

"I wouldn't want to harm a man just for a shirt-tail full of corn."

Nor for the whole cribful, I thought. That's the kind of man
Grandpa was. He was a gentle soft-spoken man.

Anyhow, when it was good and dark, we took our two guns and
a flashlight and climbed up the ladder in the aisle of the barn. We
took two old raggedy patchwork quilts and some of the tow-sack
sheets used to spread over the cured tobacco and made ourselves
beds. Grandpa raked up a thick mattress of oat hay, and we put two
bales of peanut hay in front of our heads at the open loft door to rest
our guns on. Grandpa said we'd keep our shells in our pockets; we
wouldn't load unless we heard the thief coming.

Then we stretched out, talking low for a little while. I watched the
fireflies blink on and off and the heat lightning off in the distance
toward Clayton. Millions of stars were out like shiny bits of mica, and
the moon was like a quartered cantaloupe. The light was so clear I
could see the corncrib, which set off a little ways from the big barn,
almost like it was day. I aimed my .22 toward the board window, pretending it was loaded and clicking my tongue against the roof of my
mouth for a shot.

"You think the thief will come back, Grandpa?"

"I don't know, son," he said. "It's not likely he'll come tonight.
Some other night maybe."

"If he comes, we won't shoot him, will we?"

"No, we won't shoot. It would be a terrible thing to shoot a man
for a few bushels of corn. A man whose family may be hungry."

"Ranse, he doesn't think it would be wrong to shoot him."

"Every man to his own notions."

"We'll just capture him, then, won't we, and holler for Myrtle to
call Sheriff Slade?"

"That sounds like a mighty good plan. But you ought to get a little sleep now. You've got a lot of tobacco to take off the sticks in the morning. We've got to get that curing ready for the auction."

But I couldn't begin to sleep. "Don't you think we ought to keep guard, I mean stay awake in shifts so we wouldn't miss him—if he comes?" That was the way they did in all the books I read.

But Grandpa said it wasn't necessary. He told me he'd propped some old tin cans against the door. If anybody broke in the crib, we'd be bound to hear and wake up.

But I made up my mind I'd stay awake all night by myself, and for a long time I did, after Grandpa was asleep on the oat mattress. Once when the quartered moon was way up high, I thought I heard something in the barnyard. I gripped my rifle and peered over the bale of hay. But it was nothing but a barn owl looking for mice.

After that I eased back down and scrooched under the quilt. A breeze was rising from the Cape Fear River and it was cool. For a while I lay awake on my back, smelling the oats and listening to the breathing of the brindled cow in the stable below.

Toward midnight in the hayloft I started getting sleepy. Then, before I knew it, it seemed like a hoot owl had lifted the woods up and was carrying them far, far away. . . .

Grandpa woke me, shaking my shoulder. "Joel," he called gently. Then we went down the cobwebby ladder together. I pumped a basin of water, then we washed up. Just as Grandpa always did, I sloshed the cold water on my face, drying with the towel hanging on the nail.

"We'll sleep out again tonight, won't we, Gramp?" I asked.

"Maybe. We'll wait and see, son." He looked tired, and there were worry lines around his pale eyes.

When we went in to eat breakfast, Ranse Martin and Myrtle were already sitting at the kitchen table. Like Myrtle, Ranse was from Queen City, and she had hired him herself on the spur of the moment when the old hired man quit while Grandpa was in the hospital. I suppose Josh Shipman got tired of Myrtle's sharp tongue or hard biscuits, maybe both.

Anyway, she sent for Ranse to help her tend the crops, claiming him for her dead sister's brother-in-law. One thing sure, he didn't know anything much about farming. He told me he'd been in the transportation business, but I found out all he did was drive a taxi.

I heard Uncle Sam Eller say he probably sold a little moonshine on the side.

Now the hired man smiled and put his coffee down on the checked oilcloth. "He come back?" he asked. When he smiled you could see his stained teeth, and his reddish mustache bristled beneath his hawk's nose. He wore his dark hair long and combed it so it covered a bald spot on the crown of his head.

Myrtle heaved up then and got our eggs and grits from the stove warmer. They were cold, but the biscuit toast was good and the coffee was strong and hot.

Pouring my coffee, she said, "I bet a silver dollar you two went to sleep before ten o'clock out yonder. A thief could—"

Grandpa saucered his black coffee and said, "Well, at least there's no corn gone."

The new lock hadn't been touched.

"Sure we went to sleep. We didn't have any notion he'd come back again so soon." I set to eating then, hungry from staying awake to guard the corncrib.

But Grandpa just picked at his breakfast like there was a spider in his plate. I could see he was pondering something.

"Well," Myrtle fussed, "I'd like to know what you figger to do."

"Maybe he's got all he needs now," Grandpa said.

"Maybe he heard us in the barn loft," I chimed in, "and will stay away for good." I started to tell them about the big barn owl, but I thought better of it.

Myrtle just snorted.

Ranse commenced, "Look here now, Cap'n Jim, me and you just better set us that trap this evening when we knock off." He seemed to grin, and his lips were pulled back from his gums.

"No, not yet. I wouldn't want to harm—"

"Hunh, I think it's a time you listened to Ranse, Jim Eller, and quit being stubborn as a iron-headed mule."

"It's just a few bushels of corn, Myrtle," I said.

"Who pulled your chain, Mr. Big Britches?"

"That's it," Ranse persisted. "That's all it is now, but mind you when a thief gets to stealing like that, there's no telling what he'll wind up taking. To my way of thinking he's got to be stopped."

"And I'm not going to set still," Myrtle said, her voice rising, "while some low-lived scoundrel steals us out of house and home. I'm not about to."

She sounded like she already owned the place, which someday she would. Grandpa had willed the house to her after he got sick, so he would have someone to take care of him and wouldn't be a burden to his daughters. I had heard Mama fussing with Papa against it, though Myrtle was her own blood kin.

"I'm glad she's no kin of mine," Papa had said.

Myrtle commenced to pout, but Grandpa didn't appear to pay her any mind.

But we had to listen all over again to Ranse telling about how him and his uncle once cured a corn thief. How they rigged up a shotgun in the crib, and when the man opened the door that night, it blew one of his legs nearly off.

"Simple as shooting a dove on a fence post," Ranse said, winking at me.

I gave him a sharp look. Grandpa had taught me never to shoot a bird unless it was on the wing, never to take unfair advantage of any creature, wild or tame.

Grandpa pushed back from the table. "I'll give it some thought." He stood for a minute in the doorway studying the two of them, his face older than I'd ever remembered it being.

"You do that thing, Cap'n Jim," Ranse said, slapping the table. "I tell you there's more than one way to catch a thief."

That night we slept in the hayloft again, and this time I sneaked a bullet in the chamber of my rifle.

When we woke up, it was long past daylight. My mouth dropped open when I saw the door to the corncrib was open. The thief had pried open the new lock, maybe with a crowbar, just like before. But that wasn't all: along with the corn, a power saw was gone from the tool shed. And we hadn't heard a whimper out of Wolf.

Ranse Martin was standing on the back porch grinning at us when we came down. "What'd I tell you all yesterday? You wouldn't listen to me before. I reckon you will now." He actually seemed happy the thief had come back again.

All that morning I worked hard in the packhouse. I had a notion I wanted to try out. I took the tobacco off the sticks as fast as I could, throwing the empty sticks out the window and piling the bright leaves beside Grandpa. He was grading the tobacco near the open door, holding the spread leaves up close to his eyes before dropping them into one of the three piles on the grading bench in front of him.

When I had taken off enough tobacco to last until past noon and swept up the broken stems and twine, I told Grandpa I was going to take the .22 and look for a rabbit over by the old millpond.

"You better be careful in them woods, boy," Ranse said. "I'd stay out of them woods if I was you. I seen a great big rattler near that dam, not more than three days ago." He was sitting near Myrtle, tying the tobacco in big awkward hanks.

"Your mama told me she didn't want you traipsing around—" the housekeeper began. She was tying the best grade, wearing a white sack apron to keep the sand off her flowery dress.

But I caught Grandpa's eye, and I didn't pay them any attention.

"Here, Wolf," I called, standing in the packhouse door.

Then the dog and I struck out across the pasture toward the woods. Grandpa knew I wasn't just out for any rabbit. Wolf must have sensed it, too, from the way he wagged his tail and kept his gray muzzle to the ground, sniffing and whining. Anybody would have thought he was a spry pup and not an old half-blind, nearly toothless dog.

We tracked the corn thief for nearly a mile. I could have done it without Wolf, the signs were so clear. I could see where he'd gone down the side of the cow lane, mashing down a fennel here and there or rabbit tobacco or ragweed. When he got to the woods behind the barn, he climbed the fence and turned north, headed, I guessed, for the old sawmill road that led to the Wilmington highway.

Presently Wolf sniffed all around in a clump of sumac and blackberries, then, looking back at me, headed up the dry creek bed, into the woods toward the old sawmill. I gripped my rifle and trotted after him, scaring up a hermit thrush.

In ten minutes we left the scrub oak and poplar and ran into the cutover pine. I was glad I'd put on my straw hat then because the sun was hot. Sweat trickled down my ribs, and the pine needles felt warm and soft under my bare feet. They were good to smell, too. A squirrel fussed at me, but I just waved and smiled at him.

When we came out into the clearing, Wolf barked and dashed ahead. I ran after him, crossing the old lumberyard. A blue-tailed

lizard sat gulping the sunshine on the pile of rotting slabs, and a cat-
bird flew up from eating blueberries.

When I walked around the slab pile, you could have bowled me
over with a feather.

There was the stolen corn!

I took off my hat and squatted down, putting my arm around the
dog's neck. His nose was wet and he was panting, with his tongue
hanging out. "You may be old," I told him, "but you can still track a
thief."

All the corn was there. The thief had dumped it in a sunken place
at the foot of the sawdust pile and raked down sawdust over it. But he
hadn't nearly covered it up. I guess he figured nobody would look for
corn in an old sawdust pile. Either that or he was in a big hurry. The
dog and I searched all around, under strips and old slabs covered
with vines, but we didn't find Grandpa's power saw.

That evening, after we'd packed the graded and tied tobacco down
and covered it with old quilts, Grandpa and me took our guns and
headed for the sawmill site. The guns were just for show because we
decided to keep my discovery a secret.

Grandpa stood watching Wolf scratch at the pile of stolen corn.
He took off his sweaty felt hat, scratched his head, and spit a glob of
tobacco juice onto the sawdust pile.

"Don't that beat bobtail?" I said. "What do you make of it,
Gramp?"

He just grunted and studied the situation a while, his eyes dis-
turbed.

"Ain't that some kind of funny stealing?" I asked.

Grandpa said maybe whoever it was intended to hide the corn
there until he had a wagonload. Then some night they would cut the
wire fence and drive a wagon in and take it out by the old logcart
road.

On the way back he said, "Then again, maybe they didn't really
intend to steal that corn, Joel."

Which was a puzzle to me. But I didn't have time to ask any more
questions because just then Myrtle was calling us to supper, her
voice as screechy as ever.

At the supper table Ranse said, "I reckon you'll listen to me now that thief has stole something worth as much as a power saw. I already got the stuff ready to set our little trap."

As usual Myrtle set in to backing him up, fussing and whining. I figured one reason Grandpa gave in finally was to get a moment's peace from the two of them.

"It might be the best thing after all," Grandpa said, looking away from me. "I just hope he won't come back."

I was sure surprised to hear him agree to the trap. It wasn't like him to do such a thing.

"Now you're talking sense for once," Ranse said, squinting at Myrtle, whose lips were quirked in a smile.

I guess Ranse Martin expected to get his way, sooner or later, because he had all the stuff ready. He'd nailed a board to a stanchion in the middle of the corn pile, with a V sawed in it to cradle the shotgun barrel. The stock rested on the corn. He had another board with a spool contraption fixed to it.

When Grandpa climbed up on the dwindling pile of unshucked corn and settled the gun, Ranse tightened the strong twine he had braided that ran to a staple in the door and slipped the loop over both triggers. Then he shifted the old twelve-gauge shotgun until it aimed where he wanted it.

"Now, boy, you slip out that window and open the door."

I did. And when I eased the crib door open I heard the two clicks, one right after the other.

Grandpa took the claw hammer then and knocked the board with the V in it loose and nailed it back six inches lower. That way, if the shotgun went off, it would hit the thief in the legs, not in the chest. All this time he never looked me in the eye.

At least, I thought, he's showing that much mercy.

Ranse squatted close by, his bald spot under a string of red peppers dangling from a rafter. He watched Grandpa with narrowed eyes. "Suit yourself, Cap'n Jim. You're the boss, but I sure wouldn't show him no mercy, a thief like that."

Grandpa said, "The Bible tells us to temper justice with mercy."

"Well, get me them shells now," Ranse said gruffly.

"I'll get them, Grandpa," I volunteered.

"Yeah, let Big Britches there fetch 'em."

"No," Grandpa said. "I'll get them myself, Joel. I know where they are."

"Hurry now," Ranse said. "We'll get ourselves a thief if he dares come back. I tell you, the time me and my uncle . . ."

But Grandpa had already gone, walking toward the house on his short legs, the back of his shirt stained with sweat.

It was almost dark now, and the last domineckers had already gone to roost. The hired man and I waited in the corncrib about fifteen minutes, not saying anything. Somewhere in the pile of corn a mouse was gnawing steadily.

Finally Ranse took to popping his knuckles. "What in the name of the devil's keeping him?"

"I hear him coming now."

"The Cap'n's just gettin' old," he said. "He's old like that mangy dog, livin' on borrowed time."

"Grandpa's not old," I said. "He's not as old as you think, leastwise."

When Grandpa came back with the two shells, Ranse was fidgeting nervously with the gun.

"What kept you so long?" he said, reaching for the shells.

Grandpa didn't answer him. Instead, he clambered up the pile of corn. "I'll load it myself," he said.

I watched closely as Grandpa squatted and slipped the two shells into the chamber and flicked the safety catch off.

Ranse stooped and adjusted the gun until the twine was stretched as tight as a guitar string. "I double guarantee you that won't miss."

Then we slid down the corn pile and climbed out of the window. Grandpa swung the heavy board window to and twisted the wooden latch.

"What if he comes in the window?" I asked.

"Heck," Ranse said. "Ain't he always come to the door?"

"Maybe he's got all the corn he needs," Grandpa said quietly.

That night, of course, we slept in our beds for a change. There was no reason to guard the corncrib. Grandpa turned out the light after reading a chapter in his old Bible, and pretty soon I heard him snoring away.

In a little while the housekeeper and Ranse turned off the radio in the parlor and went out on the front porch. I heard them talking and laughing, kind of low, rocking on the end of the porch shaded by the chinaberry tree.

I sneaked to the window, and when I peeked out I saw Ranse and Myrtle sitting close together in their rocking chairs. He had his arm on her shoulder.

As soon as Myrtle turned the lights out after Ranse, I slipped out of the cot and put on my shirt and blue jeans. Grandpa was breathing quietly, and I didn't disturb him.

On the back porch I picked up my .22 and tiptoed out into the moonlit yard. I put my shoes on sitting on the back steps. Then I climbed the ladder up to the barn loft and stretched out on the oats, with my rifle resting on the bale of hay. If any thief came, I made up my mind I'd capture him first, before he got blown to smithereens by Ranse's devilish trap.

I reckon my intentions were good, but, like before, I dozed off sometime before daybreak. And that made a lot of difference.

Anyhow, when I woke up it was good daylight. I guess what woke me then was Grandpa's brogans, because when I looked down he was walking toward the corncrib, his face half hid by his old felt hat. He stopped at the crib door and tested the lock. I saw that it hadn't been broken. Then he walked slowly around to the board window.

I was just about to surprise him and call out when I stopped. What made me keep still was this: I happened to glance toward the smokehouse, and there was Ranse Martin squatting down and looking over the stacks of stove wood. It looked curious. I couldn't puzzle out what he was hiding for, so I scrooched back under the oats beside my rifle.

But I could still see Grandpa standing by the crib window. He didn't open it right away. The shoats in the pigpen commenced squealing, and I heard him speak to them gently. Then he looked all around, finally toward the packhouse where Ranse slept. He spit out some tobacco juice and reached for the latch on the board window.

The minute he put pressure on that latch I sensed something was wrong. Out of the corner of my eye I glimpsed Ranse Martin stand up by the smokehouse, and I felt the hackles on my neck rise. But it was too late to warn Grandpa.

Because as soon as he pulled on the window the shotgun exploded near his head and the shot echoed in the woods behind me.

For a second Grandpa seemed to clutch at the windowsill. His finger-nails scrabbled against the rough boards as his body slumped down, and then he sprawled out beside the crib. One arm was flung over his head, and his old felt hat was still on. He didn't budge.

My heart was thumping against a button, and I was weak as skimmed milk. I just lay still for a minute, listening to the pigs squealing and the mules stamping below in their stalls. Then I told myself I had to go down. If Grandpa wasn't dead, I would have to help him.

That's when I saw Ranse, and I ducked my head back and kept still as a mouse. He was walking past the woodpile, his shotgun held down by his side. His eyes looked puffy, and there was a smile on his thin lips.

For a minute he stood in front of the corncrib. I heard a door slam, and then Myrtle was running across the backyard. "Is it all right, Ranse?" she cried.

He waited for her. "Hush now," he said. He put his arm around her waist, and together they walked around the edge of the crib, with Ranse keeping the shotgun down by his side, away from the pudgy housekeeper. I watched them studying Grandpa's body. I could hear every word they said, and it was enough to turn my blood cold.

"Well, Myrt, what'd I tell you now?"

"I don't want to think of anything going wrong, hon."

Ranse patted her on the rump. "All you got to say is the old man set the trap and then forgot about it and killed himself. Everybody knows he's not been himself since that stroke. Leastwise, nobody's going to guess I turned the gun to cover the window instead of the door. And that house there is all yours—ours."

"I reckon you know best. But I feel so sorry for—Oh, I do hope nothing goes wrong."

"There's nothing to go wrong, I've been tellin' you."

"But what about the boy? He saw you-all—"

"I've thought about that, too," Ranse said, tapping his head with a finger. "I'll just say the old man changed his mind, and we reset the trap to cover the window."

Then I heard her scream. Ranse put his hand up to her mouth, but it didn't help. She cut loose as loud as the shotgun had, louder.

But what made her holler was enough to stop the tears in my eyes.

It was Grandpa. He was getting up. I saw him rise to his knees, and then he stood up, with the two of them gaping at him and Myrtle's shoulders shaking.

He turned to face them, but he wasn't in any hurry to speak. I watched him brush the dirt off his work shirt and khaki trousers. There was a little smile on his lean face as he took off his felt hat and wiped the white hair away from his forehead. He was standing up straight, and in the morning light he didn't look so weak or old any more.

Ranse blurted out, "We—Cap'n, we thought you was shot. I'm mighty glad—"

"I reckon I know what you thought, Ranse Martin. You, too, Myrtle." Grandpa looked at the window where the gun had gone off near his head. "Mighty lucky thing for me I took all the shot out of them shells," he said.

Ranse rapped out, "What do you mean? What the hell's going—"

"You're going," Grandpa said calmly. "That's what's going, Ranse. The both of you are going to Queen City this morning." His jaw was set in that stubborn Eller way that Ma always remarks on when I act up. "I may be old, but I'm not blind. Not yet I'm not."

"That's what you think, old Cap. There's more than one way to skin a cat." Ranse swung his shotgun up then, holding it at his waist, aiming it right at Grandpa's chest.

"No, Ranse!" Myrtle cried. "I back out now. That weren't in the bargain."

"You'll back out of nothing. Shut your damn mouth."

Grandpa didn't flinch. He just got a little smile on his face.

"No, Ranse," Myrtle said. "I mean it."

Grandpa said, "You've not got to worry, Myrtle. Ranse here's been talking about killin' something ever since he came on this place. But I've got him pegged. He wouldn't kill a tick unless he could set a trap and go off somewhere and hide while the dirty work was done."

"Is that so?" Ranse snarled, steadying his gun.

That's when I stood up in the barn loft. I aimed the rifle at the corn thief, and I didn't tremble a bit. "Drop it, Ranse," I said. "Drop that gun now."

Ranse swiveled his head around and up, his eyes almost as wide as Myrtle's.

"You'd better do what he says," Grandpa advised. "I taught Joel how to handle that rifle, and he don't miss." He smiled up at me. "Come on down, son."

Ranse just let his shotgun fall out of his hands, his shoulders slumping.

I scrambled down the ladder. When I got there Grandpa was holding the shotgun, not pointing it at anybody. Myrtle was whimpering, and Ranse looked like a suck-egg dog that had eaten an egg with red-devil lye in it. He even looked blue around the mouth. Wolf was sitting by the crib door looking at them with his one good eye, puzzled.

"I'll go call the sheriff, Mister Jim," Myrtle said in a low voice.

"I hope this teaches you a lesson, Myrtle," Grandpa said.

From the look on her face it had. I almost felt sorry for her myself.

Ranse turned to walk toward the house with her. He didn't say a word more to us.

"Another thing," Grandpa called after them. "Joel and me are goin' fishing. When we get back, if that power saw has turned up, I won't mention it to Sheriff Slade."

I guess that's what's meant by tempering justice with mercy. Anyway, when we got back from the Cape Fear River with a string of perch a yard long, there the power saw was on the back porch. And Myrtle and the corn thief had gone and turned themselves in to the law.

GUY OWEN (1925–81) was a novelist, poet, editor, critic, and teacher who received his undergraduate and graduate degrees from the University of North Carolina at Chapel Hill. He taught at North Carolina State University for many years. Owen may be best known for his novel *The Flim-Flam Man*, which became a motion picture starring George C. Scott and Michael Sarrazin. Among his many honors were a Sir Walter Raleigh Award, a North Carolina Award for Literature, and a Pulitzer Prize nomination.

THE CHOICE

Margaret Maron

"**K**ate?"

She whirled around, the blood draining from her face, then returning so rapidly that she flushed like a guilty schoolchild.

"I'm sorry," Sam said. "I didn't mean to startle you. I thought you heard me when I came in."

He peered over his wife's slender shoulder through the tall narrow window slit that gave light to the stair landing and realized suddenly that this was not the first time he'd found her here.

"What do you see out there?" he asked.

He himself saw nothing except bright sunlight playing on an overgrown pasture that sloped down to a creek. He couldn't even see the creek for it was hidden by the trees and underbrush that grew thickly along its sandy banks. They had talked about horses when they first moved here, when the children were little, and they'd had a few chickens and, briefly, some goats to eat the poison ivy and stinging nettles. The youngest child was in college now. Their only animals were a couple of dogs and some stray cats that nobody had the heart to take to the pound, and small pine trees were starting to spring up in the pasture.

Although they'd both grown up on working farms—or maybe it was more accurate to say that because they'd both grown up working on farms right here in Colleton County, North Carolina—they had no romantic illusions about getting back to the earth. Tobacco was already loosening its stranglehold on the area, and even if it weren't, neither Sam nor Kate had any desire to spend their lives doing such hot, sweaty, dirty work. No, when they came back to the country, it was on their terms: with college degrees that allowed them to work in Raleigh yet still raise their children in a loving community of aunts and uncles and grandparents on a ten-acre piece of land where there was space for the children to run and play freely, safely.

"What are you looking at?" he asked again, his chin brushed by the softness of her hair, hair that was gently going gray, like the first random flakes of snow falling lightly on brown autumn leaves.

"Nothing," she said, leaning back against his chest in the circle of his arms. Yet she continued to gaze out the window, so he did, too.

And then, of course, he saw it. How odd that he'd never noticed before. By some trick of architecture, this was the only window in the house that was high enough to overlook the trees along the creek bottom to where the land rose beyond. Near the top of the rise was a ruined chimney, two stories tall, a visible reminder of the house that once stood there.

"Do you ever feel time fold back against itself?" she asked him. "Sometimes I stand here and I can almost see the house the way it used to look with Tim and me racing down the hill with our fishing poles, heading for the creek after a day in the fields. As if those two kids were the reality and I was a ghost out of their future."

"The future doesn't have ghosts."

"Doesn't it? Remember when we were building this house? I stood right here—it was the same day they put the roof trusses on— and you and the children were outside picking up nails where the doorway was going to go. I remember thinking to myself that I'd grow old in this house and I would stand at this very window and watch a grown-up child come up from the creek. It felt so real, I could almost see it. Last weekend, when Chris was out here . . ." Her voice trembled and broke off.

He turned her in his arms then and looked down into her troubled face.

"Kate, the kids are back and forth all the time. Of course they're going to go down to the creek. They spent half their lives splashing around down there. There's nothing odd about seeing Chris through this window."

"No? Then why did I have the exact same feeling I had twenty years ago? As if I ought to be able to look up and see the sky through the trusses."

"Deja vu all over again?" he teased. Then, as he felt her shoulders tighten, he added sympathetically, "You've been working too hard. And all this strain with your mother. You were out there this afternoon, weren't you?"

She nodded. "It's not that though. She's adjusting to the place very nicely. Likes the food, likes the staff, likes her room."

"What then?"

A small shrug of her shoulders. "The aide was changing the sheets when I got there, and Mama was up in her wheelchair. The aide said something about her cold feet, and Mama said that was one of the things she missed the most after her husband died. Not having somebody there beside her that she could warm her cold feet on."

"And?" he asked in puzzlement.

Even though his family had known the Cole family when they were children, they were in different school districts and hadn't met until high school. Like the rest of the community, he'd heard of the tragedy though—how Mr. Cole had fallen asleep with a lighted cigarette after being up half the night with his wife when she miscarried their third child, how Kate and her older brother Tim blamed themselves because they might have noticed the fire in time to raise the alarm if they hadn't skipped their chores and gone fishing. Not that Kate ever talked much about it or about their father either, for that matter. Even after they were married, it was years before she confided that her father had been drinking that day. In that time, in that churchly community, excessive drinking—drunkenness—had been a shameful secret that every affected family tried to keep hidden. She chattered freely of the poor but loving grandparents who took them in, the aunts and uncles who'd helped out. Only rarely did she speak of her father and never about his death. When Tim reminisced about the waterwheels Mr. Cole built for him on the creekbank or the times they went hunting together, Kate would somehow drift away to the kitchen to make coffee or fill a glass or check on the kids.

It was years before Sam actually noticed, and when he did, he put it down to the pain and embarrassment she must have felt.

Mrs. Cole was a different matter. A sickly woman who shied from any sort of confrontation, she had bravely borne her widowhood, devoting herself to the welfare of her two children. Her two fatherless children. She had a way of reminding you of how she had sacrificed her health to make up to them for their loss. And hers, too, of course. A hot-tempered man, folks said, but a good man and a hard worker. Made the children work hard, too, they said. Hard work never hurt anybody, and look how good those children turned out, both of them teachers, both of them upright pillars of the community.

"After all these years, don't you think it's sort of sweet that she still misses him?"

"Daddy's been dead almost thirty-five years," Kate said. "And she quit sleeping in his bed long before that."

That surprised him. "But I thought that was why she was in the hospital with a miscarriage."

"Even a poor marriage can still have sex," Kate said dryly as she turned back to the window. But someone to warm her cold feet on? Kate wondered what Mama would say if suddenly reminded of the way she flinched whenever he grabbed her breast in front of them and pulled her up the rickety stairs to his bedroom and slammed the door, leaving Kate and Tim to pretend nothing unpleasant was happening up there? Not that she had really understood, but Tim was two years older and he certainly had. That must have been why he always tried to distract her during those bad times. Protecting her emotions. Unable to protect his own. She shuddered to think of the lasting damage to his emotional psyche if their father hadn't died when he did. So why should it bother her if Tim had managed to bury the pain and angry humiliation of their childhood, if Mama pretended her marriage had been as warm and loving as Sam and Kate's?

Most of the time, she didn't care, just let her mind go blank. But today, standing at this window, staring across to the ruined house of her childhood, Kate wondered if she were the only one who remembered how things really were. . . .

They were tenant farmers. Sharecroppers. Unlanded gentry. Maybe that was the acid that ate at him and corroded his soul. Moving from farm to farm every few years. Living in tiny little shacks or huge dilapidated houses like this one, with no indoor plumbing as though it were the 1870s, not the 1970s. Knowing that the labor of his body and that of his wife and children would never earn enough to buy back the land that his own father had gambled away in the forties. Or maybe it was just the alcohol. Rotgut whiskey or a case of Bud when he had a few dollars. Fermented tomato juice or aftershave lotion when he didn't.

Not that he was drunk all the time. That's what made it so horrible. The unpredictability of his rages. He could go months without a drop, months where, when the field work was done for the day, he'd help little Katie plant flower seeds or whittle slingshots and, yes, waterwheels for Timmy. Then, for no reason they could ever fathom, he'd go roaring off to town and come home in a black drunken rage that could last for days. Near the end, those rages seemed to come more often, with more violence. Like the day he'd carried Mama to the hospital because she was bleeding so badly. She and Timmy were scared and wanted to go with them, but he'd ordered them out to the field.

"And I'd better see every one of them tobacco plants suckered by the time I get back," he'd told them.

All morning, they'd toiled up and down the rows of sticky green plants, snapping off the suckers that tried to grow up where the money leaves met the plant's stem. At lunchtime, they stopped just long enough for sandwiches and glasses of cold milk before heading back into the broiling field with only their wide-brimmed straw hats for shade. Feet bare on the hot dirt, their bare arms and legs burned brown by the sun.

An hour later, Timmy had gone back to the house for a jug of water, and that's where he was when their father came home and accused him of slacking off while his sister was out there working as she'd been told.

Katie heard his screams from the edge of the field, but experience had told her there was nothing she could do except blank her mind and keep on snapping the suckers. When Timmy took his place beside her in the next row, his legs were red and raw. The welts from the belt marched up and down her brother's backside like rows of newly seeded corn.

"Did Mama come home?" she whispered. Not that Mama had ever been able to step between Timmy and the belt. Timmy shook his head and kept moving.

They finished the field a little before four. Timmy didn't want to go back to the house, but Katie was bolder. Their father almost never hit her. Just Timmy and Mama.

"Besides, I'll bet he's passed out on the bed by now."

Something else that experience had taught her.

But Timmy couldn't be persuaded. Instead he fetched a hoe and headed for the vegetable garden. "He said for us to start chopping grass if we got through early."

She crept into the old wooden house quieter than the mice usually were. Silence was all around. At the foot of the staircase, she hesitated until she heard deep snores from above. Relief flowed down like healing waters on her sore heart then, and she tiptoed up the stairs, the stairs he'd knocked Mama down this morning, though he said it was an accident when he saw all the blood.

His bedroom was at the top of the stairs, and as her eyes got level with the landing, Katie could see him sprawled on his back, his head on the pillow, loud ragged snores issuing from his open mouth.

She tiptoed closer. The sheet had come untucked and there was a cigarette-shaped scorch mark on the mattress ticking. At least this time, he'd put his cigarette in the ashtray on the night stand, she thought. It had burned right down to the filter, leaving an acrid smell in the room. There were more little scorch marks all around on the carpet where cigarettes had dropped from his fingers when he fell asleep. Last winter, he'd actually burned his chest and fingers when he passed out with a freshly lit one. Mama kept saying they'd all be burned in their beds one night.

She thought of Timmy's raw legs, of Mama's bloody dress and the way she'd held her swollen belly and moaned as she hobbled to the car.

Timmy's legs.

Mama's blood.

"It's okay," she told Timmy, whose eyes were almost as red as the welts on his legs from crying. "He's drunk as a skunk and won't remember how much chopping needed doing today. Let's you and me go fishing, okay? Catch a few sun perch for supper."

She pulled a couple of cane poles from the shed and sidetracked Timmy when he headed for the compost pile with a small shovel to dig for worms. "Wait and dig 'em out of the creekbank," she said. "It'll be cooler there."

As they hurried along toward the path that led through the thick underbrush down to the creek, she paused and looked back. A tendril of gray smoke leaked from the upstairs bedroom window.

Abruptly, like a startled doe who feels the hunter's eye upon her, she whirled around and searched with her own eyes the pasture that rose on the other side of the creek, an empty pasture where no house was yet built.

No one was there though. No one had watched her before and no one cried out in alarm now.

No one.

"So your mother sees her marriage through rose-colored glasses," said Sam. "After thirty-five years, let the old woman rewrite her past if she wants to. Haven't you ever wanted to?"

Kate stood so long without answering that Sam tightened his arms around her. "Hey, it was just a rhetorical question. It's not as if you really have a choice."

No choice? When out there, across the creek, she could almost see the ten-year-old child she'd once been looking straight at her? If she leaned forward, rapped on the window, would the child turn? Run back to the house? Raise the alarm?

"No, of course not," she told Sam. "And even if I could rewrite the past, I wouldn't."

"C'mon, Katie!" Timmy called impatiently. "Whatcha looking at?"

"Nothing," Katie said. "Not a thing." And ran down through the underbrush to join her brother.

The debut novel in MARGARET MARON's second mystery series, *Bootlegger's Daughter*, was the first book to win all four major mystery awards, the Agatha, the Edgar, the Macavity, and the Anthony. Since then the series, which stars Judge Deborah Knott and the fictional Colleton County, North Carolina, has reaped more awards and become a best seller in the mystery field. Maron received the Sir Walter Raleigh Award for *Last Lessons of Summer* and was elected president of Mystery Writers of America for 2005. After spending some years in New York and Italy, Maron now lives on her family's homeplace in Johnston County.

Brynn Bonner

eborah's sharp intake of breath came like the *whoosh* of a hydraulic brake as she entered her mother's dining room and saw her father sitting at the head of the table. A cup of steaming coffee was on his saucer, and the morning paper was folded neatly beside his plate. It was a homey sight and wouldn't have been at all out of the ordinary—except for the fact that her father had been dead for well over two years.

"Deborah!" her mother startled, a hand to her sagging bosom as she came through the swinging doors from the kitchen. "You almost gave me a heart attack! I didn't hear you come in!"

"I-I-I," Deborah stammered, her eyes still fixed on her father. He had remained entirely motionless and silent throughout the exchange—as he would have, being made from canvas and cotton batting.

"You caught me before I had a chance to clear up breakfast," her mother fussed, grabbing at a plate soiled with poached egg and toast and heading back to the kitchen.

Deborah stood rooted to her spot, tilting her head and examining the specimen of her father as if trying to understand some alien species. The face was painstakingly sculpted and painted, the gray hairs applied individually and so skillfully she wondered idly if they had to be trimmed occasionally. "Mama, what is this?" she asked, her voice now taking on an exasperated tone.

"It's nothing, Deborah," her mother called from behind the door. "Don't trouble yourself about it. It's just a doll. Mrs. Leiberman told me about a woman who makes life-sized dolls, and I decided to have one made of Shelton. Don't make more of it than it is," she said as she pushed back through the doors and used her hand to brush a few crumbs of toast from the tablecloth. She pushed in her chair, picked up the newspaper, and placed it on top of a neat stack in a wicker basket. Then she grabbed her pseudo-husband by the hair and hoisted him up, swinging him unceremoniously around the back of the chair and depositing him with a thump in an armoire in the hallway. "There," she said, wiping her hands on her housedress, "all tidied up. What are you doing here so early, dear?"

"I came to bring you your prescription, Mama. I knew you were almost out," Deborah said, squeezing the bridge of her nose and struggling to keep her voice level. "Now tell me about this—" she hesitated, motioning vaguely toward the armoire, struggling to fit a word to the situation. In the end she could find no better characterization than her mother's—"this *doll*."

"What's to tell? It's nothing, Deborah. I told you. It's *just* a doll," her mother said, trying to sound defiant, but her voice was now quivering.

Deborah sighed and pulled her mother into the living room and sat her down. The plastic her mother insisted on keeping over her davenport crinkled under Deborah's legs as she sat down beside her.

"Mama, this can't go on," she said softly. "Pops has been gone for a while now. You're going to have to accept it. You've got to find a way to get on with your life. It's time."

"I *am* 'getting on with my life,' as you say." She mimicked Deborah's delivery. "I get on just fine. You're just blowing this up all out of approportion, Deborah."

"Proportion," Deborah corrected absently.

"Whatever," her mother said, patting her hair. She wore it skinned back into such a tight bun that the tension in her face gave her a perpetually questioning look. "I know very well that Shelton is gone. I've accepted it and I'm getting on just fine."

"Mama," Deborah said, throwing up both hands and letting them fall helplessly on the couch's cushions, "you have pictures of Pops in every room of the house, you've kept all his clothes and things— you still keep up all his magazine subscriptions, for God's sake!" She plucked a copy of *Popular Mechanics* from its place in the fan configuration on the coffee table, presenting it to her mother as evidence.

"I like to look at that magazine sometimes, too," her mother said, turning away from the offending issue and feigning interest in the arrangement of chotchkes on the coffee table: a silver cigarette lighter, though no one in the house had ever smoked; a candle carved into the shape of a fish, which she'd never allowed anyone to light; and a cut-glass candy dish filled with buttermints circa 1970, which no one ever ate. "It's inter-resting."

"Oh, it's inter-resting, huh?" Deborah asked, flipping open the pages and reading, "'Toolbox Treasures: Great New Picks from the Hardware Show'; 'The Best Wet-Dry Vac on the Market'; 'The Car Clinic: Fixing a Leaky Radiator.' Yeah, Mama, this is right up your alley," she said, slapping the magazine shut.

"You don't have to get sardonic with me, Deborah," her mother said, pulling herself up straighter and arranging the magazines back into their perfect fan.

"*Sarcastic*, Mama," Deborah said through clenched teeth. "I don't have to get *sarcastic* with you."

"No, you don't," her mother agreed, smiling as she patted her daughter's hand and picked lint off the sleeve of Deborah's new coat.

Jimmy squinted at the brownstone, concentrating. The woman had gone in a good ten minutes ago. She was dressed in a long black coat and looked all business. A fed? But alone? *Feebs* almost always worked in pairs, he was pretty sure. Somebody from the prosecutor's office? Whatever—he didn't like how this was shaping up. Too many loose ends.

He'd never had things go bad like this. He was a meticulous planner. His brother Joey had given him the nickname Jimmy the Nitpick for his attention to detail. It had bugged Jimmy at first, but it was better than what they called Joey—behind his back, anyway.

Joey'd had only one ambition from the time they were snot-nosed little boys. Joey wanted to be a wise guy. He wanted to be connected. He started carrying a switchblade when he was fifteen and calling himself Joey the Blade. But Joey had one problem—he just didn't have it in him to hurt anyone. When this became obvious his buddies had started calling him Joey the Butter Knife.

Jimmy had never had the kinds of ambitions Joey had. He didn't want to be connected. He didn't care about rank or respect. He pretty much just wanted to be left alone. But he did like money. Jimmy would do anything for anyone if the price was right. No loyalties or constraints. He took a job, or he refused it, his choice. An independent contractor.

No, Jimmy didn't share his brother's ambitions. He also didn't have his brother's sweet nature. That was for people who wanted to end up having friends snicker behind your back. Jimmy didn't want the snickering—or the friends.

What Jimmy had was a flourishing assortment of idiosyncrasies and urges. Like now he really needed to step over and check the return-change slot on the pay phone outside the little bodega where he was skulking in the doorway watching the brownstone. He'd already checked it five or six times since he'd been waiting, and no one had used the phone in the meantime. But he felt a pressing urgency to check it again. This time it might have a coin in it. There was no reason to believe it did, but Jimmy's brain was wired to allow for a continual string of maybe-this-times—logic be damned. And so what if it did have a coin in it—chump change. The coin wasn't the point. The point was that when he put his finger into the slot, there might *be* a coin in there. The fulfillment of the maybe—that was the point.

Jimmy had made it this far—three weeks from his twenty-fourth birthday—without being popped. Not once, not even juvie stuff. His record was as clean as his apartment, and you could perform surgery in there. He didn't get caught because he never left anything to chance. He planned to the last detail and checked—and rechecked—everything, way past the point of caution or reason.

Until now Jimmy had never taken on the big job—never taken a contract to dust anyone. Not out of faintness of heart or any jiggle of his moral compass—Jimmy's only true north was a dollar sign. But the big job always brought heat, and Jimmy definitely preferred a cool climate. If the big job was ever required, however, Jimmy knew just how he'd do it. He'd use the Glock, one to the body, one to the head, by the book. And he'd stay around until the close of business.

Jimmy stayed with second-layer stuff where the pay was good and nobody got all lathered up about things. He applied his skills like any craftsman. He studied and he planned. But as the most recent job had taught him, there are some things you just can't anticipate.

It should have been a walk in the park. He'd just been supposed to stick the guy up. Make it look like a routine robbery, something he did with regularity. Take the guy's watch, the diamond cuff links, and the wallet. Jimmy would get the jewelry, whatever cash was in the wallet, plus his fee for the job. All he had to do was hand over the small white card with a list of numbers on it that was tucked inside the lining of the wallet. The guy was a short, overweight, pasty-faced accountant. If he'd had half a brain he wouldn't even have been hurt —not bad, anyway. He'd have had a doozy of a headache the next day and a lump the size of a golf ball on the back of his head—but he would have been alive. And he'd have been wise to the error of his ways and very eager to make amends.

If the pitiful little toad hadn't decided to fight it out, if he hadn't thought he stood a chance of getting to the gun he had stashed in his glove compartment, Jimmy would never have shot him. Wouldn't have had his ski mask torn off by the flailing man, wouldn't have ended up chasing the bleeding man out into the street and up onto the front stoop to finish him off. Wouldn't have been spotted as he stood bathed in light from the street lamp outside the brownstone.

And after all that, he hadn't even gotten the card. Sometime during their tussle the guy's wallet had gone airborne. The little worm had pulled it out and run with it, like he was going to find a place to hide it or something. Like they were a couple of kids playing Keep Away! By the time Jimmy took care of him and started to look for the wallet, people were yelling and he could hear sirens coming closer, so he bolted. The wallet was probably sitting in the property room of the local precinct at this very moment. But it wouldn't be there for long, Jimmy knew that. Somebody on the inside would get the job of lifting it from there.

Jimmy's contact had told him that all was forgiven for the botched job, but he was watching his back just the same. The tension was activating a facial tic that made him blink in a series of three, then two, then three again, like some berserk Morse code.

He shifted from one foot to the other. If the old grayhead was talking, by this afternoon there could be flyers out all over the neighborhood with an artist's sketch of his face looking out at every person he'd ever ticked off. There were a few people around here—okay, more than a few—who would just love to see him with a can tied to his tail. Jimmy wasn't much of a people person. He started to make a mental inventory of everything he owned that he could turn into quick cash for a getaway. It didn't amount to much. He'd be lucky to get to Jersey.

He shrank back into the doorway and watched as the woman in the black coat emerged. "I've got to get to work, Mama," she called back over her shoulder. "I'll call you later today. We *really* need to have a long talk."

Just the daughter. He huffed a sigh of relief. There was still time to head this off. Jimmy knew one thing: Old people didn't usually want trouble. They liked being left alone, too; they were usually scared to get involved. Odds were pretty good that nothing had been reported. Not yet.

He looked down at his highly polished brown shoes and bent down to adjust the laces. This was only partly to avoid having the departing woman see his face. The laces *did* need his attention. They weren't tied evenly, and Jimmy couldn't abide that. He retied them, careful that the loops were equal on either side. That done, he needed to move on quickly, get some other noises into his ears. Jimmy's auditory system couldn't tolerate voices in a certain register, usually carried by old ladies and sometimes by whiny young ones. It was almost as if his hearing were allergic to the sound. It made his head feel swollen and his neck muscles clench. He moved on down the street and turned the corner where the soothing sounds of traffic, cursing taxi drivers, and blaring horns made him smile with relief.

"Now, Mama," Deborah said as they sat down at the dining room table that evening, cardboard cartons from the Chinese takeout aligned in a neat row beside plates, napkins, and silverware. Her mother fidgeted, looking for some task to perform. She finally settled on filling the water glasses. "Tell me how you've been doing," Deborah continued, trying to sidle up to the subject of the doll.

"I've been doing just lovely, dear," her mother replied. "I have so much to do, you know? Taking care of the apartment, and we play canasta now every other day. Plus, I help out at the Center two days a week now, did I tell you? So much to do." She spooned rice onto Deborah's plate and continued, "And I'm feeling well. A little touch of the arthritis, but that's to be expected." She flexed her hands and winced to demonstrate the pain the motion caused. "And how are you doing, Deborah? We haven't really talked in a while. Is your job going well? Are you seeing anyone?" For the last question her mother's voice went down half an octave, and she leaned forward to await the answer.

"Ma, we have dinner together at least once a week. We talk plenty! And things haven't changed since last week. Yes, my job is going fine. And yes, I'm seeing someone—two or three someones—but no one special. I'll give you a heads up if a good marriage candidate enters my radar field, okay?"

"Sure, Deborah," her mother said, reaching over to push a stray strand of hair out of Deborah's face. "It'll happen, honey, don't be discouraged. I just meant—well, you *are* twenty-six years old."

Deborah slumped and cradled her forehead in her hand. "Ma, what am I? A piece of cheese nearing my expiration date? Listen to me. I'm in no hurry to get married. I like my life just the way it is. You understand?"

"Yes, Deborah, I understand you," her mother said softly. "Do *you* understand me?"

Deborah looked at her mother, who returned her gaze with an iron stare. "Tell me, Mama," she said finally, heaving a sigh. "Tell me about the doll."

Her mother paused, smoothing the lace tablecloth over the edge of the table. "Again with the doll? Deborah, it's simple. I miss your father. You don't spend that many years together and not have a big hole in your life when they're gone. I miss having him to talk to. And that's all this is about. When Mrs. Leiberman told me about the woman who makes the dolls, I thought it would be a comfort to have it around, just to talk to. It makes me feel like a crazy old woman to talk to myself. Like I've got that All-the-timers."

"Alzheimer's," Deborah corrected.

"And it's not like Shel ever chattered on or anything. He mostly just rustled the paper or grunted," her mother continued, then smiled to herself, remembering. "But just the same, he was there."

"Mama," Deborah said, her voice melting, puddling the word out.

"Anyway," her mother went on, sitting erect, her words coming brisk, brooming away any emotional litter, "about that same time, I read in the paper that some women out in California were buying those blow-up dummies to put in the passenger seats of their cars so it didn't look like they were driving alone. As a divergence to crime, you know?"

Deborah frowned and hesitated. "As a—oh, a deterrent?"

"Yes," her mother replied, rushing on, "so I figured it couldn't hurt for me to have another person silhouetted on those shades." She motioned to the dining room windows facing the street and paused. She stared at the shades for a moment, narrowing her eyes, then shook her head and went on. "So that was another good reason to have the doll made up. You can't be too careful, you know? Only last week a man was shot to death, right out there on that street. While I was sitting right here, having a cup of tea."

"Yes, Mama, I know that. I came over after it happened, remember? I was with you when the police were knocking on doors looking for witnesses. I wish you'd give some more thought to moving."

"Deborah, we've had this conversation, we've conversed it to death. I'm not going to reallocate. This is my home."

"Relocate," Deborah corrected automatically. "I just worry about you, that's all," she said, noticing for the first time the slight tremor in her mother's hand.

"You don't need to worry about me, honey," her mother said, starting to stack the empty food cartons. "I'm just hunky-dory. I like everything just the way it is. I don't want anything stirred up. I didn't tell you about the doll before because I figured you'd start to think your ol' Ma was a little moonstruck." She held up her hand like a crossing guard. "Which I am *not*. But I just didn't want to have to convince *you* of that. Who needs it? So I kept it to myself. Sometimes it's better just to dummy up, no joke intended there," she said, nodding her head toward the armoire.

"I don't think you're anything like that, Ma," Deborah said, "I just want you to be happy. I don't want you to shut yourself up in this house and be lonesome. And you know Pops wouldn't want that, either."

"I'm not doing that, Deborah. I'm really not. You can ask anyone. I'm even thinking of taking a cruise with the seniors group. One of my friends is going." She gathered cartons and dishes and rose. "I'm doing just wonderful. If you don't believe me, ask your father; I can go get him out of the armoire if you like."

Deborah's head snapped in her mother's direction, and she saw the sly grin on the old woman's face. "I'm just indirigible, aren't I?"

Deborah smiled and, yanking on her mother's lace-trimmed apron, said, "Incorrigible—you're definitely incorrigible."

"That's what I said!" replied her mother, balancing Deborah's Kung Pao chicken container on top of the growing tower and hipping her way through the swinging door.

Getting in the front door of the brownstone was a piece of cake. The lock wouldn't have discouraged a seven-year-old with a pair of safety scissors. Jimmy had circled the building several times, checking for the telltale wiring of alarm systems. The inner door to the apartment he was interested in turned out to be more of a challenge. Old people were getting crafty. There were double deadbolts and, he suspected from what he could see in the tiny sliver of a crack underneath the door, a bar slide in the floor. He'd have to creep the place.

Under cover of night, the kitchen window turned out to be an open invitation. He didn't even need the glass cutter. The pane was so in need of glazing he was able to pry the whole thing out with a couple of twists of a screwdriver, then remove the security bars—which someone had put on from the outside. Jimmy loved stupid maintenance men!

Jimmy had an incredibly light touch—not a sound going in. He looked around the kitchen approvingly. Very neat, orderly—correct, except for the tray on the countertop by the coffeemaker. It held several bottles, a spiky potted plant, and two tiny cloisonné boxes. The arrangement was all wrong. Jimmy reached out to fix it, then caught himself. He wasn't here to feng shui. He was here to gather information and maybe even go ahead and get the loose ends tied up.

He crept into the living room, catlike. He wore coverings over his shoes that his cousin Sonja had gotten him from the hospital where she worked—so he could protect his shoes from the grease when he worked on his motorcycle, he'd told her. He wore latex gloves, no finger or palm prints. And he wore a balaclava, not only to hide his face, but to make sure he didn't leave any forensic evidence, like hair. Jimmy knew about these things; he watched the Discovery Channel. He checked and rechecked his pathway to the window.

It would be an incredible stroke of luck if he could get this over with the first time in. Old people went to bed early. It was a reasonable hope. He crept silently up the stairs and paused at the top, listening hard. He heard the muted sounds of classical music coming from the room at the end of the hall on his right. The door was slightly ajar, and a faint shaft of light fell in the hallway.

Jimmy eased down the hallway until he could see between the door and the jamb. The old woman sat up in bed, a book propped on a pillow in her lap, huge round glasses perched on her nose. Her wiry gray hair spilled down on her shoulders. Jimmy had been watching the place for four days now and had seen the old broad a half-dozen times. Now that she'd let her hair down out of that stranglehold of a bun, her skin had relaxed into a series of loose wrinkles. She looked like one of those Shar-Pei dogs. All loose skin. Jimmy shivered involuntarily.

He squinted through the slit and moved his head slightly, trying to get a fuller view of the room. The phone on the old woman's bedside table shrilled and she jumped. So did Jimmy! He flattened himself against the wall and calmed his breathing, listening.

"Oh, hello, Edith. No—no, I was just reading. What's on your mind? Oh, you don't say. Well, you want to hear something? You know what I got from Marge Styler? She said their daughter ran off with a cruise ship singer two days before her own wedding. . . ."

Jimmy clenched his teeth. The noise coming from the old ninny was making his head balloon, and his neck was starting to stiffen. No way to do this now without bringing attention from the outside. And he couldn't risk that. And he couldn't wait around here all night, not with his head expanding and his neck starting to feel like some guy with a blowtorch was welding it in place.

He retraced his steps to the kitchen and slinked up onto the counter to make his exit. He was halfway out the window, one leg dangling down into the bushes, when he stopped. He hauled himself back in and scampered along the countertop to the tray. Tall things go in the back, everyone knew that! He arranged the tray in its proper configuration, tilted his head to admire it for a moment, then let himself out the way he had come in. He was careful to replace the glass and the bars at the window, just as he'd found them, sticking the pane back in place with tiny globs of insta-putty he carried in his gym bag, into which he now stuffed his surgical booties, his balaclava, the gloves, and the screwdriver.

Jimmy walked purposefully back out into the street. One more young guy returning from a late-night pilgrimage to the gym. One more seeker of buffdom. Jimmy knew how to blend in. So what if he had to go into the brownstone again. He knew the layout now. He knew which bedroom was occupied. He'd be back. Then it would be finished. No more loose ends.

Deborah was sitting at her desk trying to organize the mountain of paperwork she had to finish by Friday, when the auditors were scheduled to arrive. The accounting secretary, Alison, put her head around the door jamb.

"Deborah, your mother's on line 1; she sounds a little upset."

"Ma?" Deborah asked as she snatched up the phone. "You okay? What's wrong?"

"Oh, Deborah. Everything's okay. I'm fine, dear," came the answer, though she didn't sound fine in Deborah's ears. "It's just that, well, I have this feeling. . . ." She paused.

In the silence Deborah felt pressure in her chest and realized she'd been holding her breath. "Ma," she said, letting it out, "what's the problem?"

"Well, you're going to think I'm hallucinogenic," her mother said, "but I think someone's been in the apartment."

"What do you mean you *think* someone's been in there?" Deborah asked, ignoring her mother's fractured syntax. "Do you think someone's in there *now*, Ma?"

"No, honey. I'm sure no one's in here just now."

"Well, are things missing? Has someone forced the locks?"

"No, no, nothing like that. I—well, you're going to think this is a silly thing—but my medicine tray was out of order this morning."

"Out of order?" Deborah asked. "What exactly does that mean— out of order?"

"Well, I always arrange it a certain way, you know. By how I take my pills—my vitamins, and herbs, and calcium—throughout the week, and it was all a mishmosh this morning. You didn't bother it last night, did you?"

"No, Ma," Deborah said, now relieved—and exasperated. "I didn't rearrange your tray. Are you so sure that it's in a different order?"

"Deborah Elaine!" her mother said sharply. "Think about who you're talking to! I know how I had my tray set up, and it's been moved. I'm very fastudious about these things."

Deborah sighed. "*Fastidious*," she said. "Yes, yes, you are, Ma." It was true. If her mother said things were rearranged, odds are, they were! Now, what to do about it? Call the police and say, *My mother's apartment has been broken into. No, no, nothing's missing. No, no sign of forced entry. How do I know? Well, I know because her pill bottles are arranged in a different order than they were yesterday. Could you please send someone out to investigate this crime of the century?* She wondered if they'd bother to reply or just hang up on her.

"Ma, make sure your doors are all locked and call Mrs. Leiberman to come over and sit with you for a while, okay? I'll be over right after work, and we'll have another look around. You're sure everything is okay in the apartment now, right?"

"Yes, Deborah, everything but my tray."

"Yeah, aside from that," Deborah said as Alison came in to plop another pile of folders on the end of her desk. "Okay, I gotta go. I'll see you later. Everything'll be fine. Just relax."

Jimmy lined up the apples in the wooden crate out front at the little greengrocer's so that all the stems pointed in the same direction. Mr. Kwan didn't like him to do that. He always seemed to think it was some elaborate scheme on Jimmy's part to steal one of them, but Jimmy didn't see how a person could stand to look at them all going this way and that. The oranges bothered him a little, but they didn't have stems, so he could teach himself to pretend that they were just balls, with no this-end-up about them.

Didn't that old bat ever leave her house? He'd been waiting here for two hours. It'd be good if he could get in while she was out. Have the element of surprise on his side. Loose ends just drove Jimmy crazy. He walked down to the coffee shop and ordered a cup of regular coffee to go, then stopped in the bathroom. The reason he needed to buy the coffee was so that he could use the bathroom. They were really picky about people using their facilities without buying something. And then, because he'd bought another cup of coffee, he'd soon be needing to come in and use the bathroom again. What a racket!

Just as he took up his perch again outside the greengrocer's the old lady came out the front door with another old hen. They were both bundled up and carried pocketbooks the size of suitcases. They trundled off down the street, both of them talking in that jet-engine whine. He could hear it from here, over the traffic and everything. Jeez! He shook his head to clear it.

They turned the corner. Jimmy picked up his gym bag and sprinted across the street, looked around, and slipped behind the brownstone. Daytime was risky, but he'd checked out all the windows that looked out onto the back of the brownstone, and no one had a straight-on view. And he had a great friend in the form of this tall shrub by the kitchen window. He took out his telescoping mirror and used it to look around the kitchen. Then he took out the glass and then the bars again, just as he'd done before. He used the mirror to check that the kitchen was clear. Now for the split second it would take him to hoist himself up—and he was in.

He drew the blind to obscure the open windowpane and sat very still listening. Nothing. He crept around the kitchen wall and noticed, with considerable irritation, that the tray he'd arranged properly last night had been messed up again. *Keep your mind on your business, Jimmy! Loose ends!* he reminded himself. He looked out onto the dining room, then crossed to the opposite wall and peered into the living room. All the furniture was covered with plastic, and the magazines on the coffee table were laid out in a symmetrical fan. Jimmy stared at the arrangement for a long moment. He nodded his head as if blessing the room.

He listened again, then crossed to the dining room table, stood in the appropriate place, and looked out into the street. He needed to check. No use doing an unnecessary job. His heart sank. Loose ends, all right. The view was unobstructed, and with that streetlight where it was, he would have been lit up like he was on stage to sing an aria.

He eased over to the stairs and made his way up them, his back flattened against the wall. A painting in a gilt-edged frame hung on the landing at the top of the stairs. He gave it a scornful frown. Fruit in a bowl—very original. It was hanging about three degrees off kilter, and Jimmy straightened it as he slipped past down the hall.

He checked the bedrooms. Empty. He went into the bedroom where he'd seen the old lady reading and looked through the closets. Old guys' clothes, old guys' shoes, old women's clothes, junk jewelry. He was glad he wasn't here to burgle the place. Nothing here worth taking. He looked again at the old-man clothes. Where *was* the old codger? They must have one of those social rooms in the building, or maybe he was in someone else's apartment. The coffee had made its journey, and Jimmy needed to use the bathroom again. He didn't dare risk a flush, suppose the front door opened at that time? Couldn't anything go right on this job? He squeezed his eyes shut and memorized the layout of the place, then made some calculations. Nighttime. Nighttime was better anyway. And he could do it clean and disappear into the dark.

No one had squealed on him yet. At least he didn't think so. He'd have heard on the street by now. But there was always the chance with old folks that they'd get all civic-minded. He had to follow through.

Jimmy made his way back down the hall, no longer bothering to creep. The painting he'd just straightened was hanging crooked again. Jeez! He took a tiny piece of insta-putty from his pocket and placed it under the bottom of the frame and pushed it against the wall. Now the sucker would hang right! One thing accomplished, anyway.

He made his exit, willing himself to leave the tray on the kitchen counter alone. If the old bat liked it that way, let her have it. Soon it wouldn't matter anymore.

Deborah threw her coat over a chair and dropped her shoulder bag on top of it. Her mother's admonitions—Hang things up as soon as you come in the door—rang in her ears, but she was too tired to care. The auditors had been there for two days—this one a *very* long one—laboring over the books. After they had pronounced them clean and healthy, the gang from accounting had all gone out for a late dinner. And the boss had given them tomorrow off. All she wanted now was a long hot bath and her flannel pajamas.

In the morning she'd need to go over early to check on her mother. This paranoia about break-ins was getting to be a real concern. The neighborhood had seemed safe enough, all things considered, until recently. That business with the man being killed in the street outside her apartment building had been unsettling. But the police had told Deborah they didn't think it was a random mugging. They had reason to believe that the man was involved in some high-stakes financial shenanigans with the "wrong people," as the cop put it, placing his finger beside his nose. He'd been moving money that wasn't supposed to move to a numbered account offshore. "I guess someone objected," the cop had said. "It's always good to be careful, and your mother should always take precautions, but I don't think this was a sign that the neighborhood's going to hell."

Still, her mother had been adamant that someone had been in the apartment again when she went to see her yesterday afternoon.

"Was your tray out of order again?" Deborah asked, trying to keep the scepticism out of her voice.

"Well, no, it was okay. It was the way I left it."

"Was anything missing or anything else out of place?"

"No, I couldn't see anything. But someone had been in here. I could just tell. The place felt different. I have good initiative about these things, you know that, Deborah."

"Intuition," Deborah amended. "Well, intuition or no, let's check through the apartment and see if we can find anything a little more concrete."

They walked through every room in the apartment, with Deborah checking in cupboards, under beds, and in drawers. Her mother's house was so exactly arranged and organized that anything out of place would be instantly apparent. Nothing.

"Well, Ma, just make sure you lock all the doors and keep your phone right by the bed. If you hear anything, anything at all, you call 911 right away, then call me. Okay?"

Deborah didn't believe her mother was in any danger. Everything looked perfectly normal. But she appreciated how much the recent crime had upset her, and she knew, despite her mother's protests, that she wasn't adjusting well to being alone. She wished she could get her to reconsider moving to another building with more security. But her mother wouldn't even entertain the idea.

She was luxuriating in a deep tub of lilac-spiked hot water when the telephone jangled in the other room. She focused on her watch on the bathroom counter. Eighteen minutes past midnight. Who'd be calling her at this hour? She thought of her mother and sprang from the tub, grabbing a towel and wrapping it hastily around her, dripping water and lilac bubbles over her hardwood floors as she sprinted out to the phone.

"Deborah, come over, please," her mother's voice, sounding strangely mechanical, warbled over the wire.

"Ma, are you okay? What's happened?" she asked.

"I—he—I . . . Don't ask! Just come over, Deborah," she said, and the line went dead.

When Deborah arrived, her mother was in the kitchen. A young man dressed in sweat clothes was sitting in one of her kitchen chairs— no, that wasn't quite right—was *tied* to one of her kitchen chairs with four or five pairs of support hose. Two police officers were there, a male and a female. The male was taking notes in a little notepad as her mother bustled about making coffee.

"What in the world is going on here?" Deborah shouted.

"Do you have to yell?" the young man tied to the chair asked, bobbing his head back and forth in misery and blinking his red eyes.

"I told you, you've got the right to remain silent," said the female cop. "Now why don't you just exercise it?"

The male cop was tall, older, and fit. He obviously hadn't fallen victim to the doughnut epidemic. He stopped scribbling and aimed his ballpoint at the window. "This young gentleman came in to see your ma without a proper invitation. Came in through that window there. Your mother here," he gestured toward her, "pepper-sprayed him and coldcocked him with a sock full of quarters. Then she tied him up, doctored his eyes, and called us."

"She WHAT?" Deborah exclaimed.

Jimmy had been watching the place for over an hour when he saw the old woman come into the dining room and bend down to plant a kiss on the old guy's head and gesture toward the stairs. *Toddling off to bed, goodnight, dear.* He picked up his bag and scooted behind the building. If he went in quiet, he could have this done and be gone before the old woman could even get her feet on the floor. He peered up over the kitchen window ledge. He couldn't believe his luck. The swinging doors to the dining room were open. It was a clear shot.

Now he was getting a preview of hell. The old woman had ambushed him coming in. She'd been sitting there in the dark, pepper spray in one hand and a homemade sap in the other. She'd let him have it just as he took aim and fired. And all because of that stupid piece-of-crap crooked painting. If he'd let the thing alone, she'd never have gotten on to him. She'd been in the habit, she told the cops, of straightening the picture every morning when she came down for breakfast. And as she tramped up and down the stairs during the day, it slowly leaned all akimbo again by nightfall. What kind of person would put up with that? Jimmy couldn't understand it. She'd found the putty when she'd gone to straighten it this morning, and that had set her off on her own little Miss Marple tour of her apartment. Who'd ever have imagined she'd spot the tiny pieces of putty in the window. They were so small, and he'd applied them so neatly. If he hadn't used the putty. . . .

Jimmy was blinking his eyes furiously, trying to clear the pepper spray. He had come to tied to the chair by a tangled web of old-lady stockings. The old broad had him by the chin and was squirting eye drops in each eye as he thrashed around in the chair. She held his eyelids open and flooded them with water, none too gently, all the while telling him it was more than he deserved. His eyes still felt like lit cherry bombs. He needed to get his vision clear. He could have sworn he'd hit his target. Why wasn't she telling the cops about that? Why wasn't she doing something?

And all the while, she'd been talking in that voice. And now the daughter was doubling her. Hell in stereo. His head throbbed where she'd whacked him, his face felt like it was on fire, and now the two of them wouldn't shut up.

"He was going to rob me," the old woman was screeching.

"Lady, you ain't got nothing worth stealing in this place," Jimmy responded before he could stop himself. He willed himself to stay calm and said in a low voice, almost pleadingly, "Stop talking, just stop talking."

"And maybe rape me, too," the old hag went on.

"Not on my darkest day," Jimmy shouted back, then winced as the pain of the effort ping-ponged inside his skull. Rape her? The thought triggered his gag reflex.

The woman cop had put cuffs on him and was now untying his

hands, though his feet were still bound to the chair. "Behave your-self," she told him. "And I warn you again, you might want to keep your mouth shut."

Jimmy pushed his feet on the floor tiles and inched the chair back until he could see into the dining room, if only he could get his eyes clear enough to focus. Yes, there he was, lying on the floor, the gray hair just visible behind the legs of the dining room chair. Why wasn't the old woman doing anything to help him?

"And just look at this, would you, Deborah?" she was rasping, her voice now sounding like a thousand fingernails on a thousand blackboards in Jimmy's ears. "Somebody put these bars in back-ward. Probably our nincompoop super, Mr. Cervalles." She stopped to suck in a breath, then pointed to Jimmy. "He might have killed me in my sleep. Raped me, then killed me. What kind of a divergence to crime is that?" she asked, gesturing her flabby arm toward the win-dow, looking like some giant geriatric version of a flying squirrel.

Divergence! That wasn't even the right word. Jimmy's head now felt twice the size of his body, and his neck muscles were locked and loaded in the put-me-out-of-my-misery position. She was talking in that leaf-shredder voice—and now she wasn't even using the right words. A strangled protest spewed out of him. "I wasn't even after you, you stupid old cow. I was after the guy!" He half stood, his hands cuffed behind him. His face was red and his voice strained. "It was the old fart. He's the one who saw me!" He jerked his head, with con-siderable effort, toward the dining room, then shook his head back and forth like a dog with a rag, trying to unknot his neck muscles. He could feel the foam at the corners of his mouth and realized sud-denly that there were more and more loose ends and that now he was creating them himself. Everything was coming unraveled.

"Everybody stop talking, just stop talking!" He slumped back into his chair and let out a few frustrated whimpers. He was caught, and the old guy might be in there dying while she bumped her gums. He'd be facing murder one. He blinked his bloodshot eyes at the female cop. "Check on the old man. I fired, but I don't know. . . ." His voice trailed off and he closed his eyes tight. Through lips drawn tight across his teeth, he hissed, "Just check on him." As they all looked at one another in confusion, Jimmy opened his eyes, which had taken on the vacant stare of surrender. They bobbed along until they came to rest on the tray on the countertop. "And for God's sake, fix that! Please! Everybody knows the tall things go in the back," he said and groaned.

Deborah had seen the cops sneaking sidelong glances at one another as she'd explained, as best she could, about the Shelton doll. She'd gone with the male cop into the dining room, where they had found the doll with a "through-and-through" in his head, bits of stuffing clumped around the exit wound. Throughout her explanation, Jimmy sat rocking back and forth, keening and repeating, "A dummy, a dummy, popped for a dummy," like a mantra.

Her mother had sat calmly sipping her coffee and steadfastly refusing to look at the officers or at her daughter as she told them about her mother's reasons for having the doll made and how she made a habit of having meals with him sitting at his customary place. Deborah saw her mother sitting up straighter and fidgeting more with her clothing or her hair with every new detail her daughter provided. She knew she was robbing her mother of her dignity, but she wanted her out of the middle of whatever mess this Jimmy character had dragged her into when he'd decided to do his dirty business right in front of her apartment building.

The male cop stage-whispered to his partner as they marched Jimmy out of the apartment, "This is one for the books, the perp and the victim are *both* dummies." They chuckled discreetly, and Jimmy, completely morose but still Jimmy, reached out a foot to straighten the rug by the front door as they took him away.

Now they were all gone and she was alone with her mother. She came up behind her where she stood at the kitchen sink and placed her hands gently on her shoulders. "I had to tell them about it, Ma. I'm really sorry if it embarrassed you."

"That's all right, Deborah," her mother said, busying herself scrubbing the coffee cups in a sink generous with suds. She worked on them industriously for a few moments, then stopped abruptly. "Actually, Deborah, I have a question for you," she said as she dried her hands on a dish towel, slowly and deliberately. "Do you think it's technicality correct to say that it's not making a false statement to the police if you don't say anything?" her mother asked finally, flipping her hands palms up, then palms down to navigate her way through the upside-down question.

"A false statement? Ma, you didn't make a false statement, *technically* or otherwise!"

"I know I didn't, dear. That's what I'm saying. You did all the talking. I just didn't argue with you."

"Well, why would you argue with me?" Deborah asked with a nervous laugh. "Did I get something wrong about the doll?"

"Oh no, not at all, honey," her mother said, reaching over to pat her cheeks. Deborah blinked as she got a whiff of lemon-scented Palmolive liquid. "You did a fine job of explaining the Shelton doll and all that business. It's just that . . ." Her voice trailed off as she began to twist the dishcloth in her hands. "Deborah, do you remember Mr. Feldman? He and Trudy—Mrs. Feldman, God rest her soul—they used to play canasta with your father and me and some other couples in the neighborhood?"

A tiny trench of thought formed between Deborah's eyebrows as she conjured up a picture of Mr. Feldman. He was a short, round man who always had a strange little smile on his face, as though he was thinking pleasant thoughts—that, or indulging in some fairly powerful narcotics. He wore Mr. Peepers glasses, magnifying his pupils to fun-house size.

"Well, yes, Ma. I know Mr. Feldman." She swiped crisscrossed hands in front of her face as if to refresh her mental screen. "What does this have to do with the police, or the statement, or the doll, or that psycho who broke in here—any of it?"

Her mother tilted her head to one side as if trying to hear distant music, ignoring Deborah's agitation. "Mr. Feldman is a very nice man, you know," she replied finally. "He lives up in 4B still."

Deborah extended both hands and opened her mouth, producing a chuff of impatience. "Yes, I know that, Ma. I see him sometimes when I come to visit." In fact, Deborah had run into Mr. Feldman last week when she'd come to borrow her mother's rice steamer. She remembered exchanging hello-how-are-yous on the front stoop. Whenever Deborah saw Mr. Feldman she was always reminded of a toy her cousin Rhonda's little girl played with. It was a tabletop contraption that featured a disembodied plastic head and a lever. Little Vicky would put a big glob of Playdough into a tiny compartment and pump the lever and spikes and strings of Playdough hair were squeezed up through holes in the head. Then she'd trim the hair with scissors or squish it into different styles. Except Mr. Feldman seemed to have a clog somewhere, and the hair that was intended for the head was being diverted—squeezed out in the form of ear hair, nose hair, a shaggy beard, and antennae-like eyebrows. The top of his little gnome head remained smooth and shiny, while the rest bristled.

"I'm sure you're right," Deborah said now, slumping into a kitchen chair. "I'm sure Mr. Feldman is a perfectly nice man. But can we get back to this thing about the police, Ma? I told them just what you told me about the doll and all. Why are you talking about what's a false statement and what's not?"

"You said it was the doll, the doll of Shelton that Jimmy person was after. That the doll was sitting at the dining room table the night of the shooting."

"Yeah," Deborah answered. "That was why he broke in here. He thought Pops saw him gun that man down, you heard him. Only, obviously, Pops is a little beyond witnessing anything." Deborah laughed softly and gestured toward the ceiling and, by extension, heavenward. "Or if he did, he's beyond making a statement. And his stand-in—while I grant you it is very accurate—" she said, holding up a hand to quell her mother's argument, "it doesn't exactly have twenty-twenty vision."

"Actually, Deborah," her mother said, drawing out the words, "your father was in the armoire that night." She paused, tilted her head downward, and gave Deborah a meaningful look. "All night."

Deborah arched her eyebrows—a silent question.

Her mother continued, "But the person who was sitting there doesn't have twenty-twenty, either. Not even close," she said, fanning the dish towel. "He can barely see his hand in front of his face. I mean, have you ever seen those thick glasses of his? He wasn't a witness, either. Not by a long shot. So I don't see any reason to complicate things by getting the police involved in our private business."

Deborah made several attempts to formulate a question but could only form the initial "Wh—"; she sounded like a helicopter hovering in her mother's kitchen. "Wh—Wh—Wh—"

"Mr. Feldman," her mother said, hanging the dish towel over the handle of the oven and spreading it evenly. "Well, him and me have been," she paused and searched the air for a term, "we've been *keeping company* lately." She put a hand to her forehead and rested a fist on her ample hip. "I just cannot believe I forgot to pull the shades that night. I've always been so careful when Mr. Feldman comes over to—" she paused again and cast a sidelong look at Deborah, her cheeks turning rosy pink "—to socialize," she concluded. "Imagine what Mrs. Leiberman—or, God forbid, Edith—would do with this. Mr. Feldman and I would like to have our confidentiality. And Edith is, you'll pardon the expression, a number-one gossipmonger!"

The thought of her mother *socializing* with round, hairy little Mr. Feldman made Deborah grimace. "Ma, what are you talking about?" Deborah demanded, then gave a little gasp and clapped her hands over her ears. "No, don't tell me. This is too much information." She pressed her hands tighter and bent over in her chair. "Way too much information."

"That's right, honey," her mother said, rubbing her shoulders. "It'll take time. I really don't think you're ready."

Deborah's mother paid meticulous attention to her packing. The bun was gone in favor of a short, styled coif. The housedress replaced by a snappy new wind suit.

"Ma, are you sure about this?" Deborah asked, not for the first time.

"Very sure, Deborah. I'm looking forward to this cruise. I've never been anyplace like this. The Cayman Islands. It sounds so exotic. Edith would positively die if she knew about this. But Mr. Feldman and I have been the soul of deception."

"Soul of *discretion*." Deborah smiled. "I'm glad you're happy, Ma, and I hope you have a wonderful time." She rose from the edge of the bed and kissed her mother on her rouged cheek. "Call me the minute you get home. I want to hear all about your trip." She scrunched her eyes shut. "Well, maybe not all of it, but most of it...." Her voice trailed off.

"I know, Deborah," her mother said, patting her daughter's cheeks. "Honey, not to worry. I'll call you the minute I get in. I'll see you in two weeks."

Deborah gave one last backward glance as she left the bedroom and tried to picture her mother and Mr. Feldman playing shuffle-board, JUST shuffleboard, aboard the cruise ship.

When she heard the front door close, Deborah's mother went to the closet and brought out the Shelton doll. The hole had been neatly patched, and she smoothed the hair over it and sat the doll in the side chair by the window, placing a newspaper on its lap.

"She's trying, Shel. But she's going to need more time." She laughed softly and patted the doll's canvas hand, then went back to her packing.

"I could have told her that I didn't misspeak that time. I meant just what I said. Mr. Feldman—Aaron—and I *have* been the soul of deception. But she's had so many things to adjust to lately. I don't think she needs to hear all the details. But I could always tell you everything, Shelton."

She sighed and sat down on the edge of the bed, still folding things into her suitcase. "That night when that poor man was shot, Aaron was sitting at our table, just like old times when we all used to get together, you know? Except that you and Trudy and some of the others are gone. I was having a cup of tea, and he was having some wine. We heard the shot, but we thought it was just a car backfiring. What do we know from gunshot sounds? Anyway, we were listening to music on the phonograph. Then Aaron decided to go up to his place and bring down a record he wanted me to hear. A Mendels-sohn, I think it was. But that's neither here nor there." She shooed the issue away with a fan of her hand.

"So, when he started up the stairs he saw a little piece of white paper stuck under the front door. He thought maybe somebody dropped it when they were getting their key or something. He picked it up and looked at it, then stuck it into his watch pocket and con-tinued on his way. He intended to tack it up on the bulletin board by the mailboxes the next day. He was still up in his apartment looking for the record when the police came to question us all."

She sighed, leaning her head to one side as she gazed at the doll. "You know, Shelton, I miss you terribly, but Deborah's right. I have to get on with my life. I know that's what you'd want."

She got up to fold a new dress she'd bought for the captain's din-ner into tissue paper and placed it carefully into her suitcase. "You remember, Aaron was a CPA for a lot of years. He understood right away what the little white card was, after the police talked to him." A smile of satisfaction crept across her face. "And he understood right away what it can mean for a *very* comfortable retirement. That's why we're going on this cruise. This specific cruise. To the Cayman Islands, where there are some very specific banks. He's found out what he needs to know, and he says one of our stops will feature something lush and green — ripe and ready for the picking." She did a little cha-cha step in place.

"Do you know what he asked me yesterday?" she queried the doll, her voice playful. "He said, 'What do you think — Europe next summer?' Europe next summer! 'What's to think about?' I said. Can you imagine?" she asked, her smile fading as she walked over and picked up the doll, giving it a squeeze. She smoothed the hair again.

"Aaron isn't you, Shelton, I know that. He's short, overweight, bald, and wears coke-bottle glasses." She danced the doll across the floor and put it gently into the closet. She closed the door and put her back to it, leaning in until she heard a click of finality. "But a dummy, he's not!"

BRENDA WITCHGER, who often writes under the name of Brynn Bonner, is a former teacher and journalist who lives in Cary. Witchger's stories appear regularly in *Ellery Queen's Mystery Magazine* and other mystery and literary publications. She won the Robert Fish Award, given by the Mystery Writers of America for best first short story, in 1999 and the Doris Betts Prize in 2004.

clyde Haywood

ince one paper clip straightens pretty much like another, and since there are not many different ways to review the same eighty-six mostly thin files, and since the view from a single small window into a blind alley doesn't change much, Allen Wade was bored. In the fall of 1968 when he started with the finance company, the title of management trainee had convinced him he would soon be on his way up in Atlanta, or at least in Charlotte. But when the title of office manager became his after only six months of training in Richmond, he found himself shuffled, cut, and dealt out to a small town on the North Carolina coast where he managed one lonely secretary vainly battling middle age armed with mascara and miniskirts, one part-time collector supplementing his salary as one of the county's six deputy sheriffs, and himself.

True, the office saw lots of traffic in the summer. But that was mostly vacationers who had underestimated their ability to spend money at the beach and needed the $100 or $200 their national cards —issued by some other office—guaranteed them. That kind of business didn't give much opportunity for the kind of "creative credit management" Allen had heard about before he took the job. Even worse, it provided no chance for follow-up work during the slow season to come.

Allen's social life was as seasonal as his business. When he went to North Carolina in the spring of 1969, living in a beach town frequented by vacationing or weekend college girls seemed quite the life for a twenty-three-year-old bachelor. So what if there was a professional vacuum? That just left more time and energy for the girls.

From a small inheritance he made a down payment on a neat little cottage miles up the coast from the public areas, with its own little patch of sand and no near neighbors of any sort. He had

Playboy-inspired dreams of college cuties—or working girls for that matter, dropouts can't be intellectual snobs—romping bare-bottomed in the surf, soaking up the rays on his tiny beach, and satisfying his greatly overestimated needs all over the quaint little place in all the ways that a horny young male egotist can imagine.

The girls did come, starting with two he found huddled on the beach on a rainy night when all the motels were full, then some of their sorority sisters. By the end of the summer, he was calling them his "Beta Bunnies," and "Wade's Warren" was the most popular beach accommodation for the summer students of a genteel old southern girls' school. He was known in every beach joint around as a genuine party animal.

But there was the rub. The end of summer did come. On the weekend after Labor Day, the beach joints began to empty. By October they were closed for the season. The summer girls were back to full-time classes and frat parties at the boys' schools. Beach weekends at Allen's gave way to football weekends a long way inland and sorority balls that didn't include a loan officer some of the sisters had met at the beach.

In June, July, and August he usually left the office early on Fridays. On that gray Friday in October he had no reason to leave when closing time finally dragged itself to his door. Not that he could fail to notice closing time. His secretary, Miss Just-call-me-Sherry Bailey, would see to that.

She pecked on the glass that partly separated Allen's cubicle from the rest of the loan office and called to him as though he were on the other side of a wide chasm instead of behind a three-foot desk.

"Oh, *Al*len," she said, tapping her watch.

He had never told her to call him by his first name. That had been her own idea.

She half closed her eyes in what he took to be an unconscious imitation of a Hollywood seduction. "Mother's visiting her sister in Greenville this weekend, so you'd be welcome to keep me company for supper, or—" she paused and blinked at him "—whatever."

Thirty-nine if she's a day, Allen thought, and she knows as much about being a woman as I do about being an antelope. This is her idea of how to seduce her handsome young boss.

"No, thanks," he said aloud, barely lifting his eyes from the half-memorized file on his desk. "I've got plans."

"Well, you know the way if your plans should change. Toodle-oo," she called as she waved from the door.

Toodle-oo, Allen thought. Nobody says toodle-oo, not even in the movies. Oh well, I said I had plans for the weekend. What are they?

"I plan," he said aloud to the empty office, "to drink beer and see if I can pick up Jenny."

Jenny was the only barmaid left in town worth picking up. She worked in the only bar left in town worth drinking in. All the beer joints and beachfront motels had closed, but the Holiday Inn remained open through the winter, serving Sunday dinner to North Carolina farmers and hardware merchants and providing lodging to traveling salesmen and occasional tourists, tiring early on their way to or from the year-round beaches farther south. The inn featured what passed for a lounge in North Carolina in the 1960s — a dimly lit room off the restaurant where you could buy beer or a glass of wine but not a mixed drink. The lounge, in turn, featured Jenny.

Jenny was Allen's age, more or less. She came from a farm community a hundred miles inland, and as far as Allen knew, she had never been any farther from home than she was now. He estimated her I.Q. at 90 percent of her bust measurement. She was loud, overpainted, and not the sort of girl Allen's mother would have wanted him to bring home. But Allen wasn't planning to take her home, just back to the beach cottage as he had done a couple of other times since Labor Day when he couldn't find anybody better and she wasn't already taken by some salesman or trucker.

He hurried through the lobby, barely slowing at a greeting from Clarence, the night clerk-manager-franchisee of the inn, and on into the lounge. He had hoped and half expected to find Jenny alone. Not only was it too early for most of the regulars, but there was a high school football game that evening. The contest held no appeal for Allen, but it would draw most of the locals away from any other form of entertainment. As his eyes grew accustomed to the near darkness, however, he saw Jenny seated with two strangers at a table near the far end of the bar.

Allen had never learned whether Clarence didn't mind his lounge waitress's sitting with the customers or whether Jenny just didn't care if he did mind. Either way, that's what she was often doing when she wasn't actively serving customers.

"Come on over, Al," she called to him with her usual siren volume.

Allen saw one of the customers motioning to her to be quiet.

A hopeless task, he thought as he started toward them. If the man didn't want him to come over, Allen figured, he must be trying to pick Jenny up himself. All the more reason to get over there and cut him out early.

Jenny was sitting sideways to the door where she could see any arriving customers. The man who had been motioning sat to her left, facing Allen as he approached the table. He was huge, obese, and now folded his hands across his enormous belly.

He looks, Allen thought, like a big fat frog.

Allen greeted Jenny with a peck on the cheek and nodded to the fat man.

"I'm Allen," he said. "Allen Wade."

The frog man took Allen's extended hand in a big soft mitt and said in a surprisingly high, squeaky voice, "Webb Wickersham's the name. Some folks call me Wide Webb, but I don't know why. This here is Billy Webb. His last name's the same as my first because we're related. He's my step-neighbor-in-law."

The big man laughed harder at his own joke than anyone else did. Billy Webb, who looked to Allen like a typical lanky redneck, took the loan officer's hand in a corn-grinder handshake like a country politician's.

"Hey, y'all," said Jenny as Allen sat down. "Maybe y'all ought to talk to Al. He's in the money-lending business."

"Who needs money?" Allen asked of no one in particular.

Wickersham forced his wide mouth into an unconvincing smile, almost closing his eyes with the rolls of fat he pushed up his cheeks.

"Jenny, you talk too much," he said. "Get Allen a beer on me. And bring me and ol' Billy another round."

Jenny hopped up to fill the order. Allen gave her a familiar pat on the bottom to establish his territoriality against the two men he now saw as most inferior rivals. He was sure she'd prefer him to either of these homely fossils.

"Kitchen open?" he asked.

"Sure," she said. "But they ain't doing no business either. They'll sell a bunch of hamburgers and french fries later on when the game lets out, but we won't do no good in the lounge all night. About all the regulars but you got families, and they'll be with them for the game instead of out drinking beer."

"I didn't want a local business report," said Allen. "I just need some supper. Bring me a sandwich platter of some kind."

Jenny slipped around behind the bar, yelled "Cheeseburger and fries" through an order window into the kitchen, and trotted back to the table with three bottles of beer on a small plastic tray.

As she served them, she asked Wickersham, "Why'd you want me to shut up? You said you needed $2,500 to make $10,000 in a week. Allen's a loan office manager. Maybe he can loan you the money."

The big man laid his head back and sucked deeply on his beer, his eyes half closed. Foam flecked his grizzled mustache.

It's not a frog he looks like, Allen thought, it's a bull walrus enjoying himself in a rainstorm. I wonder if walruses have shaggy gray manes like his.

At last the man set his beer down and responded to Jenny's question.

"My dear child, not every business can deal with every other business. Now I think the time has come to talk of other things."

"That's right," said Billy Webb. "This guy might be a police."

"Al ain't no po-lice," said Jenny. "He don't even like po-lice. Least he don't when they drive up to his little beach place when we're skinny-dipping." She giggled and patted Allen's cheek.

"That don't matter none," said Billy. "We don't need him hearing about our business."

"Now, now, children," said Wickersham. "Let's just all forget the subject of mine and Billy's finances and talk about something more pleasant, like having a tooth pulled or perhaps the war in Vietnam."

Again he laughed heartily at his own joke and steered the conversation to country music, sending Jenny to the jukebox for a quarter's worth of his favorite selections.

They spent the next two hours chatting about car racing, state politics, television shows—topics that would not normally have held Allen at the table for twenty minutes. But he had become like a housecat outside a closed door—the more they wanted to shut him out of their business, the more he wanted in. He bought them round after round of beer, trying to pace himself at one beer to two each for the others.

The beer seemed to have no more effect on Wickersham than on the bottles he drank it from, but Billy Webb's eyes grew ever more bleary, his speech ever more slurred. At last, when Wickersham left for the men's room, Allen saw his chance. He sent Jenny to the juke-box with a handful of change and told her to pick the six songs she liked best. That should give him plenty of time. She couldn't decide what day it was in less than twenty minutes.

"What was it you guys were needing that money for?" he asked softly as the first record started.

His conspiratorial tone seemed to work.

"To buy a truck," Billy whispered back.

"A truck?" said Allen. "What's the big secret about a truck?"

"It ain't the truck that's the secret," said Billy. "It's what we're going to haul in it."

"What are you going to haul?"

"We was gonna haul moonshine," answered Billy. "We got a still. We got a load made. But we ain't got a truck. Webb's got this friend named Johnson that was going to front us the money, but he just up and disappeared. We got a $10,000 buyer all lined up, but we ain't got no way to get the load out to him, and a moonshine buyer don't never front you nothing."

At that a squeaky voice behind Allen said, "Billy Webb, have you never learned that a wise stillhand should be seen and not heard?"

Wide Webb Wickersham had returned. He eased his bulk onto the little tavern chair.

"Why should he be seen and not heard?" asked Jenny, who had just finished punching in her selections.

"Because Billy just told this lad too much, my dear," the wide man answered. "Well, at least now Allen knows why he doesn't really want to lend us any money. Little lads from loan offices help schoolteach-ers buy Chevrolets. They don't help bad men buy booze buggies. Right, Jenny?"

He patted Jenny's thigh as he spoke. She giggled, looked at Allen, and giggled again.

Allen felt his face grow warm. Everything about Webb Wicker-sham was beginning to bother him, from the way he called Allen "lad" to the way he kept his big soft hand on Jenny's thigh after his first pat.

"I wouldn't have to write it up as a truck," he snapped. "I could say Jenny's buying a Chevrolet."

"And just what would you show the company for title papers on that Chevrolet?" Wickersham asked.

Allen couldn't respond. To his surprise, Billy could.

"I had a cousin that worked in a bank over in Raleigh," said the lanky bootlegger. "He used to get money to gamble with out of the bank. He took a bill of sale and what he called—I think—a contract for a title or something like that."

"Was it a contract to furnish title?" Allen asked.

"That sounds right," said Billy. "And he'd put down that the car was from Alabama on account of he said that wasn't a title state."

"It's still not," said Allen.

"Anyway," Billy went on, "if anybody in the bank was to check behind him, that held them off for a month or so, and if he was winning he'd pay off the loan, and if he was losing he'd roll it over."

"What does that mean, 'roll it over'?" Jenny asked.

"He'd write another one up the same way and use it to pay off the old one," said Billy. "Maybe Allen could do that, or maybe he's got some money of his own he could throw in with us."

Wickersham shook his massive head. "No, he doesn't, and he doesn't want to make any phony loans and put up the company's money either. He's the rabbit kind."

"What do you mean, Al's the rabbit kind?" asked Jenny.

"There's two kinds of people," said the fat man. "There's the kind that live in holes like rabbits. That kind finds a quiet little job in a quaint little town. They stay out of everybody's way, and sooner or later they get to be a deacon in the church. And later on they die and they're buried by their grandchildren.

"Then there's the kind that weren't made to live in holes—the kind that runs with the foxes, feasts on the hare, flees from the hound. Me and old Billy are the fox kind. Maybe you too, Jenny. You look like a vixen."

As he said her name, he slid his hand up her thigh and patted her fanny under her little black cocktail-waitress skirt.

That did it!

I won't run, Allen thought, because I won't have to. But I will have this one feast.

"I can get your damned $2,500," he said.

Wickersham shook his head again. "No, my boy, I can't let you do that. I bet that's more than you make in three months, isn't it? You can't afford to take that kind of risk."

"Never mind what I make," fumed Allen, who wouldn't make $2,500 in four months. "What about the risk you and Billy take?"

"We thrive on risk," said Wickersham. "You stick with the Chevrolets."

His hand was still on Jenny's bottom. He patted again, then squeezed. Jenny looked at Allen and giggled again.

"You worry about your risk, and I'll worry about mine," Allen stormed at the big man. "I'll get you your damned money, but I'll have to have it back with carrying charges, plus I want a third of the profit."

Wickersham stared at him for several seconds, then turned and looked at Billy. Billy nodded.

Wickersham turned back to Allen. "By God, you're serious, aren't you? Well, if you're fool enough to give $2,500 to a couple of rascals to run illegal alcohol, we're fools enough to take it. Let's shake on it."

They shook hands all around and agreed to meet at the lounge early Monday evening when Allen could bring the money. At closing time Jenny left with Allen, but she didn't help his ego much when he heard her tell Wide Webb that she would get in trouble with Clarence if he caught her going to a motel guest's room.

The next morning Allen rolled Jenny out of bed well before noon, her usual Saturday starting time, and drove her down to his office. He pulled an old file to find a Chevrolet vehicle identification number. He changed a couple of digits and typed out the paperwork for a used car loan in Jenny's name in the gross amount of $2,640 with $2,500 net to borrower. He dated the check for the following Monday and instructed Jenny about when and where they would meet to cash it.

Jenny had to work Saturday night, the busiest time at the lounge. Allen hung around until closing time and took her back to his place again. He tried to persuade her to stay over Sunday. She wasn't working that night. But she insisted on going "up country" to see her parents. So the Sabbath passed more slowly for Allen than even his October weekdays.

He went to the lounge, but under local blue laws he couldn't even buy a beer on Sunday. He just sipped soda, watched a dull football game between two teams he didn't care about, and tried to avoid talking to the two other stranded customers and the gray-haired waitress who worked there on Jenny's days off.

Finally Monday came. As he had instructed her, Jenny met him at ten o'clock at the bank where his employer maintained its accounts.

"Joe," he told the branch manager, "Jenny's making a private purchase of a Chevy from a guy in Alabama, and he won't take a check. Can you cash her out?"

Joe could and did. After Allen and Jenny left the bank, he slid the money into his pocket and went back to his office, dreading the rest of the day. He handed Sherry the paperwork on the Chevrolet loan and gave her the same story he had given Joe the banker.

Processing the loan took all of twenty minutes and left a long, empty day ahead. Unfortunately Sherry tried to fill it for him, sitting in his office most of the time with her micro-miniskirt halfway up her stomach and the slack white flesh of her inner thighs shining at him like dead fish bellies. She prattled on endlessly, spouting vague generalities about the wild weekend she had spent with her mother gone, even though he was sure she hadn't shared her bed with anything more interesting than a paperback novel and a cat.

At last it was five o'clock. For the first time since Labor Day, Allen beat Sherry out of the office. He was at the Holiday Inn by 5:15. He rushed through the lobby. Clarence looked up from a mystery magazine as he passed.

"Don't get mixed up with Webb Wickersham," called the innkeeper. "He's bad news, Allen. He's been coming around here off and on for fifteen or twenty years, sometimes spending big bucks, and he ain't had an honest job the whole time. I saw you with him and his cousin or whatever he is the other night, and they're back in here now asking for you. Whatever they're up to, boy, it's bad business. Listen to me now. Stay away from them."

Clarence couldn't have known it, but he had just removed Allen's last bit of fear that Wickersham might take his money and never be seen again. If he had been coming around for fifteen years, he wouldn't leave for $2,500. Besides, he hadn't wanted Allen to put up the money in the first place.

"Don't worry, Clarence. I can take care of myself," he called over his shoulder.

But he thought, let your grandchildren bury you, rabbit; this time, I'm feasting with the foxes.

Wickersham and Billy Webb were seated at the same table as before. Jenny stood beside Wickersham's chair with her tray dangling at her side. It was early on the slowest night of the week, and there were no other customers in the lounge. Allen joined them and handed the money openly to Wickersham. The big bootlegger pocketed it without counting it.

"We'll meet you back here on Sunday to settle up," he told Allen as he got up to leave.

Allen looked at Jenny. "You working Sunday?" he asked.

"No," she replied. "Maggie James has got that shift, and as nosy as she is, with you and two strangers she'd be snooping around and telling tales. You better meet someplace else."

"She's right," said Allen. "You'd better come to my place. Can you be there by noon or so?"

The other men agreed to the time and place. They all left the bar together. As they walked through the lobby, Clarence nodded to them.

"Take care, Allen," he said as if he were just making a pleasantry.

Just before Billy drove away in a beat-up Cadillac, Wickersham rolled down the passenger window and yelled to Allen, "See you next time, boy!"

"Boy" again. Damn him. He'd show them.

The next Sunday morning Allen kept Jenny in bed until almost noon. She was just making coffee when they heard a loud knock and an unmistakable voice squawking, "Hey, Allen! You in there, boy?"

They had not dressed yet, and Allen tried to get Jenny to answer the door in the nude, to show the men how sophisticated they were. One of his "Beta Bunnies" had done that to his collector in July, and it had blown the man's mind so bad it was after Labor Day before he quit making up excuses to drop by every weekend.

Jenny just said, "Don't be silly, Allen," jerked on one of his T-shirts, and let the bootleggers in, all of them laughing at Allen as he struggled into his shorts.

The three men sat down around Allen's dinette table. Wickersham drew a roll of cash from his pocket and started to peel off bills.

"You said $2,640 would cover what you got in this? Okay. Here it is. That leaves about $7,300. Me 'n' ol' Billy got about $1,300 in sugar, corn, barrels, and a small gift to a friendly sheriff. So there's — say — $6,000 to divide. Here's your third."

He counted off another $2,000 and gave it to Allen.

"Two thousand dollars," Allen said, holding his profit in his upraised hand. "Not bad for a one-week investment of somebody else's money."

Billy laughed, and Wickersham snorted. "Hell. If me and Billy could get going right away, we could turn $15,000 into $50,000 in a month or less. But if we can't do it soon, we'll never make it."

"How's that?" Allen asked.

"If we had that kind of money, we could add more barrels, speed up production, buy a big old truck, and make a real gift to the sheriff. We could make and sell a $50,000 load and be in and out before Old Perk even knows we're there. When we got in this, we thought my friend Johnson was going to put up most of the cash, but now he's gone missing and here we are with nothing but a few thousand bucks and a few barrels. Even that beat-up little truck you helped us get is probably too hot to use again.

"See, you can't build up gradual when you're moonshining around Old Perk's territory. You have to get in and out fast or forget it. I guess it's time for us to forget it."

Allen hated to ask one more naive question, but he had to know. "Who's Old Perk, some kind of federal agent?"

Both older men laughed. Even Jenny giggled, although Allen doubted that she had any more idea who Old Perk was than he did.

"Old Perk," said Billy, "is Adam Perkinson. He's the biggest danged moonshiner on the East Coast."

"He's the biggest in the whole country," said Wickersham. "And the Carolinas are his home territory. He owns it like the mob owns Jersey. And if you're moonshining in his territory, he'll wipe you out. If you're small, he'll let you alone, not even pay any attention to you.

But if you get big enough to make some real money—" he drew his open hand across his throat like a knife.

"How would he wipe you out?" Jenny asked.

Allen noticed they didn't laugh when Jenny asked a question.

"He wouldn't do it himself," Wickersham answered. "He used to have his boys dynamite the still, maybe shoot the stillhands. But he doesn't need to take that kind of chance any more. Now he lets the sheriff do it."

"I thought you were going to buy the sheriff," said Allen.

This time Wickersham didn't laugh at Allen. He just shook his head sadly and said, "They don't stay bought. If you pay his asking price, he's got to let you get one good load out or nobody will ever do business with him again. But once you've got that one load out, he's up for bids again, and Perk can outbid us every time. Since Johnson is missing and presumed permanently unavailable, we're going to abandon ship, take our meager earnings, and get out of business."

By then Jenny had served sandwiches and coffee all around and joined them at the table. They ate in a mix of silence and small talk.

"It's been a pleasant meal, Jenny," said Wickersham. "And a pleasant venture, Allen. Now Billy and I need to take our little profit and find something better to do than push small loads of whiskey out of a few miserable barrels. And you, my boy, need to get back to helping old ladies buy Chevrolets."

"Wait a minute, Webb," said Allen. "You and Billy have $4,000. You just need $11,000 more, right?"

Webb shook his head. "No, my boy, we need $15,000. We've made little enough out of this venture. We're not risking what little there is. Unless an angel with $15,000 in his wings flies down and gives it to us, we're out of the business."

"Look, old man," said Allen, glancing at Jenny as he tried out a new way to deal with being called boy, "I think I could do it. I could roll that loan we've got on the books now and add three or four more. If you can get a load out in a month, there wouldn't be any problem. I'd want $20,000 off the top to cover the loans and my trouble. That should leave us $10,000 apiece on a one-month investment."

"No," said Wickersham. "You've made your one fast run with the foxes. Go back and sleep in the hutch where it's safe. I can't be a party to your taking that kind of risk."

"What kind of risk is there really?" asked Allen. "You said the sheriff would have to let you make one good run, and Old Perk doesn't take chances on using violence himself."

"There's always risk in every enterprise, and a lot more in an illegal one," said Wide Webb. "You get strung out on your company's money to the tune of 15,000 bucks and something goes wrong, you're done for. That's as much as they pay you in—what—two years?"

"Two and a half," said Allen. "That's why I need the $10,000 I can make in a month on this. Don't worry about me, old man, I can cover my tracks at the company. Let me get you the money and give us all a chance to make a score."

"Yeah, Webb," said Billy. "You ain't his daddy. When you and me was his age, we was already pulling off some pretty good deals."

Jenny had hopped up to get more coffee. She set the pot down, bent over, and grabbed Wickersham by the neck with both hands. She pretended to choke him.

"You give Al a chance to make some money, or you won't get any more coffee," she said.

The fat man hung his tongue out and made choking sounds. He gasped out, "I give up. I give up. If he wants to take the risk, I want to take the money. Now give me my damned coffee."

By Tuesday evening Allen had it done.

He had paid off the Chevrolet loan and entered on the books three new auto loans and a signatory note in the name of a fictitious doctor. Together the four totaled just over $17,000, with $15,000 net to the borrowers. That gave him enough to give his partners what they needed and still have $2,000 on hand to make any necessary payments on the loans if the profit was slower than expected.

Wednesday he took Webb, Billy, and Jenny around to three different branch banks to cash out the car loans. He ran the signatory loan proceeds through his own account. That was a little risky, but none of his partners looked enough like a doctor to introduce to a banker as one. Finally he gave Wickersham all the cash in return for the Wide One's assurance that he would have $50,000 in four weeks, thirty days tops.

For twenty days, Allen managed to feel pretty good. By the twenty-fifth he wasn't eating well. By the twenty-eighth he wasn't sleeping at all, worrying all night about what would happen if Webb and Billy didn't come back.

On the morning of the thirtieth day, well before sunrise, Webb Wickersham did come back. But he didn't have Billy with him, and he didn't have $50,000 to divide. He came banging on Allen's door, screaming, "Allen, let me in, boy, for God's sake, hurry!"

Allen unlocked the door, and the big man almost knocked him down rushing in. He was flushed and shaking. His breath came in great rasping pants.

"Billy's dead," he blurted out before Allen could speak. "Old Perk came in with a bunch of men while we were loading. I was off in the woods, and I hid, but they shot Billy and a black guy we had helping us load. Blew the bodies up with the still, so the sheriff won't even call it murder. Just say two stillhands got blown up with their still."

Webb's voice choked off into sobs for a moment. Allen was too shocked even to speak.

Finally he said, "What am I going to do, Webb? I've lost $15,000 of the company's money."

"To hell with money, boy. Billy's dead, and Perk's liable to kill me if he figures out that I'm in on it. You're lucky. Perk doesn't know you. I've got a thou left. Half of it's yours. I'll need the rest to run on." He handed Allen five $100 bills and patted him on the shoulder. "I've got to put some miles between me and Ol' Perk. If you keep rolling those loans over, you'll be okay in time."

He was gone as fast as he'd come.

A few hours later Allen called the office and told Sherry he was sick. She offered to close the office to come take care of him, but he ordered her not to, telling her he would be going to a doctor. Instead, he spent the day figuring.

With what Webb had given him and what he had held out of the loan proceeds, he had just enough to pay off the signatory loan and make payments on the car loans for a couple of months. If he sold his car and his equity in the cottage, he could pay off one more loan. Then he could move to a ratty apartment in town, walk to work, and by living like a miser afford payments on the other two loans.

If he did all that and it all worked as he planned, he could pay the last two loans off in three years. Even then there was the risk that someone in the company would learn of his change in lifestyle, pull a full audit on his office, and have him prosecuted for fraud or embezzlement. Even a routine audit could do it, especially if someone noticed that four recent loans all had post office box addresses.

If he rolled the loans occasionally, he could spread the payments, but the new carrying charges would make his balance bigger and leave him exposed longer. The sooner he could get the loans off the books, the better his chances of surviving undetected. He had a desperate idea. He would marry Jenny.

Not only would such a marriage give him her earnings to add to his and hurry the payout, but he thought he could cut expenses that way. He knew two couldn't really live as cheaply as one, but he figured half of two lives more cheaply than one living alone, especially since Jenny had a little efficiency apartment at the motel that Clarence let her live in dirt cheap. Allen could move in with her cheaper than anywhere he could find by himself. He drove to the inn to tell her about Webb and Billy and start selling her on the marriage idea. But as he dashed through the lobby, Clarence called out to him. "If you're looking for Jenny, she don't work here anymore."

"She, uh, she . . . you fired her?" Allen stammered.

"No," said Clarence. "I didn't fire her. She just up and quit. Come in here an hour before her shift was supposed to start and drew her pay. I had to call Maggie James in without warning. Had to pay her overtime to get her to come. You know any girl looking for a job?"

"No," said Allen. "Did Jenny say where she was going?"

"Said she was going back home," said Clarence. "But I don't believe her. I think she's taking off with Webb Wickersham."

Allen tried to sound uninterested. "Why would she leave with that ugly lump of lard?" he asked.

Clarence snorted. "No man's ugly to that little chickie when he's got a wad of money on his hip."

Allen would at least show Clarence he knew something about running with the foxes. He forced himself to laugh as he said, "Webb hasn't got any money. Ol' Perk blew up his still and killed his partner."

"His still!" Clarence hooted. "He ain't never had a still. That hasn't kept him from selling part interest in one to suckers all up and down the East Coast, but he ain't never had one."

It dawned on Allen for the first time that when foxes feast they must always invite one rabbit.

CLYDE HAYWOOD is the pseudonym of Judge David B. Sentelle of the U.S. Court of Appeals for the District of Columbia. Judge Sentelle published several short stories before his "secret identity" was disclosed by an investigative reporter for the *Legal Times* in 2003 after the publication of his nonfiction first book, *Judge Dave and the Rainbow People*, under his own name. Judge Sentelle graduated from the University of North Carolina School of Law, has practiced privately, has served as an assistant U.S. attorney in Charlotte, has taught in two law schools, and has held three judicial seats, including his current position.

MANIAC LOOSE

michael malone

Holding a yellow smiley-face coffee mug, Lucy Rhoads sat in her dead husband's bathrobe and looked at two photographs. She had just made a discovery about her recently deceased spouse that surprised her. Prewitt Rhoads—a booster of domestic sanguinity, whose mind was a map of cheerful clichés out of which his thoughts never wandered, whose monogamy she had no more doubted than his optimism—her spouse Prewitt Rhoads (dead three weeks ago of a sudden heart attack) had for years lived a secret life of sexual deceit with a widow two blocks away in the pretty subdivision of Painton, Alabama, where he had insisted on their living for reasons Lucy only now understood. This was the same man who had brought her home Mylar balloons proclaiming "I Love You," white cuddly Valentine bears making the same claims, and an endless series of these smiley-face coffee mugs—all from the gifts, cards, and party supplies shop he owned in Annie Sullivan Mall that was called The Fun House. This was the same man who had disparaged her slightest criticism of the human condition, who had continually urged her, "Lucy, can't you stop turning over rocks just to look at all the bugs crawling underneath them?"

Well, now Lucy had tripped over a boulder of a rock to see in the exposed mud below her own Prewitt Rhoads scurrying around in lustful circles with their widowed neighbor Amorette Strumlander, Lucy's mediocre Gardenia Club bridge partner for more than fifteen years; Amorette Strumlander who had dated Prewitt long ago at Painton High School, who had never lived anywhere in her life but Painton, Alabama, where perhaps for years she had sat patiently waiting, like the black widow she'd proved herself to be, until Prewitt came back to her. Of course, on his timid travels into the world beyond Painton, Alabama, Amorette's old boyfriend had picked up a wife in Charlotte (Lucy) and two children in Atlanta before returning to his hometown to open The Fun House. But what did Amorette Strumlander care about those encumbrances? Apparently nothing at all.

Lucy poured black coffee into the grimacing cup. Soon Amorette herself would tap her horn in her distinctive pattern, *honk honk honk* pause *honk honk*, to take Lucy to the Playhouse in nearby Tuscumbia so they could see *The Miracle Worker* together. Lucy was free to go because she had been forced to accept a leave of absence from her job as a town clerk at Painton Municipal Hall in order to recover from her loss. Amorette had insisted on the phone that *The Miracle Worker* would be just the thing to cheer up the grieving Mrs. Rhoads after the sudden loss of her husband to his unexpected heart attack. "I always thought it would be me," said Amorette, who'd boasted of a heart murmur since it had forced her to drop out of Agnes Scott College for Women when she was twenty and kept her from getting a job or doing any housework ever since. Apparently, Lucy noted, the long affair with Prewitt hadn't strained the woman's heart at all.

Lucy wasn't at all interested in seeing *The Miracle Worker*; she had already seen it a number of times, for the Playhouse put it on every summer in Tuscumbia, where the famous blind deaf mute Helen Keller had grown up. The bordering town of Painton had no famous people to boast of in its own long hot languid history and no exciting events either; not even the Yankees ever came through the hamlet to burn it down, although a contingent of Confederate women (including an ancestor of Amorette's) was waiting to shoot them if they did. A typical little Deep South community, Painton had run off its Indians, brought in its slaves, made its money on cotton, and then, after the War between the States, gone to sleep for a hundred years except for a few little irritable spasms of wakefulness over the decades to burn a cross or (on the other side) to send a student to march with Martin Luther King or to campaign against anything that might destroy the American Way of Life.

In its long history, Painton could claim only three modest celebrities. There was Amorette Strumlander's twice-great-grandmother who'd threatened to shoot the Yankees if they ever showed up; she'd been a maid of honor at Jefferson Davis's wedding and had attended his inauguration as president of the Confederacy in Montgomery. Fifty years later there was a Baptist missionary killed in the Congo either by a hippopotamus or by hepatitis; it was impossible for his relatives to make out his wife's handwriting on the note she'd sent from Africa. And thirty years ago there was a linebacker in an Alabama Rose Bowl victory who'd played an entire quarter with a broken collarbone.

But of course none of these celebrities could hold a candle to Helen Keller, as even Amorette admitted—proud as she was of her ancestral acquaintance of Jefferson Davis. Indeed no one loved the Helen Keller story as told by *The Miracle Worker* more than she. "You can never ever get too much of a good thing, Lucy, especially in your time of need," Mrs. Strumlander had wheedled when she'd called to pester Lucy into going to the play today. "*The Miracle Worker* shows how we can triumph over the dark days even if we're blind, deaf, and dumb, poor little thing."

Although at the very moment that her honey-voiced neighbor had phoned, Lucy Rhoads was squeezing in her fist the key to her husband's secret box of adulterous love letters from the deceptive Amorette, she had replied only, "All right, come on over, Amorette, because I'm having a real dark day here today."

Still Lucy wasn't getting ready. She was drinking black coffee in her dead husband's robe and looking at the photos she'd found in the box. She was listening to the radio tell her to stay off the streets of Painton today because there was a chance that the streets weren't safe. In general, the town of Painton didn't like to admit to problems; the motto on the billboard at the town limits proclaimed in red, white, and blue letters, "THERE'S NO PAIN IN PAINTON. THE CHEERFULEST TOWN IN ALABAMA." There was always a patrol car hidden behind this billboard with a radar gun to catch innocent strangers going thirty-six miles an hour and slap huge fines on them. If Deputy Sheriff Hews Puddleston had heard one hapless driver joke, "I thought you said there was no pain in Painton," he'd heard a thousand of them.

The local billboard annoyed Lucy, as did the phrasing of this radio warning; she thought that a town so near the home of Helen Keller had no business suggesting life was "cheerful" or that the streets were ever safe. The reporter on the radio went on to explain rather melodramatically that there was a maniac loose. A young man had gone crazy at Annie Sullivan Mall on the outskirts of Painton and

tried to kill his wife. Right now, live on the radio, this man was shooting out the windows of a florist shop in the mall, and the reporter
was outside in the atrium hiding behind a cart selling crystals and
pewter dwarves. No one was stopping the man because he had a
9mm automatic assault weapon with him, and he had yelled out the
window that he had no problem using it. The reporter had shouted
at him, "No problem," and urged the police to hurry up. The reporter
happened to be there broadcasting live at the mall because it was the
Painton Merchants Super Savers Summertime Sale for the benefit
of the Painton Panthers High School football team, 1992 state semi-
finalists, and he'd been sent to cover it. But a maniac trying to kill
his wife was naturally a bigger story, and the reporter was naturally
very excited.

Lucy turned on her police scanner as she searched around for
an old pack of the cigarettes Prewitt had always been hiding so she
wouldn't realize he'd gone back to smoking again despite his high
cholesterol. He'd never hidden them very well, not nearly as well as
his sexual escapades, and she'd constantly come across crumpled
packs that he'd lost track of. Lucy had never smoked herself and had
little patience with the members of the Gardenia Club's endless conversation about when they'd quit, how they'd quit, or why they'd quit.
But today Lucy decided to start. Why not? Why play by the rules when
what did it get you? Lighting the match, she sucked in the smoke
deeply; it set her whole body into an unpleasant spasm of coughing
and tingling nerves. She liked the sensation; it matched her mood.

On the police scanner she heard the dispatcher rushing patrol
cars to the mall. This maniac fascinated her, and she went back to
the radio, where the reporter was explaining the situation. Apparently the young man had gone to the mall to shoot his wife because
she'd left him for another man. According to the maniac's grievance
to the reporter, his wife was still using his credit cards and had been
in the midst of a shopping spree at the mall before he caught up with
her in the Hank Williams Concourse, where they'd fought over her
plan to run off with this other man and stick the maniac with the
bills. She'd fled down the concourse to the other man, who owned
a florist shop at the east end of the concourse. It was here that the
maniac caught up with her again, this time with the gun he'd run
back to his sports van to collect. He'd shot them both but, in trying

to avoid other customers, had managed only to hit the florist in the leg and to pulverize one of his wife's shopping bags. Plaster flying from a black swan with a dracaena plant in its back gouged a hole out of his wife's chin. He'd allowed the other customers to run out of the shop but held the lovers hostage.

Lucy could hear the sirens of the approaching patrol cars even on the radio. But by the time the police ran into the atrium with all their new equipment, the florist was hopping out of his shop on one foot, holding on to his bleeding leg and shouting that the husband had run out the back door. The police ran after him while the reporter gave a running commentary as if it were a radio play. As the florist was wheeled into the ambulance, he told the reporter that the maniac had "totally trashed" his shop "terminator time." He sounded amazingly high-spirited about it. The reporter also interviewed the wife as she was brought out in angry hysterics with a bandage on her chin. She said that her husband had lost his mind and had nobody but himself to blame if the police killed him. She was then driven off to the hospital with the florist.

Lucy made herself eat a tuna sandwich, although she never seemed to be hungry anymore. When she finished, the maniac was still on the loose and still in possession of the 9mm gun that he'd bought only a few months earlier at the same mall. News of the failure of the police to capture him was oddly satisfying. Lucy imagined herself running beside this betrayed husband through the streets of Painton, hearing the same hum in their hearts. The radio said that neighbors were taking care of the couple's four-year-old triplets, Greer, Gerry, and Griffin, who hadn't been told that their father had turned into a maniac in Annie Sullivan Mall. The couple's neighbors on Fairy Dell Drive were shocked; such a nice man, they said, a good provider and a family man. "I'dah never thought Jimmy'd do something like this in a million years, and you ask anybody else in Painton, they'll tell you the same," protested his sister, who'd driven to the mall to plead with her brother to come out of the florist shop but had arrived too late.

The reporter was obliged temporarily to return the station to its mellow music program, *Songs of Your Life*, playing Les Brown's Band of Renown doing "Life Is Just a Bowl of Cherries." Lucy twisted the dial to OFF. She did not believe that life was a bowl of cherries, and she never had. In her view life was something more along the lines of a barefoot sprint over broken glass. She felt this strongly, although she herself had lived a life so devoid of horror that she might easily have been tricked into thinking life was the bowl of sweet fruit that her husband Prewitt had always insisted it was. The surprised reaction of the Mall Maniac's neighbors and family annoyed her. Why *hadn't* they suspected? But then, why hadn't she suspected Prewitt and Amorette of betraying her? At least the maniac had noticed what was going on around him—that his wife was stockpiling possessions on his credit cards while planning to run off with the florist. Lucy herself had been such an idiot that when years ago she'd wanted to leave Prewitt and start her life over, he'd talked her out of it with all his pieties about commitment and family values and the children's happiness, when at the exact same time, he'd been secretly sleeping with Amorette Strumlander!

Lucy smashed the smiley mug against the lip of the kitchen counter until it broke, and her finger was left squeezed around its yellow handle as if she'd hooked a carousel's brass ring. There, that was the last one. She'd broken all the rest this morning, and she still felt like screaming. It occurred to her there was no reason why she shouldn't. She didn't have to worry about disturbing her "family" anymore.

It had been twenty-one days now since the death of the perfidious Prewitt. Last Sunday the Rhoadses' son and daughter had finally returned to their separate lives in Atlanta after rushing home to bury their father and console their mother. These two young people, whom Prewitt had named Ronny after Reagan and Julie after Andrews, took after their father, and they thought life was a bowl of cherries too, or at least a bowl of margaritas. They were affable at the funeral, chatting to family friends like Amorette Strumlander about their new jobs and new condo clusters. They liked Amorette (and had Lucy not distinctly recalled giving birth to them, she could have sworn Amorette was their mother, for like her they both were slyly jejune). Ronny and Julie were happy with their lifestyles, which they had mimicked from trendy magazines. These magazines did not explain things like how to behave at a father's funeral, and perhaps as a result Ronny and Julie had acted during the service and at the reception afterward with that convivial sardonic tolerance for the older generation that they had displayed at all other types of family functions. Amorette later told Lucy she thought "the kids held up wonderfully."

Lucy was not surprised by her children's lack of instinct for grief. Their father would have behaved the same way at his funeral had he not been the one in the casket. "The kids and I are day people," Prewitt had told his wife whenever she mentioned any of life's little imperfections like wars and earthquakes and pogroms and such. "You're stuck in the night, Lucy. That's your problem." It was true. Maybe she should have grown up in the North, where skies darkened sooner and the earth froze and the landscape turned black and gray, where there wasn't so much southern sun and heat and light and daytime. For life, in Lucy's judgment, was no daytime affair. Life was stuck in the night; daytime was just the intermission, the waiting between the acts of the real show. When she listened to police calls on the radio scanner, the reports of domestic violence, highway carnage, fire, poison, electrocution, suffocation, maniacs loose in the vicinity of Annie Sullivan Mall always struck her as what life was really about. It suddenly occurred to her that there must have been a police dispatch for Prewitt after she'd phoned 911. She'd found him by the opened refrigerator on the kitchen floor lying beside a broken bowl of barbecued chicken wings. The scanner must have said, "Apparent heart attack victim, male, Caucasian, forty-eight."

Prewitt had died without having much noticed that that's what he was doing, just as her day children had driven off with whatever possessions of Prewitt's they wanted (Ronny took his golf clubs and his yellow and pink cashmere V-necks; Julie took his Toyota) without having really noticed that their father was gone for good. If Prewitt had known he'd be dead within hours, presumably he would have destroyed the evidence of his adultery with Amorette Strumlander since marriage vows and commitment were so important to him. But apparently Prewitt Rhoads had persisted in thinking life a bowl of imperishable plastic cherries to the very last. Apparently he had never seen death coming, the specter leaping up and grinning right in his face, so he had died as surprised as he could be, eyes wide open, baffled, asking Lucy, "What's the matter with me?"

Amorette Strumlander had been equally unprepared when she'd heard about Prewitt's sudden demise from their Gardenia Club president Gloria Peters the next morning. She had run up the lawn shrieking at Lucy, "I heard it from Gloria Peters at the nail salon!" as if getting the bad news that way had made the news worse. Of course, Lucy hadn't known then that Prewitt and Amorette had been having their long affair; admittedly that fact must have made the news harder on Amorette. It must have been tough hearing about her lover's death from Gloria Peters, who had never once invited Amorette to her dinner parties, where apparently Martha Stewart recipes were served by a real maid in a uniform. In fact, that morning after Prewitt's death when Amorette had come running at her, Lucy had actually apologized for not calling her neighbor sooner. And Amorette had grabbed her and sobbed, "Now we're both widows!" Lucy naturally thought Amorette was referring to her own dead husband Charlie Strumlander, but maybe she had meant her lover Prewitt.

Honk honk honk pause *honk honk*. *Honk honk honk* pause *honk honk*.

Amazingly it was two in the afternoon, and Lucy was still standing in the middle of the kitchen with the yellow coffee mug handle still dangling from her finger. She quickly shoved the photographs she'd found in the bathrobe pocket as Amorette came tapping and whoohooing through the house without waiting to be invited in. She had never waited for Lucy to open the door.

"Lucy? Lucy, oh, why, oh, good Lord, you're not even ready. What are you doing in a robe at this time? Didn't you hear me honking?" Mrs. Strumlander was a petite woman, fluttery as a hungry bird, as she swirled around the table in a summer coat that matched her shoes and her purse. She patted her heart as she was always doing to remind people that she suffered from a murmur. "I have been scared to death with this maniac on the loose! Did you hear about that on the radio?"

Lucy said that yes she had and that she felt sorry for the young man.

"Sorry for him?! Well, you are the weirdest thing that ever lived! You come on and go get dressed before we're late to the play. I know when you see that poor little blind deaf-and-dumb girl running around the stage spelling out 'water,' it's going to put your own troubles in perspective for you, like it always does mine."

"You think?" asked Lucy flatly, and she walked back through the house into the bedroom she had shared with Prewitt. She was followed by Amorette, who even went so far as to pull dresses from Lucy's closet and make suggestions about which one she ought to wear.

"Lucy," Amorette advised her as she tossed a dress on the bed, "just because this maniac goes out of his mind at the Annie Sullivan Mall, don't you take it as proof the world's gone all wrong, because believe me most people are leading a normal life. If you keep slipping into this negative notion of yours without poor Prewitt to hold you up, you could just slide I don't know where, way deep. Now, how 'bout this nice mustard silk with the beige jacket?"

Lucy put her hand into her dead husband's bathrobe pocket. She touched the photos and squeezed the key to the secret letters into the fleshy pads of her palm. The key opened a green tin box she'd found in a little square room in the basement, a room with pine paneling and a plaid couch that Prewitt considered his special private place and called his "study." He'd gone there happily in the evenings to fix lamps and listen to vinyl big band albums he'd bought at tag sales, to do his homework for his correspondence course in Internet investing in the stock market. And, apparently, he went there to write love letters to Amorette Strumlander. Lucy had never violated the privacy of Prewitt's space. Over the years as she had sat with her black coffee in the unlit kitchen, watching the night outside, she had occasionally fantasized that Prewitt was secretly down in his study bent over a microscope in search of the origins of life or down there composing an opera or plotting ingenious crimes. But she was not surprised when, the day after her children left for Atlanta, she'd unlocked the "study" door and discovered no mysterious test tubes, no ink-splotched sheets of music, no dynamite to blow up Fort Knox.

What she had found there were toy trains and love letters. Apparently Prewitt had devoted all those nights to building a perfect plastic world for a dozen electric trains to pass through. This world rested on a large board eight feet square. All the tiny houses and stores and trees were laid out on the board on plastic earth and Astroturf. In front of a little house, a tiny dad and mom and boy and girl stood beside the track to watch the train go by. The tiny woman had blonde hair and wore a pink coat, just like Amorette Strumlander.

Lucy found the love letters in a green tin box in a secret drawer built under the board beneath the train depot. There were dozens of letters written on legal pad, on pink flowered notepaper, on the backs of envelopes, hand-delivered letters from Amorette to Prewitt, and even a few drafts of his own letters to her. They were all about love as Prewitt and Amorette had experienced it. There was nothing to suggest to Lucy that passion had flung these adulterers beyond the limits of their ordinary personalities, nothing to suggest *Anna Karenina* or *The English Patient*. No torment, no suicidal gestures. The letters resembled the Valentines Prewitt sold in his gifts, cards, and party supplies shop in downtown Painton. Lacy hearts, fat toddlers hugging, fat doves cooing. Amorette had written: "Dearest dear one. Tell Lucy you have to be at The Fun House doing inventory all Sat morn. Charlie leaves for golf at ten. Kisses on the neck." Prewitt had written: "Sweetheart, you looked so (great, stretched out) beautiful yesterday and you're so sweet to me, I couldn't get through life without my sunshine."

Beneath the letters at the bottom of the box, Lucy had found the two Polaroid pictures she now touched in the bathrobe pocket. One showed Amorette in shortie pajamas on Lucy's bed, rubbing a kitten against her cheek. (Lucy recognized the kitten as Sugar, whom Prewitt had brought home for Julie and who, grown into an obese flatulent tabby, had been run over five years ago by a passing car.) The other photograph showed Amorette seated on the hope chest in her own bedroom, naked from the waist up, one hand provocatively held beneath each untanned breast. After looking at the pictures and reading the letters, Lucy had put them back in the box, then turned on Prewitt's electric trains and sped them up faster and faster until finally they'd slung themselves off their tracks and crashed through the plastic villages and farms and plummeted to the floor in a satisfying smashup.

Now, in the bathroom listening to Amorette outside in the bedroom she clearly knew all too well, still rummaging through the closet, Lucy transferred the key and the photos from the bathrobe pocket to her purse. Returning to the bedroom, she asked Amorette, "Do you miss Prewitt much?"

Mrs. Strumlander was on her knees at the closet looking for shoes to go with the dress she'd picked out for Lucy. "Don't we all?" she replied. "But let time handle it, Lucy. Because of my murmur I have always had to live my life one day at a time as the Good Book says, and that's all any of us can do. Let's just hope this crazy man keeps on shooting people he knows and doesn't start in on strangers!" She laughed at her little joke and crawled backward out of the closet with beige pumps in her hand. "Because there are sick individuals just opening fire whenever and wherever they feel like it, and I'd hate for something like that to happen to us in the middle of *The Miracle Worker* tonight. Here, put that dress on."

Lucy put on the dress. "Have you ever been down in Prewitt's study, Amorette?"

"Ummum." The dainty woman shook her head ambiguously, patting her carefully styled blonde hair.

"Would you like to see it now?" Lucy asked her.

Amorette gave her a curious look. "We don't have time to look at Prewitt's study now, honey. We are waaay late already. Not that jacket, it doesn't go at all. Sometimes, Lucy . . . This one. Oh, you look so pretty when you want to."

Lucy followed her dead husband's mistress out to her car. Amorette called to her to come along: "Hop in now, and if you see that mall shooter, duck!" She merrily laughed.

As they drove toward the interstate to Tuscumbia through Painton's flower-edged, unsafe streets, Lucy leaned back in the green velour seat of her neighbor's Toyota (had Amorette and Prewitt gotten a special deal for buying two at once?) and closed her eyes. Amorette babbled on about how someone with no handicaps at all had used the handicapped-parking space at the Winn-Dixie and how this fact as well as the Mall Maniac proved that the South might as well be the North these days. Amorette had taken to locking her doors with dead bolts and might drop dead herself one night from the shock of the strange noises she was hearing after dark and suspected might be burglars or rapists. It was then that Lucy said, "Amorette, when did you and Prewitt start sleeping together?"

The little sedan lurched forward with a jolt. Then it slowed and slowed, almost to a stop. Pink splotched Amorette's cheeks, until they matched the color of her coat, but her nose turned as white as a sheet. "Who told you that?" she finally whispered, her hand on her heart. "Was it Gloria Peters?"

Lucy shrugged. "What difference does it make?"

"It was, wasn't it! It was Gloria Peters. She hates me."

Lucy took one of Prewitt's left-behind hidden cigarettes out of her purse and lit up. "Oh, calm down, nobody told me. I found things."

"What things? Lucy, what are you talking about? You've gotten all mixed up about something—"

Blowing out smoke, Lucy reached in her purse. She thrust in front of the driver the Polaroid picture of her younger self, flash-eyed, cupping her breasts.

Now the car bumped up on the curb, hit a mailbox, and stopped.

The two widows sat in the car on a residential avenue where oleander blossoms banked the sidewalks and honeysuckle made the air as sweet as syrup. There was no one around except a bored teenage girl in a bathing suit who rollerbladed back and forth and looked blatantly in the car window each time she passed it.

Lucy kept smoking. "I found all your love letters down in Prewitt's study," she added. "Didn't you two worry that I might?"

With little heaves Amorette shook herself into tears. She pushed her face against the steering wheel, crying and talking at the same time. "Oh Lucy, this is just the worst possible thing. Prewitt was a wonderful man, now, don't start thinking he wasn't. We never meant to hurt you. He knew how much I needed a little bit of attention because Charlie was too wrapped up in the law office to know if I had two eyes or three, much less be sympathetic to my murmur when I couldn't do the things he wanted me to."

"Amorette, I don't care to hear this," said Lucy.

But Amorette went on anyhow. "Prewitt and I were both so unhappy, and we just needed a little chance to laugh. And then it all just happened without us ever meaning it to. Won't you believe me that we really didn't want you to get yourself hurt."

Lucy, dragging smoke through the cigarette, thought this over. "I just want to know how long?"

"Wuh, what, what?" sobbed her neighbor.

"How long were you screwing my husband? Five years, ten years, till the day Prewitt died?"

"Oh, Lucy, no!" Amorette had sobbed herself into gasping hiccups that made the sound "*eeuck*." "No! *Eeuck. Eeuck*. We never . . . after Charlie died. I just didn't think that would be fair. *Eeuck. Eeuck*."

"Charlie died a year ago. We've been in Painton fifteen." Lucy squashed her cigarette butt in the unused ashtray. She flashed to an image of the maniac smashing the glass storefronts that looked out on the concourse of the shopping mall. "So, Amorette, I guess I don't know what the goddamn shit 'fair' means to you." She lit another cigarette.

Amorette shrank away, shocked and breathing hard. "Don't you talk that way to me, Lucy Rhoads! I won't listen to that kind of language in my car." Back on moral ground, she flapped her hand frantically at the thick smoke. "And put out that cigarette. You don't smoke."

Lucy stared at her. "I do smoke. I am smoking. Just like you were screwing my husband. You and Prewitt were a couple of lying shits."

Amorette rolled down her window and tried to gulp in air. "All right, if you're going to judge us—"

Lucy snorted with laughter that hurt her throat. "Of course I'm going to judge you."

"Well, then, the truth is . . ." Amorette was now nodding at her like a toy dog with its head on a spring. "The truth is, Lucy, your negativity and being so down on the world the way you are just got to Prewitt sometimes. Sometimes Prewitt just needed somebody to look on the bright side with."

Lucy snorted again. "A shoulder to laugh on."

"I think you're being mean on purpose," whimpered Amorette. "My doctor says I can't afford to get upset like this."

Lucy looked hard into the round brown candy eyes of her old bridge partner. Could the woman indeed be this obtuse? Was she as banal of brain as the tiny plastic mom down on the board waving at Prewitt's electric train? So imbecilic that any action she took would have to be excused? That any action Lucy took would be unforgivable? But as Lucy kept staring at Amorette Strumlander, she saw deep down in the pupils of her neighbor's eyes the tiniest flash of self-satisfaction, a flicker that was quickly hidden behind a tearful blink. It was a smugness as bland and benighted as Painton, Alabama's, history.

Lucy suddenly felt a strong desire to do something, and as the feeling surged through her, she imagined the maniac from the mall bounding down this residential street and tossing his gun to her through the car window. It felt as if the butt of the gun hit her stomach with a terrible pain. She wanted to pick up the gun and shoot into the eye of Amorette's smugness. But she didn't have a gun. Besides, what good did the gun do the maniac, who had probably by now been caught by the police? Words popped out of Lucy's mouth before she could stop them. She said, "Amorette, did you know that Prewitt was sleeping with Gloria Peters at the same time he was sleeping with you, and he kept on with her after you two ended things?"

"What?"

"Did you know there were pictures, naked pictures of Gloria Peters locked up in Prewitt's letter box too?"

Mrs. Strumlander turned green, actually apple green, just as Prewitt had turned blue on the ambulance stretcher after his coronary. Amorette had also stopped breathing; when she started up again, she started with a horrible-sounding gasp. "Oh, my God, don't do this, tell me the truth," she wheezed.

Lucy shook her head sadly. "I am telling the truth. You didn't know about Gloria? Well, he tricked us both. And there were some very ugly pictures I found down in the study too, things he'd bought, about pretty sick things being done to naked women. Prewitt had all sorts of magazines and videos down in that study of his. I don't think you even want to hear about what was in those videos." (There were no other pictures, of course, any more than there had been an affair with Gloria Peters. The Polaroid shot of Amorette's cupped breasts was doubtless as decadent an image as Prewitt could conceive. Every sentiment the man ever had could have been taken from one of his Mylar balloons or greeting cards.)

"Please tell me you're lying about Gloria!" begged Amorette. She was green as grass.

Instead Lucy opened the car door and stepped out. "Prewitt said my problem was I couldn't *stop* telling the truth. And this is the truth. I saw naked pictures of Gloria posing just like you'd done and laughing because she was copying your pose. That's what she said in a letter; that he'd shown her the picture of you and she was mimicking it."

"Lucy, stop. I feel sick. Something's wrong. Hand me my purse off the backseat."

Lucy ignored the request. "Actually I read lots of letters Gloria wrote Prewitt making fun of you, Amorette. You know how witty she can be. The two of them really got a laugh out of you."

Unable to breathe, Amorette shrank back deep into the seat of her car and whispered for Lucy please to call her doctor for her because she felt like something very scary was happening.

"Well, just take it one day at a time," Lucy advised her neighbor. "And look on the bright side."

"Lucy, Lucy, don't leave me!"

But Lucy slammed the door and began to walk rapidly along beside the oleander hedge. She was pulling off fistfuls of oleander petals as she went, throwing them down on the sidewalk ahead of her. The teenage girl on rollerblades came zipping close, eyes and mouth big as her skates carried her within inches of Lucy's red face. She shot by the car quickly and didn't notice that Amorette Strumlander had slumped over onto the front seat.

Lucy walked on, block after block, until the oleander stopped and lawns spread flat to the doorsteps of brick ranch houses with little white columns. A heel on her beige pump came loose, and she kicked both shoes off. Then she threw off her jacket. She could feel the maniac on the loose right beside her as she jerked at her dress until she broke the buttons off. She flung the dress to the curb. Seeing her do it, a man ran his power mower over his marigold beds, whirring out pieces of red and orange. Lucy unsnapped her bra and tossed it on the man's close-cropped emerald green grass. She didn't look at him, but she saw him. A boy driving a pizza van swerved toward her, yelling a war whoop out his window. Lucy didn't so much as turn her head, but she took off her panty hose and threw them in his direction.

Naked in her panties, carrying her purse, she walked on until the sun had finished with its daytime tricks and night was back. She walked all the way to the outskirts of Helen Keller's hometown.

When the police car pulled up beside her, she could hear the familiar voice of the scanner dispatcher on the radio inside, then a flashlight was shining in her eyes and then Deputy Sheriff Hews Puddleston was covering her with his jacket. He knew Lucy Rhoads from the Painton Town Hall, where she clerked. "Hey, now," he said. "You can't walk around like this in public, Mrs. Rhoads." He looked at her carefully. "You all right?"

"Not really," Lucy admitted.

"You had something to drink? Some kind of pill maybe?"

"No, Mr. Puddleston, I'm sorry, I've just been so upset about Prewitt, I just, I just . . ."

"Shhh. It's okay," he promised her.

At the police station back in Painton, they were handcuffing a youngish bald man to the orange plastic seats. Lucy shook loose of her escort and went up to him. "Are you the one from the shopping mall?"

The handcuffed man said, "What?"

"Are you the one who shot his wife? Because I know how you feel."

The man tugged with his handcuffed arms at the two cops beside him. "She crazy?" he wanted to know.

"She's just upset. She lost her husband," the desk sergeant explained.

Prewitt's lawyer had Lucy released within an hour. An hour later Amorette Strumlander died in the hospital of the heart defect that Gloria Peters had always sarcastically claimed was only Amorette's trick to get out of cleaning her house.

Three months afterward, Lucy had her hearing for creating a public disturbance by walking naked through the streets of Painton, the cheerfulest town in America. It was in the courtroom across the hall from the trial of the Mall Maniac, so she did finally get to see the young man. He was younger than she'd thought he'd be, ordinary-looking, with sad, puzzled eyes. She smiled at him, and he smiled back at her, just for a second, then his head turned to his wife, who by now had filed for divorce. His wife still had the scar on her chin from where the plaster piece of the swan had hit her in the florist shop. The florist sat beside her, holding her hand.

Testifying over his lawyer's protest that he'd tried to kill his wife and her lover but had "just messed it up," the maniac pleaded guilty. So did Lucy. She admitted she was creating as much of a public disturbance as she could. But unlike the maniac's, her sentence was suspended, and afterward the whole charge was erased from the record. Prewitt's lawyer made a convincing case to a judge (who also knew Lucy) that grief at her husband's death, aggravated by the shock of the car accident from which her best friend was to suffer a coronary, had sent poor Mrs. Rhoads wandering down the sidewalk in "a temporarily irrational state of mind." He suggested that she might even have struck her head on the dashboard, that she might not even have been aware of what she was doing when she "disrobed in public." After all, Lucy Rhoads was an upright citizen, a city employee, and a decent woman, and if she'd gone momentarily berserk and exposed herself in a nice neighborhood, she'd done it in a state of emotional and physical shock. Prewitt's lawyer promised she'd never do it again. She never did.

A few months later, Lucy went to visit the maniac at the state penitentiary. She brought him a huge box of presents from the going-out-of-business sale at The Fun House. They talked for a while, but conversation wasn't easy, despite the fact that Lucy not only felt they had a great deal in common but also thought she could have taught him a lot about getting away with murder.

MICHAEL MALONE is one of North Carolina's most successful writers, among both critics and readers. His range is immense. He has written mainstream novels, comic novels, short stories, and mysteries. He was head writer for the soap opera *One Life to Live* for many years. He's won both an Edgar and an Emmy. His mystery series, set in a fictional North Carolina town resembling Hillsborough, features "two of the most memorable detectives ever to appear in mystery fiction" (Cuddy Mangum and Justin Savile V), according to the *New York Times Book Review*. Malone, a native North Carolinian who graduated from the University of North Carolina at Chapel Hill, lives and writes in Hillsborough.

BEAUTY IS ONLY SKIN DEEP

Gallagher Gray

"Absolutely not." There was no way T.S. would relinquish the wheel to Auntie Lil. Fat flakes of snow whipped against the windshield and dark clouds above promised more. Besides, she never drove more than twenty-five miles an hour. At that rate, it would take them a week to get to Highland Lake Lodge.

"I'm an excellent driver," Auntie Lil protested. She crossed her arms firmly and glared out the window. The trouble with Auntie Lil was that, at age eighty-four, she was not only a horrible driver herself but firmly convinced that everyone else was much worse.

"You owe me one for this weekend," T.S. said, ignoring her sulking.

She ignored him. "A mystery weekend jaunt will be fun for both of us. We can relive old glory."

"I don't see how a bunch of bad actors screaming lousy dialogue can ever approach solving the real thing." An unwelcome fantasy unfolded before him: suppose he was trapped in a blizzard with an entire houseful of Auntie Lils? It was enough to make him turn around and speed home to New York City.

"Besides," Auntie Lil added. "We had to come. I promised Clarabelle. I believe we are part of the draw. That's why we attend for free."

Oh Lord, it really had to be a low-rent crowd if they were the celebrities, T.S. thought grimly as he steered his way through the storm.

The snow was approaching blizzard proportions by the time they neared Highland Lake, making the steep ascent perilous and Auntie Lil's attempts at backseat driving all the more maddening. The town was no more than an intersection marking the final crest of a mountain overlooking the Delaware River. Following Clarabelle's directions, they passed a small community of deserted summer homes blanketed with snow, then turned left down a narrow road. They abruptly came upon a converted Victorian house that was splendid

in its overgrown majesty. A porch wrapped around the entire structure, and snow-dusted bushes grew wildly over the carved wooden
railings. Through a large bay window, a cozy sitting and smoking
room could be seen, complete with crackling fire.

"I see my room," T.S. remarked cheerfully as he helped Auntie Lil
up the steps. Ice made the going slippery, and he was forced to perform several heroic maneuvers in order to preserve his elderly aunt's
dignity.

"I can't think why they don't have someone to help the guests,"
Auntie Lil muttered as she grabbed a fence post to keep from tum-
bling ass over teakettle.

Before they could ring the bell, the door was opened by a small
woman with impossibly orange hair. She was in her early fifties and
dressed in a purple leotard topped by an elaborately embroidered
blue vest. She collapsed into raptures at the sight of Auntie Lil. "You
made it!" she squealed in a babyish voice that made Marilyn Monroe
sound like a truck driver with congestion. "I knew you would come
through for me."

"Neither rain nor sleet nor snow nor . . ." Auntie Lil began.

"I'm T.S. Hubbert, Lillian's nephew," T.S. interrupted, before
Auntie Lil moved on to quoting Tennyson.

"I'm Clarabelle Clarke," their hostess replied, leading them into
a huge hallway with the highest ceilings they had ever seen in their
lives. A curving stairway led upward past a wide landing to a three-
sided balcony area that served as the second-floor hallway. Huge
oil portraits of dour ancestors crowded the walls. Dozens of sour
expressions caught the casual observer in a cross fire of ancient
grumpiness.

"Are these all yours?" Auntie Lil inquired faintly.

"Of course not. But don't they just lend the place the most fabulously rich and exotic aura?" Clarabelle spread her arms wide and
breathed deeply.

Uh-oh. Clarabelle was heavy into aura, T.S. deduced. He hoped
her enthusiasms would not rub off on his aunt over the weekend.
Auntie Lil didn't need anything remotely New Age in her life. A dose
of Old Age would be far more appropriate. She was impossible to
control as it was.

Their one tantalizing glimpse of a cheerful sitting room hurried both T.S. and Auntie Lil through the unpacking. Before long, they were ensconced in a cozy sitting room, warming themselves by a fire while they waited for other guests to arrive.

"Who else will be here? Where are the actors?" Auntie Lil looked about as if hoping a body might tumble from the cupboard.

"Unfortunately, we've had quite a few cancellations," Clarabelle explained, "because of the weather. A few have already arrived, however. Technically, it's cheating to know in advance because that's part of the game—figuring out who's a guest and who's an actor. But just between us, the guests already here include two elderly sisters, Dotty and Agnes Baird; Mr. Charles Little, a retired gentleman; Donald and Marion Travers, he's the real estate mogul; and Dr. Sussman, a well-known Park Avenue dermatologist who is napping at the moment."

"Donald Travers?" T.S. asked, mystified. "That's a surprise." Travers was the last person T.S. had expected.

Clarabelle looked smug. "I know his wife. A lovely woman. He brought her here for the weekend as an anniversary gift. I better go see how they're doing." She scurried away so quickly that T.S. was left wondering if Clarabelle was angling for an infusion of capital into her bed-and-breakfast from the famed Donald Travers.

"There you are. Hiding from us, I see." This booming voice was followed into the room by a woman in her early sixties who looked like a domesticated Gertrude Stein. Her nose was prominent and shaped like a fat banana, her eyes were exceedingly large and somewhat protruding, and her cheeks hung down in pronounced pouches. She bore down on T.S. as inevitably as a steamer.

"T.S. Hubbert," he said quickly, extending his hand. It was crushed in a powerful grip.

"I'm Dotty Baird." The large woman laughed as if this were a tremendous joke.

"Is it safe, Dotty? Can I come in?" The second voice from the hall was soft and tentative.

"Oh, for God's sake," Dotty broadcast in reply. "They aren't going to kill the paying guests. Of course it's safe." She dropped her voice and explained. "My sister Agnes has quite an imagination. She gets carried away."

Agnes had a headful of wiry gray curls springing about in every direction. Her general air of unconscious distraction was enhanced by the too-large cardigan sagging about her shoulders. "Are you a guest or an actor?" she asked Auntie Lil excitedly. "You look a lot like a fat Lillian Gish."

Astonishingly enough, Auntie Lil took this as a compliment. "Me?" she said in a pleased voice. "Well, actually . . ."

"Now, now," Dotty interrupted. "You can't just ask if a person is a guest. You have to figure it out or you're cheating and you know it."

"I know one person who is not a guest," Agnes declared in small triumph.

"Who is that?" Auntie Lil asked politely.

"Maria Taylor. She's going to be here this weekend." Agnes beamed in awe. "She's famous for having the most beautiful skin on television. I can't wait to see it up close."

Auntie Lil's eyebrows raised briefly. She clearly had no earthly idea who Maria Taylor was. T.S. knew but could not admit it without also admitting that he watched soap operas. He wisely decided to keep silent.

Dotty grabbed Agnes by an elbow. "Come on, dear. We've got to get a jump on everyone. Let's look for clues." She led the way out of the sitting room, nearly bowling over Clarabelle, who had an expensive-looking couple in tow.

"May I present our honored guests for the weekend, Mr. and Mrs. Donald Travers," Clarabelle gushed, clearly in awe of their net worth, if not their aura.

Donald Travers ignored everyone. He ambled over to a window and stared morosely at the falling snow. He was trim as only a man with access to racquetball courts and a private gym can be, with a face so completely tanned that it looked as though it had been burnished with walnut oil. Marion Travers proved more gracious than her husband and nodded at Auntie Lil as she made her way to an empty seat by the fire. She was fashionably slim but possessed a sweet face, with kind eyes and gentle features. Her hair was a becoming silver gray, and whether or not it had been treated to produce that color, the overall effect was more in keeping with her age than could be said for her husband's suspiciously blond hue.

"We're off to a roaring start," T.S. whispered to Auntie Lil as he sipped his drink. "What have you gotten us into?"

Auntie Lil smacked his hand lightly. "You must admit that there are far worse places to be in the midst of a snowstorm."

She was right. The fire crackled merrily in the hearth, the bar was well stocked, and, outside, a terrible blizzard raged. T.S. snagged a chair by the fire and dozed off in hopeful anticipation of, at the very least, a decent dinner. He awoke to find the sitting room full of occupants. The weekend had begun.

A bored-looking butler lounged against one wall without even a pretense at working. He took out a pocket watch and exclaimed, "What? What's this, I say?" in an utterly wretched British accent. Suddenly, a girl dressed as a French maid charged into the room with a tray of champagne and nearly plowed down Auntie Lil. She apologized profusely and went careening off in another direction.

T.S. removed himself to a safer spot behind the bar, but Auntie Lil dragged one of the armchairs into the middle of the room and sat down in the flow of traffic. She beamed at everyone and waited for the real action to begin.

An elderly gentleman with a head as oval and smooth as an egg grinned at Auntie Lil from the doorway. The reflection of flames danced over a backdrop of his slick pink scalp. A few tufts of white hair about the top of the ears gave evidence to earlier glory. His tie was wide and orange, with a hula dancer painted on it. He flipped it flirtatiously at Auntie Lil when she made the mistake of glancing his way.

Auntie Lil stood abruptly and joined T.S. at the bar. "Be a darling and make me a Bloody Mary, will you, Theodore? Champagne isn't nearly quick enough."

T.S. hid his smile and went to work. The old fellow was Charles Little, he remembered Clarabelle explaining. A retired gentleman. Well, Mr. Charles Little would just have to take a number and get in line behind the rest of Auntie Lil's unrequited suitors. Auntie Lil was so full of life that elderly men surrounded her like beggars at a temple, hoping some of her joie de vivre might rub off.

An imperceptible humming filled the room as the weekend's star arrived. In person, Maria Taylor was smaller than expected. But the familiar dark eyes were there, flashing in a catlike face. She had a mane of black hair, arched brows, and thin red lips. She smiled, revealing a row of tiny teeth so feral and sharp that T.S. half expected her to drop to her knees, seize his trousers in her teeth, and shake him into submission.

It would have been entirely in character for her to have done so. Maria Taylor played a vixen, as the entertainment magazines so politely put it. Every day for an hour, in living rooms across America, she schemed, plotted, lied, cheated, and killed. All the world loved to hate her, and she reveled in her image. She surveyed the assembled guests and asked in a bored voice, "What must one do to get a drink around here?"

T.S. offered his services and was roped into making a complicated concoction involving milk and three kinds of liqueur. He was soon sorry he had asked.

"Let the games begin," Maria Taylor said, raising her frothy green drink in salute.

With impeccable timing, a thin and extraordinarily pale man appeared in the doorway. "How do you do," he announced, with a slight bow. "My name is Dr. Ronald Sussman."

His mannerisms were so flamboyant that, had Auntie Lil and T.S. not known he was the real thing, it would have been impossible to say whether Dr. Ronald Sussman was a guest or an actor. His voice fluttered as if a vocal cord had snapped loose. He mixed a drink, all the while darting his eyes around the room, toting up people like prices on a cash register. He sipped his drink speculatively, then raised his eyebrows in approval as he spotted a suitable conversational partner.

Marion Travers, wife of the Wall Street millionaire and an heiress in her own right, according to all press reports, was sitting by the fire, apart from the others. Dr. Sussman pulled a stool up by her feet. "You have incredible skin," he told her. "The skin of a goddess. I feel it's my duty to help you protect that gift." His enraptured expression focused on her face. "I can tell you take excellent care of your body."

"I eat no meat or dairy products," she said, returning to her book.

"Even the most perfect of complexions must be protected," the dermatologist declared. He leaned closer. She shifted her leg away from him and ignored his comment. "I have a fabulous skin care system," the doctor continued. "I developed it myself. Some of the most beautiful women in the world swear by it. Their wrinkles disappear virtually overnight."

"I believe in inner beauty, doctor," Marion Travers said brusquely. "I'm not ashamed of my wrinkles. God knows I've earned them."

"I would be happy to give you some free samples," Dr. Sussman persisted smoothly. "After all, someone of your social standing could do me a lot of good. Help me attract more clients."

"It doesn't appear to me that you need any more patients," Mrs. Travers said. "I understand you're responsible for Miss Taylor's skin, and isn't it supposed to be the most beautiful on television?" The glare she sent the actress was quite out of character, as was the alarmed look that Maria Taylor returned.

"Then you've heard of me," the doctor insisted. "Perhaps some of your close friends rely on me to enhance their own inner beauty, shall we say?"

"Dr. Sussman—" Marion Travers put her book down. "I like the way I look. I have no intention of wasting three hours a day slathering overpriced oils and creams on my face. Please go away."

"Honestly," T.S. thought, inching toward the bar. "I'm not the only one around here who could use a drink."

Suddenly, a young girl dressed in a shimmering green evening gown dashed into the middle of the room. Her face was contorted in fury, and she held a small pistol in her hand. She cast a murderous gaze at Maria Taylor. "I hate you, but I can't kill you!" she screamed at the star, collapsing in a heap on the rug. The gun flew across the carpet, and the fake butler retrieved it, tossing it carelessly on top of a bookshelf. The young girl burst into enthusiastic sobs, her face buried in the folds of her green dress. T.S. wondered whether her shoulders were shaking from actual tears or from helpless laughter at how silly the guests were to watch this nonsense.

"She's ruined him for life," the young actress sobbed. "The only man I'll ever love! Now he'll never marry me!"

The assembled crowd watched the proceedings with expressions ranging from delight to suspicion. Auntie Lil looked confused, but the sisters quickly produced notebooks and feverishly scrawled information. The elderly man, Charles Little, placed his empty glass at his feet and clasped his hands, his face shining with excitement.

"I haven't a clue as to what the little snip is talking about," Maria Taylor said, rising majestically from her chair. But just as she started across the room, the young girl flung herself at the older actress, grabbing her around the ankles. It was a dangerous improvisation. Maria Taylor produced a hiss that could never have been faked, then unceremoniously dragged the girl toward the door. The green evening dress zigzagged across the blue rug like a trout being brought to shore.

The exit was further spoiled by the arrival of an enormous maid, who fixed the actresses with an uncomprehending stare that T.S. deeply understood. "Dinner is served," she announced, shaking her head in amazement. "If you can tear yourselves away from all this excitement, that is."

Despite the welcome arrival of personality in the form of the no-nonsense maid, dinner was a resumption of the tepid plot unfurled in the sitting room earlier. The assembled guests ate nervously, unsure if or when the plot might once again explode. All was quiet until just after the main course, when the young actress, apparently deciding that the guests' digestive tracts had enjoyed enough of a headstart, gave a shriek and stood, swaying dramatically against her chair. She clutched her throat and screamed, "She's poisoned me! She's poisoned me!"

Maria Taylor rose from her chair, eyes flashing as she stared haughtily into the distance. "Rubbish." She dismissed the girl with a wave. "Simple indigestion. I'd never be so indiscreet. I won't listen to any more nonsense."

"Hear! Hear!" T.S. wanted to agree, but before he could follow this impulse, Maria Taylor swept from the room and headed upstairs, leaving the girl to swoon to the floor. Unsure of the protocol, guests crowded around and stared down at the inert body. Only Donald Travers remained at his seat, staring sourly at the dessert before him.

When no one stepped forward to take the lead, Clarabelle intervened. "That's it," she announced loudly, clapping her hands. "Murder most foul. And, if any of you can sleep tonight, we'll get started solving it tomorrow."

T.S. fled to his room as soon as was decently possible, noticing with amusement that Auntie Lil gave him a wide berth. She was in no mood for a round of "I told you so's." He dressed carefully in his favorite silk pajamas. He'd get his revenge on Auntie Lil, he vowed, then amused himself with several possible scenarios as he lay awake in the darkness, drifting off to sleep. Before long he was oblivious to anything but a delicious dream in which he lay beneath a pristine Caribbean sky, the hot sun baking his winter-weary bones as he sipped an endless supply of rum funnies.

His fantasy was shattered by a reverberating gunshot that echoed like deep thunder through the house. Within seconds a pounding threatened to lift his door from the hinges.

"Theodore!" Auntie Lil demanded. "Open up."

He stumbled to the doorway, groggy with sleep. "This is too much," he protested. "They should let the guests sleep."

"This can't be the play," Auntie Lil said sharply, drawing him into the hall. "I feared something like this might happen."

"Like what?" T.S. asked. He tried a light switch. It did not work. "Was that thunder and lightning? The power is off."

"It was murder," she said. "Real murder. Follow me." Doors opened as they passed, sleepy faces peeking out in bewilderment. They acquired a small parade of confused guests by the time they reached the far side of the staircase.

"What's going on?" Auntie Lil demanded.

"The power's out," Clarabelle wailed from the darkness. "And I heard a gunshot. A gunshot in my own home!" She was waving a small flashlight wildly in her nervousness. In front of her, a tall figure bent down in the shadows, fiddling at the lock of a closed door.

"It's locked," the figure announced. It was the fluttery voice of Dr. Ronald Sussman.

"The gunshot sounded like it was right outside my room," Clarabelle cried. "The doctor is on the other side of me, so it has to be this room."

"Whose room is it?" Auntie Lil demanded.

"Maria Taylor's," Clarabelle said, her cry escalating into a wail. "She won't answer our knocks."

"Open up!" Dr. Sussman shouted, pounding vigorously on the door. He stepped aside. "You try it," he ordered T.S.

T.S. took up the challenge, turning the knob, lifting and pushing, jiggling and shoving, all in vain.

"Oh, get out of the way," the doctor ordered again, and T.S. backed off. Dr. Sussman stepped back until he was pressed against the second-floor railing, then hurled himself against the door. It flew open with a wrenching crack as the lock plate gave way. The doctor dashed through a small sitting room into the back. He returned to the hallway within seconds. "Give me your flashlight!" he ordered Clarabelle, snatching it from her hands. "Keep everyone back," he told T.S. and Auntie Lil. "There's trouble. Call an ambulance. Now!"

The others shrank back and stared in horror as he shut the door in their faces.

"Call," Auntie Lil told T.S., pushing him gently toward the steps. "Pray the phone lines are still up. And call the police at the same time."

"What should we do?" Agnes asked, her voice breaking. "Dorothy, I'm scared."

"Do nothing," Auntie Lil ordered. "Stay here. I'm going in. I'll see if the doctor needs any help. And keep this door open. The poor woman may need air. Clarabelle, stop that crying! Take charge of the crowd."

Auntie Lil marched back into the darkness of the suite, determined not to let the doctor bully her. The smell of cordite hung heavy in the air, and it took her eyes a few seconds to adjust to the deeper darkness of the inner room. Dr. Sussman was bent over the bed, gazing down at the lifeless figure of Maria Taylor. His delicate fingers probed beneath her throat, searching for a pulse.

"What are you doing here?" he asked brusquely. "This is no place for amateurs."

"I came to see if you needed help," Auntie Lil explained. "I can hold the flashlight for you."

"It's no use," he told Auntie Lil abruptly. "She's beyond help. Gunshot through the temple."

Auntie Lil was not surprised. She went to work examining the room. Maria Taylor had occupied a spacious suite with windows opening onto the back lawn. Auntie Lil checked the frames for signs of forced entry. They were firmly locked from the inside with heavy old-fashioned brass half-moons. She stared into the backyard. The blizzard had stopped, and a heavy blanket of snow coated the lawn in one unending and undisturbed blanket. No footprints at all. Above, the clouds had cleared and a nearly full moon shone down, reflecting off the snow. Auntie Lil drew open the curtains, and enough moonlight entered the room to allow her to get a better look at the scene.

A huge canopied bed was sumptuously covered with a ruffled pink satin comforter that cascaded to the floor on one side. Across the sheets, sprawled so dramatically that she might have been styled by a photographer, lay Maria Taylor. Her famous black hair fanned out around her upturned face in luxuriant snakes of dark color. Her arms were outstretched, and her mouth was slightly open. She was clad in a luminescent white dressing gown that pooled around her in shimmering waves and revealed a matching slip.

Dr. Sussman opened one of her eyes with his thumb and forefinger, then gazed into her pupil. "It's just happened," he said confidently. He examined her face. "The wound goes right through the forehead. There's absolutely no question about it."

"Well, then, for God's sake, get out of this room and stop contaminating the evidence," Auntie Lil answered briskly.

The doctor glanced at Auntie Lil. "I apologize, but I took an oath to save lives and fulfilling that oath is my first priority. I had an obligation to see if I could help. I assure you I touched nothing."

"Well, now that you know you can't help," Auntie Lil said sensibly, "get out and stop spoiling things for the police."

Dr. Sussman snapped his black bag shut, annoyed. "It's a suicide, you silly old bat. This isn't one of those dismal murder mystery games."

Auntie Lil looked him over quietly. "That's all the more reason to let the police take over," she said.

The doctor had been outflanked. He marched from the room, head held high, and slammed the door pointedly behind him.

This was just what Auntie Lil had hoped. Scurrying over to the bedside, she examined the actress, gently stroking her face and noting that the skin was already cooling. Without makeup, Maria Taylor's celebrated beauty was decidedly pedestrian. Fine wrinkles spread out like miniature fans from the corner of each eye. Heavy lines traced from each side of her nose to the edges of her too-thin lips. Her famed complexion looked splotchy and reddened by death. And it was indeed a fresh bullet wound: small, deadly, and perfectly placed in the center of the forehead like a Brahmin's mark. How odd that so precise and neat a hole could destroy a life. But where was the gun? Auntie Lil lifted the edge of the comforter where it had slipped to the floor. There, deep beneath the folds of satin, lay a flat gray gun. She touched it with the tip of her elbow. It was still warm. No sense leaving fingerprints, not with this crowd. They'd read clues into everything.

Which wasn't a bad idea at all. Auntie Lil hurriedly detoured into the closet, where she discovered a small box containing a spectacular jewelry assortment, including a costly diamond necklace and bracelet set. The actress had not been robbed. She quickly scanned the bathroom as well, where a collection of cold cream and beauty jars on the windowsill drew her attention. She examined the labels in the bright moonlight, chose two, and slipped them into the enormous pockets of her housecoat.

T.S. was waiting for her by the door. "What were you doing?" he hissed. "The police and ambulance are on their way."

"Never mind what I was doing," she murmured, looking up at the crowd huddled in the darkness. "The doctor is right," Auntie Lil announced. "Maria Taylor is dead."

"Dead?" someone called out. "How?"

"Suicide," Dr. Sussman said sadly. "The graceless exit of yet another aging actress. The gun is right there by the bed where it slipped from her hand." He shook his head sadly. "Such a waste of talent and beauty."

"An actual death," Charles Little said with reverence.

"I've never seen a real dead body," Agnes ventured.

"Me either," Dotty agreed. "It would be so interesting to—"

"No," Auntie Lil said firmly. "Absolutely not. We must not disturb the scene."

"She's quite right," Dr. Sussman agreed. "Perhaps we should guard it against curiosity seekers. I am used to such things. I shall be glad to wait by her bedside until the police arrive."

"Theodore, go with him," Auntie Lil said. "Don't argue. Just do it."

T.S. knew better than to debate. He followed the doctor inside, taking a position by the window where he could gaze out at the clean snow and forget that a suddenly still life force was lying void on the bed before him.

After a moment, the doctor excused himself and almost ran to the bathroom. T.S. could hear the sounds of repeated flushing. Thank God he wasn't that squeamish himself. And Sussman was a doctor.

Outside in the hallway, the assembled guests waited anxiously. The maid had appeared with a Coleman lantern. Clarabelle hovered beside her, her bright orange hair bulging at odd angles where the pouf had been flattened on one side from a pillow. Mr. Little crept toward the beacon, blinking like a baby owl in the glare from the lamp. He had obviously fallen asleep in his clothes, and his vest had fallen open to reveal a large red wine stain spread across the breast of his white shirt like a pool of blood. The sisters stared at it with keen interest and exchanged glances that threatened to erupt into accusations.

A distraction averted such a disaster. The door opposite the murder scene opened, and Donald Travers, Wall Street mogul, appeared with suitcases clasped in each hand. He ignored the crowd and called back into his room. "I said, let's go. I didn't come here for the weekend to get tangled in this nonsense."

"I'm not leaving with you," a determined voice answered. Marion Travers appeared in the doorway of her room and stared at her husband.

"This place is dangerous," her husband said. "I forbid you to stay."

"No." Her voice grew in confidence as she surveyed the many onlookers. "I refuse to leave with you. If you pursue the matter, I will start screaming."

"What?" Travers stared down at his wife. So did everyone else. The thought of the proper Marion Travers screaming was startling indeed.

"If you so much as move one more step closer to me, I'm going to start screaming." She opened her mouth silently, as if practicing.

Auntie Lil butted in with little hesitation. "Could I be of assistance?" she asked Mrs. Travers.

"Yes, thank you. I would like someone to remove my things from the room I am currently sharing with my husband," she replied with quiet dignity. "You may put them in Clarabelle's room, if you like. I'll wait there for the police."

"Stop this nonsense at once, Marion. You're coming with me." Donald Travers looked around, challenging anyone to interfere.

Auntie Lil parked herself directly in front of Mrs. Travers. "We won't let you take her anywhere against her will," Auntie Lil declared firmly. "In fact, I don't think it's a good idea for anyone to leave until the police get here. Perhaps it would be best if we all gathered together in the dining room to wait."

The thrust of her strong jaw and the glint in her eye dared anyone to disagree. Slowly the group began to trudge down the stairs, exchanging theories in low voices. Auntie Lil followed behind them, peeking out each window as she passed, examining the snow for fresh tracks. When they passed the sitting room, she popped in for a few seconds, emerging with a satisfied look.

They gathered in silence in the dining room, taking their places around the large table and gratefully accepting mugs of hot tea from the maid. Sipping in silence, they eyed one another suspiciously until the doorbell finally rang. The maid hurried to answer it as tension in the room rose palpably.

A burly man in a heavy down jacket appeared in the doorway. A gold badge was pinned to the lapel of his coat, and he wore a sheriff's hat pushed back on a graying crew cut. Behind him, a small group of uniformed men stood holding battery-operated lanterns, as if they were a particularly mature group of Halloween trick-or-treaters.

"Who's in charge?" the sheriff asked in a growl.

No one answered. "In that case, I am," he announced. "Everyone stay in their seats. Who was injured?"

"Not injured—dead!" Agnes cried out and other voices joined in.

The sheriff efficiently dispatched several officers and the ambulance crew to Maria Taylor's room. Soon T.S. and Dr. Sussman joined their fellow guests in the dining area. The sheriff nodded for them to be seated. As soon as everyone was still, he placed two lanterns in the center of the table, making them all look spectacularly guilty, their faces alternately shrouded in darkness or glare.

He waved an arm expectantly. "Who's the person who phoned me?"

"I am," T.S. admitted.

"Then start," the sheriff ordered.

"But I saw the body first," Dr. Sussman interrupted. "I was lying awake, unable to sleep, when I heard a gunshot. The sound was unmistakable. I met Miss Clarke here in the hallway"—he nodded toward Clarabelle—"and together we ascertained where the shot had come from. As these people can attest, the outer door to Miss Taylor's room was locked, and I was forced to break it down. She had clearly committed suicide. The gun is lying right by the bed."

The silence that descended on the room after this seemingly inarguable synopsis was interrupted when Auntie Lil rose from her chair and pointed to the doctor. "That man," she announced calmly, "is a murderer. And I can prove it."

The room erupted in murmurs, and Dr. Sussman raised his hands in a gesture of friendly helplessness. "Officer, this is a murder mystery weekend," he explained. "Everyone's imagination is on overdrive, shall we say. I'm afraid you'll find your progress hampered by all kinds of theories. Please don't hold it against this nice woman." He smiled kindly at Auntie Lil.

"Wipe that smirk off your face, you cold-hearted killer," Auntie Lil retorted. "And don't you dare patronize me."

"This is ridiculous," Dr. Sussman said, looking to the sheriff for help. "I was in my room when the gunshot occurred. Everyone saw me. The door was locked. I can't possibly have killed her."

The sheriff stood mutely between them, content to watch the play unfold. Several officers entered the room and were directed to stand around the table.

"You most certainly did kill her," Auntie Lil snapped back. "But not with the gun." She took two round bottles of face cream from her pocket and slammed them down on the table. Everyone jumped. "You killed her with these."

The sheriff stared at the objects. "Please continue," he said calmly.

"Maria Taylor is supposed to have the finest skin on television," Auntie Lil explained. "Yet when I examined her right after her death, her skin was red and splotchy."

"Did you happen to notice the gunshot through her head?" the doctor interrupted, his voice tight with anger.

"There was a gunshot wound, all right," Auntie Lil agreed. "But Maria Taylor was dead well before she was shot. I touched her skin. She had started to cool. She'd been dead for at least an hour."

"So now you're a pathologist?" Dr. Sussman challenged.

"Let her continue," the sheriff ordered.

Auntie pointed toward the beauty jars. "These are the murder weapons," she insisted. "If you let me, I can explain."

"Continue," the sheriff said.

"I knew at once it had not been a suicide," Auntie Lil said, "because of the body's temperature. But murder? Only by an outsider. It would have been impossible for anyone to shoot Maria Taylor and return to their room in time without being noticed by another guest. Yet when I checked the snow all around the house, it was undisturbed. No one had entered. So that left only one explanation: events had not happened as they seemed. A murder had been staged after all. I had to figure out how—and why—Maria Taylor had really been murdered."

"This is ridiculous." The doctor rolled his eyes and stood. "Is everyone going to get a chance to play this game?"

"Shut up and sit down," the sheriff ordered. Dr. Sussman quickly complied.

"There were plenty of oddities to consider," Auntie Lil went on. "For example, traveling here this weekend was quite difficult, yet everyone made an effort to get here. My nephew and I came simply because we had promised Clarabelle. But why had the others traveled through sleet and snow to get here? And why had Maria Taylor agreed to take the part in the first place? No offense, Clarabelle, dear. But what was the doctor doing here—he thought the whole idea 'dismal'? Or Mr. Travers, who clearly thought it beneath him?"

"I resent the insinuation," Donald Travers said.

Auntie Lil eyed him carefully and continued. "The staged mystery was really very silly. People drank too much, the acting was wretched, and we all retired early in defense. The alcohol, the fatigue, the weather all combined to encourage heavy sleeping. No one heard a door opened here or there, no one heard footsteps in the hall. No one heard the murder being committed—because it all happened hours before the gunshot rang out." She stopped and glanced around the table. "The gunshot was merely to establish an alibi for Dr. Sussman here, who had decided to murder the wrong woman. And he's not the only murderer among us."

"What do you mean?" one of the sisters asked.

"I believe that Miss Taylor had recently started an affair," Auntie

Lil answered. "An affair with a very rich man. I'm speaking, of course, of Donald Travers. There can be no other credible explanation for his presence here."

The millionaire rose from his chair and stared at Auntie Lil. She shrugged. "It will be quite easy to prove, you know. While searching Maria Taylor's room—you needn't look so shocked, I'm not bound by rules of search and seizure—I discovered a fabulously expensive bracelet and necklace set. You can trace its purchase back to Donald Travers. Or simply ask Marion Travers—Maria Taylor does not strike me as a very discreet woman."

"It's true," Marion Travers confirmed quietly, as her husband abruptly reclaimed his seat. "I never dreamed she would be here this weekend. I thought my husband wanted to get away together to repair our marriage."

"He wanted to destroy your life," Auntie Lil explained sadly. "You have a great deal of money on your own, do you not? Forgive me if I pry."

The woman nodded, not looking up.

"Money I believe your husband needed," Auntie Lil confirmed. "And this need coincided with Maria Taylor's own need to marry quickly and to marry well, before the bloom faded even more from her rose, shall we say. She and your husband conspired to have you killed, I am sure, and turned to Dr. Sussman for help. There was a very curious conversation earlier in the sitting room that helped me make the connection. Dr. Sussman attempted to force his beauty creams on Mrs. Travers." Auntie Lil pointed toward the graceful woman. "Her skin is flawless. Why in the world attempt to alter perfection? What Dr. Sussman was really trying to do was force his poison creams on her."

"How dare you?" Dr. Sussman shouted.

"Chemical analysis will confirm it," Auntie Lil said simply, sliding the jars toward the sheriff. "I suspect a topical poison capable of soaking through the skin. Some sort of insecticide, perhaps Parathion."

The sheriff took the jars without comment, storing them in a jacket pocket for safekeeping. He was not smiling.

"It had to be done that way," Auntie Lil said. "Marion Travers couldn't be poisoned any other way because she is very strict about what goes into her body. She eats only the purest of foods with the blandest of tastes. So Donald Travers came up with a plan worthy of a successful businessman when Marion Travers mentioned to her husband that she'd met a woman named Clarabelle at a New Age convention. Clarabelle owned a lodge, she told her husband, and staged mystery weekends. People paid a lot of money to participate. How much fun it all sounded." Auntie Lil nodded an apology toward Clarabelle. "It was terribly rude of them to involve you," she said.

"This is just too awful," Clarabelle choked out, her hand massaging the base of her throat.

"Because Donald Travers had always been vain himself—and had had affairs with vain women—he assumed that his wife must be as well," Auntie Lil continued. "He based his plan on vanity and that was his undoing. He cultivated an acquaintance with Dr. Sussman at Maria Taylor's suggestion and offered him a significant sum of money, I suspect, to prepare a special set of face creams for his wife. Dr. Sussman appears quite vulnerable to offers of money." Auntie Lil shook her head in great distaste; this was a clear sign of poor breeding in her book. "Executing the plan was easy. Maria Taylor was part of it. She simply called up Clarabelle and asked to be in one of her weekend mysteries."

"It's true," Clarabelle confirmed. "I could not believe my good luck."

"Donald Travers then invited his wife up here that same weekend," Auntie Lil continued. "The plan was to compliment Maria on her skin, to make Mrs. Travers jealous enough to try Dr. Sussman's remedies. But Marion Travers would not accept the cream, and the doctor saw his payment slipping away."

"Then why was Maria Taylor killed instead?" Mr. Little asked.

"You'll have to ask Dr. Sussman," Auntie Lil said. "I think he had a deeper grudge against Maria Taylor in mind all along, despite the fact that he had offered to commit murder on her behalf. Perhaps Dr. Sussman had wanted more from Maria Taylor than she cared to give him, in terms of both money and affection. I noticed Miss Taylor snubbed him in the dining room. She pretended not to know him at all. Certainly her murder was premeditated."

"You have no proof of that!" the doctor cried.

"Don't I?" Auntie Lil said. "Last night, for whatever reason, you entered Maria Taylor's room and switched her regular creams for your poisons, making it look as if the jars were half-used. I am sure if these nice young officers search thoroughly enough, they'll find plastic gloves and poison residue in this house somewhere. Try the drains in Miss Taylor's bathroom first. Thanks to my nephew Theodore standing guard on the body, the doctor here was unable to remove the creams from Miss Taylor's room. But perhaps he tried to flush away other evidence."

The doctor's back stiffened and he looked away.

"But why the gunshot?" the sheriff asked, intrigued.

"To take attention away from her skin," Auntie Lil said, "and to give the doctor an alibi. I suspect that Maria Taylor had left her door open for late-night visitors." She coughed discreetly and glanced away from the stricken Marion Travers. "That made it easy for Dr. Sussman to check on her later, to confirm that she was dead. When he saw the unexpected condition of her skin, his plan became all the more important. He stole a prop gun from the sitting room, where one of the actors had left it last evening. When the time was right, he shot off the blank gun in the upper floor stairwell. That was why it boomed so loudly. He has admitted he was the first to examine the body. In fact, no one else had a chance. He made sure that everyone knew the door was locked, even using my own nephew to establish that fact, then shut it in our faces and was alone with the body long enough to shoot her for real, using the gun you will find by the side of her bed and a silencer. His own words convict him. He told us all that the gun was right there by the bed; yet I had to lift up the covers before I spotted it—and he claimed not to have touched a thing. I am sure you'll find the silencer somewhere in this house." She looked at the doctor. "It proves premeditation, wouldn't you say? The fact that he brought the gun and a silencer along. He had agreed to kill Mrs. Travers, but his real victim had been Maria Taylor all along. Or perhaps he had intended to kill them both, earning a tidy sum and gaining revenge at the same time. If you decide to search for the silencer, I'd try Donald Travers's luggage first. He seemed extremely anxious to leave before the police arrived."

There was a thump as Donald Travers recrossed one of his legs.

"Travers had to agree to help Dr. Sussman cover up," Auntie Lil explained. "He could not say anything without implicating himself in another murder plot. I suspect blackmail would have been the doctor's next step."

Auntie Lil finished her story, and her bright eyes darted around the room.

The sheriff stared at Auntie Lil, his face an impassive mask that was threatening to crack. "What did you say your name was again, ma'am?" he asked, pushing his hat even further back and scratching at his hairline.

"My name is Lillian Hubbert," she told the sheriff crisply. "But you may call me Auntie Lil."

KATY MUNGER is the author of two mystery series: the Casey Jones series set in Raleigh and, writing as Gallagher Gray, the Hubbert and Lil series set in New York. Her Casey Jones series has won an Anthony and a Shamus award. Munger's father is Guy Munger, and she grew up on Park Drive in Raleigh. Munger now resides in Durham, where she writes, operates a communications consulting company, and reviews mysteries for the *Washington Post*.

Copyright 1998 by Kate Munger. First printed in *Murder They Wrote*, volume 2, edited by Elizabeth Foxwell and Martin H. Greenberg (New York: Boulevard Books, 1998). Reprinted with permission of the author.

THE WISH PEDDLER

Lisa Cantrell

he path through Graham Park was lined with aged oak trees that had, over the years, grown to need each other. Their gnarled old branches held hands overhead, and one passing underneath and looking upward could not be sure which arthritic limb belonged to which distended trunk. Despite their antiquity, new foliage was busy emerging, for it was spring and though the trees were old they were not yet too tired to try.

A slippery breeze cavorted between spatters of moonbeams and did surface dives through the balmy air. There was the scent of greenness, of the ripening year, of things new and renewed. The evening wrapped itself languidly on the park and sidled down the path and around the trees. It was a velvet night, a honeyed night, the perfect accompaniment—complete with cricket murmurings and silvered moonlight—to the moment when one Randall P. Wodenhaus became dead.

Not that Mr. Wodenhaus immediately recognized this august happening for what it was (he had declined setting the precise time and place of his demise himself, opting for the added enjoyment of spontaneity). Rather the reverse, in fact, for several moments had passed before the first inkling of what was transpiring tickled the edges of Mr. Wodenhaus's reverie. By then it was much too late to change his mind (had he wished to), and the faint stirring of rebellion that was his initial response fizzled out. An Epilogue was, after all, an Epilogue and should be greeted as such with dignity and a certain amount of savoir faire—if, that is, one was getting what one asked for; and that was exactly what Mr. Wodenhaus was getting, for he had bought and paid for twenty-four hours of death.

Mr. Wodenhaus glanced at his wristwatch. Eight P.M. on the dot.

It was mildly interesting to note, thought Mr. Wodenhaus, that so far none of the venerable prophecies had come to pass. Mr. Wodenhaus was unsure whether or not to be disappointed (some forecasts *were* a bit intense for his taste) and decided to reserve judgment. He had harbored no fear of suddenly finding himself flung into a fiery furnace, as it were (though it didn't hurt to have this belief confirmed); nor had he expected to be greeted by a heavenly host of angels gloriously in chorus. Mr. Wodenhaus had never suffered from the religious illusions or cultist superstitions that plagued so many.

Yet death had always held a strange fascination for him, particularly as the years advanced and its dark specter loomed more and more ominously on Mr. Wodenhaus's horizon. Perhaps its status as the sole inevitability of life (taxes could be gotten around) caused the question of what death would be like to gnaw with increasing voracity at Mr. Wodenhaus's patience until at last he decided to jump the gun a mite (no pun intended). It was important, thought Mr. Wodenhaus, to be prepared. Mr. Wodenhaus had always liked to know beforehand just what he was getting into and didn't mind paying for the knowledge. His contract with the Wish Peddler had cost him more than he'd wanted to pay, but once a rider had been attached assuring that no physical harm would come to him during the twenty-four-hour period and guaranteeing his safe return at the end of that time, Mr. Wodenhaus had been quite satisfied.

Drat! He'd forgotten to pay special attention to the initial *feel* of being dead. Then he realized it was not too late, for looking over his shoulder he discovered his body was still in the process of settling to the ground. It was as though "he" had simply walked on while "his body" had stopped its forward movement and slowly begun to crumple.

Freedom was the word that popped up first regarding his temporary state, yet that single word fell just short of perfect. Mr. Wodenhaus searched for an appropriate analogy and conjured up a somewhat too vivid picture of a snake slithering out of its skin—then discarded it for the more pleasant image of a butterfly, flitting with capricious abandon from its cocoon. Ah, yes. A butterfly. That was much more to his taste. A yellow butterfly.

Mr. Wodenhaus continued to regard his body, which was still involved in its slow-motion slump. It lent a certain graceful symmetry to his angular frame. Mr. Wodenhaus smiled, seeing himself through new eyes and liking what he saw. Death wasn't so bad. It smoothed the creases, rounded the edges, eased the pace—

For just a moment, something scratched at a door in the back of his mind, something cold and ghoulish. Mr. Wodenhaus tightened his lips and bolted the door firmly shut.

Mr. Wodenhaus looked around at the world he would inhabit for the next twenty-four hours. Right off, he could detect no major changes. The trees were still trees, their budding branches at rest now in the absence of the earlier breeze. The path continued on its winding way through the park. The crickets—wait a minute, what had happened to the crickets? Only moments before, the night air had been filled with their raspy songs. In fact, their chirring was not the only sound Mr. Wodenhaus now realized was missing. He no longer heard the muted rumble of the evening traffic over on Fifty-fourth Street . . . nor the soft strands of guitar music coming from the young man seated on a bench farther back along the path . . . nor . . . big deal. Noise could be so distracting to one's peace of mind— yes! yes, of course—that was it! Peace. Quiet. That was part of death, wasn't it? "The Silence of the Grave" and all that rot (uh, no pun intended). Something to enjoy. For twenty-four hours.

Mr. Wodenhaus glanced over his shoulder once more, only to be a bit disconcerted now by the sight. His body seemed suspended . . . immobile . . . one knee slightly bent, the foot turned sideways and pointed inward . . . an arm just beginning to act upon orders from the brain to prepare for an impending fall . . . head tilted back, eyes staring . . . staring . . . dead eyes . . . dead, dead eyes . . .

Should be closed, thought Mr. Wodenhaus, repressing an involuntary shudder, zeroing in on a point he could deal with and, for the moment at least, disavowing knowledge of the cold thing tapping on the door in the back of his mind.

Resolutely Mr. Wodenhaus approached the body, intent only on closing the gaping, sightless eyes. He pressed thumb and forefinger to the lids—and immediately recoiled. There was no sense of touch. He put his hand out toward, then *through* his body.

Mr. Wodenhaus walked through his body.

He did it again.

He went over to a tree and mimicked the act.

He waved his arm through a bush.

He scooped his hand through the ground.

But Mr. Wodenhaus could not close his body's eyes; and for some reason, at the moment, this was the *only* thing Mr. Wodenhaus really wanted to do.

Mr. Wodenhaus shrugged. Apparently certain norms were in effect here, just as in the real world. There were a million things one could do and a million things one couldn't. Just different things. Adjustments could be made, and Mr. Wodenhaus would make them. After all . . . it was only for twenty-four hours.

The best thing to do, decided Mr. Wodenhaus, was to branch out a bit and see what other new accomplishments he had acquired. This was going to be fun. Mr. Wodenhaus chuckled merrily. It was like being invisible. Who hadn't pondered the possibilities of such a state? He headed toward Fifty-fourth Street. First a little snack, then—wait a minute . . . he couldn't eat!

Never mind, never mind. He didn't need to eat. He was dead—temporarily dead, he amended—and there were infinite . . . uh, *lots* of other things to do. Mr. Wodenhaus's agile mind flicked over a wide range of activities: from such trivialities as playing fiendish tricks on some of his cronies to more serious endeavors such as altering bank records and property titles. But how was he to do any of those things when his fingers wouldn't hold a pen? . . . when his hands passed through solid objects? . . . when he had no substance, no effect, no—

Stop it! This would not do. It would not do at all! There was no real problem. Maybe it wasn't turning out so well after all, but it would soon be over. Nothing could go wrong, the Wish Peddler had assured him of that; and besides, it was all neatly spelled out in his contract. Mr. Wodenhaus patted his pocket. Right there in the fine print just above the line where he'd signed his name (in blood, of all things, but the Wish Peddler had been a stickler on this point, no pun intended). Mr. Wodenhaus always read fine print, *particularly* read fine print, so he knew that in exactly the specified time his contract would become null and void—without exception!

Mr. Wodenhaus was ashamed of himself. His twenty-four hours was just beginning, and here he was already allowing emotionalism to replace logic. He'd never done so in life; why should he in death? *Temporary* death, he quickly amended. He must simply get his thoughts in order, adjust his thinking. Mr. Wodenhaus resumed walking. So what if taste and sound and touch were denied him during his tenure here. He could see, couldn't he? And there was so much to see.

Oof! Mr. Wodenhaus staggered backward. He'd walked into something solid. He didn't *see* anything—Mr. Wodenhaus put out a tentative hand—but there was something in his way. He moved his hand up and down, left and right. There was an invisible barrier of some sort. Mr. Wodenhaus drew back his hand. He glanced around him, looked above him, suddenly recalling one of those "venerable prophecies"—something about restless spirits doomed to spend eternity within the spatial limits of their earthly passing. Could this barrier possibly extend—

Something cold started pounding on the back door in Mr. Wodenhaus's mind. It was the ghoul. It wanted out. It had something to tell him.

No no, not now, thank you. Not now. Don't want to know now, thank you very much. Not now . . .

Mr. Wodenhaus moved back from the barrier. He didn't look at his body again. He sat down on the ground instead, his back toward it. He couldn't feel the ground, but that didn't matter. He had to make plans. There were other things he could do, he was sure of it. Mr. Wodenhaus glanced at his wristwatch. Eight P.M. on the dot. He must not waste any of his precious time. After all, he only had twenty-four hours. . . .

LISA CANTRELL is the author of four horror novels and several short stories. Her first novel, *The Manse*, won the Bram Stoker Award in 1987. She was born in Birmingham, Alabama, but has lived in Madison, North Carolina, for thirty years. She continues to write, teaches writing at the local community college, and lectures at conventions and writing workshops.

SPILLED SALT

BarbaraNeely

"I'm home, Ma."

Myrna pressed down hard on the doorknob and stared blankly up into Kenny's large brown eyes and freckled face so much like her own he was nearly her twin. But he was taller than she remembered. Denser.

He'd written to say he was getting out. She hadn't answered his letter, hoping her lack of response would keep him away.

"You're here." She stepped back from the door, pretending not to see him reach out and try to touch her.

But a part of her had leaped to life at the sight of him. No matter what, she was glad he hadn't been maimed or murdered in prison. He at least looked whole and healthy of body. She hoped it was a sign that he was all right inside, too.

She tried to think of something to say as they stood staring at each other in the middle of the living room. A fly buzzed against the window screen in a desperate attempt to get out.

"Well, Ma, how've you—"

"I'll fix you something to eat," Myrna interrupted. "I know you must be starved for decent cooking." She rushed from the room as though a meal were already in the process of burning.

For a moment she was lost in her own kitchen. The table, with its dented metal legs, the green-and-white cotton curtains, and the badly battered coffeepot were all familiar-looking strangers. She took a deep breath and leaned against the back of a chair.

In the beginning she'd flinched from the very word. She couldn't even think it, let alone say it. Assault, attack, molest, anything but rape. Anyone but her son, her bright and funny boy, her high school graduate.

At the time, she'd been sure it was a frame-up on the part of the police. They did things like that. It was in the newspapers every day.

Or the girl was trying to get revenge because he hadn't shown any interest in her. Kenny's confession put paid to all those speculations.

She'd have liked to believe that remorse had made him confess. But she knew better. He'd simply told the wrong lie. If he'd said he'd been with the girl but it hadn't been rape, he might have built a case that someone would have believed—although she didn't know how he could have explained away the wound on her neck where he'd held the knife against her throat to keep her docile. Instead, he'd claimed not to have offered her a ride home from the bar where she worked, never to have had her in his car. He'd convinced Myrna. So thoroughly convinced her that she'd fainted dead away when confronted with the semen, fiber, and hair evidence the police quickly collected from his car and the word of the woman who reluctantly came forth to say she'd seen Kenny ushering Crystal Roberts into his car on the night Crystal was raped.

Only then had Kenny confessed. He'd said he'd been doing the girl a favor by offering her a ride home. In return, she'd teased and then refused him, he'd said. "I lost my head," he'd said.

"I can't sleep. I'm afraid to sleep." The girl had spoken in barely a whisper. The whole courtroom had seemed to tilt as everyone leaned toward her. "Every night he's there in my mind, making me go through it all over again, and again, and again."

Was she free now that Kenny had done his time? Or was she flinching from hands with short, square fingers and crying when the first of September came near? Myrna moved around the kitchen like an old, old woman with bad feet.

After Kenny had confessed, Myrna spent days that ran into weeks rifling through memories of the past she shared with him, searching for some incident, some trait or series of events that would explain why he'd done such a thing. She'd tried to rationalize his actions with circumstances: Kenny had seen his father beat her. They'd been poorer than dirt. And when Kenny had just turned six, she'd finally found the courage to leave Buddy to raise their son alone. What had she really known about raising a child? What harm might she have done out of ignorance, out of impatience and concentration on warding off the pains of her own life?

Still, she kept stumbling over the knowledge of other boys, from far worse circumstances, with mothers too tired and worried to do more than strike out at them. Yet those boys had managed to grow up and not do the kind of harm Kenny had done. The phrases "I lost my head" and "doing the girl a favor" reverberated through her brain, mocking her, making her groan out loud and startle people around her.

Myrna dragged herself around the room, turning eggs, bacon, milk, and margarine into a meal. In the beginning the why of Kenny's crime was like a tapeworm in her belly, consuming all her strength and sustenance, all her attention. In the first few months of his imprisonment she'd religiously paid a neighbor to drive her the long distance to the prison each visiting day. The visits were as much for her benefit as for his.

"But why?" she'd kept asking him, just as she'd asked him practically every day since he'd confessed.

He would only say that he knew he'd done wrong. As the weeks passed, silence became his only response—a silence that had remained intact despite questions like "Would you have left that girl alone if I'd bought a shotgun and blown your daddy's brains out after the first time he hit me in front of you?" and "Is there a special thrill you feel when you make a woman ashamed of her sex?" and "Was this the first time? The second? The last?"

Perhaps silence was best, now, after so long. Anything could happen if she let those five-year-old questions come rolling out of her mouth. Kenny might begin to question her, might ask her what there was about her mothering that made him want to treat a woman like a piece of toilet paper. And what would she say to that?

It was illness that had finally put an end to her visits with him. She'd written the first letter—a note really—to say she was laid up with the flu. A hacking cough had lingered. She hadn't gotten her strength back for nearly two months. By that time their correspondence was established. Letters full of "How are you? I'm fine. . . . The weather is . . . The print shop is . . . The dress I made for Mrs. Rothstein was . . ." were so much more manageable than those silence-laden visits. And she didn't have to worry about making eye contact with Kenny in a letter.

Now Myrna stood staring out the kitchen window while Kenny ate his bacon and eggs. The crisp everydayness of clothes flapping on the line surprised her. A leaf floated into her small cemented yard and landed on a potted pansy. Outside, nothing had changed; the world was still in spring.

"I can't go through this again," she mouthed soundlessly to the breeze.

"Come talk to me, Ma," her son called softly around a mouthful of food.

Myrna turned to look at him. He smiled an egg-flecked smile she couldn't return. She wanted to ask him what he would do now, whether he had a job lined up, whether he planned to stay long. But she was afraid of his answers, afraid of how she might respond if he said he had no job, no plans, no place to stay except with her and that he hadn't changed in any important way.

"I'm always gonna live with you, Mommy," he'd told her when he was a child. "Always." At the time, she'd wished it was true, that they could always be together, she and her sweet, chubby boy. Now the thought frightened her.

"Be right back," she mumbled, and she scurried down the hall to the bathroom. She eased the lock over so that it made barely a sound.

"He's my son!" she hissed at the drawn woman in the mirror. Perspiration dotted her upper lip and glistened around her hairline.

"My son!" she repeated pleadingly. But the words were not as powerful as the memory of Crystal Roberts sitting in the courtroom, her shoulders hunched and her head hung down, as though she were the one who ought to be ashamed. Myrna wished him never born, before she flushed the toilet and unlocked the door.

In the kitchen Kenny had moved to take her place by the window. His dishes littered the table. He'd spilled the salt, and there were crumbs on the floor.

"It sure is good to look out the window and see something besides guard towers and cons." Kenny stretched, rubbed his belly, and turned to face her.

"It's good to see you, Ma." His eyes were soft and shiny.

Oh, Lord! Myrna moaned to herself. She turned her back to him and began carrying his dirty dishes to the sink: first the plate, then the cup, the knife, fork, and spoon, drawing out the chore.

"This place ain't got as much room as the old place," she told him while she made dishwater in the sink.

"It's fine, Ma, just fine."

Oh, Lord, Myrna prayed.

Kenny came to lean against the stove to her right. She dropped a knife and made the dishwater too cold.

"Seen Dad?"

"Where and why would I see *him*?" She tried to put ice in her voice. It trembled.

"Just thought you might know where he is." Kenny moved back to the window.

Myrna remembered the crippling shock of Buddy's fist in her groin and scoured Kenny's plate and cup with a piece of steel wool before rinsing them in scalding water.

"Maybe I'll hop a bus over to the old neighborhood. See some of the guys, how things have changed."

He paced the floor behind her. Myrna sensed his uneasiness and was startled by a wave of pleasure at his discomfort.

After he'd gone, she fixed herself a large gin and orange juice and carried it into the living room. She flicked on the TV and sat down to stare at it. After two minutes of frenetic, overbright commercials, she got up and turned it off again. Outside, children screamed each other to the finish line of a footrace. She remembered that Kenny had always liked to run. So had she. But he'd had more childhood than she'd had. She'd been hired out as a mother's helper by the time she was twelve and pregnant and married at sixteen. She didn't begrudge him his childhood fun. It just seemed so wasted now.

Tears slid down her face and salted her drink. Tears for the young Myrna who hadn't understood that she was raising a boy who needed special handling to keep him from becoming a man she didn't care to know. Tears for Kenny who was so twisted around inside that he could rape a woman. Myrna drained her gin, left Kenny a note reminding him to leave her door key on the kitchen table, and went to bed.

Of course, she was still awake when he came in. He bumped into the coffee table, ran water in the bathroom sink for a long time, then he was quiet. Myrna lay awake in the dark blue-gray night listening to the groan of the refrigerator, the hiss of the hot-water heater, and the rumble of large trucks on a distant street. *He* made no sound where he lay on the opened-out sofa, surrounded by her sewing machine, dress dummy, marking tape, and pins.

When sleep finally came, it brought dreams of walking down brilliantly lit streets, hand in hand with a boy about twelve who looked, acted, and talked like Kenny but who she knew with certainty was not her son, at the same time that she also knew he could be no one else.

She woke to a cacophony of church bells. It was late. Too late to make it to church service. She turned her head to look at the crucifix hanging by her bed and tried to pray, to summon up that feeling of near weightlessness that came over her in those moments when she was able to free her mind of all else and give herself over to prayer. Now nothing came but a dull ache in the back of her throat.

She had begun attending church regularly after she stopped visiting Kenny. His refusal to respond to her questions made it clear she'd have to seek answers elsewhere. She'd decided to talk to Father Giles. He'd been at St. Mark's, in their old neighborhood, before she and Kenny had moved there. He'd seen Kenny growing up. Perhaps he'd noticed something, understood something about the boy, about her, that would explain what she could not understand.

"It's God's will, my child—put it in His hands," he'd urged, awkwardly patting her arm and averting his eyes.

Myrna took his advice wholeheartedly. She became quite adept at quieting the questions boiling in her belly with "His will" or "My cross to bear." Many nights she'd "Our Fathered" herself to sleep. Acceptance of Kenny's inexplicable act became a test God had given her. One she passed by visiting the sick, along with other women from the church; working on the neighborhood cleanup committee; avoiding all social contact with men. With sex. She put "widowed" on job applications and never mentioned a son to new people she met. Once she'd moved away from the silent accusation of their old apartment, prayer and good works became a protective shield separating her from the past.

Kenny's tap on her door startled her back to the present. She cleared her throat and straightened the covers before calling to him to come in.

A rich, aromatic steam rose from the coffee he'd brought her. The toast was just the right shade of brown, and she was sure that when she cracked the poached egg it would be cooked exactly to her liking. Not only was everything perfectly prepared, but it was the first time she'd had breakfast in bed since he'd been arrested. Myrna couldn't hold back the tears or the flood of memories of many mornings, just so: him bending over her with a breakfast tray.

"You wait on people in the restaurant all day and sit up all night making other people's clothes. You need some waiting on, too."

Had he actually said that, this man as a boy? Could this man have been such a boy? Myrna nearly tilted the tray in her confusion.

"I need to brush my teeth." She averted her face and reached for her bathrobe.

But she couldn't avoid her eyes in the medicine cabinet mirror, eyes that reminded her that despite what Kenny had done, she hadn't stopped loving him. But her love didn't need his company. It thrived only on memories of him that were more than four years old. It was as much a love remembered as a living thing. But it was love, nonetheless. Myrna pressed her clenched fist against her lips and wondered if love was enough. She stayed in the bathroom until she heard him leave her bedroom and turn on the TV in the living room.

When he came back for the tray, she told him she had a sick headache and had decided to stay in bed. He was immediately sympathetic, fetching aspirin and a cool compress for her forehead, offering to massage her neck and temples, to lower the blinds and block out the bright morning sun. Myrna told him she wanted only to rest.

All afternoon she lay on her unmade bed, her eyes on the ceiling or idly roaming the room, her mind moving across the surface of her life, poking at old wounds, so amazingly raw after all these years. First there'd been Buddy. He'd laughed at her country ways and punched her around until he'd driven her and their child into the streets. But at least she was rid of him. Then there was his son. Her baby. He'd tricked a young woman into getting into his car, where he proceeded to ruin a great portion of her life. Now he'd come back to spill salt in her kitchen.

I'm home, Ma, homema, homema. His words echoed in her inner ear and made her heart flutter. Her neighbors would want to know where he'd been all this time and why. Fear and disgust would creep into their faces and voices. Her nights would be full of listening. Waiting.

And she would have to live with the unblanketed reality that whatever anger and meanness her son held toward the world, he had chosen a woman to take it out on.

A woman.

Someone like me, she thought, like Great Aunt Faye, or Valerie, her eight-year-old niece; like Lucille, her oldest friend, or Dr. Ramsey, her dentist. A woman like all the women who'd helped feed, clothe, and care for Kenny; who'd tried their damnedest to protect him from as much of the ugly and awful in life as they could; who'd taught him to ride a bike and cross the street. All women. From the day she'd left Buddy, not one man had done a damned thing for Kenny. Not one.

And he might do it again, she thought. The idea sent Myrna rolling back and forth across the bed as though she could actually escape her thoughts. She'd allowed herself to believe she was done with such thoughts. Once she accepted Kenny's crime as the will of God, she immediately saw that it wouldn't have made any difference how she'd raised him if this was God's unfathomable plan for him. It was a comforting idea, one that answered her question of why and how her much-loved son could be a rapist. One that answered the question of the degree of her responsibility for Kenny's crime by clearing her of all possible blame. One that allowed her to forgive him. Or so she'd thought.

Now she realized all her prayers, all her studied efforts to accept and forgive, were like blankets thrown on a forest fire. All it took was the small breeze created by her opening the door to her only child to burn those blankets to cinders and release her rage—as wild and fierce as the day he'd confessed.

She closed her eyes and saw her outraged self dash wildly into the living room to scream imprecations in his face until her voice failed. Specks of froth gathered at the corners of her mouth. Her flying spit peppered his face. He cringed before her, his eyes full of shame as he tore at his own face and chest in self-loathing.

Yet, even as she fantasized, she knew Kenny could no more be screamed into contrition than Crystal or any woman could be bullied into willing sex. And what, in fact, was there for him to say or do that would satisfy her? The response she really wanted from him was not available: there was no way he could become the boy he'd been before that night four years ago.

No more than I can treat him as if he were that boy, she thought.

And the thought stilled her. She lay motionless, considering.

When she rose from her bed, she dragged her old green Samsonite suitcase out from the back of the closet. She moved with the easy, effortless grace of someone who knows what she is doing and feels good about it. Without even wiping off the dust, she plopped the suitcase on the bed. When she lifted the lid, the smell of leaving and good-bye flooded the room and quickened her pulse. For the first time in two days, her mouth moved in the direction of a smile.

She hurried from dresser drawer to closet, choosing her favorites: the black two-piece silk knit dress she'd bought on sale, her comfortable gray shoes, the lavender sweater she'd knitted as a birthday present to herself but had never worn, both her blue and her black slacks, the red crepe blouse she'd made to go with them, and the best of her underwear. She packed in a rush, as though her bus or train were even now pulling out of the station.

When she'd packed her clothes, Myrna looked around the room for other necessary items. She gathered up her comb and brush and the picture of her mother from the top of her bureau, then walked to the wall on the left side of her bed and lifted down the shiny metal and wooden crucifix that hung there. She ran her finger down the slim, muscular body. The Aryan plaster of Paris Christ seemed to writhe in bittersweet agony. Myrna stared at the crucifix for a few moments, then gently hung it back on the wall.

When she'd finished dressing, she sat down in the hard, straight-backed chair near the window to think through her plan. Kenny tapped at her door a number of times until she was able to convince him that she was best left alone and would be fine in the morning. When dark came, she waited for the silence of sleep, then quietly left her room. She set her suitcase by the front door, tiptoed by Kenny, where he slept on the sofa, and went into the kitchen. By the glow from the back alley streetlight, she wrote him a note and propped it against the sugar bowl:

Dear Kenny,

I'm sorry. I just can't be your mother right now. I will be back in one week. Please be gone. Much love, Myrna.

Kenny flinched and frowned in his sleep as the front door clicked shut.

With her debut novel in 1992, *Blanche on the Lam*, BARBARANEELY joined a growing number of African American writers who write mysteries set in black America. Blanche is a middle-aged, eggplant-black, African American domestic, full-time mother, and part-time sleuth who lives and works in Durham. Neely's first book in this series garnered three first-novel prizes: the Agatha, the Macavity, and the Anthony. Neely now lives in Massachusetts, but she resided for some time in North Carolina, where she wrote for *Southern Exposure* and produced radio shows for the African News Service.

Elizabeth Daniels Squire

"Mama's gone, Peaches," Lola said to me, "and I need your help."

I held the phone tight, and a shiver of sadness went through me.

I knew Lola meant that her wonderful eighty-three-year-old mother, Bonnie Amons—my next-door neighbor—had died. Lola liked soft-pedal words—"gone" or "passed on" for died, "indisposed" for vomiting all over, and so forth.

Bonnie's death was my fault. Now, why on earth would I feel like that? I'd been good to Bonnie. I even helped train her dog. "I heard she was much worse the last few weeks since I've been away from Asheville," I said. I looked out into my sunny garden where a robin took a morning dip in the birdbath. Bonnie's garden adjoined mine on the right. That blooming apple tree was on her land.

"She'd been declining," Lola said. "Even her mind was going. She talked about changing her will to leave Doc James everything she had if he'd just get her well. Of course, she couldn't do that without a lawyer." Suddenly Lola sounded smug, but then properly sad again. "You're never ready for loved ones to go, are you? And I arrived to look in about eight this morning and . . ." She sighed.

I figured there was no easy way to say what she found. But she hadn't called me right away. My watch said quarter to ten.

Strange, I thought, that Bonnie got so sick so fast. Three weeks before, she'd been a little vague about time, she'd been almost blind, but there was still a lot of spunk in the old gal. She did have to take heart medicine, but otherwise she was full of ginger. Still, she *was* eighty-three. And nobody lasts forever.

"And now," Lola blurted, "somebody is trying to shoot George."

"Shoot George?" Why on earth would anybody want to shoot my neighbor's little black-and-white volunteer dog? I say volunteer because he simply appeared a year or so ago. And Bonnie couldn't bear not to feed him, so George—which is what Bonnie named him—moved in and became her mainstay.

"But everybody loves George," I said. "What on earth happened?"

"Right after I found Mama"—silence while she pulled herself together—"Peaches, she had plainly passed on. I found her and then I called Doc James and Andrea Ann." Andrea Ann was Lola's older sister.

"George barked to go out and I let him out and then I heard a gunshot. But thank the good Lord I hadn't closed the door tight, and George came running in and had one of his shaking fits."

I knew it didn't require a gunshot to scare the dog. He had those shakes with new people, especially men, and especially men wearing boots. Somebody had mistreated that dog. But somebody had been good to him and trained him right, because he was an affectionate little dog who would sit or come on command. I figured we'd never know the whole story.

"I didn't see a living soul," Lola said, "but the mountain is in back of Mama's house here. Somebody could shoot down from among the trees and then slip away."

"It's probably some crazy mean kid," I said, "with a new gun. What do you want me to do?"

I said that bit about a kid to ease her mind, but I found myself wondering: Was there someone from that dog's past who wanted him out of the way? Silly idea, I told myself. But the idea grew: Was there some guilty secret the dog knew? Oh, come on! What imagination! First I'd asked myself if it was my fault that Bonnie died because I wasn't around to look in. Then I wondered if a little dog knew guilty secrets. But I never entirely dismiss my wild ideas. Some of them turn out. If you have a lousy memory, and I admit to that, sometimes you just know something without remembering the little signs that made you know it. I file my strange ideas under "Way Far Out," but I don't erase them.

"People will be coming and going here," Lola said, "paying respects to Mama. Would you take care of George till I get time to take him to my place?"

"And are you going to keep him for good?" I asked.

"I don't know," she said. "Mama would want him to have a good home, but Victor doesn't care too much for dogs."

I didn't like Lola's husband, Victor. Why did my wonderful friend Bonnie's two daughters both marry stinkers?

Unsuccessful stinkers. One from the city, one from the country. Andrea Ann's Arnold had run a tired trailer park out in the county where he grew up, except he'd finally sold it and put a down payment on a house near Bonnie's (which is to say, near me) and announced he was going to be a salesman. Now they were neighbors. And Arnold had to shave more often. Funny thing, though, Arnold had always had bedroom eyes even without shaving. Gave every woman he met the once-over like he was checking her out for sex, like his imagination was extra good in that department. Carnal Arnold. From the day I met him, I'd remembered his name that way.

Lola's husband, Victor, had a craft shop in Asheville. He'd always shaved. In fact, he overdressed. Slick Vic. He wore suits with vests to work. But most of his mountain-type "handmade crafts" came from Korea. He couldn't understand why, in an area with so many real and beautiful crafts, his shop didn't do well. Also, Victor was selfish and wanted to be the center of everything. And Lola was, I am sorry to say, a doormat. A mealymouthed doormat. Victor and Lola were made for each other. But not for a little dog with boot-kicks and God knew what else to get over.

"I'd like to have George," I said. "He has character. I'll come get him right now."

"Now, where has that dog gone?" Lola groaned as she let me in the front door. Why on earth had she worn a pink satin blouse to drop by her mother's in the morning? It went with her teased hairdresser hair and her carefully painted rosebud mouth. On a woman of fifty-plus. No doubt Slick Vic liked it.

We traced George to Bonnie's room, where the unmade bed looked so forlorn. Doc James must have arranged for the funeral home to come and get the body. Lola seemed too upset to have thought clearly and worked that out. Doc was getting a little senile himself. At least, I didn't think he'd come to see Bonnie as often as he should. But Bonnie would never change doctors.

George stuck his little black nose out from under the dust ruffle when he heard me and gave the single bark that means hello. "Good dog," I said to encourage him.

I looked around the room and choked up. The picture of praying hands, as worn as Bonnie's, hung as always on the wall above the old brass bed. Across from it was the plain bureau with Bonnie's hairbrush and comb and the old crazed mirror that had belonged to her mother. On the bedside table was a framed picture of the two girls as kids, Lola and Andrea Ann. Pouting in Sunday dresses. Also a glass of water, Bonnie's bottle of heart pills, and a box of dog biscuits. Everything was just like it had been at my last visit when I'd slipped in early before I left for my plane. I was glad I'd said that good-bye.

I walked over and picked up the pills and sighed. Heart medicine almost killed my father. As-much-as-you-need can save your life. More-than-you-need is deadly poison. "Lanoxin" (Digoxin), the label said, Rite-Aid. "Bonnie changed pharmacies," I said out loud. "I used to get her pills for her sometimes from Barefoot and Cheetham when I got my thyroid pills." Who could forget a name that made a picture like Barefoot and Cheetham? The two are actually old mountain names. Several in the phone book.

"Rite-Aid is a chain, so it costs less," Lola said primly. She stood near the bed nervously, watching me. Twitching like she wanted me to hurry up.

George edged out from under the bed. His small straight tail began to wag. He fastened his bright little black eyes on me.

"Bonnie really counted on George," I reminisced. "He even helped her remember her pill." Silence. Lola didn't like to admit that before the dog came, her mother sometimes forgot to take her heart pill at all. Which was dangerous. So I had come to the rescue.

I take pride in the fact that my friends count on me for memory tricks. In fact, I'm writing a book called *How to Survive without a Memory*. My only problem is that sometimes I forget to take my own advice. But the dog-pill trick really works. A dog's stomach can tell time as well as an alarm clock. Give him a treat at the same time two or three days running, and he'll come ask for it on the button after that. Especially if he's a hungry type. And before George showed up on Bonnie's doorstep, goodness knows how long he'd been hungry.

George nudged my leg to be patted. I stroked his velvet head.

"Yes," Lola admitted, "George was a help, although my Victor was always afraid the dog was going to give us fleas."

Fleas! I'd taken on the job of seeing that George never had any. Bonnie's daughters never took time for that. Lola was always off at Victor's beck and call.

Andrea Ann, who was a trained nurse, did look in more often. She kept an eye on her mother, now that they'd made up a long-standing fight. You see, Andrea Ann had thought her mother had ruined her marriage by not lending her money. A dumb idea, but Andrea Ann had spells of dumb. And she had a talent for getting mad. Angrier Ann. She had evidently forgiven her mother, but she wasn't about to take on dog care.

Sometimes I wondered if Andrea Ann had any warm feelings — even for people, much less dogs. She'd told me that when she was a child she'd dissected small animals — mice, chipmunks, and once (to my horror) a squirrel — because she wanted to know what was inside. Which maybe made her a better surgical nurse, especially since her patients were anesthetized while she was with them. Human interaction was not required.

I don't think Andrea Ann knew how to show love. And Lola wasn't much better. George was the one who quivered with love whenever Bonnie came near. Who jumped with joy when she fed him. George knew she'd taken him in and saved his life. Fleas, indeed!

"Why, George told your mother by his bark whether a friend or a stranger was at the front door. He went crazy over strangers."

"And she felt safer that way, Peaches," Lola admitted, shrugging those satin shoulders.

"And George may be small and scared of strangers," I added, "but he can be fierce. He used to come steal my cat's supper. Now I put it on a high shelf."

"Mama called him a feist." Lola eyed his bowed legs, white chest, and funny little black body. "But he looks like a mongrel to me."

Out in the country, feists are kind of a breed. Not all exactly alike, but all small and fierce when they need to be. That's where the word *feisty* comes from. The dictionary says so.

"It's our mountain thriftiness, I guess," I said. "To breed a fierce watchdog in a small size that won't need much to eat."

George came out from under the bed and began to bark. Someone at the door? Andrea Ann should certainly be here by now. We went to look. No one was there. George raced back into the bedroom. He stood by the bed and barked. All of him quivered, and he pranced up and down, stamping first one front paw, then the other.

"Oh! It's time for your mother's pill!" I could have cried. He was barking, as always, because it was time for the treat that Bonnie gave him each time she took a pill. George wanted his dog biscuit. I gave him one for old times' sake. I looked at the pills. Take one at 10:00 A.M., the label said. And sure enough, the clock said ten. George was going to have to be deprogrammed so he didn't bark every day at ten o'clock.

I picked him up, and he wriggled with delight and licked my nose.

"Where's Andrea Ann?" I asked. Now she and Arnold lived just a few houses down the street, and Lola said she'd called her sister before she called me. Andrea should have arrived.

"She said she had to get dressed," Lola said. "She and Arnold." Arnold the new salesman. Shallow and insincere. He'd kept trying to talk Bonnie into selling the large tract of land with a lake and a little cabin on it, out at the edge of town. Bonnie'd never gotten there the last few years. But she was attached to that place. Carnal Arnold was too thickheaded to understand that. Or maybe he and Andrea Ann had wanted to borrow the money that Bonnie could get by selling the land. They tended to gamble. They'd been on vacation to Acapulco and Atlantic City and I forget where else.

You might think I don't like anybody the way I talk about Bonnie's girls and their men. I like most everybody. But something had gone wrong with those girls. I never knew their father. He was gone by the time I moved in next to Bonnie. Maybe he was the bad apple. Bonnie refused to talk about him.

"Do you think your father is still alive?" I asked Lola. "Do you need to let him know?"

She glared at me. "That," she said, "is not your business." At the same moment Andrea Ann walked in the door. No pink satin for her. Nurse's white and laced shoes. Andrea was the practical type. Dumb spells and all. Her mother said she never wasted a thing. Even saved odd bits of string. She glared at me too.

So I took a hint and went home, carrying little George against my shoulder.

I put my old barn coat on the floor for him to lie on. Silk, my cat, who used to belong to my mother, came through the cat door. My father didn't really want Silk, and I seem to inherit animals. Silk and George were friends from outdoors. No problem. I poured myself some cornflakes, added milk. I did some wash. I answered two letters. George was restless. He knew something was wrong. He kept going to the door and asking to get out. He didn't know how to use the cat door. "You've been out," I said, remembering the gunshot, "and it nearly killed you." I looked out the window. I saw Lola talking to Carnal Arnold on her mother's front porch. Even from a distance I could see her preen and him leer. A car drove up and out got Victor. A traffic jam. About time that joker got there; it was early afternoon.

All of a sudden George began to bark again. It wasn't quite his stranger-at-the-door bark. But insistent. He didn't go to the door and hop up and down to get out. Still, I glanced outside. Nobody. I looked at the clock. Two o'clock. Not the right time for the pill routine. What on earth was he trying to tell me? I gave him a dog biscuit. He stopped barking.

Then I heard a thump on the side of the house, over toward the bedroom—the side away from Bonnie's house. I went in the bedroom to investigate. Both animals followed me. I looked out the bedroom window, past the stained-glass cardinal fastened to the glass. Nobody in sight on that side of the house. Though there was a hedge. Someone could have slipped behind that. Nothing seemed to have fallen in the bedroom. The picture of an old man playing a mountain dulcimer hung securely in place. So did the picture of the barn owl. No explanation for the noise. Only then did it occur to me that that thump was designed to get me out of the kitchen. That someone actually banged the side of the house.

I hurried back into the kitchen, and George began to run toward the cat door. I saw what he was after—a big piece of juicy raw hamburger. I ran so fast, I grabbed it before he did. I wiped the floor with my sleeve before either animal could lick any juice. I put the meat in a square freezer box and called the police department.

I was lucky to reach an old friend, Lieutenant John Wilson— whom I call Mustache, for obvious reasons. "I hate to hear from you," he said, "in case somebody else has been murdered." He said it like a joke. But of course, it wasn't. I've been mixed up in several murders. Not, thank God, on the wrong side.

"You're right. My next-door neighbor, Bonnie Amons, has been murdered," I said. "If you'll get right over here, I can tell you how to prove it, even though she was eighty-three and everybody thinks she died of natural causes. Or," I said, "I can give you the proof if you come at 5:30."

"I can't come now," he said. "I can't even talk long now. I'd have to send somebody else. I'll come at 5:30 or quarter of six."

"Nothing is going to change before then," I said. "But don't be late."

You can bet I took good care of George for the rest of the afternoon, and Mustache arrived as promised, about 5:35.

"Okay," he said, "tell me your theory. I bet it's something that nobody but me would ever believe. But I've had practice." He sighed. I know he wishes I wouldn't get mixed up in strange deaths. Like finding my poor Aunt Nancy in the goldfish pond or stumbling on the fact that a serial killer was coming up I-40 our way and had my father on a list. Mustache wishes I wouldn't throw him curves. He has an orderly side that wants the world to make sense. You can tell by his crisp blue suit. No wrinkles. And by his straight firm mouth and intelligent eyes.

On the other hand, if he stuck to the tried-and-true way, he probably wouldn't have that scar next to his eye. He probably wouldn't have that wry manner—that was kind of nice. "Why do you believe that your neighbor, Bonnie Amons, was murdered?"

I introduced him to George. "This little dog belonged to Bonnie Amons, and he was trained to bark for a dog biscuit at ten o'clock every morning," I said. "That reminded her to take her heart pill."

George eyed Mustache's feet. No boots. George stood his ground.

"Now, someone has trained this dog to bark for a dog biscuit more times a day than Bonnie was supposed to take pills. Today he's barked at ten and two, and I'll bet he'll bark at six. That would make a regular pattern." Even my friend Mustache looked doubtful. Mustache looked at the kitchen clock. Quarter of six.

"And then, if you want to be sure of the whole pattern, let your police gal who works with the drug-sniffing dog keep George for a day and see," I said. "If she gives him a dog biscuit after he barks for it, he'll keep on barking at regular intervals, and you can use that for evidence."

"I might laugh at that evidence," Mustache sighed, "except I know you. But we need more. That dog-alarm-clock stuff could be laughed out of court."

"Well, I'm willing to bet an autopsy on Bonnie Amons will show she's been taking more Lanoxin than she should, maybe three times as much," I said. "The amount will match the number of times a day that George barks in a certain way. I showed Bonnie how to train this little dog to bark when she was due to take her medicine, but now her daughter, Andrea Ann, has trained the dog to bark more often. And I believe the overdose killed my friend."

"Well, you know about heart medicine, all right," he sighed, pulling at his mustache, "since the attempt last year to kill your father with it. So you think this Andrea Ann killed her own mother?"

"Sure," I said. "Andrea Ann had a fight with her mother because Bonnie wouldn't lend her money. Then Andrea Ann made up and helped nurse her mother. Maybe just in order to kill her. Andrea Ann is a little strange. But very determined. She didn't like to live in a trailer park."

"But how could anyone prove Andrea Ann was the poisoner, even if the autopsy and the dog check out? And we can't even ask for an autopsy without some proof that something is wrong." He chewed the end of his mustache. "I hate to let you down," he said kindly, "but this one may be too preposterous if all you have is the dog and speculation."

"Luckily," I said, "Andrea Ann thought the dog could incriminate her by barking too often. She thought I'd figure out what happened. She had one of her dumb spells. So she gave me proof.

"Here," I said, "is some hamburger laced with poison. I'm sure of it. If you look in Andrea Ann's refrigerator, I think you'll find unpoisoned hamburger that matches it. Andrea Ann never could bring herself to waste anything. She may possibly have thrown out the poison, but she can't have thrown it far. She needed to be over at her mother's house with her sister, looking innocent. She could slip out while her sister was busy flirting with her husband and drop the poisoned meat into my kitchen, the louse. But she didn't have time to go far away. And she didn't expect to have to use poison. Earlier she had shot at George, but she missed. Then she probably poisoned this meat with what she had handy—some household pesticide. You'll find the evidence. I have faith."

But Mustache was staring at the clock. The hands said six. George was lying quietly on the floor by my feet. I sighed. So okay, my imagination led me astray. But I didn't believe that. George yawned.

And then he stood up and began to bark. He jumped up and down and ran back and forth. He stamped his feet.

I handed Mustache a dog biscuit. "Here, you give it to him," I suggested. He did, and George wagged his tail and stopped barking.

I am happy to say that when Mustache got himself a hurry-up search warrant, there *was* hamburger in Andrea Ann's fridge, and it matched. Modern science can spot those things. The rat-poison box was still in her garage. She was overconfident. So sure that once the dog was dead, nobody could spot those extra pill-barkings. So sure she could prevent us from discovering the secret of the dog.

Mustache found one thing I missed. Andrea Ann was going to three different pharmacies to get Lanoxin, using stolen and forged prescription forms she got from her nursing job.

As for George, he settled in with me and is a big help. I used to take my thyroid pills when I thought of it. Or else I didn't. Sometimes it was hard to remember. Now I take them every day at ten o'clock.

ELIZABETH DANIELS SQUIRE (1926–2001) came late in life to the mystery field. As you might expect of a scion of the Daniels family, founders of the *Raleigh News and Observer*, she spent the first years of her career as a reporter, covering everything from school boards to murder trials. For a time she wrote a syndicated column about the character and talents of the famous as divined from their palm prints. Her seven mysteries, set in the mountains of North Carolina where she lived, featured an absent-minded sleuth named Peaches Dann. The short story featured in this collection, "The Dog Who Remembered Too Much," won an Agatha Award and an Anthony nomination in 1996.